VIKING

THE PLAINS OF ALTHING

by

Katie Aiken Ritter

ISBN 13: 978-0-9978765-7-4
ISBN 10: 0997876573

eBook ISBN 978-0-9978765-6-7

With thanks to Peter Smith, PhD, MDiv, LCSW-C:
psychotherapist, professor. priest, and
family counselor rock star

Never woulda got here without your help

VIKING
THE PLAINS OF ALTHING

Series in chronological order:

The Plains of Althing

Thunder Horse

The Green Land

Alphabetical List of Characters

Aldís   an itinerant healer with some 'second sight'

Ankya   Naldrum's oldest daughter and favorite child

Eilíf   a widow, badly scarred in a farm fire

Friedrich   bishop of a monastery in Germania

Haakon Sigurdsson   *Jarl* (earl) of Lade Garde, Trondheim, Norway

Josson   a ne'er-do-well cart-trader

Konradsson   young Germanic priest, once native to Iceland

Mani   Lawspeaker of all Iceland

Naldrum   headman of Bull Valley

Nenet and Nikea   Tor's children

Rota   agent for Haakon Sigurdsson, Jarl of Lade

Sauthi   a reclusive shepherd

Thorgest   a landowner friend of Tiller

Tiller   a *vikinger* (sailor) sent to steal The Nubian

Tor   an enslaved Moroccan man

Iceland, circa 979 A.D.
a valley in the north-western quarter

The longhouse nestled on a strip of land between a steep hill and a narrow fjord, a stalwart little dwelling that promised shelter from windy gusts, chilly even in these warmer days. As Kel Coesson rode towards the home, sheep chewed and stared at him, their mouths full of fragrant grass. Their pale long wool lifted in the fresh breeze.

Kel swung off the saddle and went straight to the doorway. Geese honked and chickens clucked, scattering in his path. Kel steadied himself. *Last time this year,* he felt certain. Hoped.

He lifted his hand to knock. Reluctant, he tightened his fist and paused. His eyes drifted along the door separating him from the people inside. *I could just walk back to my horse. I could just ride away.*

The massive slab of dark wood, rounded at the top, fit tight against the tidy turf wall. These people took care of their modest property.

The door itself showed signs of generations of use. Kel imagined sparks flying, as some long-dead ancestor had hammered apart the iron hinges that holding it tight to another distant longhouse. He pictured its heavy weight thudding onto the deck of a ship, one that would carry it across waves to a new start in a new land; the door, now a last connection to life before the Great Settlement, a story told to children about the old ones who had lived far away.

Cracks ran along the thick timber. Bright green moss clung to those crevices, its soft mounds defying the cut of the wind.

The bitter taste in Kel's mouth worsened. The farmer who lived here had come to Naldrum's compound some days ago, his body stiff with nervousness. *Fear of being mocked. Fear of being denied.* His kind all arrived looking the same. Like all the others, when the man left his shoulders were straight and strong, every line in his body exuding proud joy, eager to return home with good news.

Kel had followed the man, staying well out of sight. Just before they reached the tidy holding, Kel had seen him rein in his horse and attach a strap of bells to its harness. The sound of bells had jingled the man's triumphant arrival. People had run from the fields to greet him.

I can't do this much longer.

Kel lifted his fist again to pound on the door, but once more put it down. He raked windblown hair away from his brow and looked around the property.

Scraped animal hides hung stretched over frames, curing. These people had begun to slaughter their animals well ahead of the traditional time. The meat would help keep the family alive, but it would cost, because the next year they would have fewer cows, fewer goats and sheep, less milk, less cheese, fewer chickens, fewer eggs. He had seen the same downward spiral in other farms. Without a decent harvest this year, this farm might not last much longer.

At least they'll have one less mouth to feed when I'm finished.

The thought brought no consolation. Might as well get it over with. He raised his hand for a third time. This time the knock sounded, firm and forceful.

Laughter bubbled as the door opened to an intoxicating smell of fresh bread. Smiling faces peered out.

"It's chieftain Naldrum's steward Kel," the man exclaimed. "I've just arrived home and have been telling my family about my meeting with your headman. We didn't expect you quite so soon."

He stepped back, his arm extended to include his family. "Meet Kel Coesson, who the headman said would bring silver to us."

Silver? No. I bring only death. Kel let anger fill him; it would help. *Not his fault another silly girl had gotten herself with child and blamed Naldrum.* Not his fault this man had come knocking with a dubious claim of the chieftain's responsibility, followed by a demand for payment. Wheedling, respectful, shouting, or pleading, it happened every spring, as regular as lambing; one, two, three times. Four, on bad years. *One of the perils of being a rich man,* Naldrum always said. *We must nip this practice in the bud, year after year.*

Kel felt his throat grow tight with dread at the task ahead. It wasn't his job to question, he reminded himself. Only to make the problem go away. Defying Naldrum created other, worse troubles.

Kel's gaze slid away from the farmer to the two women who stood behind him. The one holding the baby looked familiar.

Please tell me I don't know her.

Kel reminded himself again that this should be the last time for the year. Just get through it, and he'd not have to face doing it again until next spring. The thought brought a bit of relief.

"Don't just stand there in the doorway. Come in and eat with us," the man gestured. "My wife has just taken a loaf from the oven." He gestured to the older woman behind him. The fragrance carried the promise of welcome, of comfort.

"I'm not hungry."

"Something to drink, then—? My niece's baby has a bit of colic, so they're behind on making small beer, but I could offer you—" The farmer trailed off at the steward's harsh expression.

Kel stepped inside. He turned, every movement deliberate and slow, and closed the door behind him. Pulled in the leather latchstring, leaned against the old wood timbers. Spoke, guttural and grim.

"Never mind about the bread…or the beer."

. . .

Curse the greed of these people. The first time Naldrum had sent him on such a mission, Kel had been young and angry, eager to prove himself to his headman. Even then, his stomach had turned over at taking the infant in his arms. Across the years, stopping the ridiculous demands had become more and more disturbing. Now it was all but impossible. He used to bring a servant with him, but the last few years Kel could no longer face even a slave afterwards. Better to sleep rough and do his own cooking. Better to trace his return route alone without someone riding alongside, wondering exactly what Kel had done to change warm greetings into bitter anger and silent fear.

. . .

When it was over, Kel left the farmstead, now grateful for the wind and the threatening clouds. Images needed to be forgotten and shame purged. He would spur his horse back to Naldrum's holdings until both he and the stallion were soaked with rain and sweat.

But before the hills hid the farm from view, Kel yanked hard on his horse's reins. The animal reared, wheeled, stopped. It snorted while its rider sat staring back at the longhouse.

The face of the young woman—*that girl who clutched the infant*—had cast everything Kel believed into doubt and confusion. Kel had eyed her as he forced himself to say the real actions Naldrum had ordered. *There would be no silver. Moreover, the infant would not be allowed to live. Orders of the headman; since you have claimed he is the father, Naldrum has the legal right to deem if the child is fit to survive. He determined that the creature carries defects and must be—*

"…exposed." Kel choked out the last word. Such a bland term for the murder of an innocent child.

Naldrum had never laid eyes on a single one of his supposed offspring, but Kel had held each of the wee beings in his hands. All of them perfect, but law was law. He had given what gentleness he could, taking the small bundles with their round trusting eyes and tiny fists curled around his rough fingers away where the family would not see.

Kel had reached for this infant, too, still hoping he imagined that the young woman looked familiar. But when she argued, tears running down her cheeks, recognition finally came: Sóma, one of the daughters of an iron-smelter from the northern bogs. The earnest expression Kel remembered from his youth now graced the face of this young mother.

. . .

Kel sat motionless in the saddle. Every part of him yearned to race back to the farmhouse, to somehow undo the act, to leave without ever knocking on that cursed door. His horse Thor-Thunder, sensing Kel's unease, knickered and stamped on the grassy ground.

He stroked Thor-Thunder's silky mane. The smell of saddle leather, warmed by the horse's big body, drifted up.

Even as a child she had lived up to her name: *Sóma,* honor. Always one to make calm observations, to speak with quiet integrity. *Ask Sóma,* people always said, *if you want the truth.*

Naldrum had ranted that the claim of his fatherhood was false, but always-honest Sóma told a different story. Kel had blanched with fury listening to her account of what had happened the prior summer.

It did not change what he had to do. "I am so sorry, Sóma," he had said, his jaw clenched as he looked her straight in the eyes. "Whether it seems so or not, you're all better off this way." *All except the child.* "Naldrum gives me no choice."

. . .

In the end, Kel had done what Naldrum had instructed, but the act had been harder than ever before. He felt vile. Without thinking, he wiped his hands on the legs of his pants, as if to clean guilt from them.

If Sóma told the truth, that meant it was Naldrum who had lied— and raped. His headman had defiled that young woman.

Kel felt ill. *Sóma told the truth.* His gut knew it, even though his mind did not want to admit it.

His thoughts swirling, he stared at the little longhouse as if he could wring answers from it. Much as he disliked this particular duty, Kel had never doubted its necessity before. If one woman got away with it, dozens more would follow her example, Naldrum always claimed. But now, questions filled him. Sóma never lied.

No sign of distress showed at this distance, only a quiet, well-tended property. Kel let Thor-Thunder drop his head to graze. *What might it be like, to live here so far from Naldrum?* No wealth, but plenty of freedom; none of the prestige that came from being a powerful headman's steward, but the sweet peace of this isolated valley, the serene sameness of daily farm chores.

Another remembered face came to Kel, and along with a sweet ache, the familiar caution to himself. *Don't think of Aldís. Not ever, not ever, not ever.*

Half to protect her, half to protect himself.

But her memory defied his efforts. In his mind, it was not Sóma who stood against that moss-covered door but Aldís, a child of their own in her arms, her smile brightening the day. A warm fire crackled and hams hung from the ceiling, the smell smoky and rich.

He spun a story for himself. *We met that time at Althing. We talked of law and ideals, and we fell in love.* Instead of parting in pain and anger, they had stayed together, riding away from Althing hand in hand. They had searched for just the right place to start a life together. They had found this small farm and had made a life together.

Kel, caught in the dream, felt brief relief remembering how fiercely Aldís had debated with him and defended her hopes. *Can you imagine me, the daughter of a slave, being one of the law-arguers?*

But the reprieve was fleeting. How would she have reacted to what Sóma said? *Aldís would law-argue Naldrum into banishment.* And if that didn't work, there was her other skill, her uncanny ability to hold a plant and know if it would kill or cure. The way she could touch a person and somehow see disease deep inside—and most of all, the way she connected with spirits of land and water, who spoke to her in tendrils of understanding, of warning, and of help.

No, Aldís would never be a farm wife or a mother. She was too fierce, too free, and she hated him besides. He was stuck with Naldrum.

Kel flinched. Were her invisible land-spirits staring at him, right now? If Aldís was here, would she hear them describe what he had just done, and look at him with cold loathing, the way she had before?

Bitterness flooded him. *Time I should be getting back.* The chieftain demanded speedy confirmation that his orders had been fulfilled. with assurances that the family would never dare mention it.

"Hargh!" Kel wheeled his horse around and dug his heels into the stallion's flanks. "What choice do I have? I'm tied to him by law and by threat. No matter what I might want, I'm bound!"

Thor-Thunder charged forward, eager to run, his strong spirit ready for the long ride home. But despite Kel's burst of frustration, doubt squirmed, a wicked little worm eating away beliefs that had long kept Kel sane. The questions kept time with Thor's hoofbeats.

Kel gagged as the ideas grew. What if other claims had been true? It had been hard enough to do the deed, thinking he was righting a wrong. But if Naldrum had lied other times—

Kel thought of the headman's bloated face back at the compound, always impatient and testy. Resentment Kel had buried years back began to bubble up, hot and furious as lava. But just as fast, the familiar trap closed. *Defying Naldrum meant destroying Aldís.*

His chieftain could wait. What Kel wanted was a visit with a friend who asked no questions and spoke to no spirits. He pictured another distant valley, a place of respite, silent except for cries of birds and the bleating of sheep herded by old Sauthi.

"Hargh!" Kel shouted again. Thor's hooves pounded on the grassy track, curving up over a low hill. The fresh clean breeze chased them. Kel sucked in great gulps of air. He couldn't help Sóma, and he would never have Aldís, but he could find temporary escape from troubling questions. Kel turned the horse towards the far hills where his old friend would be grazing his flock this time of year. He rode hard, trying not to think or feel.

. . .

Chapter Two

southern coastline of Iceland, late summer

The fragrance of bitter-oranges—Tor's favorite, when he had been a free man—finally caused the slave to revolt. That, and the stupid selfishness of the trader Josson. Once the perfume of oranges had meant lovemaking on long sweet nights, but the stupid, drunken selfishness of the trader Josson gave them a new meaning: defiance.

Josson had bought the oranges at the same trading in which he acquired Tor. Even though he had barely scraped by this season, Josson still believed himself a great merchant. His failing profits were never his own. The fault lay with those from whom he had bought wares and those to whom he had sold them. This year he had many to blame, and the trading season was nearly over.

"Still some summer left. Plenty of time for another ship." Josson fidgeted in the door of his meagre dwelling, ignoring chores, watching daily for a sail. *Please, just one more ship.* He had counted his small stores of food over and over. Not enough to survive the winter.

When a square sail finally appeared on the horizon, Josson rushed to harness his bedraggled horse, desperate for decent trade goods.

The journey from his rude homestead to the trading-beach took most of a day. As his cart lurched along the rutted track, its ancient wooden wheels creaked. Josson struck at his horse, urging it to go faster, fretting. "Damned rain! Damned tide! Damned horse and cart!"

At the last turn, Josson sighed in relief. A small group of buyers and sellers remained, and the vessel still lay on its side on the wet shoreline. But the sea rose steadily. Foam edges of wavelets already licked at the curved hull. Shipboard merchants were reloading their wares, their eyes on the weather and the water. The sea goddess did not grace those who ignored her drifts and flows.

Josson hobbled his horse and plodded to where the last few tables displayed goods for trade. Sellers, pausing at his arrival, quickly assessed Josson, his cart, his horse, his clothes. *Nothing much here,* their expressions signaled to one another. They resumed packing.

"Anything left for barter?" he asked. "Where do you trade from?"

"Northumbria, mostly, and some things from beyond," came a listless reply. "We have hops and honey. For metals, we have some tin and a supply of bronze-bars. A container of black pepper, if you have a wealthy client, and along with that, a box of oranges from Al-Andalus. Very rare, very expensive."

"I'll pass on the pepper and the oranges," he said. "Too rich for me. Nobody's trading for luxuries this year."

"This is our last run for the season. Maybe the price is not that much after all." A tease, and it worked. Josson pursed his lips. No one would buy a whole box of peppercorns, but with harvest suppers coming, perhaps he could trade a berry or two at a time as a novelty.

"I'll take it if your price is right. What do you want in exchange?"

"We need meat, fresh or cured. We've none left. Also, two passengers want a falcon as a wedding-present for themselves. Brimstone's always welcome, as well as cloth. Tell us what you have."

"No brimstone," Josson said, "but I have linen cloth, and good spun wool." He eyed his cart. It held a barrel of salted meat, but it was his own supply for the coming winter. "I'd need something of great value in exchange for meat. And I have a falcon."

The bird huddled in a basket in Josson's cart, fluffing its feathers. *Probably sick*, he thought, but with the raw air from the incoming storm, the buyers might not notice. "Tell me about the bronze bars," he said. "I have a fellow who might use them."

Someone roused a sleeping form on the deck. "Got a customer."

The small figure rolled over and detached itself from a burrow of blankets. It sat up, and yawned mightily, revealing a woman as slight as a sparrow. As she hopped over the side of the ship, Josson prepared to bluster and wear down her price.

"What's your offer for the bronze?" she asked abruptly.

"What, no greeting? No parlay?"

"Don't use Frankish words on me. You're not even saying it right," she said. "If you want these bars, tell me. Otherwise I should get them loaded before the tide gets higher. Did you look at them?"

Josson rubbed his thumb across the narrow metal rods. He took out a knife and scored one. "I don't like the way it looks."

"It's serviceable, but it's not good enough for weapon-work. That's why I still have it. Your best sale is to someone who can make cheap fairing trinkets for those who can't afford gold or silver."

The effect of such honesty unsettled Josson. Before he realized it, he found himself agreeing to take the bronze in exchange for all the wool and linen he carried.

As the ship merchants began to pull down the trade-booth tents, the woman gestured to the water. "Sailing tide won't wait much longer. My man will help you load it onto your cart."

She called, and Josson laid eyes on the first dark-skinned man he had ever seen. His jaw dropped open and he stared.

. . .

"You've never met someone like him before, have you?" The merchant woman's voice cut into Josson's astonishment.

"No…no, I've seen plenty." He closed his mouth and opened it again. At her skeptical expression, he backed down. "Well, I've heard of them, anyway. They're from Byzan— Byzanty—? His tongue struggled to get out the strange word. He could not take his eyes from the man's huge height and that skin, lustrous and dark as charcoal.

"Do you even know where Byzantium is?" The woman peered at Josson with her thin mouth pursed. "No, he comes from much farther away than that. He works for me, trading between Northumbria and Iceland and around the North-way lands."

Josson had heard stories of people whose skin was the burnt-black color of lava-fields. He had tried unsuccessfully to picture them. With a living example right in front of him, Josson stared in fascination. *Were they all this large,* he wondered? The man towered over him, too thin, but with powerful muscles under his threadbare clothing,

Josson hardly dared ask his other question. Was it true about the staggering prices paid for these fantastic dark-skinned beings captured far away by slavers and brought north for sale? He'd never heard of anyone having one of these exotic creatures, not in all of Iceland. Plenty of thralls here, yes, but all Saxon and Gaelic, and usually women: they were easier to acquire and able to do almost the same work as men, they ate less and produced valuable children. Some had dark hair like this man, and some dark eyes, but their skin was as pale as Josson's.

He could feel his pulse, hard and fast. He swallowed. "How much for him? Just wondering, of course."

Past years of buying dejected beings from slave ships and selling them to valley farmers had brought good returns to Josson. But those same trades had produced an abundance of slave-child births. Now the valleys were full of them, and no one wanted to buy. Josson had practically had to give away the last thralls he had acquired. Since then, he resented being stuck in a miserly living dealing in sundries: metals, whetstones, cloth, and tar. *But this creature…he could bring the profit of a lifetime.*

Josson twisted his threadbare cap, wistful that for once he could make a stupendously profitable trade. *But I could never afford him.*

"Do you see a collar on him, you ignorant fool?" the woman retorted. "You assume he's a slave just because he's dark-skinned and working for me? Entire countries of people like him work and travel and trade, free men and women, just as you and me." Her sigh spoke of regret and frustration. "But in fact, I do have the rights to him."

Josson watched the man as he loaded the bars onto the cart as if the heavy bronze weighed nothing. "What's his name?"

"I call him *Sám Tor.* It means *Black Mountain.*"

"How did you get him?"

She debated telling Josson, decided it could do little harm. Enough other people knew anyway.

"A slaver captured his wife several years ago. Tor spent all his wealth and borrowed a great deal, trying to find her. Facing enslavement in a galley ship, he offered me his freedom. In return, I paid his debts. That way he could keep searching for his wife along our trade routes. His journey, sadly, has been fruitless."

Josson cared little for the man's problems. "Is he for sale or not?"

The woman asked a question in words Josson did not understand. The enslaved giant considered Josson. He shrugged, as if to say *it cannot be helped.* She asked again, her voice sharper. Tor looked at her sadly, touched his hand to his chest, and nodded his head.

"How much?" Josson repeated. Thoughts of what he might earn made him salivate. *I'll be rich. I'll be so rich.*

The female merchant's voice quavered as she tried once more, still speaking to the man in the language Josson did not understand. "Tor, this trader seems deceitful to me. I don't trust him, not even a little bit. I have a terrible feeling about this. Please stay with the ship. We'll find you something else, I promise."

Again, those sad eyes, but Tor shook his head. He pointed towards the ship, gestured something with his hands, their movement a question, waiting for her response.

"Yes, I do know this is our last trading stop before we put in for winter," she replied. "And yes, I understand the need for a safe haven. But please, not this man. Look at his face. No honesty in it at all."

Tor gave her a slight wink, as if to say *fear not. All will be well.*

"It appears that my *maurus-man* agrees to being sold." She drew a deep breath. "But you need to know the whole deal. He comes with two others. You have to take all three."

"Three men?" Josson nearly drooled, thinking of the riches that *three* dark slaves could bring. But, anguished, "I can't afford that."

"Not three men." She asked Tor another question. In reply, he pointed.

She tapped on her trading-table. "Out here, you two." A bit of scuffle, and something squirmed from under the table covering, followed by another something.

Josson could not believe his eyes. Before him was astonishing magic: two children, each of them a miniature copy of the man Tor.

. . .

Josson lifted his hands to the sky, his heart full of an uncommon feeling: gratitude. The gods did not often bless him. In fact, he felt certain that the gods had *never* blessed him, but right here in front of him stood a pair of wondrous things. His fingers reached out, grasping towards them. What a story to tell as he wound his way through the valley farms, where good tales usually ensured better trades.

"They belong to you also?" he asked the merchant.

"Not mine. They're his children, and they're free-beings. He wears their soul-stones." She gestured, and Josson noticed the string with blue beads that hung around Tor's neck.

"What's your price?" he wavered.

"Your falcon," she said. "And all the meat you have."

Josson shrank back as he considered handing over his precious store of salted meat, his only safeguard against starvation that winter. But surely, he could trade these creatures for far, far more.

The trader imagined himself strutting to farms that still had wealth despite the last few lean years. He would carry a stick, would tap the dark man, *turn this way, turn that* as he had with thralls he had sold, but instead of bickering over price, his audience would rush to get a purse, not just silver but gold clinking inside.

Not one maurus, *not two, but three of them? I'll be able to eat beef for the rest of my life. Even lamb and horsemeat.* His mouth watered as he pictured the barrels being loaded onto his wagon.

Josson made up his mind. Best not to seem too anxious.

"If you've had trouble getting meat, so have I." It was true. His small supply of porridge-oats would be his only food. "You want my falcon *and* the meat? Then I want your oranges along with the man."

"Done," she said.

Josson's mouth dropped open, astonished at the deal he had just struck. *Three exotics and six oranges...* He turned to leave before she could change her mind, but the merchant woman grabbed his tunic.

"Remember our deal. When you sell him, they all stay together. Only Tor is for sale. He keeps his children with him, as freeborns."

"Of course. I heard you the first time."

She still gripped his shirt. "Swear it. On your own blood."

A blood oath? What if the gods heard and held him to it? But eager to escape with his prize, he dipped his knife in a wave, then pricked his forearm, said the sealing-words of sea and blood, and Tor was his.

As the wind grew stronger, cold drops began to fall. The great negotiator rode off with a huge slave, plus two ragged children, a partial box of peppercorns, a half-dozen oranges that would spoil in a week, and a load of low-quality bronze. In return, he had parted with a prized gyrfalcon, good linen and wool, and most of the food that had been his defense against the long bitter winter to come.

. . .

The merchant woman Indaell had argued with Tor when that year's spring trading runs had begun. He had been firm that she must sell him. She had protested, to no avail.

"My children cannot stay on the ship another year," Tor had said. "They're getting too big to hide when we beach for trading. Always someone's eyes on them. That look, calculating what they'd bring on the market. I need to find somewhere they can live safely."

"Why not take them back to your own homeland? To family? To relatives?" But his wife's disappearance had ruined Tor's faith in the people of that sun-drenched land. She knew he would refuse again.

"You know the reasons," he replied. "No, I want them here in Iceland. I like what I've seen of this country. It's a land of law. It raised a woman like you; strong, brave, independent. People here are mostly hardworking farm folk. They have no rich kings collecting taxes off the backs of their poor to buy curiosities like me. Best of all, it's remote and isolated. My daughter and son will be safer here than anywhere else. I want you to find a local trader and sell me to him. We'll end up at a farm where I can raise them in safety."

"Do you really trust that will happen?"

"In years of searching for my wife, there's never been even a trace of her. I'm weary, Indaell. I need to protect my children."

"I'll keep looking. If I find her, I'll find you. I promise."

His face had softened in a rare smile. "You have my gratitude. Now cheer up, friend. My children will grow up calling themselves Icelanders. Even I will be, from now on. Should make you proud."

. . .

Indaell held back her tears until after Josson left, with Tor walking chained behind the cart. The Danish passengers on the ship quickly approached her, stripping off their silver bracelets, holding them out, excited to get the gyrfalcon, but she turned away from them.

"They say falcons mate for life." Indaell looked at the bird's bright eye, peering between the staves of the willow basket. She choked, thinking of Tor and his wife.

More silver bracelets extended. More pleading. Gold bracelets.

Again, she spoke as if only to herself and the bird. "Is your mate somewhere out there, searching for you? Like Tor?"

The Danes pressed her again, offering a fortune for the coveted bird. It was double what she'd spent to buy Tor so long ago.

Indaell shook her head at their entreaties. With trembling fingers, she unbuckled the leather straps and lifted the top from the falcon's cage. The bird's sharp beak twisted back and forth. Its piercing eyes turned from her to the sky.

"For my friend," she said. "I can't give him freedom, but I can give you yours. Find your mate. And as you fly, please watch out for Tor."

The bird hopped from the basket and perched on the rim. Indaell ignored the Danes' angry shouts of protest and the calls from her shipmates to hurry and get on board before they sailed.

With a last look around, the falcon screamed, a cry of raw power. It lifted its wings, beat them, and leapt aloft, soaring upwards. The bird climbed towards the ragged clouds. Indaell watched as its black silhouette dwindled to a dot, as tears and rain rand down her face.

. . .

Chapter Three

Afraid that Indaell would somehow change her mind and defy the sea and come running after him, Josson drove his horse hard, his cart lurching wildly on the rutted track. When the cove was out of sight, he breathed a sigh of relief and considered his good fortune.

Could Tor sing? Dance? Juggle, or do tumbling tricks? An exotic with such skills would fetch the best price. He watched, eager to see signs of unusual talents, but to Josson's frustration, the man showed no amusements as he plodded along, as silent as the looming hills.

"*Black Mountain,* eh? Has that always been your name?"

With no answer, he tried again. "Where do you come from?"

Still only silence in return. The trader frowned. His tunic, wet from rain, lay plastered against his skin, and he ached all over from the long, hurried trip to the beach.

"We'll stop here," Josson growled when they reached a sheltered spot along the trail. "We'll make camp for the night instead of traveling to farms ahead. I need to see what you can do, so I get the best deal for you. Surely you have skills besides lifting bronze bars."

Josson pulled a filthy cloth from the side of the cart, untied a bundle of sticks, and hauled out his small rusty kettle. Squatting beside the wood, he struck his flint, worked at starting a cooking fire. When the flames began to crackle, Josson stood and tried again. "You! Where from?" he asked louder, pointing at Tor.

The enslaved man sat with his back against the cart's wheel, weary, his eyes closed. His wrist oozed where the chain cut into it. The two children sat wide-eyed and silent, side by side on the cart.

The trader leaned over Tor. He poked the silent man in the chest with his walking stick, but Tor did not acknowledge the poke.

His silence deepened Josson's annoyance, who sneered. "Maybe your wife wasn't captured. Maybe she just ran away."

Still nothing. Tor sat as if he were stone.

Josson cursed. "No one is going to offer gold or silver or meat for a sulking silent hulk. I'm ruined if I can't find a buyer for you. Not just me, either. Who do you think is going to feed you and your children? I don't have enough for all of us. I'm not going to starve because of you. Better cooperate if you want them to eat."

Growing despair suddenly overwhelmed the trader. He struck at Tor with his stick. "Answer me! Speak when I ask you a question!"

The chained man lifted his head. For a short while he stared straight ahead toward where the setting sun glowed under the departing storm clouds. Josson could hear the man breathing, *in,* slowly, and *out,* even more slowly, …*in, out,* …*in, out.* Afterward, Tor blinked, just once, turned his head, and surveyed Josson.

Josson held his stick aloft, his arm stilled. For the first time, he had a direct view of Tor's eyes. They did not have the look of a man about to lose his temper. Josson saw in those dark orbs a calm assessment of how far Tor would tolerate the trader, and a weighing whether Josson had crossed that line.

Josson stepped back, frightened. He swung his stick to strike again, but with one fluid motion, Tor grabbed the stick and pinned it to the ground. He stared at Josson, his expression calm but defiant.

Shaken, the trader found himself muttering a rough, rare apology. Tor nodded imperceptibly and lifted his hand, releasing the stick. He resumed looking at the sunset, and Josson, shamed, went back to poking the fire.

. . .

A flaw in the trader's character began niggle at him. He could not bear to have someone triumph over him in even the smallest way. Despite his apology, he seethed at being bested by the other man. *I can even that score up if I want,* Josson told himself. *I have his children. If he tries something like that again—*

Josson turned to the two children huddling together. Up until now he had pointedly ignored them, unused to offspring.

"Good thing you did not make trouble today like your father. I suppose you're hungry. Too bad; I only have enough for myself until I make more trades. Your father'll have to figure out how to feed you."

Josson felt smug for having established his superiority to the children. Turning to Tor again, Josson boasted with a small taunt.

"You don't want to talk? You don't want to understand my words? Your brats will pay for your stubbornness."

As he slurped porridge, a horrifying thought occurred. *Could* Tor speak? He had not actually heard the slave man utter a sound.

"Damn the gods if that woman sold me a mute. I know you're not deaf, but you had better not be dumb."

Tor said nothing. He did not look at Josson. The trader, infuriated, uttered a curse. Afraid to admit he may have made a ruinous trade, he busied himself with his meagre meal. "Too bad for all of us if it's true.

In the meantime, there's only enough food for me tonight. Maybe tomorrow you'll find a way to ask for some."

In the gloaming, he did not notice Tor lift his chin towards his children or shake his head ever so slightly at them. The smallest nods in response told him that they understood.

. . .

The next morning, come first light, Josson's rickety cart creaked along the broad gravel streambed that served as the valley road. As they passed farm after farm, Josson turned onto the track that led to each holding and tried, mostly without success, to trade.

By nightfall, Tor's legs felt weary and his stomach growled. A line of red dots trailed him on the gravel, drops of blood from where the iron band had chafed his wrist raw.

The next day the track crossed the mouth of a narrow valley. Josson flinched. "We'll not turn in this way. Only one farm in this valley, and it's pretty far back," he announced to no one in particular. He pointed to where the barest trace of a path showed through long grass. "Used to be a good customer, but I never stop here anymore."

He clicked his tongue at his skinny horse. "The next place is still quite a way ahead. It'll be dark by the time we arrive. Let's get past here as fast as we can. Evil spirits." The cart lurched over a boulder in the rough roadway. Josson slapped his horse's flank to hurry it, then pointed. "See the marks on that stone?"

Tor observed where lines had been scored onto a large gray rock, beside the indistinct track. He nodded.

"That mark is how we show someone's an outlaw in these parts. They get an *X* like that put onto the back of their hands. Some headmen burn it in with a hot brand. Some use a knife. I scraped the stone that way to remind myself to stay away from here."

Josson laughed at his cleverness, then suddenly stopped. "It's a widow woman who lives there. Not old, though. Quite young, actually. Attractive, once, and a damned good cook. She always used to trade with me. Expensive things, too. Her husband had a forge, like most farms do. He was good at it, better than most. Made stuff for her to trade. He died in a fire a little while back. She got burned too, pretty badly. Never remarried. I can guess why…her face."

Josson demonstrated the damage she had sustained, scraping his grimy fingers from his hairline to his jaw. He grimaced. "It was ghastly. Made me sick to see it, the last time I stopped in here. She doesn't want anyone around her now. Lives solitary. Milks her pathetic little herds, grows her own food, weaves her own cloth. Without her husband to make her trade goods, she's poor. Won't even barter for anything either, not even the smallest bit. Not worth my time. Just as well. I can't bear seeing those hideous scars." Josson flicked the horse to go faster. "Nice weather today. The moon's getting towards full. We'll be able to see long enough to make the next farm. I'll claim hospitality rights to stay there. Make them give me a bit of supper. Maybe they'll throw in a scrap for you."

He scratched his head. Had it been two days or three since the ship? Each meal, Josson had moved his cooking fire farther away, resentful of the two small hungry faces staring at him. At Tor's look of scorn, Josson added, "You'll have to do the asking. I won't beg."

Fate, however, decided otherwise. Almost as soon as the words had left Josson's lips, a loud crack came from the cart. It skewed sideways. Josson bent to inspect the fittings and groaned.

"Just my luck. The axle has partly split. We can't move a step unless it's repaired. What am I going to do?" He kicked the ground, cursing, "It'll take too long to carry the parts back to the next place."

Tor thought of the words *her husband had a forge* and *she was a damned good cook.* He pointed at the cart. "Children food. Tor fix."

Josson stared at him. "You *can* talk? In Icelandic, too?"

"Children food here. Tor fix here." The man gestured with his head toward the forsaken valley.

Josson's surprise switched to the angry frustration he had felt the night before. "You deceitful wretch!" Profanity flowed from his lips.

"Food for children." Tor gestured, implacable. "No food, no fix."

"Fine. We'll talk later about tricking me. As for the widow, I can manage that hideous face if she lets you repair my cart."

Josson unhitched the horse and the chain that held Tor to the cart. The two men wrenched the axle from underneath the cart. Josson handed Tor the shorn fitting. "It's a long walk up the valley. You carry this. As for food, you'd better hope she has something to eat. If not, you fix it anyway. A deal's a deal."

. . .

At their insistent knocking, the slimmest crack finally opened in the small longhouse's doorway.

"Wh—who is there? What do you want?" A young woman's voice, stammering a little in fear.

Josson thrust his face toward the crack. "You know me. It's the trader Josson. I used to stop here."

"I don't allow anyone on my farm." She offered no explanation.

"My axle broke. Law of hospitality requires you to offer help."

The woman stayed silent. Tor could smell something delicious coming from inside. His stomach growled.

At length she said, "What exactly do you need?"

"You have a forge here?" Josson winked at Tor. In a not-very-subtle whisper, he said, "Of course she does. It's where she and her husband got burned. Question though, is enough of it left?"

"Yes," her voice trembled. "But no one has used it since... since..." A small sob.

Tor heard shame and heartbreak in the few words. *She feels guilty.*

"Does it still work?" Josson demanded.

"I don't...I don't know. I never go near it. You can try. But you can't come into my house." She started to close the crack.

At the look on Tor's face, Josson jammed his fingers in the door.

"Wait. I need something else. Food...two children..." Josson said. "They're hungry."

"Children? Hungry?" Her voice changed. "Of course I would not deny children. I can feed them while you work on your harness."

The crack opened. The children started forward eagerly. Tor caught a glimpse of a strong young forearm and a much-patched apron when the woman screamed and slammed the door shut against them.

. . .

"What's the matter with you?" Josson asked.

"Why are you doing this to me?" Muffled crying came through the thick wood. "Haven't I suffered enough? Go away!"

"We're not doing anything. We just need to fix our harness."

"But that man...those children..." The devastating last memory of her husband swept over her, the ghastly sight when she had heard his screams of pain and run to the burning forge. She rushed in just as he fell, his clothing and hair in flames, and the nauseating sick-sweet smell of charred human flesh and burning leather hit her. She had tried to claw him out of the fire as the flames ate burned her hair and skin. She could not remember running out of the forge, but guilt and grief had been her constant companions ever since.

"*Revenants,*" she whimpered. "Why did you bring them here?"

Josson rolled his eyes in disgust. "She thinks you're her dead husband's ghost."

"Why?" Tor did not understand.

"Your skin, man. You're black as can be, and your children too."

The widow wept. "Did you bring them to punish me because I no longer trade with you? I didn't mean for the fire to happen. Please...I am so sorry..."

Josson shouted against the doorframe. "Quit your wailing. I didn't bring your burned-up husband's ghost to haunt you. It's just the color this man is, the way the gods made him. Like Danes have red hair."

No sound came back. Tor pictured the woman sagging against the doorframe, her body trembling. He pushed Josson aside.

"Tor not burned." He spoke in a soft voice, but she would hear it. "Tor not revenant. Children not burned."

"Children," she gasped.

"Children hungry," he said. "Need help."

With effort, the widow forced herself to open a tiny slit in the door again. Her legs felt as if they would not hold her up.

Tor nudged the small ones forward. "Children *very* hungry," he said, his voice pleading.

An eye, rimmed white with fear, peered out at them. Tor put his hand near the crack, turned it in the light that came from behind her. He flexed it to show healthy whole flesh.

The widow's finger came through the door. Shaking, she traced his skin. After a little while, the door creaked a bit wider. Tor took his daughter's hand to cradle it in his where the widow could see it.

She touched for the child's fingers. Bit by bit, the doorway opening enlarged. At last, the woman knelt, trembling, her face level with the girl, ignoring Tor and Josson.

Tor's small daughter studied the woman's face carefully. She pushed away the light linen cloth that covered the woman's head. The widow did not stop her. The girl's tiny fingers explored scars where an ear should have been and where bone protruded, and where hair would never grow again. She ran her hand over the other side to touch a plump cheek and a pale blonde braid tied in a bit of rag.

"Something hurt me," the woman said simply. "Long ago. It doesn't hurt now." She did not know if the child could understand her words. In turn, the widow could not help herself from reaching toward the little girl's face. Her own strong young fingers touched skin that felt the same but looked utterly different from her own, in an almost-identical movement of gentle curiosity. Her lips parted in wonder. "What *are* you?" she asked.

Tor's daughter took the woman's hand in hers. She reached back for her brother's small fingers. "We are *hungry*," she answered firmly.

"Oh, you darlings," the woman cried. She rose to her feet and led them into her home.

. . .

Tor carried the broken axle to a charred outbuilding and kicked open the half-burned door. Light filtered in on a scene of utter disarray. Everything lay covered with burnt wood and ash. The roof had caved in, but amid the wreckage he could make out a small anvil.

Tor remembered Josson's words about the fire, and how the woman's voice had shaken as she opened the door for them. He imagined the screams of the man caught in the flames and the woman rushing in to try and save him. "Those poor people," he murmured.

He propped open what remained of the door and started clearing the mess, putting the blackened pieces of wood to one side. The bellows leather was charred but still looked usable. Tor raked through the ashes that covered the tool shelf. He found a blacksmith hammer with its wooden handle almost intact and located a pair of tongs.

"Seems you know what you're doing," Josson was leaning against the opening. He got no response and tried again. "I know you understand me now. You could say something occasionally. Makes life easier if I don't have to always guess what you're thinking." Why was he pleading with this man? *He's a damned stubborn stone. I paid a falcon and my winter meat-barrel for him.* He cursed again and stomped away, glaring across the fields.

The damned stubborn stone paid Josson no mind when the trader returned. Tor methodically put stacked burned pieces wood on the forge. *He's using it as charcoal,* Josson realized. *Clever.*

Tor lit the fire. He inspected the axle and measured with his hands. In what seemed no time at all, a bit of iron reddened on the forge and the hammer clanged as Tor formed a collar to join the broken pieces. Soon he plunged the hot metal into water and steam hissed.

. . .

As Tor checked the cooled piece against the axle and prepared to reheat it, the young widow called. Tor stepped outside. She stood at some distance from the small building, her face turned away.

"Your children have eaten," she said.

Tor nodded, a simple movement that conveyed deep thanks.

"Do you two need food as well?"

"I have not had anything for days," he said. "The trader has eaten, but not much."

"Come inside when you're finished," she said. She hurried away, pulling the linen cloth closer to her face.

Inside the forge, Josson was inspecting the repair to the harness. "That's a complex bit of smithy you just did. What else can you do?"

"Make weapons. Tools. Fix things. Jewelry. Anything metal."

Josson rubbed his hands together, pleased. He leaned back to consider the tall man who sweated in the heat from the fire. *Perhaps not such a bad trade after all.*

. . .

Tor sighed in relief when they entered the small longhouse. His son and daughter no longer had the starved and desperate look in their eyes. Their thin bellies were rounded and their faces relaxed.

"It's just pottage," the young woman apologized. "But I used to be known as a fine cook."

The food tasted as good as her word as the men ate eagerly. Josson scraped the wooden bowl with his fingers, licked it, and considered having a morning meal from her as well.

"You've fed us and let us use your forge. Manners demand that we help with something. This man knows how to repair things. Anything on your farm he could do? Not long until sunset. We'll sleep here. You'll have to feed us again tomorrow, of course."

"You don't need to fix anything. But do stay. It would be wonderful…" she broke off, and then began again. "I have no children. It's a joy to see young faces."

Josson fingered the scrape where he had sworn the blood-oath to keep Tor's children with him. With his mouth full, he mumbled. "You ought to leave these two here with her. Does 'em no good dragging about with you. Better to get rid of them."

Anger flashed in the slave man's eyes. "Do not ever speak to me regarding my children."

Josson squinted at Tor. "Regarding your children? When did you suddenly learn to talk so good?"

Tor ignored the trader. He handed the widow his empty bowl and strode outside. In the forge, he picked through the mess and retrieved a flat piece of iron. As he pounded with the hammer, Tor's anger at

Josson cooled. In short order he had created a brace for where the longhouse door had begun to rot along the bottom.

"Looks as if we're staying," Josson grunted to the widow. He spent the rest of the evening scuffing about outside, avoiding the scarred young woman as if the sight of her might poison him. Tor moved steadily from one task to another. When dusk softened into darkness, he came into the longhouse and washed his hands at the bowl, lathering the tallow-soap up to his elbows. Josson followed him in, lurking away from the widow.

"I've made a decent supper," she offered. "Your son and daughter have eaten more." She indicated where the two children played happily with a kitten.

The widow had killed two chickens and plucked them. In a cauldron over her fire, she had turned the chickens over and over, letting the sizzling fat turn them golden brown. Tor pulled the crisp skin from the meat, relishing the rich taste. When only gnawed bones remained, Tor fixed Josson with his gaze.

"She gave up two chickens for us. Give her an orange," he said.

Josson licked his fingers to get the last bit of savory taste. "Chickens do not merit an orange. Besides, you've fixed half her broken-down farm today. She made out better than I did, I think."

"Give her an orange."

"They belong to me." Josson did his best to glare, but he wavered under Tor's calm insistence. "No orange," he muttered, feeling for the fruit-box key that hung around his neck. He turned away and climbed onto the sleeping bench. "You want to take what's mine. Well, you can't. They belong to me."

. . .

As the firelight flickered to embers, Josson's snores filled the small homestead. Tor watched the young woman. She sat wrapped in a soft blanket, her hands clasped together as she gazed at the sleeping children. For a long while they did not speak.

"What's your name?" Tor finally asked.

"Eilíf" she replied.

"You have no sons or daughters, Eilíf?"

She shook her head. Firelight reflected on shimmering tears. "I was carrying when the fire happened. Twins, I learned later. I lost them soon afterwards; stillborn. Maybe from being burned myself, perhaps from grief. That's why I was frightened by you and your two children. I thought… you know."

"That they were the spirits of your infants."

"Yes. I never saw them. I don't even remember it happening. A woman came to help me. Aldís, they call her. She walks the countryside, doing healing work, helping on farms. A *druid-vitki*…a truth-seeing one. You know of them?"

Tor saw that Eilíf wanted to explain. He shook his head no.

"*Druid-vitki* have powers beyond what most of us understand," Eilíf said. "Some can discern truth when a man or woman speaks. Those are often called to speak at *thing* law councils, to help settle matters between feuding people. Others can sense weather, or good planting times. Some have second-sight of the future. This one, Aldís—she hears a calling when someone has been hurt."

Tor cocked his head sideways, frowning. "She hears something?"

"No, it's not like that. She just…senses it. She said she's never sure, but she follows it anyway. I remember waking in agony to find her caring for my wounds. I had no idea when she arrived. She told me later that she had had a sensation as if her own skin was burning, and that she had walked towards the feeling."

"Why does she do that? Is she paid by those she helps?"

"No. She refuses to take anything for her services. And I don't know why she does it. She's a good person, that's for certain—but there's something more. Something…sad…about her. I think she is trying to forget something."

"In any case, good fortune for you," Tor said.

"Yes. She saved my life, worthless though it was. I went in and out of the darkness for days. The pain…" Lines along Eilíf's mouth deepened. "She stayed with me until the burned skin fell off and I healed. When I could bear to touch it—when the pain had lessened— my fingers told me I must look terrible." She sat silent, her eyes downcast. As if she had just remembered, she turned slightly away from Tor and adjusted the light veil that covered her scars.

"Aldís is the only reason I survived. One day she was gone," Eilíf continued. "After that, other people came. Men who had been widowed. Others came thinking to marry me as a second wife, to get my land." She choked. "But the look in their eyes spoke the truth: no land was worth the ugliness they saw. No offers were made. They all left. It humiliated me, at first, but later, I realized I preferred it that way, to be alone here. I wanted nothing from them anyway, and I wanted to never see that look again in anyone's eyes." She paused again. "The shock, and their staring. There hasn't been another chance to have children. But I wanted some, desperately."

"You're a good woman. I'm sure life will bring a family one day."

"I can't imagine how that might happen." Eilíf's voice held only resignation. "Besides, I don't deserve them."

The logs in the fire crumbled softly, the once-bright flames now a soft flicker among embers.

"One never knows." Tor leaned forward, his expression earnest. "Keep your hope. What I have learned is that goodness flows through life, but not always how we might expect."

"A remarkable attitude for a man who himself has no freedom," Eilíf said. She looked pointedly at where the iron had cut into his wrist. "And whose son and daughter were all but starving."

"But I *have* my children," Tor said. "Without them, I might feel differently. Yes, things are difficult now, but I will somehow find a way for us to live safely together. That is all that matters."

"This man Josson will sell you? I would offer to pay him if I had anything to barter. You could stay here. I certainly could use help on the farm. I wouldn't expect you to…I mean, I would care for your children, but we wouldn't…I wouldn't…we would just…" A pink blush suffused her cheek and she looked away.

"I thank you for being willing to help," Tor smiled gently. "But he traded a gyrfalcon for me. I expect he'll want quite a bit in return."

Eilíf changed the subject. "You spoke in broken sentences when you first came. I heard Josson's surprise when you answered about your children. How did he not know that you and your children can speak Icelandic fluently?"

"It's a silly thing, perhaps. But it's a way of protecting us from others, until I have a chance to see what they're like. Imagine this trader's astonishment if he knew that I speak four languages well, and a few others badly." He chuckled a little.

Eilíf marveled. "How far you have travelled! More than I can possibly imagine." She glanced around the sparsely furnished room. "This small farm, so far from anywhere, has been my whole life."

"Travel doesn't make a better person," he replied. "Nor wealth or possessions. A good life may have those but does not require them."

She turned her sweet gaze back to the children. "You, who have no hope for freedom, embrace goodness. You show kindness, even to that trader who locked you to his cart. But I know only sorrow. My husband loved this farm so I tend it as my last way of honoring him. I just live day to day in lonely regret."

Tor got up to stir the fire. He cleared his throat. "Hate nearly destroyed me, twice in my life. Because of it, I choose to walk a path of kindness." His mouth eased in another reluctant smile. "But it does not come easily. In truth, I must choose calm and kindness over fear and anger every single day. But I have learned that such small choices, day after day, shape our lives more powerfully than we might guess."

Eilíf sensed the truth in those quiet words. Their meaning sank into waters deep inside her. Understanding spread in slow ripples that lapped at the edge of a lie.

The reason why. Guilt had tormented her since the fire, and Eilíf had dared tell no one. Now it had grown into a formidable wall. For the first time, she sensed that keeping her dreadful secret hidden had not protected her but instead had imprisoned her.

I, too, have made a choice each day, she wanted to say. *To hide the truth of all that happened.*

Eilíf tried, but the words stuck in her throat. Instead, she said, "Sometimes our choices set us free, even when enslaved. Sometimes they enslave us even if we are free. You may be a thrall, but you are far freer than I ever will be."

They did not speak again, but simply sat in silence. From time to time, one or the other of them added wood to the longfire. Finally Tor yawned, rose, and bowed slightly to Eilíf. He stretched on the sleeping bench alongside his children and wrapped himself in the woolen blankets. They murmured and she heard Tor say mysterious fluid words to them, then watched him drift quickly into dreams.

She rubbed her arms where the fire warmed them and leaned forward, staring at it and thinking. At some point, her eyes closed and Eilíf slept as well, with a peace that she had not known in years.

. . .

Chapter Four

In the morning, Eilíf dropped chunks of onion and smoked ham into hot butter in a forged skillet over her fire. Josson ate greedily. After that he chafed, anxious to get on his way again. Knowing that Tor could speak *and* had marketable skills had greatly revived Josson's hopes of recovering some gain. He listed on his fingers the various farmsteads he would try.

"Let's go, mountain-man," Josson said.

Tor gestured his children toward the longhouse door. They stepped out, squinting at the bright sparkles of dew in the morning sun.

When they had hefted the repaired axle in place and resumed their way along the track, Josson swore vehemently.

"Good food or not, that's the last time I'll stop at that poverty-stricken farm. I never want to lay eyes on that grisly woman ever again." He cracked his whip at the horse. Its hooves clopped against the stones in the path and the cart creaked forward.

Tor had taken a last look at the longhouse before it was lost from their view. Eilíf's carefully tended garden was lush with cabbages and abundant leaves of turnips, beets, onions, and carrots. A row of firkins on a shelf held cheeses, and the bright-eyed goats in her pen promised milk for more. Her loom held a blanket she was weaving.

Tor shook his head at the trader's foolishness. Josson did not know the riches this woman had.

. . .

By nightfall, hunger had again begun to cramp in Tor's stomach.

"She fed you well enough for two days," Josson said, peevish.

"You're eating again. We're hungry too."

But Josson did not offer to share, turning his back as he ate.

Tor could see the worry return to his children's eyes. He held them and rubbed their small stomachs as they tried to sleep.

. . .

The next day, Josson gobbled a solitary breakfast. Three sets of eyes followed every spoonful of food to his mouth. Josson wiped his dirty hand across his lips.

"Quit watching me, you vultures."

"My children need food."

"Your children are not my problem."

. . .

Farms grew plentiful along the roadway. All showed great interest in Tor, asking questions and poking his muscles, pulling his jaw down and examining his teeth, but none made an offer.

"But these young ones—are they for sale?" Tor flinched at the question each time.

"No," Josson replied. "They're his. Free-beings."

"Are you sure? We'd love to buy one of *them*. Maybe both."

"No, they're not really for sale." But Tor noticed that each time, Josson's voice sounded a little less certain. Tor thought of the oranges and Josson saying *you can't take what's mine.* Would the trader respect those same rules?

By that second night, Tor's daughter wept when Josson ate, but he ignored her. She sniffled and wiped her nose with the back of her hand.

Josson spoke directly to Tor, ignoring the children. "I hardly have enough for myself. But I can't have you looking too thin if I'm trying to sell you. I'll give you a share of oats for supper, but you'll have to divide it with those two."

Tor gave his children all the food. They tried to get him to take some of the porridge, saying *please, papa, eat*, in their strange musical language, but Tor refused, kissing the soft brown curls of their hair and murmuring to them, and glaring at Josson.

. . .

The following midday, Josson turned his wagon into a farm with many outbuildings. The bright noon sun gleamed on broad golden fields where a score of workers scythed wheat in rapid strokes. The sound of an ancient harvest-song reached the cart as they bumped along over the grassy approach to the longhouse.

My children will live safe here, Tor thought. To Josson, he said, "This place seems well-managed. Their workers look fit. They must have plentiful food. There's lots of work here. Sell me to them, whatever they offer. I'll find a way to make it up to you."

Josson, still nursing a grudge over Tor's demand of an orange for the widow, snorted. "It's up to me to decide who I'll sell you to. No promises. Maybe they won't even want you, saddled with those two extra mouths that can't do anything worthwhile."

"I'm able enough to do the chores of three men, and the children are both old enough to work. You know it." He told the horse to halt.

"I said we'll see. Stay here." Josson pushed the children inside an outbuilding and gestured for Tor to follow them.

The landholders greeted him with food and ale. Josson, looking at the dishes served and the servants who carried them, could not see any pinch from poor harvests. To his delight, the couple quickly bought the whole package of peppercorns and four of his bitter-oranges.

Now, for the trade of his life. Josson licked his lips.

"I have a *maurus-man,* an exotic. Dark, from—" He tried to remember the place the ship merchant had named but failed. "You saw him as we arrived, perhaps? That huge creature is for sale."

As Josson described Tor's excellent blacksmithing, he saw his hosts glancing at one another. He felt certain an offer would come soon. He grew more eloquent about Tor's skills.

The woman whispered to her husband, who nodded. She beckoned to a servant, spoke quietly again.

Then to Josson, she said, "Before we discuss a possible trade, let us enjoy more refreshments. The oranges we bought for our *Jül glögg*…have you ever had it? Perhaps you would like to try some of the wine we use to make it?"

Josson had never tasted the extravagant spiced treat, nor the expensive beverage used for it. "Of course. It's my favorite drink."

The woman handed him a hard clear item, amber in color.

"Oh, you have glass-horns," Josson admired. He held the vessel by the talons worked in its base and the woman filled it. He gulped, as if she might snatch the wine back after a sip.

A taste, tart like berries and sweet as honey, filled Josson's mouth. He lifted the vessel, admiring how light shone through it, then held it out for more. As they talked, Josson noticed that his feet felt oddly large and warm. He clutched his wine-glass and knew with certainty he was a powerful man, not one to be trifled with. *These folks know; look how well they treat me.* He could smell meat cooking on the fire.

"Bring your man in. We want to look at him," said the freeholder.

As he led Tor into the hall, Josson proffered his wine-glass towards table-girl again as the man and woman walked around Tor, inspecting him. Josson guzzled the whole glass, and then another one. When the table-girl cleared the food bowls, he seized the opportunity to sneak an unopened skin of wine under his ragged tunic.

"What's the cost for this man?" the woman asked

Josson racked his brain but now could not remember the prices he had heard paid for dark-skinned slaves. He ran his eyes around the rich longhouse, grew bold, and shouted out an appalling number.

"Too much," the woman replied. "I saw two children as you arrived. You must expect that for all three. We only want the man."

"Yes. All three. They come as one lot." Josson burped.

"I said we don't want the children." The woman's friendly tone had turned hard. "They will be a distraction to the other workers. Name your price for just the man. You can sell the small ones at another farm along the way."

Josson puffed himself up, sure of his skills in haggling. He would make the landowner work for it. *Push the price higher.* He drained the wine-glass again and held it out.

The freeholder husband ignored the gesture. "Your price," he said. "For just the man. We won't ask again."

Josson, his hand still outstretched with the glass, realized that he had somehow lost control of the situation, but he did not know how to stop. The wine made him feel dizzy and powerful all at once.

So what if Tor wore those blue beads, the soul-stones of a free person? So what if Josson had promised the ship merchant to keep them together? No one knew that now besides him and Tor. And it would serve Tor right for tricking Josson about not talking, the liar.

"Just the man, then," said Josson. With his ability to count now in hopeless disarray, he called out an even higher number. "You want less, you pay more. Compensate me for being stuck with two sprats."

"Your greediness beggars belief!" the hostess said.

Tor closed the distance between him and Josson in one furious leap. Gripping Josson's tunic, his face close to the trader's, Tor roared.

"You swore a blood-oath that my children would stay with me."

The freeholders backed away, blanching at the sight of a thrall threatening the man who owned him.

"That thing is a menace," the woman shouted. "Get him off our property this instant!"

The trading interview ended abruptly, as Josson found himself hustled unceremoniously to the door.

. . .

Josson had planned to ask for scraps from the welcome-meal to give to the children. When he and Tor returned to the stable yard, they stood up, their small faces hopeful. Josson thought for a brief instant of going back to ask for food but pictured the farmer's disdain. In anger, he turned on Tor, his words slurring from the wine.

"Look what you did! You ruined that sale. Keep your precious children if you want, but from now on you'll have to find food for them. I won't provide for three mouths when I paid for only one."

Tor chose not to argue. He had won the most critical issue.

"Still plenty of light to get to the next farm," Josson said. "We can sleep along the road after that if we have to." *Better to make haste before a servant carried news of this disaster along the valley.* Josson fumbled with the slave-chain as he fastened it to Tor's wrist.

When they reached the roadway, Josson turned his cart-horse the wrong way on the path, in the direction that led back towards the widow's house. Tor noticed the error and started to speak but changed his mind and said nothing.

As they headed along the road, Josson flopped onto the cart. "Do you know how foolish you are, dragging these two everywhere with you? You think whoever buys you won't sell them? You'll wake up one day and they'll be gone. Sold and gone! You should cut them loose. Look out for yourself. I learned that long ago," he mumbled. "Look out for yourself." At this, he pulled his patched cloak over his eyes and fell asleep, snoring heavily, his mouth open.

The children looked at Tor, worried. He kept his tone gentle.

"Do you see where we are headed? This old man must want to go where we were before. Eilíf's home is this way. You remember?"

In reality, Tor felt desperate at Josson's words. He had convinced himself over the years that somehow, he could keep the children with him. The words he'd spoken to the ship-merchant Indaell were true: Iceland was a land known for its laws. But Josson had spoken a truth Tor had not dared let himself consider.

The widow's longhouse ahead felt like a safe harbor beckoning. The thought gave him something to hold on to. He slapped the horse's flank, urging it along the road like a madman, glad that Josson was too soundly asleep to notice how they bounced and lurched over the ruts.

I could kill this man with one snap of his neck, Tor thought. *I could toss his skinny old body into the woods. No one would ever be the wiser. I could sign as a bond-worker to some farm, and my days as a slave would be over.*

But even as he thought the words, Tor abhorred them. He had learned the hard way that one could not control hate once invited in.

He looked at the pathetic trader. "If you die in your sleep, I'm a free man. But you'll not die by my hand—not today, or any day. As you said, a deal's a deal."

He did not explain his words to the children who bounced on the cart alongside Josson, but simply urged the horse onwards.

. . .

Stars began to twinkle against a rosy evening sky when they reached the same rocky grove in which they had sheltered the night before. Tor pulled the cart and horse off the road. When the movement stopped, Josson sat up. He looked around, confused. "Where are we? We slept here last night. How'd we get here?"

"You chose the way," Tor said.

"You tricked me somehow. Is this a *maurus*-enchantment?"

"Hardly. It's called drunkenness."

Josson held his head. "My head feels like a rotten turnip. It's getting dark and the moon's not up yet. This is a good enough place to stop for a while. Safe. Nobody will see us. We'll sort it tomorrow."

He staggered off to relieve himself, then returned to unlock Tor to allow him the same. "I'm watching your children, so don't run off." Josson made the same threat every time, keeping his gaze fixed on the children as small hostages. He groaned. "Be quick."

When Tor got back, he found Josson thrashing on the ground, clenching his temples and muttering.

"Look out for myself. Children…soul beads… need to get those beads from him…get the beads…"

Tor, exhausted and furious, held his daughter and his son in his arms, trying to calm himself. The trader did not hear the *slow breath in, slower breath out*. Neither Josson nor Tor realized that Tor's wrist chain swung loose on the cart.

. . .

Tor dreamed of oranges.

The sweet smell drifted through the night, and his body responded to the scent and what it meant. His wife had always used that seductive perfume to signal a private message to him.

Tor inhaled deeply. The delicious fragrance filled him with desire. He saw her neck, her ebony skin lustrous where she had smoothed the orange's skin. She tipped her head back, lifting her throat to his kiss.

His mouth moved along her jaw, across her collarbone, wanting more. Tor took his time, hearing her faint moan.

He glanced up to see her expression, with her lips parted and her eyes closed. Fire filled him. His lips explored every muscle of that taut body, breathing in the orange fragrance; her favorite, and because of her, his favorite.

She sat up and arched her back. The light silk covering her breasts slid from her shoulders. The sound of her laughter floated on the air.

Full of yearning, Tor pulled her close, and she pressed, knowing full well that her every movement aroused him even more. That aroma, *yes*. That fragrance, *I want you, now*. He wrapped her in a tight embrace, and they twined their legs around one another. *Yes, now*.

Tor's lips moved as he whispered his wife's name. He did not hear his daughter whisper beside him, *mama*.

His wife kissed him. He ran his teeth across her soft mouth, felt her tongue smooth against his. He could never recall when laughter turned serious or when sounds of play turned into gasps for breath.

Afterwards, when the urgency had drained away, she would feel chilled by the smallest breeze on her naked skin. He would pull a light sheet over her to keep her warm. They would lie together in perfect symmetry, her head nestled against his shoulder and her fingers twisted in his hair, their legs still entangled, the only thing not spent into softness the gold circle that gleamed on her finger. Deeply in love, Tor would drift into sleep, hearing the rustle of orange-tree leaves in the courtyard of their home, breathing the lustful, exciting aroma.

. . .

Aching with readiness, reaching for his wife, Tor woke. *Why was it so cold? Why did the moon shine on his bed? Where was he?* His daughter murmured again, and Tor realized that he lay cramped in the dirt on hard ground. The scent of orange still drifted on the summer night. He came suddenly alert.

The rising moon flooded the ground with pale light. Tor heard the horse snuffling in sleep, and Josson's uneven snorting for air. The stolen wineskin lay beside the trader, empty.

"You stupid, stupid man," Tor said. "Look what you've done to your precious oranges!"

Sometime in the night, Josson had staggered to the wagon. He had pried his last two oranges from their box, intending in his inebriated state to protect them from Tor. But Josson had fallen unconscious after drinking the stolen wine, and he lay clutching the fruits, squeezing them to a pulpy mess.

Tor looked at the trader with growing fury. The treasured scent in his dream had come not from his beloved wife's skin, but from oranges mauled by a filthy man who lay drunk in the dirt, who had refused to feed Tor's children. Josson lay on the ground, intoxicated, wasting the very fruits he had refused to share with the widow.

Tor squatted. He forced himself to stay motionless. He did not trust himself to move with such bitter rage surging through him.

"Papa…" came a small whisper. "I can't breathe."

Inebriated and stumbling, Josson had tied a rope around the neck of Tor's son. At some point the trader had entangled his feet in the rope. The boy lay sideways, wedged between the trader and the cart wheel, the harsh fibers twisted tight around his neck. He shook with cold on the hard ground, unable to move. "I'm choking, Papa," his small voice gasped.

Choking. From Tor's youth came the memory of another helpless boy trembling in fear. He saw his fingers wrapped around a man's throat, his hands squeezing until the one who had tortured the boy stopped thrashing and kicking. Screams had happened after. His anger had saved no one.

Tor pushed away that terrible memory day by day, but tonight, once more the desire to right a wrong burned fierce. His high-minded words to Eilíf were swept away in desire for brutal vengeance.

That flaccid neck. How right it would feel to circle it with his strong hands, to force the breath from that miserable trader. Long-pent-up fury surged in a rogue wave, unstoppable.

Tor bent over Josson. He gripped skin and bone and tunic and lifted the trader with one hand. Josson came snorting awake. His eyes bulged from fear as he clawed at Tor's arms.

May those who show cruelty feel it. Tor squeezed harder, relentless. *May those who teach fear feel it in their own bones. May those who hurt young innocents know the anguish of being dominated and controlled.* Loathing hardened his grip and Tor knew nothing but a desire to destroy. He squeezed until Josson's head flopped and his body went limp. HE threw the lifeless form to the ground.

"Look at you now, you horrid, useless husk." At the sight of the body, Tor's fury began to die. As it ebbed, horror filled him at what he had just done...the thing he had sworn to never, ever do again.

. . .

Tor fell backwards, scrambling to get away from Josson's corpse, panting. How had he let this happen? How had he let himself yield to hate enough that it had consumed him again? *I thought I had beaten it. I thought I was no longer a demon who took the lives of other men.*

Tor buried his face in his hands. He gagged in revulsion. *I murdered this man in front of my children.* Desolation filled him.

As Tor fought to breathe, Josson snorted something unintelligible, thrashing in his sleep. Tor jumped back.

"You're alive? I don't understand…" Josson's throat under Tor's fingers had felt all too real, but the trader rolled in the dirt, unhurt.

"Papa," his son whispered. "Why have you been staring at him like that? Your face scares me."

Tor sagged to his knees. "I'm sorry, my son."

"I'm afraid, Papa." The boy's chin trembled. "Please help me."

"I can't get to you. I'm chained."

"No, Papa." With his free hand, the boy pointed to where the chain dangled, hooked to the side of the wagon.

In a rush of gratitude, Tor crawled to his son, the rocks cutting into his knees. With fingers that trembled with haste, he carefully unwound the choking rope from his son's neck and wrapped him in the blanket with the little girl. Tor held them, rocking back and forth.

Guide me, Infinite Goodness. That stupid trader was not born intending to become selfish and mean. Somewhere in his life Josson had been treated unkindly, had been taught by the weak to be weak.

Tor told himself the same truths he had many times before about humans who seemed to have no good in their souls. *Hating him only deepens those same traits in my own soul. Hating him makes me be what he is. I don't want to be what he is.*

There were other ways to fight. "I will find a way forward for us," Tor whispered against his children's nestled heads. "I will."

He breathed until the angry feelings subsided into nothing more substantial than sea foam on sand. Soon the deep, careful breaths *in, out… in, out* blew even that away.

At length, Tor removed the damaged bitter-oranges from Josson's fingers. He took the key on Josson's neck-string and started to lock the oranges in their box again, but suddenly he stopped as he heard chilling words come clearly from the sleeping trader.

"I'm selling those children at the very next farm. Need to look out for myself. Need meat for the winter."

. . .

Tor could not deny the truth any longer. Today, he had barely escaped being separated from his children. Josson's words made it clear where the road forward would lead.

In pain, he spoke a sad truth aloud, fear and hopelessness swirling.

"My precious ones. As long as you are with me, Josson will see you only as profits. I will never be able to keep you safe." He nuzzled his son's forehead. "What have I done, bringing you here?"

As Tor held the children, another realization broke through. His long dedication to the Almighty had led him to this moment. At that realization, the ground itself felt unsteady beneath him.

"What can I believe in, if not the faith you have given me? Is there no way to protect my beloved children?"

A quicksand of despair sucked at Tor. He grasped for hope but found none. The weary man cried out in mortal pain. To see them in bondage would be unbearable. To be separated from them would tear apart what was left of his ability to survive. And yet, as he held them in agony, Tor realized it was the only way *they* would survive.

"Holy One, give me another path, please, I beg you. My children mean everything to me. I cannot leave them."

No answer came. Profound sadness swept over Tor. He stayed motionless. Finally, he put the oranges carefully to one side. He stood very tall, his tattered tunic moving in the light breeze.

Squared his shoulders. Set his jaw.

Tor locked the empty orange-box and returned the key on its string to the trader's neck. Lifting the heavy wrist-manacle and chain from the wagon, Tor carried it to where Josson lay, the metal links clinking softly. When he had securely locked the trader to the wagon, Tor tied a gag across Josson's mouth. He stood in the moonlight, thinking.

It had taken nearly two day's travel from the widow's house to this grove. But they had gone up many farm tracks and had stopped at many homesteads to trade. Could he cover the same ground tonight, with the two children on the horse and him walking? Could he get back quickly enough before anyone might find Josson?

Most farms were busy with harvests. The roads had been largely empty, only wind traveling along the isolated tracks. *I'll risk it.*

He whispered to his children to hush. His heart nearly broke at the feel of their trusting arms lifted to a father about to abandon them.

. . .

Chapter Five

Eilíf sat up in the dark, looking around the longhouse. What had woken her? Then she heard it again: a knock at the door. Eilíf held the blanket to her mouth, afraid to answer.

Then she heard Tor's voice. "Please let us in. I have my children."

Eilíf peeked through the crack as she had before. "What has happened? Why are you back here? Where is the trader Josson?"

"Don't waste concern on him. He will sleep soundly all night."

"Does he know you are here?"

"No. He must not."

A sinking feeling filled Eilíf. She had imagined the possibility since Tor had left, but, seeing the children in the flesh, fantasy yielded to sharp reality. "You brought them to leave them here, don't you?"

"Yes, I did." He said it flatly, without apology or emotion.

"No," she refused. Their sweet voices and trusting eyes had deepened the old wound in her heart. "Having them here was wonderful, but what you want is impossible. I won't allow it!"

"Please," was all Tor replied.

"I cannot," Eilíf cried. "There are things you don't know."

"There are things about me you don't know either." Tor stood stubbornly at the door, his frame silhouetted by the moon. "I need your help. Let us come in. They've barely eaten since we left you."

At that she could hold out no longer. The door swung wide. Soon the small ones were gratefully gulping pottage, spooning it into their mouths so fast that his daughter hiccupped. Eilíf scraped the pot and refilled the little girl's bowl. At the child's tearful thanks, Eilíf knew she would not be able to turn them away.

. . .

Tor's voice fell to a hush as he spoke of precious memories.

"We lived as a family, my children, my wife and I, in a place called Al-Andalus. Far from here, and very different. Always warm. Always sunny. But people are the same everywhere. Most are good, but a few are evil. One day she did not come home from the market. I asked questions from everyone I could. She had been taken, fighting and screaming, to a slave ship. They had bribed the port master, snatched as many people as they could, and sailed again before anyone realized what had happened."

Eilíf knew that kind of grief from loss, tangible and unhealable.

Tor continued. "I have been searching for my wife since then. I sold our home when I had no more silver. I borrowed from everyone I could. When that was gone, I sold my freedom so that I could keep looking for her in every port in the world, on the condition that I could keep our children with me. It's not being a slave that bothers me. That means nothing to me, truly. It's that she is likely in danger, or misused. I *expect* it, with dreadful certainty. The worst is that I don't even know if she still lives, if there is even the slimmest hope for us to be together again. It eats me, wondering if she is warm and safe or has enough to eat. I torment myself imagining what she must be going through, all alone, and wondering why I don't come to her."

"I'm so sorry." Eilíf felt his heartbreak.

Tor took a breath to steady himself. "There is more. Imagine, if you will, the same kind of slavers who stole my wife, but looking at my children. Imagine them, when our ship stopped for trades; they would narrow their eyes and put their fingers to their beards as they considered how much silver or perhaps even gold they could get from the sale of a beautiful dark-skinned child."

"I don't want to think of that. It nauseates me."

"While they were small, I could keep them hidden. But that became harder every day as they grew. Even you, living alone here, must sense how vulnerable they are. People would pay a great deal for an exotic, a pet to parade for guests. Their skin and hair, so strange and beautiful in these parts, are desired by those who crave a new…" He gagged, and his voice grew more harsh. "*Distraction* is the word they use. To have my daughter and son become perfumed bed-slaves for some man's perverted pleasure? I cannot allow that to happen."

Eilíf looked doubtful, not able to comprehend such a travesty. "Those dear little faces. Who could do such a thing?"

"I speak the truth!" Tor insisted. "Everywhere in the world are those who force, who take pleasure from those too vulnerable to refuse, and must endure a lifetime of shame and pain." The gorge rose in Tor, still overwhelming after all these years, the reason he had killed. "I cannot bear for that to happen to my children. I will not allow it. I must protect them, or else what kind of father am I?"

"But why here? Why me?"

"I kept telling myself that I could keep them safe, but they are not. Maybe I was afraid *I* could not survive without *them*. But my fear— my selfish desire, really, to hold onto the last remainder of my old life with my wife—it only increases their danger. Josson will not honor my children's soul-beads. I was stupid to think he would. I know it for certain now. It is only a matter of time, and not much time at that, until he sells them away from me. What would I do then? Fly into a rage, and kill Josson and the freeholder that bought them? Die, with my children watching me bleed out, beaten to death by the servants of some stranger? No. To keep my daughter and son safe, I must do the one thing which has always been unacceptable to me. I must say goodbye to them."

Tor's chest ached. "I almost lost them today. If someone takes them, it will be my fault. How could I live, bearing such guilt?"

His pain shocked the young widow into a truth she had never dared to utter.

"I know that kind of guilt!" Eilíf flung out her hands in confession. "I am the reason my husband died. I live every day knowing that it is my fault he burned."

Her words jerked Tor from his own despair. "Why do you say that?"

"I wanted to buy things from traders, and not just ones like Josson, with his meagre supplies, but from the rich-goods traders as well. All the beautiful things that I despise now."

"Most people want nice things. That doesn't make you guilty for his death."

"I did not just *want* nice things. I *craved* them, even though we could not afford them. I harassed my husband constantly, demanding more. He would work every day in the fields, trying to increase what we could earn. Clearing frost-heaved stones, plowing seeds into the soil from sunrise until after dark every day. Exhaustion would overtake him, but he struggled on, trying to make me happy. I became so selfish that I ignored how tired he was. After he ate supper, I nagged him to go into our forge, when it was too dark to work in the fields, to make whatever items he could." Her head dropped to her chest. In shame she said, "To trade for things I wanted."

Eilíf's chest heaved. "He was bone-weary. But I insisted, night after night after night. I turned him away from our bed. But he would do anything for me. He loved me more than I loved him. To please me, he went into the forge every night and worked late, too tired to be careful. One day the inevitable happened."

She put her face into her hands and sobbed. "He was such a good man, and I didn't appreciate him. I killed him. I miscarried our children because of my greediness. I cannot forgive myself, not ever."

. . .

Silence seemed the only decent response to such tragedy. Tor waited for Eilíf's sobbing to slow.

"We all make mistakes in life," he offered quietly. "At least you admit yours. That takes courage."

"What is it worth in the face of such betrayal? Nothing. And now you know: your daughter and son would live with someone who traded love for selfish vanity. The truth is that I am glad that the fire ruined my looks. I deserved that, and more."

"I do not judge you. And it changes nothing about my children."

"But I have nothing to offer them. Food and shelter, yes, but they would be completely isolated here. I live alone. Traders do not stop. Even if I could afford to buy their things, I will never allow myself their luxuries again. Hardly anyone even comes here, from one year to the next. What life would that be?"

"Exactly the life they need," Tor said. Suddenly, his faith in the Almighty surged back. "Was it chance that Josson's axle broke at your lane? We were *led* to you! The thing I want most for them is safety, for them to stay together as sister and brother. A place where no one will see them. You, who wanted children so badly, would protect them as a true mother. Safety, shelter, food, and most importantly, love, plus honest work in clean air...what more do they need? I would far prefer that they live healthy and safe in homespun cloth than be paraded about in silks, beautiful but broken inside. Please."

Now Tor flung out his hands to Eilíf, beseeching. She could not meet his eyes. But her gaze fell upon the little girl, still hiccupping in her sleep, her thumb in her mouth as she curled under the covers.

"That horror you fear for them... the bed-slavery. You know something of that personally," the young woman observed.

"I wish I did not. But I do." Now it was Tor's turn to break from the sorrow of remembering.

Eilíf reached her arms to Tor, wrapping him in an embrace of gentle compassion. As they clung together in mutual pain, new understanding grew within her.

This man has been isolated and broken like me, but where I gave up, he never did. If he can somehow find a way to keep going, I can too, if only to help him. She stroked her hand across Tor's hair, consoling him. *He suffered in his youth, and then the loss of his wife; his children lost their mother, and soon they could lose their father.*

Eilíf knew that she was Tor's only hope. *I can help. I will help,* she told herself. But when shame, her constant companion, mocked her, for the first time since the fire. Eilíf pushed back and did not yield.

"I will do what you need," she said to Tor. "It frightens me, but I will do it." And also for the first time since the fire, Eilíf knew was it was to feel strong again.

. . .

As she unfolded her sleeping blanket, Eilíf wondered why Tor simply did not run away. He had left Josson; why not just keep going? As if he could read her mind, Tor spoke.

"Where could we go? There will be no more trading ships until spring. Unless I go back to Josson, someone will inevitably find him. He will report that I tied him up and left him to die. Where could I hide, a man my color and size? No one would question Josson's right to take my children as compensation. I dread what I must do, but I realize now that the only way to protect my children is to hide them with you and return to Josson without them."

The widow could barely bring herself to ask the next question. "What if you just killed this trader? Then no one would know."

"I imagined that I *had* done that tonight, before I came here. Much as I might want that, even the idea of doing it made me disgusted with myself." Tor shook his head. "No, my faith forbids taking the life of another human. I did it before, many years ago. And now you know this thing about me: I have murdered."

They stared at one another, the grossness of their crimes haunting their eyes.

"I never will again; since then, I have dedicated myself to Goodness. A man cannot always win against evil, but he can refuse to let it grow in him."

"Can you succeed?" She held her blanket clutched to her chest.

"Sometimes, refusing to allow evil to grow inside us is all the fighting one can manage. Is it enough? Who knows? I long ago accepted that my fate follows a strange path. I decided to trust in the ways that the Most Holy One leads me."

He helped her to spread the blanket across the sleeping bench. "Much as I loathe the idea of going back to Josson, I will do it and not raise a hand against him. My only hope is that he never learns that I have been here at your farm again. Maybe things will turn out well and one day I can come back and get my children. But no matter what, I can be at peace knowing that they will live here in safety. Your country is a land of laws. Free, away from me and as your children, your laws will protect them. That is the best I can give them."

"You feel certain? Once you leave here, you cannot change what you have set in motion."

"It is the only way."

Eilíf buried her face in her hands, aghast.

"Do not feel sad for me," Tor said. "I almost asked you when we stopped here before. My instincts told me you were the right person and your home the right place, but I could not bring myself to do it. Even when Josson even suggested it, I raged at him. It is better this way, because he will never come here again, he told me so himself. He will never find my son and daughter. They will simply disappear."

As if to convince himself, Tor repeated, "I didn't have the courage earlier. Josson helped me see the truth. For that, I am grateful."

Eilíf gave a slow nod of acceptance. She reached out her hand to seal their agreement, and Tor took it in his. In the warmth of their palms pressed together lay the mortal safety of two innocent children.

Tor undid the leather string that held the blue soul-stones at his throat. His big hands shook as he put the necklace in Eilíf's careful grasp. "All my life stays here with you now. I owe you everything." His voice rasped.

"You owe me nothing. You have given me something for which I have yearned. I thought I would live my years as a childless woman. Thanks to you, I am a mother now. It is I who am in your debt."

Tor turned to go, but Eilíf caught his arm. "You are about to collapse from fatigue. Rest here for a little while. I'll make you food to take before you go. I'll wake you when it's ready," she said.

Tor slept before his head touched the bench. In the quiet night air, the young widow went to hen coop. She lifted sleepy protesting birds, collecting eggs. Back inside, she put them in her pottage-cauldron and added water to boil them, keeping her tools quiet as she worked. While they cooked, Eilíf went to the storage alcove of her longhouse and scooped fresh creamy *skyr* into a skin bag. She pulled two wheels of cheese from her shelf, but considering, put one back. *He cannot carry too much with him, or the trader will ask where it came from.* When the eggs and warm cheese and buttered warm oat bread filled the longhouse, she touched Tor on the shoulder, waking him.

"It's no exaggeration to call you gifted," he mumbled, stuffing food into his mouth. "Perhaps I am famished, but I have known hunger many times before. A man would be lucky to live here with you."

At his words, Eilíf ducked her face and blushed. She had let go of the worry of Tor seeing her scars, but from habit had seated herself with the damaged side turned away. Tor, looking up, chanced to see Eilíf as she must have been before the fire, round-cheeked and pretty, her lips curved in shy sweetness. It brought a treasured memory.

"I brought these for you," he remembered suddenly, pulling the two oranges from his pocket. "I am sorry to say that Josson damaged them, but they are still usable. Do this. Cut the skin like so," he said, slicing with a knife to remove a sliver of peel from the fruit. "Not the white part, see, just the colored bit. Dry it. It will keep its value as flavoring for years. Squeeze the fruits now for their juice, though. They won't last but a day or two more. With honey—" He stopped, realizing that, with no traders stopping by, she would likely not have any. "If you add it to barley-beer, it tastes delicious."

Eilíf exclaimed in astonishment at the rich gift. With the fruit pressed to her nose, she inhaled, sighing in pleasure. Tor laughed, full-throated and hearty, appreciating her delight.

Something about his laughter made Eilíf look up at him and blush again. For the first time in ages, she remembered the pleasure of being close with a man, but the idea shamed her. The color on her cheeks deepened to scarlet and she looked away.

"What is it?" Tor asked.

Eilíf turned towards him, her eyes half-pleading, half-forlorn, and Tor knew. In her expression he saw the hurt in her heart, how mortified she had been when people had recoiled from her appearance. Tenderness filled him, the desire to right a wrong. But he had made a pledge to his wife. Tor hesitated.

Embarrassed, Eilíf placed the orange on the table, ever so carefully. She stood and smoothed her apron. Stared down at the table, too humiliated to look at Tor again. Picked up the sliver of orange peel in one hand, and with the other, trembling slightly, reached to remove Tor's bowl and spoon.

He put his hand on her wrist. Eilíf stood absolutely still, her fingers still on the bowl. The scent of orange filled the air.

"Yes," Tor said.

Still, the widow looked only at the bowl, the table.

Tor turned her wrist over. Eilíf dropped the bowl, her fingers curving above her palm, the petals of a flower opening. Tor moved his thumb along the inside of her wrist, up and down. He could feel the heat of her skin, the pounding of a little vein against his fingers.

"Yes," he repeated.

The young woman's breasts rose and fell under her tunic. *Her heart is beating wildly,* Tor realized.

She had agreed to perhaps the most important thing he could ever ask. He could give her something back, if only for a little while. Lying together was not what she truly needed; it was the feeling of being wanted by a man. Of being desired. Of feeling beautiful again. Yes, he could give her that.

"My wi— I mean, women in my country do this." Tor took the bit of orange peel. Keeping Eilíf's wrist in his fingers, he walked around the table, turning her slightly as he came to her side. Stood close to her, his body barely brushing the folds of her skirt. "Lift your chin."

He brushed the bit of orange along the chords of her neck, skin that shone pale and creamy, so different from his wife's. Eilíf flinched, almost like a horse shying from his touch, afraid to look at him.

"This fragrance…" Tor touched his fingertips to his nostrils and inhaled. At last, she dragged her gaze to his face, caught between terror, shame, and hope.

"I am so ugly," Eilíf whispered. She turned the scarred side of her face away again. Tor saw the tears on her cheeks.

"Real ugliness lurks within a person's spirit. Your scars are on the surface. A different thing altogether."

"But…" She pulled her hand away, covered her face to hide it. Trembled. The fire sighed as a log fell to ash.

Tor cupped Eilíf's chin. He gently moved her fingers aside. His gentle touch traced the marks where the fire had burned her.

"These little scars…they are nothing, beside the rest of you." Tor bent his lips to the crown of her head. His mouth barely moved against her hair. He held her, feeling her shaking, letting her know that she was safe, giving her time to be ready.

Little by little, Eilíf pressed against him. Bit by bit, her hands fluttered along the muscles of his arms, his shoulders, tentative at first as she reached up towards him. At last, she lifted her face to his. Her lips opened to his, and Tor knew not to hold back any longer. He lifted Eilíf and carried her to the sleeping-benches.

She moaned with desire as his body pressed down on hers. Tor buried his face in her neck, breathing in the familiar, beloved orange aroma. *So long I have looked for my wife. So long since I have loved her.* The fragrance unlocked desire too long held in check, and Tor, too, cried out with wanting.

He lifted the linen of her nightgown and his fingertips found her place of yearning. He touched the soft folds, felt them become wet to welcome him. He touched his fingers to his lips, tasting, then touching them to her own lips. Once again, she cried out. She cradled her hands around his face and pulled his mouth to hers.

Intertwined, they moved, her breasts bare against his chest, her legs wrapped around his thighs. Gentleness became urgency, and urgency became ecstasy, motion that flowed without need of words. In their coupling, each reached towards long-ago innocence, lost and never to be had again, but they found only the ecstasy of flesh. For now, it was enough.

. . .

When they finished, Eilíf and Tor lay breathing side by side, her hand wrapped in his on his chest. Tor told her what he could not say earlier, because the words would have prevented what she needed.

"You are the first since my wife. I am ashamed to take you and then leave you like this. You deserve a man who will stay here with you and help you. But I must go back to Josson. I may never return."

"I understand," she said. "You meant it when you said you have accepted your fate. I thought I had accepted mine also, but tonight, my fate has changed. Perhaps yours will change, too."

His eyes had turned sad again. "I doubt it. But Nenet and Nikea will be safe with you. Nothing else matters now."

"Do not give up hope. I had forgotten how it felt, but suddenly, I *want* to hope again. Who knows what might happen?"

Over the soft hiss of embers settling, a child murmured.

"They are still sound asleep," Eilíf said. She slid her hand down his chest. Down his belly, then further, and was pleased to find that what she hoped for was possible.

"Once more, perhaps," she said. "For good luck." Unexpectedly, Eilíf's laughter bubbled, the sound of a healthy and happy woman. "And also, because it has been *such* a long time and may never happen again, perhaps once more just for pure pleasure."

Tor laughed at Eilíf's honest courage. He pulled her close. The faint smell of orange and her hushed cries against his chest once again tore open the endless longing for his wife, even as desire for Eilíf herself grew. He felt her scars against his lips, but they mattered not at all. He had wounds inside equally deep. As they moved together, motion once again became bliss, and bliss became frenzy. In the flickering firelight, they remembered how it felt to cherish.

. . .

"Josson isn't going to Hel anytime soon. I'll get back when I get back," Tor said. He stretched and yawned, and delaying his departure, watched his daughter and son eating joyfully from wooden bowls.

When they had had their fill, Tor knelt beside them and told them what was to be. His daughter wept, as did his son, but Tor kept his face quiet and calm. Finally, they did as he said. Each took one of Eilíf's hands in theirs.

"Call her *mother*," Tor said, kissing each child for the last time. "Honor her gods. Worship as she does. The Almighty's heart is infinite and will understand. Work hard to help her. Know that I will never stop loving you."

With that, Tor stood and walked out the door. He did not let himself look back until he had taken the horse's reins in his hand.

The three stood in front of the little grass-covered home, their hands raised in *fare-thee-well*. It took all the strength Tor had to mount the horse. He wanted only to look back, *look back*, but forced himself to put his heels to the horse, to ride forward. The ache in his chest where his heart used to be... Tor gasped. He had meant it when he told the widow that whatever happened to him now did not matter, but the pain overwhelmed him. Death would bring more relief than fear.

He would never see their smiles again. Never comfort them, never hold them in his arms. Never guide them, never know their love.

Unable to even think, Tor huddled on the saddle, miserable. He pressed his heels against the warm flesh of the horse's belly and rode.

. . .

Chapter Six

Fortunately, Tor encountered no one along the roadway as he pressed Josson's aging mare hard across the dawn and into late morning. To his great relief, Josson still lay tied in the rock crevice, the gag in his mouth. But to Tor's horror, the trader had company. A woman squatted near him and a small fire crackled. Her worn boots and freckled face showed her as someone who spent a good deal of time outdoors, but she did not have the bearing of a bond-worker. A small dog sat patiently nearby, not moving.

Tor reined in and sat staring.

"Ah, there you are," she called. "I thought you might arrive soon. Breakfast is nearly ready." Her voice sounded light-hearted, almost gay.

. . .

Who was this woman? And what was she doing there? Tor shifted uneasily in the saddle, uncertain of how to respond. But he could not help taking some revenge on Josson. Through the ride back he had imagined himself saying certain words. Strange woman or not, he wanted the trader to hear them.

"Now you know what you inflicted on my children," he practically spat at Josson. "Tying them up and letting them starve."

In response, the woman reached over and pulled the gag from Josson's mouth. He immediately asked for water and drank in great gulps, wetting the front of his tunic. Then the trader choked, got his wind, and the curses began.

"You foul man! You deceitful creature, you scheming, lying..."

The woman ignored him. She calmly sat stirring the porridge.

"I'm Aldís," she said to Tor. "I sensed this man's distress and followed it here. Fetch me some more branches, please. And where does he keep his bowls? I'm not one to eat out of the same pot as others. We're not swine, are we?" She laughed.

Tor found her crisp speech impossible to refuse. He realized with a shock that this must be the *druid-vitki* who had come to Eilíf after the fire. He started to ask but realized in time that such a question would betray his visit to the widow.

"I'm Tor," he simply said.

Josson continued to rant, but Aldís completely ignored his furious words. The tirade dwindled as she stirred the thickening gruel. Tor located a pair of bowls and spoons in Josson's cooking box on the cart. When the trader finally fell silent, the woman spoke to Tor again. "You can unlock him now. But get ready. You know what to expect."

When Tor undid the chain, Josson sprang, but the trader's cramped muscles failed him, and he fell back to the ground. Josson writhed in the dirt, cursing and kicking. Aldís calmly portioned out porridge between the two bowls, leaving the rest in the small pot for the trader, still ignoring his shouted accusations.

"I never should have bought you. Nothing but bad has happened since then. My food gone...my axle broken...having to see that hideous widow...worst of all, I lost some of my best customers back at that last farm... *All... your... fault!*" Josson finally got to his feet and lunged at Tor.

Tor would not stomach such nonsense. With a roar, he lifted the trader over his head, preparing to dash him against the stony ground.

Aldís' voice came sharp.

"Put that man down this instant. Both of you, control yourselves. Trader, silence. You brought this upon yourself with your greed."

Released, Josson edged away from Tor, glaring and muttering.

"Here." She handed cooked porridge to each man and turned to Josson. "I've put some honey in it. You don't likely get that very often, so don't waste it. You can indulge your temper later if you want."

Sullen but hungry, Josson took the pot and spoon.

"Now, you. Sit there. I need to listen," she directed Tor, pointing at a spot across from her. "Yes, there." Aldís sat as well, facing him.

What is *she?* Tor wondered. One blink, and Aldís was all easygoing smiles, with an easy friendly manner. Another blink, and in her eyes glimmered a thousand years of mystery, a knowing of connections unseen, a wildness that danced to music he could not hear. He almost felt himself bowing to her. Tor covered his uncertainty by sitting and putting a spoonful of food in his mouth.

While Tor ate, her eyes lost focus.

She considered him, letting *knowing* come; from Tor, from the land sprits that were her unseen constant companions, from something even deeper and inexplicable that heard stars and breathed sunlight.

The previous night, Aldís had walked alone on the roadway. She had heard someone coming and had slipped into a grove of birches. This man had passed within an arm's length of her as he made his hurried way in the moonlight. He had led a horse that carried two children. Stealth and urgency had informed his movements.

At first, she had been worried. Did he intend them harm? But her instincts had told her that his secrecy came from other intentions. Aldís had not followed him but had noted the direction he was going.

Today, those children were nowhere in sight. The slight morning breeze carried a scent to her nostrils, something sweet like berries but different. Aldís had smelled the exact scent on the trader Josson this morning. She had seen on his hands bits of some fruit with the same smell. Mingled with it, but from Tor, came the fragrance of an unusual herb that she knew a certain young widow used for cooking. In addition to that, Aldís could see the salt of dried tears on Tor's face.

These small bits of information were things any sharp-eyed and sharp-witted person might have noted. She searched further.

Such an odd conversation, in which no one spoke but questions were asked and answered. Tor felt an odd buzzing inside his mind and body, a kind of probing but without words: inquiries about the night, about the children, about his past. He sensed that this healing-woman not only knew of his lovemaking with the widow but had somehow stepped inside the feeling, observing it, understanding it.

What enchantment is this? he wondered.

"I don't understand it myself," Aldís said, answering his unasked question. "But please stop asking *me* things. I need to concentrate."

Glimpses from places and days far ago spun past. Had she summoned them, Tor wondered. Did she know what they meant?

Aldís could not have described to another what she saw or felt. Events flashed in her mind like bits of sun glittering on water and disappeared just as quickly. She felt devastating grief at the face of a woman. She knew of an endless search, but she could not have described it to anyone. Aldís dreaded that the agony inside might stay with her, but she had work to do and would not look away.

Next came impressions of future things, images, each one liquid and yielding to the next, and the next: faces of strangers that Tor somehow recognized but did not know, a ship unlike any on which he had ever sailed, and an endless ocean ahead. Tor tried to follow the flow, but like waves in the sea, the images changed, shifted, disappeared. All sense of understanding eluded him.

"Your children are in a better place," Aldís said abruptly.

Tor frowned, dismayed. How could she possibly know? He prayed she would say nothing to Josson. "A better place?" His voice wavered.

Josson peered at Tor's neck. "He's not wearing their soul-stones. That's where you've been, looking for them? What happened? Did they run away in the dark? Fall down a cliff? Get swept away by a river? It serves you right for tying me up and leaving me like that."

Tor said nothing, nor did Aldís. *Did she just wink at me?*

Josson slammed down the cauldron and sneered. "That's what those white-christ followers say, isn't it, when someone dies, that they've gone to a better place? Like Valhalla or Hel? If she says they're dead, they're dead. Ugh, these truth-seekers and their weird knowing are ill business, if you ask me." He reached for the pot again and busied himself with the spoon, scraping what remained of the porridge from it, afraid to look at Aldís.

Tor kept his face averted and hoped Aldís would not contradict Josson. Instead, her voice angry, she retorted to the trader, "Do not speak about me in that way."

Tor had all but forgotten the woman's dog. At the sound of her words, it did not move, but he could hear a low growl from it.

The trader edged away from the dog. He glared at Tor with his small eyes narrowed. "Why'd you come back?"

"I couldn't just leave you to die," Tor answered. "Even despite what you planned to do."

"What did he plan to do?" Aldís asked.

"I didn't mistreat them. I fed them," Josson protested. "I can't help it if they ran away."

All at once, pieces fit together in the healer's mind. "Ahh...you planned to sell his children." She glared at Josson. "Children whose soul-stones he wore, children not yours to sell. Do you have any idea what a monstrous crime that would be?"

Josson sucked in his cheeks. "His word against mine."

"Not if he had their soul stones. You'd be outlawed. Even a half-wit knows the penalty for that. Yet despite your appalling behavior, this man did not leave you to become food for foxes." She nodded to Tor with respect.

Unsure of what to do, Tor shrugged.

"A better place," Aldís repeated to him. "You did what you could. Let them go. Trust me—and I know of these matters—it is better to forget and move on." Tor saw sadness and anger cross her features. "Should one be able to do that."

Josson flinched again. Could this *druid-vitki* see to the afterlife? Even to Hel? Josson made the sign of Thor. For good measure, he crossed himself as the white-christ followers did. "Don't look at me," he commanded Aldís. "Keep those witch-eyes off me."

This time she laughed as if a child had stamped in temper, then ignored Josson. Once again, her gaze unfocussed as the listening expression came over her. When it passed, she looked up, considering.

"I need to leave now," Aldís announced. She stood and twisted her hair into a braid as she spoke. "Someone else is calling."

"I'm going to report this beast to the law-courts as soon as we get to the next farm," Josson ranted.

The healer calmly intervened, her voice sarcastic. "But you still need to sell him, don't you? Reporting him certainly won't help that. Stop being fearful. He won't hurt you. He's suffered enough. Just find a buyer and get the money you crave."

Unfamiliar empathy swept over Josson. For a brief instant, he felt sorry for Tor. "I guess. I don't know. Must be hard."

The strange woman smiled, enigmatic. "Well done, trader. Now then," back to the crisp tone, "You, my strapping friend, come help me cross the stream over there. Then you and this trader can proceed on your way." She spoke a command to the dog. It immediately stood and came to her side.

But at the stream, Aldís showed no need of Tor's assistance.

"I just wanted to tell you that you chose wisely. Our widow friend will care well for your children. Rest assured that I will keep an eye on them. Call when you need me." She skipped on wet stones across the burbling flow as nimbly as a goat. Pausing on the other side, Aldís waved to him.

"And it may be that you do not call, but I still hear." With that strange remark, she whirled and left, the dog trotting at her heels.

Tor watched her go. A tiny ray of hope broke through the bitterness that consumed him. It would seem that two good women would be looking after his children. Tor turned back towards Josson, trying to be grateful, but as he looked at the cart where those small beings no longer rode, a sea of sadness filled him.

. . .

As she walked away from Tor, Aldís massaged her hand. A familiar odd tingling pulsed in it.

"You know what that means," she said to her dog. "From now on, that tall stranger and I are connected by an invisible thread."

Tor would come and go in her awareness, as had others she had encountered across the years. *So many threads bind me.* Many things about her strange knowing Aldís did not understand and could not explain. It existed nonetheless, a gift she could not control, and a feeling she often feared.

. . .

Chapter Seven

Josson, subdued, walked beside the wagon, the stiffness in his muscles easing. Tor matched his footsteps on the other side of the cart. The trader could not explain why he had offered condolences to Tor, or why he had felt no need to chain Tor.

The slave man did *come back to me. Guess she's right when she says he won't run off.*

Josson felt muddled, confused and fretful. His thoughts felt like a fish flopping on the sand. *He didn't want me starving to death. Well, I'm alive. Why did he stay, still walking along as if nothing happened?*

Josson disliked thinking. He scratched under his tunic, annoyed.

Normally, he would erupt in frustration, blaming whoever happened to be nearby, but Tor's sad, silent brooding intimidated him. Still, he needed help. Josson found himself sputtering, half in apology, half-pleading for understanding.

"I still need to find a place to sell you. Sorry, but that's the way it is. What do they say? Life isn't fair? You sold yourself into bondage. I'm just a middle-man, and I'm getting too old to tramp about the country. I have to make something on you."

He looked sideways at Tor. "You understand? Harvests have been poor. Food's scarce this year. Prices have soared. I traded all my meat to buy you. I need to buy more to keep me through the winter." One last gasp of shame. "I can't feed you all winter too."

Through his own pain and numbness, Tor saw the struggle in the man, the faltering towards kindness. Such effort merited response.

Tor sighed. "You can't afford to keep me. Yes, I understand that."

Josson laughed. "You…talking…" Something about it struck him as funny. He began to laugh. "I was so worried you might be mute." Josson doubled over with laughter now, holding his stomach. "You talk better than I do!" He laughed harder and harder, roaring with humor he could not explain.

Tor plodded along. One day his life would end, and pain with it.

. . .

Josson woke to hear his horse grazing. The sky was dark. He was on the ground. Had they made camp? He must have fallen asleep.

"Did they put a spell on me?" Josson accused the air. "Tor and the witch-woman?" He listened to the horse's soft breath, the sounds of grass being torn, the slow chewing. He fell back into dreamlike fatigue. A soft chuckle grew in the trader's chest. He felt happy for the first time in years. Josson laughed again, pure lightness in his spirit.

Then he remembered the disappearance of Tor's children. Bitterness swept away his mirth.

"Should have sold those children when I had the chance." Blaming Tor brought familiar relief, but still, Josson felt that unusual flicker of unselfish kindness. He humped over onto his other side, annoyed, and soon fell asleep again, snoring fitfully.

. . .

Chapter Eight

The holdings of Naldrum, headman of Bull Valley

Kel pulled the saddle from Thor-Thunder and handed it to the stable worker who had followed him into the stable.

"Shall I groom him for you?" the man offered.

Kel glanced at the chieftain's flags. A birch rod held them, braced in the flag-stones at the longhouse entrance.

"No. I've nothing pressing. I'll do it." He led the horse by its halter behind the stable, where no one was likely to see him and betray his return to Naldrum, brushing against flowers thick along the path.

But the chieftain's daughter Ankya was waiting and watching. She had been looking for Kel's return since he left. She'd seen him riding up the valley and had squatted in a tall stand of fragrant grass.

Now, she considered the set of Kel's shoulders. *He feels tense.* Ankya looked at his lean, hard body. The day was suddenly warmer.

Ankya dropped her shawl. Her maid could find it later. Right now, Kel was all that mattered. *His hand on the lead line, the way he strokes his horse's flanks. Reassuring it, or himself?* Ankya could not remember a time when she had not studied Kel.

She slipped around to the back of the stable, bent out of sight among the weeds and flowers. She listened as Kel spoke to Thor in hushed tones. *I know what would help, Kel,* she giggled, and stood up.

"Kel! How nice that you have returned to us." her voice was bright, coquettish. She caught his small instant of freezing motionless and smirked to herself at the power she had over him.

"*Fyrst-dottir.*" Kel acknowledged Naldrum's oldest child using the formal greeting. He resumed grooming his horse.

"Don't call me first-daughter. It's just the two of us, not a *thing* gathering." Ankya laughed and tossed her hair.

Kel had no desire to make small conversation, and especially not with Ankya. He had tolerated her besotted hovering when she was a child, but she had budded. Better to not let Naldrum's favorite get too close. If matters became awkward, he had no doubt who would get blamed. It would not be Ankya.

She ran a fingertip down the horse's spine. "How is Thunder? Did he carry you well...to...?" The question hung in the air. Naldrum told no one of the errands on which he sent his steward, and Kel had no intention of enlightening Ankya's relentless curiosity.

"Yes." The fine line between polite and rude, a line he now kept with her. Kel kept his gaze trained on Thor and brushed.

Ankya toyed idly with bits of Thor's mane. She gave no sign of the pout that she felt. She brightened. "I'll let father know you've arrived home. He'll be pleased. He's been asking for you."

I'll wager he has, Kel thought. The knot in his gut tightened. He slowed the brush, drawing out every bit of time he could.

. . .

After he had left Sóma, Kel had ridden over steep hills and down treacherous crevasses. Thor-Thunder had picked a careful way through bogs and streambeds, following the faint tracks of sheep trails to a remote valley. When he made out a group of white dots scattered across a steep hill, he had spurred his horse towards them.

A shepherd, hearing the hoofbeats, turned to watch the rider's approach. As Kel came close, he raised his hand in greeting and reached for the bridle. Kel looped Thunder's reins across the pommel of the saddle. He hopped to the ground and let the stallion graze.

"Hey, Sauthi. Good to see you. Been a while."

The shepherd nodded and made no response. He did not ask why Kel had suddenly appeared, or why he had made the long ride to this distant place. The men watched the flock in companionable silence.

"Don't usually see you once spring's over," Sauthi said.

"I had some work to do for *gothi* Naldrum that took me close to here. Figured I'd swing by." In fact, Kel had ridden a full day around the chieftain's holdings to Sauthi.

To Kel's astonishment, the normally taciturn shepherd asked a direct question. "You have something weighing on your mind?"

As Kel considered his answer, he realized, shocked, that he was considering what might be safe to say. *I'm just spooked because of Sóma. Sauthi's an old shepherd. Talks to no one, doesn't even see anyone for months at a time. Naldrum will never hear what I say.*

Still, it didn't hurt to be careful.

"The work I did. Something about it seemed...not right."

Sauthi kept his eyes on Kel, an odd intensity in his gaze. Kel, looking at the grazing sheep, did not see, nor did he notice the equal intensity in Sauthi's question. "Not right in what way?"

Kel gave a grim laugh. There was no way he could speak openly of the dilemma Sóma had inadvertently caused. "Let's just say that, for better or for worse, I've served my headman loyally, but this week…well, something changed. Things that once made sense no longer do."

"You question your loyalty to your headman?"

"Maybe. A bit." *Why was Sauthi asking all this?*

Sauthi exhaled as if he had been holding his breath for a very long time. He murmured something that sounded to Kel like *at last,* but then grimaced at Kel's next words.

"Doesn't matter anyway. Naldrum has ways of that ensuring people stay loyal. No doubt I'll be back in thrall soon enough."

Kel stood, annoyed. He had come here to escape his concerns, not to rehash them. "I need to get back. Wheat-harvest time. Much to do."

The aged shepherd watched Kel mount his stallion, the visit over as quickly as it had begun.

"Find your way, my friend," Sauthi said as Kel rode away. At first, he thought the steward had not heard, but Kel lifted his hand in acknowledgement without turning and galloped onwards.

Sauthi sagged on his staff. "So close. Will he be able?" He staggered to a stone and sat, slumped. "Can Kel do what I could not?"

. . .

As soon as Ankya had alerted her father to Kel's return, the demand came for the steward to leave off fooling with his horse and to promptly present himself in the main longhouse.

Naldrum had seated himself in his place of honor, the high seat at the head of the room. Kel noted that the headman had draped one of his best imported furs around his shoulders, even though the day was warm. *Looking to impress or intimidate me,* he guessed.

"The matter is resolved?" Naldrum asked.

"Resolved." Kel's voice was clipped.

"What took so long? You were gone far longer than necessary to ride to their valley and back."

"My horse was lame," Kel lied. "We made slow progress."

"You coddle that animal. I'll have my stable-boy check it."

"No need. Seems fine now."

The air in the longhouse felt thick with unspoken questions. Kel kept his expression neutral. He could tell that the headman was doing the same, neither of them speaking his real thoughts.

Is it true? Kel wanted to ask. *Did you force yourself on Sóma— and then claim that she lied, just to save yourself a trifling bit of silver?*

"So, your Thunder was *not* lame?" Naldrum gazed at his reflection in the mirror he kept handy.

"Was. Not now." *The others…were they liars, or were you?*

"How fortunate. Tedious, when a fine beast has problems." Naldrum twirled his finger around the top of his goblet. Kel was hiding something. "When did it happen? Following that nasty fellow?"

"No. On the way back." Kel's chest felt tight at the idea of how many wrongs he had done for his chieftain. It was not just the exposing of the infants. It was the words Naldrum had made Kel utter, threats of pain and suffering that the headman declared would be inflicted should anyone in the family ever speak of or protest his actions. He controlled them with fear, Kel knew.

He stayed stoic, meeting Naldrum's narrowed eyes. Wondering, hoping he was wrong. *Surely if he lied all those times, I would have heard something, wouldn't I?* Kel recalled faces of young women and their families across the years and felt shame. *No. I did my work well.*

For the first time, he let himself acknowledge how afraid they must have been. None had ever spoken out, afterwards, to the best of his knowledge. Terrified, they would not.

He felt revolted with himself as much as with the headman. But he must not say anything. *Aldis would suffer.* But even as he thought that, Kel was shocked to hear himself blurt out the very words he sought to quiet. "You've always told me these accusations were false."

"Of course they are. They just want payment. Don't be a fool."

The two men stared eye to eye. Naldrum began to pant. "People think it's easy, being leader of a large valley. All these rabble-rousing farmers bickering with each other. All of them poorer every year, searching for a way out when there is none. Easy, being *gothi*? No."

"They are poorer because of things you have done." Loans that should never have been made were not repaid because the headman set too-harsh terms. Naldum had claimed the lands the instant payment was late.

The headman's voice grew silken. "Kel, you do remember the terms of our contract, don't you? To act as I require, without discussion and without debate?"

"I remember."

"I need men who will serve me without question."

Kel said nothing, dreading what might come next, and it did.

"You may recall the woman I…protect…on your behalf. I haven't needed to mention her name for a while now, but your insolence has made me remember. I wonder where your wild healer-friend lives these days? I have been far too derelict about keeping an eye on her."

"She has nothing to do with this."

"This mead bores me." Naldrum dumped it into the longfire trench. "You may go."

Fiercely angry, powerless, Kel spun around to leave.

The chieftain called a brusque admonition after him. "Just remember, Kel. You pledged your loyalty to me, and me alone. Cross me, and you know exactly what will happen to her.

Naldrum smirked to himself. *Easy enough to control fearful farm folk. But what a pleasure to control even strong, virile men like Kel. Fools. They stand no chance against me.*

. . .

As Kel strode through the longhouse and out the main door, his disgust hardened into anger.

Ankya hovered outside the longhouse, waiting to trap him again.

"Look," she said. "One of our dogs had puppies while you were gone. Father is selling all of them, except this one I'm keeping. What do you think I should name her?"

"Sóma," said Kel. "I want to hear that name every day of my life."

. . .

Chapter Nine

Yet another fruitless day trudging alongside the rickety cart. Farm after farm fell behind them, but Tor remained unsold.

Tension grew steadily between the two men. Tor counted, step by step, the increasing distance between him and the widow's longhouse. *Find a buyer,* he fumed, as Josson seethed, blaming Tor.

They made their campsite that night where the narrow track ran between two steep cliffs of stone. No wind reached the sheltered, silent place. The creaking cartwheels seemed an intrusion on a profound stillness, something eternal that had nothing to do with the world of men. Even water dared not speak, sliding silently over wet rock crevices where moss grew soft and green. The two men lay down, turned their backs on one another and fell asleep without speaking.

Tor woke to darkness so deep he could see nothing at all. No light came from the sky. Their small campfire had burned to ash. He could not even make out the nearby horse or the cart. Only the hard ground against his back told Tor where he was. In utter darkness, in utter quiet, the thoughts he had been pushing away broke through. The enormity of his actions finally overwhelmed him.

"What have I done?" he cried.

He thought of his children's small hands waving farewell as they stood next to the widow. How long would it be until he could not remember what it felt like to hold their fingers in his? They would grow and change each day, and he would share nothing of it, know nothing of it. Tor struggled to sit up, but sadness drained all desire to live. He willed himself to stop breathing and prayed for death.

But his lungs stubbornly ignored him. Across the long stretch of night, they sucked in air in unwilling, unhappy gasps. He wiped his eyes, tormented and alone. *We will never be a family again.*

He imagined his wife's face, pictured her sad dark eyes searching the horizon. She lacked even the small comfort of knowing how desperately he had searched for her. Their lives, torn apart that terrible day when the slavers snatched her from the market, had no chance of returning now. *I am sorry, beloved. I failed you.*

The broken words left his lips, vanishing in the night. His children would never see their mother again—and because of what he had done, this last, desperate act, they would never see their father either.

I failed them all. To protect them, he had cast them adrift, cut them off from everything of their childhood, everything familiar, abandoned them to a stranger, stripped away the last vestiges of what had once been a family. Wracked with anguish, Tor spoke to the silent stones that rose above him, invisible in the dark night.

"Why are we humans even given life if it brings such pain? Why do we even live? Why does the Creator inflict such torments?"

In the darkness, distant, a bird called. A falcon of some kind, he realized. It, too, sounded alone and desolate, yearning. For what?

The hawk screamed again. Tor listened but heard no response.

"You are lonely, too." Compassion for the falcon gave Tor strength to speak to the stones again.

"Have I made the right choice?" he asked. "I could leave this trader right now and go back to the widow. Back to my children. Hide there and live there in isolation and peace. But this man paid all he had for me, his food even, at my request. I owe him what he bought." Tor's forehead furrowed. "And it is safer for my children to live apart from me. I cannot risk anything that might hurt them. Have I done the right thing? Or have I ruined everything?"

Imprisoned by the treachery of human beings, imprisoned by his own moral code, imprisoned by the utter blackness of the night, Tor lay on his back. Tears ran from his eyes down his temples and fell to the ground, seeping into soil that touched the stones. He listened for the bird again, wanting to hear something of hope in its cry, if only the bitter defiance of survival.

Only silence. Only silence.

Unwilling to breathe, he still drew breath. Across that long death of night, a future of emptiness and grief stretched ahead, a personal hell that promised endless, relentless, cruel, utterly alone defeat.

. . .

Yet not wholly alone; the great gray stones heard him. To them, human matters seemed a tiny flitting of gnat wings, too rapid, immaterial to their own deep rhythms. But in the same way that a human might lift a small bird back to its nest, the huge rocks, too, knew compassion. By the time they became aware of the question and considered it, and answered, years had passed—but Tor might have been relieved, perhaps, to know they agreed with what he had done.

. . .

Rain dripping on Tor's face woke him from nightmares. He sat up and leaned his elbows on his thighs and sighed, and watched the gray dawn lighten the sky. Each step forward would further seal his fate. Despair deepened.

But the body, ignorant of the heart's pain, makes demands. He got up, relieved himself. Josson's horse needed harnessing. Small everyday acts of life offered tiny distractions, tiny bridges to surviving for another breath, another morning, another day.

"Need to sell you," Josson repeated when they left the strange stone valley. "Need to get back to my holdings. Winter coming. No food...I'll die." He struck his horse viciously with his switch. "No getting around it. I know where we have to go." His eyes flicked nervous and furtive towards the road that led to the horizon. That way led to a man whom he admired, but far more, feared.

. . .

Josson could not admit to himself that perhaps he *had* known, deep inside, the very instant he bought Tor. He had dodged the truth with every strike of his horse's hooves on the stony track, but as they traveled from farm to farm with no offers, the trader could no longer avoid facing it. Only one man remained to whom he might sell Tor. It was a man he dreaded seeing again.

. . .

Naldrum. The only chieftain in all of Iceland with the arrogance to encourage people to call him by the forbidden old-land title of *jarl* instead of simply *gothi,* headman. Naldrum, fawned over by many but loathed by most of them. Naldrum, who professed to care about the landowners who pledged to him, but who cared only for himself. *Naldrum the Greedy,* people mocked behind his back.

Josson did not speak of this to Tor, but only of the headman's great riches and extensive lands. At first, Tor felt hope quicken. *A rich man? Plenty of land and wealth?* Perhaps one day he might be able to bring the children there to live with him. But as Josson spoke longer, a different image of Naldrum emerged, dashing Tor's hopes.

"I meant to pay for the tools he sold me," Josson sighed. "I meant to bring the silver I promised. But it rained frightfully, and the roads were completely impassable." Josson did not mention how much interest had mounted on the silver-debt he owed.

"Why don't you just tell him the truth?" Tor asked. "Surely a man can forgive a bad year."

"Not a year."

"How long, then? Two years? *Three?*"

Josson swallowed. "Maybe a little longer than that."

"And you've not spoken? *Shite,* man. He's going to eat you alive."

. . .

Josson rehearsed excuses in his mind again and again. He could not get it wrong. If only he had those two children to give Naldrum, he could offer than he owed. *Damn Tor to Hel.*

. . .

As they pulled into the horse-yard, Josson sweated, despite the chilly day.

"This man terrifies you. It's more than just debt," Tor said. "Are you selling me to some kind of monster?"

"I am selling you to a great man," Josson said. "You will marvel at the size of his longhouse. You should feel pride at serving him."

Tor snorted. "You think it matters to me how large this man's house is? How much gold he has? His riches make *his* life better, not mine or yours."

Josson pulled off his shirt. He rummaged in a basket for a dry tunic. Tor looked at the discarded one, soaking wet on the wagon. So much sweat. Why such fear? Clearly the man ahead understood cruelty.

Cold dread began to fill Tor. When he had sold his freedom to Indaell, he had not feared violence, but he had seen the marks on the backs of thralls who were whipped. He had seen burns from fire-tongs.

Breathe in. The children are safe.

Breathe out. The children are safe.

Breathe in. The children. They are all that matters.

. . .

The headman's steward let them in the longhouse and went to fetch his master. Waiting, they looked around the enormous room.

Tor disliked Naldrum immediately from the blatant opulence of his home. There was rich, and there was obscene. He had memories of another such man, long ago, to whom wealth and power had mattered more than anything. Tor felt rage building. *I cannot be that person of anger and killing,* he told himself. *Stop. It leads to no good.*

After a long wait, Naldrum swept into the room. He took his place in the high seat that stood between pillars ornately carved and painted in gold.

Josson stepped forward. "Sir," he started. But the headman ignored him, looking over the trader's head. "Steward, instruct this man that he speaks only after I have spoken to him."

Josson crept back to the bench and sat. He seemed to grow smaller than when he had arrived.

The chieftain ignored throughout the day, as other visitors arrived and were shown into the hall. Each one brought information about Naldrum's business holdings or messages from headmen of other valleys, or requested assistance, or offered gifts. To some, Naldrum offered food and ale. To others, he showed disdain. Tor found himself forgetting his own sadness in his growing dislike of the headman.

They waited as the day passed. Even after the chieftain had heard every visitor, Tor and Josson still remained, ignored. Tor noticed that the trader had sweated through another tunic, his lips moving in some kind of invocation.

Finally, Naldrum's steward beckoned. With caution, Josson approached, bowing as he went forward.

"I have brought you a gift, *Jarl*," he quavered. "To settle the debt which I owe you."

Naldrum continued to ignore the merchant but spoke instead to his steward. "Kel, this trader has waited long. He must be hungry. Get him something to eat." He murmured something else to his steward, who made a sour face as he left the room. The man soon reappeared in front of a servant bearing a covered bowl, recoiling. For the first time, Naldrum acknowledged Josson's presence.

"Sit, trader," he said. He gestured to the table.

Josson, relieved, shaking, did as Naldrum said. Tor watched, instinctively knowing that the trader should not be foolish. A cruelty was about to ensue.

The servant placed the bowl on the table and lifted the lid, moving quickly away. Josson shrank back from the stench.

"You don't like the food I offer you?" Naldrum asked.

"My lord…it is… this is *pig dung*." Josson stammered.

"You believe you deserve better?"

"Sir, even dogs do not eat waste of pigs." Josson's chin wobbled.

"And yet pig-shit is what you are to me." Naldrum's false hospitality changed into spiteful rage. "You cheated me and defaulted on our bargain, and you tried to harm my good name. I will have you reap what you have sown. Eat it. It is what you deserve."

Tor noticed Naldrum's steward standing behind the headman. The man stared at the floor, his jaw rigid. Tor's own stomach turned over at the vile odor that filled the room.

"Eat it, I said," Naldrum shouted.

Josson implored, to no avail. Sweat poured down his face.

"Eat it!"

With trembling fingers, Josson dipped his knife into the stinking pile and scooped a tiny morsel. As he brought the bit of filth towards his lips, the knife shaking, Naldrum burst out in hateful laughter.

"What a gutless fool you are. Who would eat such a thing? Only a man with no pride whatsoever." He beckoned to his steward again. "Get that abhorrent mess out of my hall."

Josson sagged, demoralized. He wiped his hands across his eyes. Naldrum beckoned to Tor. "Your turn now, slave."

. . .

The headman appraised Tor with an expression as if the slave had offended him in some way. "What skills do you have?"

Tor kept his eyes trained on the opposite wall. He said nothing.

Josson started to interject. "I've seen him—"

Naldrum raised his hand, silencing Josson. "I didn't ask you. I asked him."

"But he—"

"Doesn't talk?" Naldrum circled Tor. "Mute? Oh, I doubt that very much." He called to his steward again. "Kel, pull a branch from the fire and bring it to me."

"He can talk," Josson panted. "He's just stubborn."

"So, dark traveler from afar. Besides being an idle curiosity, what value would you add to my household?"

Tor stayed silent. Now he fixed his gaze on Naldrum. The headman did not notice the same measuring glance Tor had fixed on Josson when the trader had hit him with the stick.

"Blacksmith," Josson tried again. "He can fix iron, tin, bronze. Wagons. Train horses."

"Any farm hand can do those things. What else do you offer?"

Tor did not reply.

"Trader, you presented this man as repayment for the silver you owe," said Naldrum. "All I see is an obstinate burden who will complicate my life."

"He is worth it, I swear. What do you *want* from me?"

Naldrum's eyebrows shot up. "*What?*"

"I am sorry, *Jarl.* I mean, what do you desire in a slave to provide sufficient value for the silver, which I meant to bring to you, before the weather became bad and the tracks impassable."

"Stop talking." Naldrum moved his face close to Tor, breathed a mocking whisper. "What will you give me? I can see that you have strength. I have strong men already. I can see that you are exotic. Exotic means nothing to me."

Tor very highly doubted those last words, coming from a man who clearly needed to impress.

Naldrum came even closer, pressed his lips against Tor's ear. "This strength in you, how deep does it run? Will you fight me, or yield to me? What pleasures will you offer to make me forget my anger at this trader?"

Tor flinched. He heard in Naldrum's voice a music he knew too well from the past, the song of those who needed a rival to punish.

Breathe. Tor fought to not show his revulsion.

Naldrum's expression switched from seductive to a childish pout. In temper, he threw his golden drinking-horn to the floor. Wine spilled across the stones.

"You won't play? Have it your way. Maybe I *should* take you and amuse myself by starving you to death. Perhaps that would please me, to hear you beg for food and to refuse you."

The rich man turned to Josson as if speaking to a child. "Look at those elegant features. Look at the set of those shoulders under his rags. This man with his princely bearing believes himself to be superior to me. Do you know how intoxicating that is, trader?

Something for me to take, and break? Such a splendid challenge, when so few are to be had."

Josson stumbled, not knowing how to reply, but Naldrum had not wanted an answer.

"You only see a *thing* here, don't you, Josson? To you, a thrall is simply something to buy, something to sell, a bit of silver to spend on food to stuff your stupid mouth. You do not see this man for what he is. Look at the expression in his eyes. Look how he despises me. How dare he? I long to break him."

"If you say so, *Jarl.*"

"The world is larger than you will ever understand, trader. For that reason, you will always live small. You will never succeed. You will always just barely scrape through. People like you make me sick. The stench of your failure offends me even more than pig feces." Naldrum laughed as if he had amused himself.

Josson stood staring stupidly at Naldrum, but Tor understood what lay behind the little show of superiority. Crushing a weak being like Josson allowed Naldrum to rescue his ego after Tor had blatantly ignored the headman. Naldrum did not really care about getting his silver back from Josson. No, the chance to grind the trader into humiliation fed the headman's insatiable desire for self-importance.

The hideous snake. For shame, Tor thought.

Josson had tried to wrap himself in confidence when he came into Naldrum's longhouse, knowing Tor would be desirable to a man famous for showing his wealth. Now the trader shrank, hunching his shoulders. He did not understand the game the headman was playing. He struggled to regain some ground.

"I have another gift for you as well, my chieftain," Josson stammered. "Oranges. I have two bitter-oranges, to flavor your mead."

"Oranges, eh? Fetch them. Their fragrance may drive your stink from my hall."

Tor felt conflicted. He had completely forgotten the oranges, but words of warning would come too late now. Besides, those oranges—

"Here…here…" Josson pulled the string from around his neck and fumbled with the key. "A gift…" He told Naldrum's steward which box on the cart held the oranges.

When the orange-box was brought in and Josson unlocked it, his jaw dropped open and his face sagged in horror.

"What…? They were here when— I sold four, but two were left." *Had the family with the wine stolen them from him?* "I am sorry, lord. Forgive me. I thought—"

Naldrum seized upon Josson's defeat with glee. He swooped in to deliver a final humiliation. "You have come to me and wasted my time with this sullen behemoth, *and* you lost the only valuable thing you had? You worthless, stupid piece of foulness!" The headman's face contorted. "Get out of here and never set foot on my land again." He pursed his lips, hawked his throat and spat. A blob of phlegm hit the trader's cheek.

Josson, all but collapsing, staggered towards Tor. His expression wavered between a plea for help and frustrated confusion. "The oranges…you know I had them. Tell him!"

When they had arrived here, Tor had not cared what happened to himself. He cared far less what happened to Josson. But as he watched Naldrum humiliate the trader for sport, Tor saw Josson as he truly was: unlikeable and selfish, but in his own way, as vulnerable as a child, helpless against Naldrum's taunting. He watched the headman relish the petty arrogance he was wreaking upon Josson. The hair on the back of Tor's neck stood up.

How had he described such men to the widow? *They take pleasure from those too vulnerable to refuse.* The very kind of men who made Tor fear for his children.

Breathe in. Breathe out. The feeling will pass. Naldrum did not know about his children, would never find them, never lay hands on them. That was all that mattered. Not Josson's self-inflicted situation.

But as Tor watched Josson's helpless pleading, his cringing in humiliation, he realized that his children's safety was not *all* that mattered. He, too, had once longed for someone to defend the powerless. Could he stand here now and do nothing?

A sound came to Tor, the powerful cry of the gyrfalcon that had rung through the darkness in the valley of stone. Loneliness and despair had reverberated in its call, but defiance as well. The sound resonated, and strength swelled in him. *Thank you, friend.*

"Not this time," Tor muttered. "Not this time." *Today, the bully would not win.* With all his being, he wanted to stop Naldrum—but the only way lay in challenging the headman himself.

Tor cast aside any danger of being whipped and beaten. He let go of his despair over his children. A tide of fearlessness drove him. Words sharpened in his mouth, relentless and sharp, and he became a falcon bearing down on his hapless prey. Before he even realized his intent, Tor moved towards Naldrum.

. . .

Tor drew himself to his imposing full height. He lifted his chin and stared down his nose at the headman's face. His eyes shone with disgust and insolence.

"I took your precious oranges." The tone of Tor's voice clearly said *you mean nothing to me*.

"*You* took them?" Astonished echoes came simultaneously from both Naldrum and Josson. Tor threw a quick glance at Naldrum's steward. The man appeared to be having a fit of coughing. Tor smiled.

"Yes. I wanted them. For myself."

Naldrum exploded in full-blown rage. "You *stole* them? I already had a low opinion of you, Josson, but you're trying to foist off a slave who steals on me? I should have you beaten. And you, brute? How dare you? Those oranges were meant for me." The chieftain kicked the nearest stool and sent it skidding across the stone floor. *"For me! Not for your enormous ugly self or those loathsome slave-hands."*

Naldrum stomped back and forth in front of Tor. His cloak dragged on the stones of the floor and his heavy frame heaved with exertion. Tor stared down, calm, implacable, and proud. Unused to such a manner, Naldrum paused, and in the silence, Tor spoke.

"I am not the enormous ugly one here. I'm not the loathsome one."

. . .

Naldrum's fury flashed. Everyone in the hall had just heard a thrall insult him. The man might just as well have slapped him in the face. The headman's pleasure in taunting Josson instantly sharpened into something deadlier. He dropped all thought of Josson, like a dog who saw a bigger piece of meat.

A slave defied me. A slave. It was a stinging blow to Naldrum's self-importance.

"I will break you," he shouted. A storm of fury grew in the headman, and deep in his loins, carnal desire throbbed as he imagined himself inflicting devastating pain on Tor.

. . .

Tor stood waiting, knowing full well the storm he had unleashed.

"Well, Josson, you worthless fool, it appears we have a bargain," Naldrum said. "You are no match for this sly fool, but I am. I could just tie him outside for the winter and watch him freeze to death, but I am a man of profit, so I will not waste this splendid specimen, disrespectful though he may be. I will *own* this creature that the gods have blessed with such extravagant color and height but no brains or courage, and I will instruct him," the headman laughed, his meaning clear, "in manners. Consider your debt paid."

Josson held out his hand, almost, and cleared his throat. "Jarl, a favor, please? I need food. I traded all of mine to get him for you."

Naldrum called to a servant. "Give this tedious whiner a barrel of meat and load his cart with root crops." He shook Josson's hand as required to seal a deal and wiped his own on a cloth immediately after.

"Now take your horse and wagon and leave here. I never want to see your face again unless you have a true prize for me."

As Josson scuttled towards the door, Naldrum gestured to his steward. "Kel, this slave has by his own words declared himself a thief. I could wait for the courts at the valley *thing,* but why bother, since I am the law in these parts? He stole my oranges. We cannot allow thievery, or nor disobedience by thralls. He must be marked as an outlaw."

"You mean—?" Kel asked.

"Cut him!" shouted Naldrum.

. . .

'Cut him' meant the headman calling for anyone working nearby to come and restrain the tall man. They hung back, unnerved at his size, but Tor snorted in careless contempt at Naldrum and willingly held out his hands. They tied him tightly to a chair and fastened a board to each hand, to keep them flat.

Cut him meant the sound of a knife rasping against a whetstone, growing sharper with each turn, as Naldrum explained the process to Tor. His voice purred, sickening and soft.

"You know our outlaw mark? No? A fine old tradition which alerts those who honor the law about those who disrespect it. Anyone who meets you will see your hands and know at once what you are. You thought you were being brave, confessing like that? I will ensure that you suffer the full consequences of your actions. Almost ready, steward?"

"Not quite," Kel answered.

"You see my steward Kel over there, sharpening his knife? When the blade is ready, he'll cut a mark on each of your hands, along the back, where it won't hinder you from working while it heals. He'll cut deep. I like the marks to show clearly on those who defy the law. Your hands are tied flat to keep you from jerking, so that the cuts go straight; a, clear, large *X* on each."

Naldrum laughed but Tor could see that he was still furious.

"That is only the beginning of what I will teach you. When the marks begin to heal in a day or two, Kel will cut them again, and when they heal more, again, and again and again. He'll follow my orders and do it properly. Tonight, it will hurt. But when he re-opens the wound each time, making a scar that will last your lifetime," Naldrum paused for emphasis, "*you will suffer.* Soon you will beg to show me the proper deference."

He closed his mouth in what passed for a smirk and lifted his great toad neck. "Even better, you'll start serving my purposes right away. Kel, when you have the knife ready, call the entire staff. I want them to see what happens to those who defy me."

Naldrum left the room and went to the *aut-haus* chamber to relieve himself. As he stood watching his flow, he imagined all sorts of ways to beat down Tor's pride. The thoughts felt rich and seductive.

Cut him deep. Naldrum stroked his member briefly before putting it back into his clothing. *I want him to suffer.*

. . .

Josson heard the blade grinding against whetstone as he led his horse and wagon from the stable yard. He knew what it meant.

The trader felt badly for the slave, but at the same time, he wished with all his heart to be thoroughly rid of Tor. *A bad deal, all around,* he thought. Little over a week spent with the strange dark man had strained Josson to his core. At first joyous about a huge profit, he had become despondent as each chance slipped through his fingers. He had known real fear for the first time in his life, when he woke to find himself tied up, nauseous from the wine. He had known real hunger, until Tor had returned.

But Tor did *come back. And there with Naldrum, he helped me. Almost as if he was a friend.*

Confusion overwhelmed the trader. He needed to feel his life in narrow order, to keep his perceptions rigid, his ambitions small and his failures always before him. Lifelong habit demanded that he see himself maligned in all ways. *What my father said. Trust nobody.*

Josson's thoughts swirled. In the chaos, Naldrum's image came to save him. Naldrum, the rich and powerful. Naldrum the ruthless, who no one dared mock. Naldrum, who was at this instant punishing Tor.

Somewhere deep inside, a small voice in Josson argued *but Tor is the better man.* Josson shoved the thought down but it refused to be silenced, reminding him *Tor saved you from Naldrum by saying he stole the oranges.* Josson clapped his hands to his ears.

"Be quiet!" he shouted. "I need this whirling in my head to stop." The trader needed less chaos, more simplicity and order. He needed to follow without question, to not have to consider complex ideas. He needed simple and easy, even if it trapped him in servitude.

In short order, Josson made the inevitable choice. Jarl Naldrum feared no one. His wealth showed the greatness of a true leader. He gave Josson meat and roots. *I will follow the jarl. What he does to Tor is his own business. That slave brought it on himself.*

Relieved to have the matter decided, Josson headed along the track away from Naldrum's compound. *Meat for the winter. That's all that matters.* He clumped down the road and thought no more.

. . .

Tor breathed in and breathed out. Desire to feel the headman's throat in his fingers pulsed. He'd not need a sword.

He fought the urge to kill a man. *This vain creature pushes me beyond my limits—but there is no way back if one chooses hate too often.* He had nearly lost himself to it before. *Breathe.*

Tor's gaze landed on Naldrum's steward, sharpening the knife.

"You seem a decent sort. Why do you serve such a rotten man?"

Kel didn't answer the question. Instead, he said, "Naldrum meant it. The first cut will hurt badly, but re-opening it each time will be agonizing. I'm not one for brutality, but I can't defy him. No one dares." No sense thinking about it. What was, was.

Yet as he held the blade against the whetstone, Kel could not silence his thoughts. He had seen Naldrum's fury. The headman didn't care about marking this thrall. He intended to destroy the poor fellow.

. . .

The metal-against-stone grinding paused. Kel felt the edge. "A bit more, I think. The sharper it is, the cleaner it cuts. That'll hurt less. Same with the recut. It's the only kindness I can give you."

Tor heard but did not reply. *Breathe in. Breathe out.*

. . .

The steward finished sharpening the knife. He came to sit facing Tor. "I'm Kel. Kel Coesson." He held out his hand, but Tor's were tied to the planks. They nodded to each other.

Tor recognized that small offering of friendship. "You serve a loathsome man, Kel Coesson. I could see your discomfort at what he did earlier. What makes you stay as his steward?" he asked.

"What makes you stay a slave? You came here one way, and I another. People take a random path one day, and sometime after, they can find no other path to choose."

"I'm a slave, but my spirit remains free. Yours is not. Something powerful and wrong holds you to this chieftain."

"Worry about yourself. He owns you now. You'll never escape."

"I'm not looking to escape. I don't need to be free—but you do. Stay much longer and you'll never leave him, no matter how much you may want to." The two men stared at one another, one challenging, one pretending carelessness.

Kel dropped his façade. He looked suddenly haunted. "Nobody gets away from Naldrum. He's ruthless."

"Yet a mere slave defied him today." Tor's lips curved.

Kel gave a rueful nod in reply. "That you did. But you appear to be a man with no one to care about and nothing to lose. Naldrum binds me by threatening someone I care very much about."

"Who truly has nothing to lose?" *My children, waving goodbye.*

"Such unanswerable questions and mysterious observations. If you have such knowledge, then, tell me: exactly how does one defy— and escape—someone as ruthless as Naldrum?" Kel looked over his shoulder, but the headman had not returned to the room.

Tor paused, then answered. "A path my ancestors called the Third Way. It is a thing which sounds simple but is not."

"I've never heard of it."

"People believe their actions matter, but they are wrong. What matters is intention. You probably believe that your knuckling-under to this headman protects this person you care about—but I promise you, your actions weaken you instead. Each time you go against your nature in serving him, you resent it. That builds a poison in you."

"True, perhaps. But so what? I still can't leave." Kel shifted on his chair and frowned at the knife in his hands.

"It is not a matter of leaving or staying. Leaving this Naldrum will not give you power, either. In fact, leaving him without setting your intentions properly will likely result in the exact *opposite* of what you desire. What matters—what gives power—is the *deciding* to do something, not the doing of it."

"I really don't understand what you're saying."

Tor flexed his fingers, tied to the boards. "Your actions will only have power when they flow from a single, simple thing: a deliberate decision you have made. It is the first step of the Third Way path."

Kel grew impatient. "Third Way? Where does it take you?"

"It leads you exactly where you tell it to, when you make your decision of what you want, before you start your journey."

The steward kicked the whetstone into spinning again. He angled the blade against it. "Sounds like nothing."

"True. But it is *everything.* Simply make your decision of what you want to do, and trust that the means to accomplish it will come. Will you stay and serve this evil man to protect this person you love? If you do so without setting your intention clearly, you will become a crust, a shadow-being whose spirit Naldrum has sucked dry. Or if you choose to leave but do so worrying that it may cost everything and achieve nothing, you will be fearful always, blaming yourself for whatever happens."

"That sums up my terrible options."

Tor shook his head. "You see it so only because at some point, you decided your only choice was to live in frustration and anger and hopelessness. So here you are, doing exactly that."

Kel felt suddenly excited, as if he was on the edge of understanding. "I do feel that way. It started years ago." He kept his words low, barely audible over the whetstone. "But it can change?"

"Yes. You feel forced into your life now. It may be, Kel Coesson, that you end up staying here in service to this vicious coward—but if you choose to do so in a calm way, strong in your resolve to protect this woman no matter what, it will not build the poison in you."

Tor paused to let the steward absorb his words. "Or, if you calmly resolve that leaving is the right choice no matter the consequences, you will learn to be at peace with that decision. It is all about a thoughtful decision, and then refusing to concern yourself with how that choice might come to happen or the dangers it may bring."

Kel stopped turning the whetstone. He stared at the knife again.

Tor continued. "This act of calm, deliberate choosing, and then accepting one's decision, is the essence of the Third Way. It fills us with quiet power and simple peace that sustains us."

They stopped talking as two servant girls came into the hall. "I'm doing work for Naldrum. Leave," the steward said.

Hunger for goodness stirred deep with Kel. His whole being reached through the trapped feeling towards the promise of Tor's words. But with hope, the old constant fear taunted him as he heard again the threat to hurt Aldís Naldrum had made that very morning.

"Peace. I can't remember the last time I felt it," Kel said, angry and frustrated. He got up, kicked the whetstone aside, and hated life.

. . .

Naldrum still had not returned. They resumed talking.

"If I try this Third Way, this deciding-without-fear. Then what?"

"Once you make your choice, remind yourself of it each day," Tor replied. "When you wake, or every time Naldrum shows cruelty, remind yourself: *I am staying here by choice to protect—*" Tor broke off. "What is the person's name?"

Kel stared at the dark stranger. He had never spoken of her to anyone, yet he felt the desire to trust this man. "Aldís," he mumbled.

Tor looked down to control his shock. Was that a common name in these parts? Did he dare admit he may have met the same woman? *No.* She was a connection to his children.

"A fine name," he only said. "Every day, you would remind yourself, 'I choose to stay here to protect Aldís.' Or, I suppose, 'I will find a way to leave Naldrum without fearing the consequences.'"

It occurred to Tor that he, personally, very much cared about the consequences to Aldís. But this man Kel must choose his own path.

"Every time Naldrum gives you a task you despise, remind yourself. Trust that you will find the strength you need, whichever choice you make. Trust that a way will open for you to follow your intentions. Trust that the great Goodness will guide you."

Eager to believe, the steward said, "What is the great goodness? Do I pray to the gods? Odin? Freya? Thor? Loki?"

"Who knows?" Kel could not believe that Tor actually laughed as he answered. "I am only a lowly slave; who am I to put a name to That Which Is? But when you set your intention and accept your choice, your life somehow *will* align with it. If you choose to stay to protect your Aldís, you will do calmly whatever you must, no matter how distasteful. Your ability to bear it, protecting her, will grow."

"And if I decide to leave?" Kel spoke barely above a whisper.

"Every day you will become less fearful of the cost of leaving— yes, even if it brings harm to her. I see you shaking your head. What I say must seem unthinkable."

"It does. For years, I have done what I could just to keep her safe."

"The Third Way does not require you to be inhuman. It understands that we need time to grow into our decisions. It only requires only the first tiny steps: the making of your decision and setting your intention to do your best in that choice, and simply reminding yourself of that and trusting that the way will unfold for you. With those small things, you will grow daily in strength and courage and calm confidence. Peace and joy, even. True freedom springs from acceptance."

"It seems slow and ineffective."

"Slow, perhaps. One cannot change a dire situation all at once. And it can be hard. The path can be rough and uncertain. You may doubt yourself, time and again. Taking the Third Way and accepting doesn't mean your pain or heartache or fears go away. But it *is* effective, Kel. Each time that you feel fearful, you must remind yourself of your choice, and affirm and accept it again. Almost without your noticing, as your life begins to align with your choice, you will grow stronger instead of weaker. That is why you must remind yourself of your choice daily even if things are not hard, so that you will grow in that strength, and have it whenever doubt besets you."

Tor leaned forward eagerly, his troubles forgotten in the instant. "Naldrum chose for you with his threats about this Aldís. But when you choose *for yourself* instead of letting someone else force your decisions, you *will* grow stronger, little by little. Be proud of that, slow and small though it may seem at first. Remind yourself of it each day. *Every day!* One moment, without knowing how, your headman will suddenly have no power over you."

For the first time since leaving his children, Tor felt his heart lift. He gave Kel a look of genuine friendliness. His old sense of humor filled him. "Do not forget that I will live here now. My example will help you remember that not only is anything possible, *everything* is."

"How? Naldrum is branding you an outlaw. That is even worse than being a thrall—and he intends to make you suffer, I know."

"Naldrum has made a very stupid decision. Your headman thinks he has shamed and thwarted me. But every day that he sees my calm face and these marks on my hands, he'll remember that a slave—the lowest of the low, with no weapon other than courage—openly mocked him, fearlessly undermining his authority. Worse, he'll fear that everyone who hears of it will laugh behind his back."

Kel smiled. "True."

"This Naldrum will *hate* that, I promise you. He has put himself in a perfect trap." Tor gave a soft chuckle. "That ugly coward will feel today's humiliation afresh every single time he looks at me."

"That he will." Kel grinned, but quickly sobered. "But because of that, he will inflict great pain on you. You will suffer more than he."

"Will I? He fears looking powerless more than I do a beating. He thinks he will somehow break me and keep me in order? No, Kel Coesson. The more he tries, the stronger I become and the weaker he."

Kel looked doubtful "If you say so."

"Your headman will return soon. I need to say one more thing," Tor continued. "Share my words with those who are not here. Others besides Naldrum and you must see these marks knowing that I willfully provoked him into making them. They, too, must understand that I defied him knowing the consequences—that I bear these marks willingly, intentionally, in defiance, without fear. It will inspire their own resistance. Those Naldrum controls believe he has all the power—but courage triumphs when used in the right way."

The steward could not take his eyes off this man with the richly colored skin. Here, right before him, a god-hero breathed. "Who *are* you?" Kel marveled.

"No one of consequence. Use your knife well, steward. Make the scars unmistakable. My will to live had all but faded, but these cuts are my passage into a new life. I will be a living sign of defiance and hope to all Naldrum holds in bondage. My 'common loathsome slave-hands,' as he called them, will shine light to those who feel despair."

"As you wish." He wiped the blade on his sleeve to smooth burrs.

Sám Tor, the trader had called this man. *Dark Mountain.* More than a measure of height and color, the name betokened power.

"The knife is ready. I'll fetch the others," Kel said. "Brace yourself."

. . .

Naldrum came back into the room after his staff assembled. He noticed something different about his steward Kel but paid it no attention.

"You see this creature?" He strutted in front of the throng of thralls and bondservants. "This slave, new to our household, has been defiantly willful. Thanks to him, you see what happens to those who oppose me. Watch as he cries out in pain, now and in the days to come. He will never dare to defy me again!"

Tor did not look at the headman. Instead, he smiled broadly at each face in the crowd, as if he looked forward to befriending them. Contrary to Naldrum's words, those watching saw only calm in the stranger's face, which perplexed them.

Naldrum gave the order to Kel. The steward gripped the gleaming knife and held it to Tor's hand.

"Sorry," Kel said under his breath. He winced, pressed down, and drew the weapon across Tor's skin. A line of wet red chased the blade.

Tor breathed in slowly, breathed out slowly. The people watched, hands over their mouths.

Sám Tor did not feel the sharp blade open his flesh. He did not hear it grit across the tendons and bones of his hand. He did not smell the blood that gushed from the wound, nor did he taste the sweat that poured down his face. He knew nothing of Naldrum's cackling glee.

In that instant, Tor's thoughts were fixed on a distant roadway. He walked in quiet towards a secluded farm, hidden from prying eyes and gossiping voices, with only the sound of birds and the breeze to accompany him. He imagined that he held in his hands a round, expensive fruit, and he inhaled the bittersweet fragrance of its oil. As he drew closer to the farm, he could hear the sound of children laughing as they ran barefoot across tender grass, free and safe under warm sunlight. He would taste soon a supper made by kind hands.

A breeze blew soft across swaying fields of grain. With that breeze, Tor breathed love.

Kel moved the knife to Tor's other hand. Despite what was happening to him, Tor's calm, peaceful expression did not waver. He made no sound. He drifted in a realm of peace.

Those who watched the cutting hid their puzzled expressions from their vengeful headman. But just as Kel had, they wondered: *who was this man?*

. . .

Chapter Ten

In another valley at some distance, the healing-woman Aldís stood at a table in the sun. She had arrived in time to assist with a birthing. With the mother now resting, she had turned to helping with farm chores. A pile of onions lay mounded on the table.

She had pulled the round bulbs from the soft earth, to prepare them for storage. These onions would sweeten bowls of *sup* all winter.

Aldís trimmed the straggling, unkempt tops. Her small knife flashed and her fingers moved in quiet rhythm as she prepared the long strands for braiding. The pleasant task required no thought. Aldís drifted, calm and peaceful.

But as she worked in the warm sun, Aldís felt a sudden disturbance inside, as if the earth had shuddered and torn open. Without warning, Tor's spirit plunged through her, and Aldís heard the tormented cry of a gyrfalcon. She searched the sky, certain she would see a bird dropping, its smooth flight pierced by an arrow. Her knife flashed again, but not on the onion tops, and Aldís cried out in sudden pain.

She looked down in astonishment. Blood gushed on the back of her hand from a gash in her skin, a large *X* cut from side to side.

"What just happened?" Aldís asked. "How did I cut myself?"

At that, a multitude of images flooded over her. She saw people shouting on a beach at moonrise, and smelled the smoke of burning torches. Once again, she saw that strange ship, and Tor clinging desperately to it as it tossed on a storm in the distant ocean. Far in the future, she saw a young woman wearing a white robe, weeping. Worst of all, the malevolent presence of the headman Naldrum seemed to ooze through all of it. The places on her wrists where his man had cut Aldís seared with pain, as if a flame had cut them afresh. Fear ravaged her, slicing into her from every direction, choking her lungs closed and squeezing her heart so hard it must certainly stop.

Aldís fell to her knees and then to the ground, too dizzy to lift herself. Such visions came from time to time, but never had one been this intense or frightening. She could feel her fingers clawing on the ground but could not see. Her dog nosed her face, whining softly. As abruptly as they had started, the visions ended. Aldís crept blindly, feeling her way to a bench.

"What *was* that?" she cried out, wondering what god or goddess or spirit had sent the images. "What am I supposed to do with these strange things you have shown me?" But whatever or whoever had invaded her offered nothing more.

"This has to do with Tor's future?" Aldís demanded. "Am I supposed to do something to help him? If so, what? Tell me!"

Only stubborn silence met her words.

She looked around, nervous. "You mistake me for someone more powerful than I am," she pleaded. "Whatever it is, this is too much for me. I'm no match for it." Her voice dropped to a whisper. "I'm no match for Naldrum. I tried once and failed. Please do not make me face him again, I beg you."

But the afternoon remained as quiet as before. Aldís sat up, her back against the bench. She looked at her hand. Already the blood from the cut had begun to congeal.

She frowned at the sky. Those memories needed to stay buried. She dared not let herself feel them ever again.

"Tor's future will come when it comes," she told her dog. "Perhaps the spirits will be a little clearer about how or even if I am supposed to help. In the meantime, we have work to do."

Little by little, she pushed the thought of Naldrum and all he had taken from her away. She picked up an onion, and another, and twisted their dried stems together, concentrating.

My daughter is gone. The past is over. I survived it, and I will keep surviving it.

The past was to be blotted out, and the future lay far away. Only today mattered, and this day, Aldís had warm sun and a pleasant task to occupy her. She shook off the hand of fate and picked up her knife again. Today, she had onions to braid.

. . .

Chapter Eleven
Equal-Day-and-Night

Autumn approached. Grasses turned gold, the air grew chilly and nights longer as light-filled days of summer dwindled. Tomorrow, sun-sticks would confirm that equal-night-and-day had arrived—which meant *álfablót*, the autumn blood-offering to the *dökk-álfa,* the dark elves of deep-earth.

Aldís dreaded *álfablót*. Not the midday feast; that was a joy, when neighbors gathered to celebrate the harvest. But afterwards each family hurried back before dusk, when the gongs sounded to warn all to get inside for the fearful, shrouded service of *álfablót*...that part.

Thoughts tormented Aldís. What happened if a child did not get a proper funeral? Did they too trail the dark elves as hunched, hungry nightwalkers? What happened if one died on *álfablót* itself?

There were days that Aldís thought she could still feel the little girl, the faintest whisper in her heart. It was wishful thinking, she knew. She could not remember what had happened that night. But the child's last day had been that of the *álfablót*. Each year, heartsick, her dread of the blood-offering ceremony had grown.

Bolt the door.

Hang a blanket over it to block any little crack where light might leak, protection against that which might see the light and wrap yellow fingernails around the hinges, trying to force its way inside.

Clear the family table.

Sharpen the knife. Hold it aloft.

Lay the bleating kid goat, its hooves tied, across the table. Speak the ancient words, repeated from oldest to youngest, imploring.

Put the knife to the kid's throat. Catch its blood in a bowl for the sacrifice to winter-elves and once-beloved dead who had not had a proper crossing-over ceremony.

Plead with them. Ask for mercy. Fear them.

. . .

Aldís, exhausted by the past weeks of healing interspersed with harvest work, felt an insatiable demand to be alone. Tomorrow, with the harvest meal and the ceremony, she would have no opportunity.

The family she had been visiting had pressed her to stay. "Aldís, don't go. So much is about to happen. And the morning after *álfablót,* the *réttir* starts, the sheep roundups. You must stay!"

She knew the invitation came partly from enthusiasm and partly from need. The annual sheep roundup meant exhausting work, as did the next event: once all the sheep had been sorted and counted, the cooler-growing weather meant butchering of pigs, sheep, goats, cows, and horses. Entrails had to be emptied and rinsed clean, sausages had to be stuffed and meat smoked, hides scraped, and hooves boiled to make glue. As a healer, Aldís was often asked to prepare animal skulls for ceremonies. All of it made for grueling, messy work, in which every pair of hands available meant less work for others. But Aldís could not think of work or helping, not just now.

"I'll be back. I just need to walk a bit."

She picked up her small bag of belongings and whistled to her dog, putting one foot in front of another away from people and towards solitude. As soon as she had left the cluster of buildings, her chest felt less tight.

The footpath led towards the neighboring farm, but Aldís turned away from it to a trail that led high above the valley. There, she would be able to sit and watch the windswept fields with only her thoughts as company.

Overwhelmed. Aldís had managed the turmoil that had been growing inside her across the summer. It was easier when all was growing and green. But tomorrow's *álfablót* meant the beginning of winter, the sudden plunging towards the season of bitter cold. Daylight would grow rapidly shorter now.

The past winters Aldís had spoken to no one of the ache inside, the feeling of unworthiness. How could she, a healer, explain the feeling that nothing she did mattered, that life had no meaning, that the idea of death had become a comfort, beckoning to her with its cold arms and promise of mindless peace? She had barely clawed her way through until spring again. How had another autumn come so fast? She needed solitude. To prepare.

To mourn.

"I miss her," she said to her dog. "You didn't know her. She was precious to me."

The dog pressed closer against Aldís's side where she could rest her fingers on its head. They climbed the path slowly, resting often. Only when she was high above the valley could Aldís feel truly alone.

As afternoon deepened, the air grew colder. Aldís reached in her bag for a cloak and pulled it around her shoulders. Up here, the last of the birch leaves had fallen. The trees stood naked.

I miss her so much. Always, when exhaustion filled her, sadness broke through.

"I'm just tired," Aldís said, half to herself and half to the spirits that surely occupied the same footpath, those of the slender birches and those of stone and air. "These last healings took too much out of me. I just need to rest for a bit."

This was true: a young mother had suffered with milk-sickness, and days of incantations and hot compresses had been needed to draw out the poison. A cut from a plowshare that had grown red and angry, and Aldís had to cut it open to let the wickedness out, always a stressful and uncertain task. A man had had pain in his ears. Aldís had filled them several times each day with salt, warm water, and spruce oil. A slave child, hungry, had eaten from the midden pile and sickened. The past blur of days had been an exhaustion of bending, tending, making offerings and prayers, whispering incantations, losing sleep, forgetting to eat.

"Maybe I'll walk back down the mountain and rejoin the family later." Aldís spoke again to the breeze that had accompanied her up the hill. "Or perhaps I'll go down to a different farm. Any one of them will welcome a strong back during the *réttir*." The thought occurred that she could sleep up here in blissful solitude, wrapped in her blanket with the light-elves of summer watching over her this one last night before autumn began. She wrapped her arms around her dog and half-closed her eyes, exhausted.

But her fatigue, Aldís knew, had less to do with healing work than the oncoming *álfablót*. That morning, she had started weeping for no reason. She had thrown her belongings together before the daybreak meal and had all but run to the foot of the hill, desperate for solitude because the inner panic welling up inside could be hidden no longer.

The playful breeze asked, so Aldís explained. Her dog listened with its ears cocked, as if eager to understand as well.

"I cannot bring myself to say the words of invocation to the spirits of the once-living without feeling as if I will scream and fall down sobbing. I need to be ready."

The breeze wafted around her, probing, gentle, insistent.

"Something is unwell inside you?" Wind loved a mystery, loved to find a crack, to flow through it, seeking in relentless curiosity.

"Perhaps." The admission frightened Aldís.

The breeze gusted, excited. "What *is* it? What do you fear?"

Aldís burst out in anger. "You slip from summer to winter easily, happily blowing in every season—but darkness and cold push me to the edge of survival. I don't want to spend another winter wandering from place to place, but I must—and the dark elves know why."

The wind snatched Aldís's words as they tumbled from her lips. She wanted to snatch them back, but the air had already claimed them.

"I want to stop grieving," she admitted. "But I don't know how. I want back what I once had, but that is impossible." She could not admit the last hard truth to the wind: that she herself had thrown away her one chance for healing.

There would not be another. She would never try again. There would be no children, no husband, no one to call her own.

"That's why I'm here alone, chilled to the bone on this bit of rock ledge, talking to the wind like a madwoman." This time the words were directed to her companion. He wagged his tail and nuzzled her hand.

With the admission came release. "I will always miss her." For the first time in years, honest tears fell.

. . .

The wind caught that last tidbit. Satisfied with its prize, it flitted away playing with Aldís's words. It tossed and caught them, flinging the sounds from wind-curl to wind-tendril, admiring how her sorrows chimed together.

Aldís pulled her cloak more tightly around her shoulders. She leaned back against the stone, glum. Now she had given the truth to the wind, Aldís considered the matter dispassionately.

The emptiness had grown year by year until it matched nearly the entire shape of her inside. A shell of skin and smile covered the inner void. It somehow had *become* her, this unhappiness, and she had no idea how to make it go away.

Had she once been happy? Was it possible ever to be again? Years of sadness stretching unbroken ahead seemed too much to bear.

Hunger gnawed, but Aldís ignored it. As evening approached, her thoughts turned to the man responsible for her pain. *Damn you to Hel, Kel Coesson.* Bitter resentment joined the pangs of hunger as Aldís fed on hate. Welcoming its poison into her heart, she breathed it out as well. It flowed from her, an invisible dank perfume—and in the dusk, things that drank of anger crept closer.

. . .

Aldís jerked suddenly awake. *What was that?*

In the midst of her bitter reveries, a tendril had floated into her awareness, an inner calling which usually signaled an ailment troubling a nearby family. Aldís could not make out from which direction the awareness had come. That was a relief, for even if she had been able to tell, Aldís knew she did not have the energy to follow the feeling. Only one more day until *álfablót* started tomorrow night at sunset. She dared not risk sharing her energy now.

. . .

But again, the inner call came, still faint but insistent. Aldís's inner listening sharpened as tight as a drawn bowstring. She sensed intently with her whole being, but still could not fathom from which farm the need came. So weak, as if it came from a great distance, but in its feebleness, a single-minded asking.

The call felt different, a strange mix that did not carry any sensation of sickness or injury she usually felt. It spoke of devastating loss, of grief, but of timid hope as well.

"Who are you? Where are you? What is the trouble?" Aldís asked.

A forlorn wistfulness floated back. Aldís leaned back, shocked. A strange mirror of sensation had seemed to mock her, echoing her question, *where are* you?

. . .

Shaken, Aldís stayed on the mountain until nearly dark, trying to sort out that odd call. She had not really decided whether to sleep up on the heights, but now clouds blew across the sky, darkening it earlier than normal. Indecision had led to decision. It was too late to safely walk down the path in the dwindling light. Now she would have no choice but to sleep here. The idea pleased her.

Aldís yawned. The strange sensation had stopped. She unfolded her blanket and spread it on the ground, ready to wrap herself in it. She prepared to be at peace, to share the night with the quiet stars and the rising moon in utter silence. It would be a good night, so unlike the bustling, noisy longhouse with its crowded sleeping benches and someone always getting up and making noise in the night. She would curl against her warm dog and sleep well.

But as Aldís yawned again, a sound rose from the dusk of the valley below: the deep tone of a single gong.

. . .

Her eyes widened in horror. "I could not possibly have made a mistake over something as important as this!" Aldís cried.

But the gong sounded again, coming from one farm and then another, until the valley rang with the somber tones. They warned that all living things, human and beast, must get inside for safety against those who would soon stalk the nights, starting especially this night.

She had packed her belongings and left before anyone had checked the *equal-day-and-night* markers.

Álfablót did not come tomorrow. It was tonight.

Aldís scrambled back against the earth wall behind her. The whole sprawling landscape below suddenly a place of danger. She would not hear the door close safely behind her in a snug longhouse, would not see the latchstring pulled inside, would not see the blanket draped over the door. No, she was high above the valley, alone, exposed on an eve when beings not fully alive broke from the bowels of the earth.

Trapped, Aldís stared with dread at the quickly darkening skies. It would not be long now until full dark, and there was not a thing she could do. The light-elves that had guarded the land from spring until now had no power once autumn began. They would leave until spring, fleeing before the creatures that ruled the cold months.

Her fear of Naldrum fled in the face of this greater danger. All of her hate and anger at Kel, the man she had trusted and who had betrayed her, departed. Those were matters of mankind. This was not.

Eyes of birch trees, stripped of leaves, watched. In almost no time the setting sun had culled all color from the sky. The birches glowed pale in the after-light as night swept over the valley and up the hills. The dark earth-elves, clambering upwards toward the world of humans, sniffed, and desired that which was their due.

. . .

Her mother's voice came in flickers of memory: "It does not matter what name one uses, Aldís. Here they bleed a kid for the *álfablót* when the *equal-day-and-night* happens. The people of my land did the same, but we called it *Samhain* there, and we celebrated it halfway between equal-nights and shortest-day. When the priests came, they made us change; now it is *all-hallows-eve*. But they're all the same, my daughter; when the sun sinks low on the horizon and the nights grow long, when the light dwindles and the earth turns cold, something in our marrow feels the touch of death. My people understood that otherworld spirits had yearnings. We understood that the dead missed us, missed their lives, and craved hospitality from their once-loved homes. We lit bonfires to welcome them and feasted outdoors. We laughed and danced. It was a happy time."

Aldís could remember the sweet sadness of her mother's voice.

"The priests changed it into a night of fear. And here, in this land of pagan beliefs, it is also fearful, this *álfablót*. They fear *revenants*— death-walkers—lurking in every hollow. They cringe at the thought of dark elves coming up from under the land. They hide inside, afraid."

Then, the haunted look as her mother finished. "They seek protection against the reckoning." Her mother had never explained what she meant by those words.

But Aldís had grown up in this land, not the place from where her mother had been taken, and the most precious thing had been taken from her the night of a long-past *álfablót*. She could not conceive of a *Samhain* of dancing and merriment against the glow of bonfires. The beginning-of-winter meant danger, with only a bit of barley beer and the blood of a bleating goat to stand against it.

. . .

Aldís clutched her dog and listened to the wail of the wind. At any instant a clawed hand, covered with soil and damp with mold, might spurt from the ground behind her and grab her. *What was that smell?* Might she see her mother's death-body, lurking as it tried to hide its fearful decay, daring to venture forth only on this night of shadows? *Oh, mother,* she whispered. *Recognize me. Treat me kindly.*

Would she see that tiny forlorn other form?

Aldís felt her way down the hill to a small cave she had passed, tripping against stones in the path. When she reached the sheltered hollow, Aldís wrapped herself in her blanket again, too afraid to fall asleep. The companionship she had spurned just a short while ago now seemed a blissful safety. *How stupid I am.*

. . .

The air moaned. The friendly breeze of earlier had fled as well, and now all nature pulsed with menace. Even the air could not be trusted. Low clouds drifted across the pale face of the moon-god. Ghostly birch-branches scraped towards it, and the long fingers of spruce swayed as if that which walked below had brushed against it. Cold crawled along Aldís' skin. The undead that had sniffed the intoxicating odor of her hate crept closer, upwards, seeking, anticipating. *Longing.*

She could hear leaves twitching on the ground. Was that from the heavy boots of the dark *álfa* as they climbed, relentless, up to the realm of humans?

Aldís imagined their inflamed nostrils, lifted, sniffing the night air for the scent of human households. They would tromp towards places around the farm where beer-offerings had been poured onto the ground, pressing their mouths against the wet soil. When that was gone, they would prowl the buildings, snuffling their noses close to the walls, scraping their fingernails against the doors and where the roof joined the standing timbers.

Aldís forced her fist into her mouth. No telling what might remain of her come morning. Sunrise, so far away, could not come fast enough.

The night noises grew louder, and the wind increased to a shriek. Aldís held her hands over her ears, closed her eyes, tried to shut out the dreadful coming-of-the-dead, the fetid, sick-sweet breath.

The gale hit the mountain on which she crouched. The wind, so light earlier, now ripped across the hillside, trying to tear away Aldís's protecting blanket.

"You want healing from that inside you which threatens to destroy you?" it screamed. "Stop running from your past and face it."

Birch branches sang in echo. "To live again, you must travel the path of death," they clattered, striking one another in the gusts of air.

Aldís shrank back, clutching the blanket to her throat.

"You are wrong," she said. "I *have* faced my past. I did nothing wrong. The fault lies with Kel Coesson, and I never, ever want to see his traitorous face again!"

But her words were a lie, and she knew it. More than anyone else, Aldís longed to see Kel tonight. His hard-headed stubbornness and his stoic refusal to break his word had once made her angry enough to spit, but that obstinate will was the very thing she needed now. As much as she hated Kel, Aldís yearned for him—and because she would never again humble herself to ask for his help, she hated him more than ever before.

Again, she breathed out anger, and once again, creatures sniffed.

. . .

The creatures of under-earth not only caught the intoxicating scent of her boiling fury, but they heard the clamor of Aldís's shouts. Their heads turned, slowly, heavily, towards the fracas. *Yes, that poisonous perfume of anger and resentment and fear comes from over there.* The smell of that-which-weakens indicated a human ripe for culling.

The thunder of the storm covered their footsteps as they clumped towards Aldís, walking straight up the mountain, not needing the path.

She could almost make out their forbidding expressions in the drenching rain. Imminent danger stripped away any hope of safety. She was alone, and she would die alone, and it would happen tonight.

With that certainty came calm. Suddenly, Aldís knew only fury.

"Have you no sense of justice?" she shouted at those who approached. "Those who actually *did* evil, you let them thrive, yet you judge me? Make *me* suffer? Yes, you are reapers of humans, but do you need to be so cruel? Is this the night you will mark me as yours and take me, yet you give me no chance to redeem myself?"

Aldís dropped the blanket and stood. "Then I choose to go to Hel rid of *everything* that is of humankind. If I can have no help from my humanness, then I choose for my spirit to be as fierce as your storm, as dark as the underworld from which you crawled. The world has nothing left for me, so I choose my terms: I will be one of you, a *dökk-álfa*, a dark elf—or are you dark dwarves? We none of us know. Show your faces. Whoever you are, whatever you are, none of you can claim to have more darkness of spirit than I—so embrace me, welcome me as one of your own, one with your storm, a part of the mountain itself!"

She stripped her dress over her head, tore off her shift, raised her arms and arched her back, lifting her breasts to the storm. She spread her fingers, felt them stretch long and thin, birch-branches reaching towards the sky. Rain drenched her face and hair and her pale body. She clawed towards to the wild flashes of lightning, beckoning it…and in the face of death, naked, defiant, and unafraid, Aldís danced.

She danced in defiance of what had been, in wild surrender to what might be. She danced to that which gives life and that which takes it. She sang the ancient words of Samhain songs to the astonished night-elves: songs of love and loss, songs of welcome and fearful reverence.

She sang for her mother, for all those lost to death, fearing nothing for how they might respond or for what they might do to her. Desired no comfort, no thing, no person, but offered herself to whatever might be. Existed, knowing how fragile a thing life was, and exulted, accepting uncertainty, yielding to it.

During the álfablót, each year, dark-elf eyes measured and marked certain humans for later-taking. On this night, Aldís had no way of knowing that the soul-searchers sifted her spirit. They saw the emptiness inside her, the murky illness. They found her wanting. They knew the brokenness in her—but they also watched and listened, enthralled at seeing a human, an above-grounder, sharing the wild night with them; close, vulnerable, yet utterly without fear.

The *dökk-álfa,* for the first time, saw beauty.

Because of the gift of her dance, because of the song, because of her mad courage, the dark elves passed Aldís by and made no mark on her. Instead, they did the rarest of things: they blessed her. She did not know it, but they gave her strength that would sustain her for the winter to come…then left her in peace and simply walked away.

. . .

Aldís could not remember when she had dropped from exhaustion. She woke to thin clear moonlight gleaming on the birch trees. She was wrapped in her sheepskin, warm and mostly dry. Her small dog was curled in a ball, sound asleep. The fear of the night seemed an age ago. What had woken her?

In her mind's eye, Aldís saw a valley she knew well, a revered place. In it, she saw the man about whom the wind had taunted her.

"Althing? No," she protested. "I can't go there. Kel is always there. I won't."

But the image persisted, relentlessly directing her: *go to Althing. You must do it. Face him.*

"All right. I'll go to Althing next summer if it means so much," Aldís mumbled. Althing was months away. Much might change between now and then. She would have all of autumn and winter and spring to prepare herself.

Satisfied, the future released its grip and let her drop back into deep sleep.

. . .

Chapter Twelve

Spring, 980 A.D., cathedral of Aix-la-Chapelle in Germania.

The novice monk Konradsson knelt, trembling, as he waited for the great bishop to reach him.

Make me worthy, Lord God. Make me obedient in serving you.

Who would have ever dreamed that he, Konradsson, would have traveled so far from his birth land to now kneel in this great cathedral waiting for the bishop's blessing? That he would be on the verge of taking vows to spend his life dedicated to serving the Almighty, here in this hallowed community?

Heavy smoke from burning incense swirled over the cold stone floor. *It looks like the door carvings back home,* he realized. *Dragons and snakes entwining the doorframes, protecting the household from dangers.*

Konradsson was horrified at himself. What a profane thought in this holy chapel! He squeezed his eyes shut to stop looking at the swirls of smoke, but the images persisted. Dragons writhed around serpents, their fanged mouths open and claws at the ready. Konradsson had not thought of them for years. Now, in his moment of greatest joy, intolerable memories filled him.

The young monk fought back. *One day those pagan monstrosities will be gone. Those doors will be carved instead with crosses, the symbols of Our Lord.*

He felt alarmed at the vehemence of his thoughts. *Pah. What has that to do with me now? I am* never *going back to that wasteland of spirits and trolls.*

The sound of the bishop's staff striking against the huge flagstones brought Konradsson back to the present. *This smoke burns in honor of God,* he reminded himself. *It has nothing to do with dragons. The Lord reminds me of the past in order that I feel grateful for how far He has led me.*

Joy filled his heart again at the prospect of receiving the bishop's directions. He felt certain that the bishop would appoint him to stay within these walls. *I will serve without expectation of praise or reward. I will rejoice in the humblest of chores, unnoticed and ...safe,* Konradsson realized.

Bishop Friedrich moved along the row of kneeling men, placing his hand on the shoulder of one novitiate after another. His voice boomed as he proclaimed to each man the duties that would fill the rest of his life.

"You, my son, will use your gift of brew-making to serve our community." A murmured response, *as the Lord wishes.* The bishop moved to the next man.

"You, my son, will devote yourself to copying the words of St. Paul." *As the Lord wishes.*

"You, my son, will go to the seacoast, and assist our brothers in healing communities there—"

Konradsson breathed a prayer. *Please, let me stay here.*

The bishop came nearer. Only two ahead of him. Konradsson's heart banged in his chest. The words became an uninterrupted stream *letmestayhere letmestayhere letmestayhere.*

Now he felt the bishop's firm touch on his shoulder. The young monk prepared to hear the words: *you, my son, will live within these walls, tending to our gardens.* But with a shock, Konradsson heard something entirely different.

"You, my son, will return to your native land, and preach the gospel to those who worship heathen idols."

Konradsson lifted his head, rebutting the bishop in alarm. "What? *What?* No," he gurgled.

The bishop frowned slightly but said nothing in response. He placed his hand on the shoulder of the next novice. "You, my son, will stay here, weaving and washing to keep us clothed and clean."

Konradsson forgot to keep his head bowed. He stared aghast as the bishop continued to move along the line of kneeling men.

Had His Grace somehow mixed up who was supposed to do what? How did he even decide? Had the friars suggested this? *I can't go back there. Not ever.* Reeling in shock, the young monk fought despair.

The smoke swirled. He felt something slithering along the bottom of his robes. A forked tongue flickered, seeking. Konradsson clutched the railing, dizzy, coughing.

An older monk made a warning sound in his throat. Konradsson bowed his head in outward obedience, but inwardly, all his certainty and desire to serve had evaporated.

Return to Iceland? God could not possibly want him to do such a thing. The bishop had made a mistake. Shocked at his own defiance, Konradsson sank lower onto the hard stones.

I must pray, he thought. He proceeded to try but was unable to think of anything but the dragons snaking along the cold hard stones, hissing and snarling in mocking voices from his youth.

. . .

"Come in" Bishop Friedrich's secretary beckoned, a portly old priest in a worn brown robe.

Konradsson genuflected. "I must talk to His Excellency, please," he stammered.

The elderly man twinkled. *Ordination. One or two always bucked their assigned duty.* He had half expected to see Konradsson. Friedrich had mentioned the young man might be uncomfortable with the bishop's choice.

He could see Konradsson trembling. The old secretary patted him on the arm. "Sit there, son. The bishop prays at this time, but when he has finished, I will send you in to him."

Konradsson's fingers curled around the chair arms, uncurled, curled again. His eyes wide, he stared at the objects in the small room without seeing them. A crucifix on the wall. An icon of the Virgin. A small book, its pages thick with gold paintings. His fingers cramped. He felt as if he would choke.

"The bishop. Is he...difficult to talk to?" What he didn't ask: *will he be angry that I came here?*

The secretary considered making a small joke at Konradsson's expense. He decided against it. The lad looked on the verge of collapse.

"You are a child of God. His Excellency will not be harsh."

At last, the door to the bishop's room creaked open. The elderly secretary waved to Konradsson and announced him without getting up from the desk at which he worked.

"Young Konradsson to see you, sir."

Konradsson wished he had a hat to remove, or something, anything, to show deference. His footsteps barely making a sound, he crept to where the bishop sat in a carved wooden chair, resting from the rigor of his prayers, his hand over his eyes.

"Tell me what brings you." Bishop Friedrich had no energy for preambles.

Konradsson gathered his nerve. "Sir, when you ordained us—" He choked and tried again. "I know it is good and holy to serve Our Lord in any number of ways. But ever since I came here—" Konradsson decided to add divine support to his plea. "Since coming here, I have felt the Lord speaking in my heart, urging me to work in this quiet place. Today I heard you say that I am to serve Him by bringing the light of faith to my homeland." He chose his next words carefully, not wanting to seem as if he was defying the bishop's command. "I am confused, sir."

"You do not love the place where you were born, do you, brother Konradsson?" It was more statement than question.

Konradsson had not expected that. He shook his head.

"No happy memories at all? No place or people you would welcome seeing again?"

Again, no.

"Why not, my son?"

Konradsson blinked. He wished not to answer, but the bishop sat waiting.

"I cannot bring myself to say," he finally got out.

The bishop sighed, the breath going deep into his lungs and back out, heavy. He knew some of the boy's story, of his struggles. He had hoped to protect him from further damage by sheltering him here in the monastery, away from the world, from people who did not understand. He had prayed about it over and over, but the same troubling answer had come, time after time: *send him home.*

"You worry that old ills might happen again."

"I care nothing for torment visited upon me, if it is because of work I do for Our Savior." Konradsson's voice broke, belying his brave words. "But here, your honor, in this community…safe…" That word again. He realized he was babbling, and pressed his lips shut.

The bishop pinched his temples between his fingers and thumb. The headache grew stronger. Did young Konradsson sense the doubt that he, too, felt?

"Perhaps God, who knows well our hurts, wants you to help others find Him," Friedrich said. "No doubt He will give you the strength to shine His light."

"Perhaps," Konradsson quavered. "But please, Your Grace—"

"I will pray on the matter one last time, my son. Now let me rest."

Konradsson rose to leave. *Iceland, please Lord, no.* He tried to have faith but felt none.

. . .

Konradsson followed the slow procession of novice monks towards the chapel for noonday prayers. Brown robe after brown robe, heads shaved exactly alike, hands in the same prayerful posture, intoning ancient Latin words they had sung the day before, and the day before, and the day before, for decades: *'unchanging, eternal Lord, may we follow Your lead…'*

The sameness soothed the monastery into an anonymous whole, allowing the priests to lose themselves in quiet bliss. Konradsson sang the chant too, but his thoughts interrupted him.

Perhaps the bishop will decide today. He feared asking again. Nagging might result in the wrong answer. He had only one chance.

"Ubi caritas et amor, Deus ibi est..." he sang. Inward desire warred with the peaceful tones. *I don't want to go back to Iceland. They still sacrifice ewes and goats and fowl to the gods. They don't want to change. No one will listen to me.* Even the old stories, ones that told of the many in his homeland who had arrived as Christians, always ended with a steady drift back to pagan ways.

"Ubi caritas et amor..." The short phrase repeated over and over as the procession moved through the narrow hall. Usually, Konradsson loved this passageway, where the sounds tumbled against their own echoes to become one great solemn beauty. *"Glorianter vultum tuum, Christe Deus..."*

He winced, remembering long-ago names and faces. *I must not think of who tormented me. The Lord will provide the strength I need, towards anyone or against anything.*

He breathed, sang, breathed, sang, and most of all, prayed fervently that the bishop would change his mind.

. . .

"Bishop Friedrich will see you after vespers." Konradsson could hardly believe the words whispered in his ear. He turned quickly to see the bishop's portly assistant smiling at him.

"Do you know if he plans to grant my request?" Konradsson pleaded.

"I cannot say," the older monk said. He chuckled gently and continued along the stone hallway.

The vespers service seemed to last forever. Konradsson stared at the bishop, who sat at the front of the church, his eyes closed, lips moving silently during prayers. *Dear Lord, please let him say yes.* Konradsson tried to stop such selfish thoughts, knowing he should be obedient, but had little success.

When the service finally ended, the bishop left, carrying his crook, and all older monks followed. Finally, Konradsson could rise from his kneeling position and file out of the room. As the rest of the novitiates headed to their sleeping chambers, Konradsson darted along the route to the bishop's chambers, his robes flapping and his sandals pounding loud in the hallways.

He leaned against the last archway before the bishop's chambers, hands on his knees, panting for breath. When he could breathe, he forced a calm appearance and knocked at the door.

Immediately, the elderly assistant called him to enter. "His Grace will speak with you soon. Do compose yourself, Brother Konradsson. I can hear your heart beating from here." Again, the small chuckle. He dipped his goose quill into a saucer of ink.

When his audience came, Konradsson knelt before the bishop, kissed his ring, and found himself quite unable to rise. Finally, the bishop coughed, and the young monk gathered himself and stood.

"I was told you wanted to speak with me, Father," he quavered.

The bishop surveyed Konradsson, hoping he had made the right decision. "You indicated that you are reluctant to return to your home country of Iceland. I had prayed upon your novice assignment, and believe the Lord directed me to give you that path. But the Lord has also given you the urge to speak to me—*"pester, more like "*—so as promised, I have prayed again for His guidance."

"Yes, Father," Konradsson breathed. He would know soon.

"I am familiar with some of what happened to you before you arrived, young brother Konradsson. You sustained damage. It is for that very reason that I believe our Father wishes that you return there."

Konradsson's heart sank. An angry feeling began to swirl in his chest.

The bishop continued, "Our Lord, however, moves in mysterious ways. I have led this community for many years. My spirit is in need of refreshment. I have meditated upon the example of Saint Patrick, who went to a heathen island and brought its people to God. The Lord tells me that it is my duty, now, to do the same."

Friedrich hoped the young priest could not see the doubt that plagued him over this announcement. *Had the desire to follow Patrick's example truly been God speaking, or his own ego?* His headaches had worsened as he wrestled with the matter across many months. *Time to try. Succeed or fail, I cannot bear the fight any longer.*

"I have great compassion for the concerns you have about this journey. You *will* go to your home country, young Konradsson, but not alone. I will accompany you, and hope it is a relief to know that you will not travel alone. I trust that divine influence will guide us both. God willing, the journey will prove a blessing to your countryfolk and to our Church, and even to your soul and mine as well as we serve Him."

Konradsson did not know whether to weep in defeat or embrace the bishop. He sank to his knees, shaking all over, and kissed the great ring again. "As you will, Your Grace."

"We travel tomorrow to the seaport," the bishop said. "Hopefully, we will arrive in time for your country's great assembly, the one called Althing. I have heard of it for many years, and confess I would like to see it for myself. Be ready at dawn."

As Konradsson turned to go, the bishop added, almost as an afterthought, "Young man, I ask that you pray tonight, and every morning and night, giving thanks for this opportunity." He gazed at the junior monk with a mixture of tenderness and resolve. "We work for Him, not for ourselves. Sometimes the greatest good comes from loving our enemies. We must ask the Lord daily to help us do His work."

Konradsson bowed and left the room.

Yes, pray, young brother. For yourself, and for my soul as well. Friedrich crossed himself, and rose, as nervous as Konradsson, went to pack his things.

. . .

Chapter Thirteen

Germania, near Hamburg

The young monk Konradsson leaned over the side of a heaving vessel and wretched into the waves again. *How could there be anything left in my stomach,* he wondered. He started to wipe his mouth with the edge of his surplice, but another bout of nausea approached.

Konradsson longed to throw himself into the sea and drown. Only the presence of the bishop nearby, sitting on a bench and fanning his face in the warm air, kept Konradsson from begging the sea-goddess for the bliss of death. He had tried prayers to the Lord, but failing that, desperate and utterly miserable, he longed for help from any quarter. He moaned.

"You'll feel better soon." The bishop seemed to feel no ill effect from the waves. He had a fat pickle in his hand and took small bites from it every little while.

Konradsson tried to nod agreement but failed. He slumped on the half-deck in a disheveled heap, wishing to die. "I prayed," he groaned. "….to not be sick…" He could not finish.

"Poor boy," the bishop said. He offered a short prayer for Konradsson's improvement. When that failed to revive the lad, who seemed to be turning an altogether unhealthy color, the bishop pursed his lips. Perhaps the Lord preferred a more direct approach. He hoisted himself off the bench and holding onto the ship rope, swayed over to where Konradsson lay, stumbling a little as they crested a particularly large wave.

"I really must insist that you eat some of this," the bishop directed.

"Forgive me, your Grace." Konradsson leaned over the rail and threw up again.

"I command you as your bishop," Friedrich said. He bit off a piece of pickle and held it out.

Konradsson, too weak to argue, opened his mouth. The bishop dropped in the morsel and Konradsson chewed.

When his throat moved, swallowing, the bishop instructed the novice to open his mouth again, and Konradsson obeyed, looking for all the world like a damp fledgling opening its beak for a bit of worm.

After a while. Konradsson had chewed and swallowed the entire pickle. He realized that he felt much better.

Now, however, shame swept over him that he had let the bishop see him in such a state, and he rolled onto his stomach, sobbing.

"Forgive me, Father, for I have sinned," he began. But the bishop would have none of it.

"Nonsense, boy," he said. "Long before God called me into His service, my uncles had me working on their ships in the Dane-marked lands. You just had a bit of seasickness. Now get yourself cleaned up. There's a long voyage ahead, and I wager that few of those on this ship know the Lord. We have work to do."

Yes, Friedrich told himself. He would practice his skills of conversion on this stalwart crew first. He watched them pulling the sail, bare-chested, bare-footed, lean and taut. *Look at them, wandering in darkness, poor souls. Probably all pagans.* He would help them find their way to the joy of the Lord, and with that work done, would open his heart to the misguided inhabitants of far Iceland.

Friedrich pictured the distant island awaiting him in the sea far away. A shadowy mist covered it, a mist of ignorance and superstition. He felt joy at reaching out to the tall folk of that land, with their tattoos and braided hair. He had heard descriptions of the men and women of these sea-swept lands and imagined their harsh faces glowing with grateful joy at the prospect of conversion to a better way of life. *Thank you, your Grace,* they would cry. *Not for me the thanks,* the bishop would tell them. *For the Father.*

Konradsson, too, watched the men working the sail as well. He reached into the barrel for another pickle and chewed, confused at the turmoil in his thoughts.

. . .

The seasickness that had plagued Konradsson did not return. Once it had resolved, he had thrown himself into being helpful aboard ship. He had caught fish, he had cleaned fish, he had cooked fish. He had scrubbed the deck, aware of the eyes that watched him, looked away when he looked, the expressions of disdain.

"Here." A bucket of seawater and a rag shoved into his hand, a pointing towards something with no other instruction offered. Konradsson fumbled, feeling inane.

"Nay, not that. *This.*" The accents of many ports, unfamiliar, the few words too quick. Konradsson tried to follow the utter lack of directions. To stay out of the way, not be completely stupid.

"No...dump the bucket at the head, ye jack!"

"Here. Do whippings." A rough needle put into his fingers, a ball of linen thread. A nod at a rope.

"Whippings?" he whispered to the nearest sailor. The man pulled a small rope that dangled from a sail, flicked at the small woven knot at the end. Konradsson studied it, tried to follow the pattern. A grunt of sarcasm from the sailor at the first dreadful attempt. No grunt at the second. Konradsson threaded the needle again, tackled another rope.

Later that day, a pair of torn trousers thrust into his hands. "Mend these." When he had finished and returned them, the briefest of nods indicated a job done properly. Konradsson hid a shy smile as he returned to sewing whipping knots.

The next day, another torn pair of trousers. When he had mended them, the man at the steering board had jerked his chin at Konradsson's long priest's alb. "Take that off and put it in your trunk. Not good for sea work. Wear those pants."

. . .

"Pull!" The sail, caught by a sudden squall, filled too quickly. All hands grabbed what they could, frantically holding as the ship keeled half over. Afterwards, Konradsson's palms bled, but he felt proud. One of the men thumped him on his bare back.

"This be how ye coil the ropes," came gruff, terse instructions. "Nay, no' like that, it'll tangle."

From daybreak until dark each day, little by little, he learned. Little by little, the looks of disdain ebbed away. The *vikingers* taunted him repeatedly about his earlier nausea, but their humor was good-natured. Now, when they made a jest about his earlier seasickness,

Konradsson laughed with the others, but once, he had had to turn away so that they did not see the sudden wet that came to his eyes.

I have friends.

. . .

To his surprise, the young monk soon felt the same kinship with the sailors on board that he shared with brothers in the monastery.

Friedrich must have as well, he reckoned, for the bishop spoke often to them as he had to the monks in Germania. But when the bishop preached to them, they said nothing. Friedrich had not learned to notice the way the sailor's jaws tightened, but soon Konradsson did.

They may be pagans, but they're good fellows, Konradsson wanted to say to his bishop, but it was not for him to correct his superior. He said nothing, but instead, looked for more work to do.

. . .

Chapter Fourteen

The plains of Althing, during the midsummer festival of Longest-Day

Kel Coesson shaded his eyes against the harsh glare and cursed. Even at middle-night, the sun still flamed scarlet where it languished along the northern horizon.

The black silhouette of the festival tent of his chieftain Naldrum stood against the red glare. Two men Kel himself had hired to guard the tent paced, back and forth, back and forth. They were armed, of course. His headman routinely ignored the rule that banned weapons at the great Althing festival.

What by Hel am I doing here? he asked himself yet again. Damned sneaky business, spying. And then, again, *what is taking so long?* He almost turned to go but at that instant saw what he had been waiting for: the change of guards.

A new pair of men approached the tent. They chatted for a short while with the first two. One stooped to tighten the laces on his boot. Another slapped him on the back, laughing at some crude joke.

Come on, come on.

Finally, the first guards left. Only the two new men remained.

Now or never, Kel told himself. He stumbled forward.

The guards saw him coming and blocked the path. Kel stopped, swaying. Wine sloshed from his drinking horn onto his tunic.

"Well, fellows," he slurred. "Glad to see you here protecting our headman, just as I instructed. Fine work. Fine night, too. Can't really call it night, though, can we? So bright." He rubbed his eyes, slurped from the drinking horn.

The guards shifted, uncomfortable. *Was Kel Coesson drunk?* They had never seen the steward other than stone-faced and sober. Kel himself had charged them with guarding this tent in which their chieftain slept. Something was wrong.

Kel feigned a burp. "Need to speak with Naldrum. Nearly time for the festival to begin."

One young sentry replied, nervous at refusing Kel. "Do you remember, sir? You instructed us that no one, *absolutely no one,* could approach the headman's tent during the sleeping time."

"Oh, yes. I did say that. So, he's still sleeping, eh?" Kel had intended them to follow that command—until he had by chance seen the headman approach the tent earlier, telling the other guards to leave. When they had, Naldrum had yanked a woman from the shadows and pushed her inside the tent, his every movement furtive.

Kel thought about Sóma, and how the earnest young woman had accused Naldrum. *Enough,* he growled. The gods had given him a chance to find out whatever he could.

Kel spilled the wine again, this time onto the ground. The guards stared at the wet spot in the dirt. One licked his lips, wondering about the taste of the drink which only the rich could afford.

"I guess I should rest too." Kel swung his head heavily. "Where's my tent? I can't find my tent. I'm damned tired."

Not much farther. Almost there. Another slosh.

"Shall I hold that for you sir?" The guard, jealous of the waste, but also concerned at seeing Kel Coesson in such a condition—and not just any man, Naldrum's steward!

Kel shook his head. "I want to finish it." He touched the horn to his lips and drank deeply. As much went down the front of his tunic as into his mouth. Kel tucked the empty vessel in his leather belt and swayed closer to the tent. *Only a few steps more. So close.*

"Sir, you must leave. Perhaps you are testing to see if we are following your orders?" The young guard ended on a hopeful note, but his face did not match his words.

Kel's head swung again. "I'll have you whipped—"

The guards shifted, uneasy. Their eyes darted to one another and back to the steward. Kel coughed and stumbled. *Curse them for doing exactly what I told them.* "What's your name?"

The man stammered out a response but Kel paid no attention. He passed his hand over his face. "Need to sleep. This midnight sun—so bright. Shade over there—" He pointed and lurched past the men, fell to his knees and crawled towards the base of the tent wall, falling with a thump on the ground against it.

"Just let him be," the other guard hissed. "Surely our headman is sound asleep. If we wake him arguing out here with Kel, who do you think will be in trouble? Us, or his steward?"

The first man hesitated. He shrugged his shoulders in consent. At that, they moved back to their posts, and took up their watch again.

. . .

Kel pretended to snore for a moment or two, then pressed his ear to the tent wall. At first, he heard nothing but his own racing heartbeat.

Look at me, Kel cursed. *Lying here in the dirt, pretending to be drunk, eavesdropping. Not a manly act.* But craven or not, this might finally answer the questions that had plagued him since he had ridden to the farm where Sóma lived.

Slowly, sounds came. The clank of a spoon against metal. The headman talking, his mouth full. A knife scraping on something. A woman's voice, awkward and hesitant. Eventually, Kel could hear the headman's voice rising, pleading and demanding, and the woman refusing. Kel could not make out the words, but he knew the sound of denial. Naldrum, more insistent. His voice, more harsh, and hers raised stronger in reply. A struggle. A stifled scream, the sound of cloth tearing, of something falling over. A rhythmic grunting.

Another sound, muffled. The woman crying out in pain and anger.

Everything in Kel demanded that he interrupt what was happening in the tent. But an inner voice cautioned him to stay quiet. *Perhaps he hired her. Don't waste your only chance to learn the truth.*

At last he heard Naldrum cry out, then for a while, there was only silence, broken at length by sounds of things on the table being moved, of liquid poured. The woman's voice, shaking, asking to leave.

Naldrum hesitated. Kel guessed the headman was considering whether he could manage again. "Yes," he finally barked. "Get out of here. Fix your clothing. You look a mess."

"Who made me look this way? You had no right to take me like that. I intend to report you."

The sound of a slap, and her cry of pain followed by Naldrum's voice. "You won't live to see another day if you do. Is your precious virginity worth your life?"

Kel heard her crying softly, and chains jangling, the flat clang of cheap jewelry as she adjusted her apron.

"Not that way," Naldrum said. "Go out the back tent-flap. Not the front. I don't want anyone seeing you."

As she fumbled with the latch string, the headman spoke again. "I never allow my good name to be tarnished. Let me be very clear: speak to no one of this. Do you understand?"

. . .

Kel's gut churned. This matched the scenario Sóma had described. How many times had the headman protested that women falsely accused him of fatherhood? Had denied their claims, saying that such a thing was impossible, and that he only lay with his own wives?

Pressed against the tent, Kel could feel the woman's presence, his body separated from hers only by the fabric wall. He could hear her breathing, almost panting. Likely, her head down, not wanting to look at the headman. *Poor thing.* Rage filled him.

Easy enough to set the matter straight. Kel thumbed the blade hidden in his tunic. He had sharpened it that morning.

Naldrum, threatening again. "If I hear even one word of you bragging about lying with me, I will have your parents flogged for raising an indecent daughter." He considered the piece of mutton in his fingers, pulled off a bit of fat. "Flogged until they bleed." He put the fat into his mouth and chewed, savoring it. "And then you will see them die, and then you will die. I take no chances."

"You can be certain no one will hear of this from me." A sob escaped her. She finally fumbled the tent flap open and blinked in the sudden brightness outside. Her fist against her mouth, the young woman ran off. She did not notice the dusty pile of clothing on the ground, or the man who peered from it, memorizing her face.

She ran away from the guards, who whirled in dismay at the sound of her retreating footsteps. Where had she come from? Had that woman gotten into the chieftain's tent without their seeing?

The guards whispered furiously to one another. "Was she in there with him just now?"

"Maybe she's a thief. Should we wake headman Naldrum?"

"He'll be angry if we do. Besides, if he doesn't notice anything missing, no one will be the wiser."

While their backs were turned, Kel seized the chance to scramble in the opposite direction.

The guards finally decided that they could not be certain they had seen the woman leaving the headman's tent, only running *behind* it. The two young men resumed their stance, chests out, defending their headman from all manner of imaginary onslaughts—and forgetting all about the sodden steward.

. . .

Kel moved down the row of tents, staying out of sight. He turned to watch the guards pace their brave steps. *Naldrum just raped that young woman. Just like Sóma. I could go back there now and beat him within an inch of his life.*

Those two guards, even together, were no match for him. Young, wanting to do their best, they would stand their ground and fight. He pictured them cut down, and again felt repulsed. *No sense harming them. They're just doing their job*. Besides, fighting was strictly forbidden in this hallowed valley, at this great festival of Althing. Kel's reverence for the sanctity of Althing clashed with visceral desire to punish a wrong. His anger threatened to boil over at the headman, at the guards, but mostly at himself.

On some level, I must have known, Kel berated himself. *But I never objected. I never challenged what he said. No. I trusted him. I let him get away with it.*

Trust. The word felt repulsive.

The sun-goddess Sól finished her short nap on the horizon. She began to stretch and rise again. Her bright rays touched Kel's back. He shivered despite the warmth. *No escaping her gaze during midsummer.* Sól drove away shadows, forbade deception, demanded stark truths in her reign of light. Across the midnight-sun days of the festival, Sól would follow Kel, watching to see what he would do.

She will know I am a coward—and at Althing of all places, he told himself, miserable. *She will know.*

. . .

The prior afternoon, Naldrum's entourage had arrived at Althing-valley, the sacred grounds where the annual festival took place. Road-weary from the long trek from the headwaters of Bull Valley, thralls and bondsmen began to untie horse-packs and set up tents. Drovers hustled herd animals into enclosures. Hammering sounded everywhere, as stakes for sleeping tents and merchant awnings were pounded into place, and ropes stretched to pull the fabric tight. Far too many jokes about 'Thor's hammer' drew obligatory laughter.

Naldrum watched the crowd grow across the afternoon. He waited until many of his loyal freeholders had arrived, milling around his tent in anticipation.

"Welcome, my friends," he had called. "As always, a short meeting, a few details, and then I will open our first barrel of festival ale." He had beckoned Kel. "Steward Kel, we have some newcomers, as always. Say a few words. Tell them what to expect from the festival."

Kel sat tall in the saddle of his horse in order that all could see and hear. He gave the same short speech he always did.

"You all know how a *thing* works. Since before anyone can remember, our ancestors gathered at *things* to discuss important matters, to trade, to mingle. If you are new to *this* one—this Althing—know this: the first rule, always, is that no weapons may be carried, and no fighting allowed except in the *holmgang* dueling area." Kel ceremoniously handed his sword and scabbard to his servant. No one would know about the knife in his boot, the one Naldrum insisted he carry.

Kel raised his voice. His speech this year would be longer than before, and his headman would not appreciate it.

"Those of you eyeing the beer keg, pay attention." *Those louts might need this one day.* "Most local *things* consist of a tent or two, a handful of merchants, and people you already know. But this is different, for this festival is *All-Thing,* the assembly for all of Iceland."

A few rough cheers. Kel waited for silence.

"People come from every part of our land, even from over the seas, to trade and to make treaties here. Because of the distances people travel, and because of the many law readings and legal cases to be heard, be prepared for Althing to last at least two weeks, perhaps even a month."

More voices raised, more shouts.

"You will see many exciting things: merchants, games, food. But the most important part of Althing is the uniqueness of Iceland in all the world. How? *We are the only people of any known land who answer to no sovereign.* But if we have no king, what rules us?"

He waited. Soon shouts came. "Our laws lead us!"

"Yes, our laws. We give our *law* power, instead of any ruler. And that law, based on fairness, protects our people."

Those words, a mysterious call to something noble in humankind, had never failed to make chills run down Kel's back. His stallion Thor-Thunder, always attuned to his mood, had snorted with excitement and tossed its magnificent head. Kel stroked its neck. "Easy, boy. You'll be chest-deep in a meadow soon."

The people had cheered and clapped, but Naldrum frowned. *Too bad,* Kel thought. The irritation and doubt that had gnawed him across the past months made Kel reckless. He wanted to taunt the headman.

"In other lands, a king or his favorites can rule by whim. They can treat some unfairly, with no fear of reprisal. But here in this remarkable valley, everyday men and women create our laws and test them each year to ensure fairness to all."

Cheers, as expected.

"Our legal cases are heard aloud in public, where all can comment. Because of Althing, the poorest and weakest among us can demand fairness from the most powerful. Our law, this valley, and Althing make our land unique in all the world—so honor this place and what it means to our people!"

The truth of those words beat deep in Kel's heart and loins. Every year, as he crossed the ridges into the beautiful Althing valley and its sparkling lake, Kel breathed reverent gratitude for the ideals this place represented. *May I be a good man,* he always whispered to himself. *May I be a true Icelander.*

With all Naldrum's people watching, Kel had forced himself to say the final words Naldrum expected. "Enjoy yourselves, but remember that you represent our headman. During your time at Althing, *gothi* Naldrum expects us all to conduct ourselves with behavior worthy of this place—and of him."

. . .

Now, staring at the tent, lurid in the bright rays of the midnight sun, those last words burned in Kel's mind. Because of honest young Sóma, Kel now he had proof. How many times had Naldrum done the same thing, over and over? Worse, he had gotten away with it for years because of Kel's unwitting help.

Kel had come to Althing with questions, but tonight, his thoughts had shifted desire to know the truth to how to trap Naldrum. Right now it was Kel's word against Naldrum, with a frightened young woman who had just promised to not say a word. He had nothing now, but nine months might tell if a snare could be sprung.

Kel clenched his hands into fists and strode away, wanting to fight someone, anyone…but mostly, himself.

. . .

Naldrum pushed away the dish of meat and swallowed the last of his mead. He already regretted the girl in his tent earlier that night. *I should have been sleeping. Too much work ahead.*

What was that on his hand? Naldrum lifted it to the light and flinched, sickened to see a smear of blood. He spat on it and wiped it with his tunic, then pulled the shirt over his head and threw it on the ground. *Filthy creature. He had not used her that hard.*

The quiet call of *first-eighth* sounded from a Kalendar who walked among the tent-booths. Not long before Naldrum would have to be presentable for festival duties. He flopped down onto his silken bedcoverings and groaned.

But as the headman lay with his eyes closed, a different kind of lust swept over him. He gave up any hope of sleep, and instead seduced himself with memories of Harald Gray-Cloak.

. . .

Long ago, Naldrum's only ship—mired in debt and brimming with unsold goods—had languished in a port in Nor'way. He had cursed the drenching rains. His first own ship, bought with funds borrowed from his father and full of goods, but no one to buy and a rain that might last for days. From the looks of the weather, they would end up having to leave for home before the market had even started. He glumly realized the catastrophic loss that would greet his return. *I'm done for. He'll disown me.*

"But the gods smiled," Naldrum reminded himself. The rains had created opportunity, for his display of heavy cloaks caught the attention of a hunting party riding on the beach, wet to the skin.

"Look, sire…these mantles. Shall I buy one for you?"

At '*sire,*' Naldrum had perked up. The handsome young man indicated wore the color restricted to royalty. Naldrum, astonished, found himself greeting the dashing young Harald, new ruler of the Nor'way lands. Drenched and cold, Harald had reached for one of the shaggy wool garments.

"Take it, your Majesty…a gift!" Naldrum had cried.

The handsome young king had tossed the thick cloak over his shoulders and declared it the best thing ever to shield against the foul weather. By the next day, everyone in the entire port desired a gray shaggy-wool cloak in emulation of the king. Naldrum sold out of his entire inventory in a day and promised to bring another shipload as fast as he could return to Iceland and load up again.

His first trading voyage had been a roaring success. Harald had given Naldrum access to the best trade routes, the richest households. Even the nickname given to the young ruler, *Gray-Cloak*, perpetuated Naldrum's fame. He and Harald had enjoyed excellent trade relations after that, to their mutual great profit.

Naldrum smiled. The next part of the memory had become his favorite, even more than that feeling of first, unexpected success.

Gray-Cloak, brimming with health, had seemed destined for a long life of rule. But a few years later, word came of his sudden death. Gray-Cloak's uncle—another Harald, called Bluetooth—had lured his nephew into a trap and had him murdered.

All-powerful, beautiful, and then maggot-meat. Just like that.

The news of Gray-Cloak's death had shocked Naldrum. But afterwards, he had traded with Bluetooth; business was business, after all. But the brutal seizing had come to fascinate Naldrum. Each

Althing, the sight of Bluetooth's contingent from the North-way regions reminded him again of the murder. Bluetooth had let nothing, not even family, stand in his way of being king—and for a while, *he* had reigned supreme in the Nor'way lands and Denmark.

But lately, new rumors had spread that Bluetooth's local *jarl* Haakon Sigurdsson had become *de facto* sovereign of the North-way lands—not by murder, but simply by stopping paying taxes to Bluetooth in Denmark. Bluetooth, old, tired, and aware of Haakon's strength, had stayed silent.

With no bloodshed or expense—in fact, at his own great profit—Haakon Sigurdsson had outright *stolen* the Nor'way lands.

Three men, one throne. They seized control by raw force or brazen defiance. This was how true leaders behaved, Naldrum realized.

. . .

The idea spun into a frenzy in the headman's mind, for something new had happened. As his entourage had arrived at the festival grounds, a messenger carrying Bluetooth's flag had approached.

"*Gothi* Naldrum? I've been waiting for you."

"What does the ruler of all Nor'way and Denmark desire?" Naldrum's voice, proud and loud for all to hear.

"I do not speak for King Harald. I carry a message from Haakon Sigurdsson, the Jarl of Lade, who keeps order in the Nor'way lands for his Majesty." The subtlest sneer in the voice. "Haakon's emissary wishes to meet with you tomorrow. We have much to discuss about the future of your country." The messenger, cloaked and with a strange high voice, had dictated a time and place.

Since the messenger's hailing, the headman had been able to think of little else. *The future of Iceland?* What did that mean? The word '*king*' flickered in Naldrum's mind, teasing, but Iceland had no ruler, had never *had* a ruler. Only the council of *gothar* had leadership, and they had to be elected. How could a man reign in a land-with-no-king?

His thoughts twisted, desiring dominance but not knowing how to seize it. It had caused him to grab the arm of that girl and hustle her into his tent. *Filthy woman,* he thought again, and brushed the place on his hand where her blood had been.

He lay in the darkness, succumbing to the deliciousness of plotting. Bluetooth had lured Gray-Cloak and murdered him. Haakon, the Jarl of Lade, had first helped Bluetooth murder Gray-Cloak, and then he had betrayed Bluetooth. Such simple moves, yet remarkably effective. What might be possible if he, Naldrum, was daring enough?

One day, I might no longer be simply gothi of Bull Valley. I might be Naldrum, Allsherjargothi, the All-Chieftain.

But that symbolic title held no true power. *How to give it teeth?* What might Bluetooth or Haakon do? Something bold, and arrogant. He thought of the magnificent sword of silver and gold he had had made, inscribed with words of power. But a sword could not serve his purposes in this land of law.

Despite Kel's lofty words earlier, Naldrum cared little for the annual dry recitations of legal matters. He snorted in derision that something so flimsy as a list of rules was his only obstacle.

Everything's negotiable, the headman told himself. *I'll find a way around it.* The thought of supremacy enticed him as no woman could. For the first time, he dared to allow himself to mouth his true goal.

King of all Iceland.

The sun-goddess Sól blazed across the festival valley, but inside his dim tent, the headman knew nothing of her brightness. Fantasizing, he stared at the roof of his tent, alternately smirking and frowning as he turned in his mind how such a thing might come to be.

. . .

Chapter Fifteen

High above the festival grounds, Aldís, too, was deep in thought. She had scrambled up in the early light of the middle-night sun to the high *Lögberg,* the sacred Law-Rock whose perfect echo carried the words of those who stood upon it and spoke to listeners below.

Lögberg, the sacred, symbolic heart of all that was Iceland. Aldís shivered at the power emanating from the stones and shifted so that the sun touched her skin. She watched her beloved *Sól* turn the rocky cliffs to gold. *I saw you do this, Sól and I believed that I could too, in my own small way, turn shadows to light.* She wiped her eyes.

How did the sun-goddess stay so bright, year after year? *So many dreams I once had.* Joy swirled with sadness.

Below her, a light mist drifted, rising from the many small streams that ran through the festival ground. Booths and tents scattered across the sprawling green fields beyond the cliffs, bright with striped colors, each one sheltering exhausted sleeping travelers.

Nothing moved. Only the sound of water broke the early stillness, where the Axe River tumbled over a cliff into the verdant valley.

Aldís closed her eyes, enjoying the warmth of the sun on her face and the fragrance of fresh grass drifting up from the meadows. She had been so afraid to come to Althing but was surprised to feel genuine happiness to be here after so many years.

I'm allowed to be happy. I'm allowed to feel safe.

She heard the Kalendar's early quiet call as he walked among the tents and wished for more time to prepare herself for what might come.

But what might come came right away, unbidden and unwanted: thoughts of that other Althing long ago, and of Kel, the man she had loved, who she had believed loved her in return.

Bittersweet remembrance swept Aldís. She felt his hands on her breasts below her shift, his lips moving on her belly, her fingers tangled in his hair as she gasped with pleasure. The savage pleasure of strong young entwining, the craving that drove them. Her back had pressed against this same rock, the sharp stone digging into her naked skin. She had cried out, somewhere between beauty and feral need.

Aldís cried out again, this time in anger. What had she been thinking, coming to this spot? For years she had refused that memory, but today own footsteps had brought her here where memories could betray her. Aldís recoiled, half in shame and half in fury.

I came for solitude, she lied to herself. *Nothing more. I came up here to be away from everyone else before the festival begins.*

Aldís drew a deep breath, closed her eyes, and prepared to savor the last bit of silence.

As a little breeze played around her skirts, whispering *remember, Aldís, remember*, something else interrupted her reverie.

The inner knowing that Aldís could never explain alerted her: *distress weeping hurt afraid* it said, long before her eyes could see anything. From force of habit, she listened inwardly, gathering understanding from some nearby person in distress.

But as her mind opened, with her thoughts unguarded, a truth she had buried even from herself burst forth: *I cannot avoid this any longer. I have to confront him, so that I can finally begin to heal. Whether he answers with the truth or not, I must know.*

This is why she had to come to Althing, Aldís realized. She was ready to walk through the pain and at last, to heal.

. . .

Aldís sat bolt upright, shocked at her thoughts. Could she truly say the words to him, after all these years?

"I cannot!" She felt sick all over at the idea. What had made her think she could?

The breeze laughed *of course you can,* as it reminded her of the stormy night on the mountain in which she had sung and danced for the dark elves. Whatever had come to life that night had brewed inside her all winter and spring and had led her here. *You survived álfablót out of doors and alone. You can do this.*

From below, audible sounds of someone weeping drifted up. Now, Aldís welcomed the distraction. She called down, knowing that the perfect echo of the Law Rock carried her words to the person below.

"Whoever is crying, wait there. I'll come down."

The crying abruptly ceased. For a while there was silence, and then a bit of a panicked scuffle.

Aldís called again. "I can run faster than a goat on these stones. Don't make me chase you to the fairgrounds where everyone will see."

More silence. As Aldís prepared to climb down from the Law Rock, she felt another uncomfortable inward tremor, a mysterious awareness indicating additional trouble. Aldís scanned the distant fields, looking for whoever had sent that new silent signal.

Over there.

A solitary man walked away from the rows of tents towards the sheep-pens, anger clearly evident in his stiff, rapid stride. He reached the gate and leaned against it, his arms spread wide, his hands gripping the rails. He lifted his face to the sky. Even at that distance, Aldís could see the furious set of his jaw.

A weeping girl, and an angry man, while everyone else slept? Another memory stirred. This one held only bitterness, with none of the pleasure of the earlier one.

Aldís stared at the man. Even though it had been years, she knew who moved that way, recognized the set of his body.

Kel Coesson.

. . .

Her heart hammered wildly. *Not Kel already.* But she had only an instant to feel the shock, because whoever had been weeping appeared suddenly on the Law Rock beside Aldís: a young woman in a torn dress, her neck chains as tangled as her hair, her eyes red from tears.

The girl saw yellow cloth around Aldís' neck. She burst out with relief. "You're a healer."

Aldís held out her arms, and the girl rushed into them.

. . .

Aldís smoothed her hands over the girl's hair. "Shhhh. Sit up and dry your tears. We need to get you away from the Law Rock before people start arriving."

The young woman wiped her eyes with her sleeve. "You wear a yellow neck-scarf," she choked out. "Thank goodness you're here."

"Yes," Aldís said. "But I'm not one of the *systirs.* I just have truth-seeing, sometimes."

"My parents," the girl wept. "What do I tell them? The *gothi* said—he said I must not—"

Lines along Aldís' mouth deepened. "A headman?" she asked. "Which one?"

"I can't tell you. He'll flog my parents."

That Althing-vulture. Still the same after all these years, and Kel protecting him. "Naldrum?" Aldís asked, bitter.

The girl looked about wild-eyed, and blanched. "I cannot say!"

. . .

Aldís longed to tell the girl to ignore what Naldrum said, that her parents would survive any flogging. *But did I have the courage to defy him when I was her age? No.*

"The opening ceremony starts soon," Aldís said, her words terse. "Let me get you back to your tent where you can calm down."

. . .

Aldís hurried the girl along paths where they were unlikely to meet anyone. They slipped between the back rows of booths, where holding-ropes and sturdy wooden pegs had been driven into the ground. But as the girl gestured towards the corner—*there, the next row over*—who would they come face to face with but Kel Coesson?

Aldís gasped in surprise. She heard the same shock in Kel's voice.

"Aldís! You're here!" he cried in astonishment. Instinctively, he reached for her, but Aldís jerked back. Kel yanked his hands away.

Aldís' face flushed with fury and humiliation. She turned aside, refusing to look at him. "So what?"

He took her shoulders, pulling her to face him. "Aldís, talk to me."

Defiant, Aldís met his gaze. Kel searched her features. He saw eyes that had once sparkled with life now sullen and weary. Lips that had curved in easy laughter were pressed together, straight and thin.

Aldís glanced at Kel. Still strong. Still handsome. His shoulders as straight as ever. *What do I care?* She pushed away his plea.

Kel, so used to giving commands and having them obeyed, faced Aldís with a sense of helplessness. "I look for you every year," he said. "You never come."

"I *always* do." She had not intended to lie, but the words had already left her lips.

"Then why have I never seen you?"

"If you had really wanted to see me, you would have." The old anger in her voice. "Perhaps you didn't look hard enough."

In truth, she had avoided the festival. How long had it been? *For the gods' sake, you know exactly how long,* Aldís reminded herself.

"I live in plain sight," she said, a little less harsh. "I hide from no one. If you wanted to see me so badly—" She did not finish. It would be weak to suggest that he might have come looking for her. The battle to be done with him yet together raged inside her, vicious and familiar.

Kel stared at the young woman standing next to Aldís. He frowned. "That girl—"

"Your headman just misused her. Your great *gothi* Naldrum."

Kel winced, but not at the scorn in her words. "Yes," he agreed.

The girl's frightened gaze went from one to the other. How did that man know what had happened? How had the woman guessed?

At Aldís' obvious surprise, Kel felt a need to explain. "Naldrum makes it hard to catch him in a lie, but I found a way tonight."

Aldís spoke in fury. "I told you long ago how despicable he is. My word was not good enough for you."

Kel closed his eyes. *She rejected me. Why does she keep punishing me?*

"Aldís," he whispered again.

For a heartbeat, the stone in her chest softened. The words that she had carried for so long pressed against her lips, demanding to be said. But facing him, courage failed Aldís. What good would it do to dig up the painful past? Besides, he could not undo what he had done.

"You made your choice years ago. Right now, this girl needs shelter," Aldís muttered. Chin up and eyes averted, she slammed tight the door inside her. *Kel Coesson, you will never hurt me again.*

The unyielding wall that they had built long ago—no, that *she* had built—stood between them, as hard and tall as the Law Rock.

Kel made his face impassive. He bowed, his movements cold and carefully polite, and stood aside to let them pass in the tight space.

As Aldís brushed against him, he smelled birch smoke in her hair. He breathed in and remembered, and hope leaped in his heart.

No, he told himself. *It's not possible. Not anymore, not ever again.* But his heart refused to listen. *I saw a flicker of it in her eyes. The old connection. I saw it. I know I did.*

But had he, really? "Damn this doubting myself about everything," Kel shouted to the empty footpaths.

But it was safer for Aldís to stay away from him. "I'm going to risk everything," Kel reminded himself. "Better that she has nothing to do with me."

. . .

Kel did not get to wonder long about Aldís. Covered with wine-sops and dirt, he needed to clean himself up before the headman saw him. The Kalendar was now calling the second *day-eighth*, his voice a little louder. After the next call, *third-eighth*, Althing would officially begin.

The empty paths between the tents and booths began to fill with people. Soon Kel could not walk without brushing against the growing crowds. As people recognized him, the fawning began.

"Steward—Steward Coesson—We've a gift for *gothi* Naldrum."

Kel walked on, pretending not to hear.

Another one. "You there, the headman Naldrum's steward? You're called Kel, aren't you? I need to talk with the headman. We've had a bad year—a year of hunger—I need to ask you—" Another after another after another, all begging for access to his chieftain. "Steward, please...a small gift for you, to encourage the *gothi* to visit our booth?" "Steward Kel, sir?"

When he had started working for Naldrum, he had felt proud to work for a man held in such high regard. Today, every person who plucked at his tunic pricked at Kel's conscience.

"Steward Coesson, glad to see you this Althing! Would you—"

Kel pulled his cloak over his face and walked faster. Tomorrow the council of *gothar*—the elected headmen from every area of

Iceland—would be called to order. Could he really stand in front of the entire Althing and pretend loyalty to a *gothi* who disgusted him?

Odin's eye. What do I do?

Kel shoved against the streaming crowds and headed for the common-labor grounds to find Naldrum's slave Tor. As he walked, Kel's resolve hardened. By the time he arrived where Tor worked, he had made up his mind what to do.

. . .

Rumors had spread like a meadow-fire among clans arriving at Althing: a remarkable being had come, a rare and expensive thrall, bought last autumn by *gothi* Naldrum. The stories grew with each telling. Worried people craved distractions, and this enthralling talk offered respite from endless speculation about failing crops.

"*A man as tall as a giant—*"

"*His skin is the color of the lava-flows, lustrous and dark—*"

"*They call him Sám Tor—*"

"*Sám Tor? What does that mean?*"

"'*Black Mountain'...I heard Naldrum paid as much for him as for two other thralls—*"

"*—as five others—*"

"*—as ten others—*"

"*He comes from a land so far away that it lies near the very edge of the earth!*"

Growing with every telling, the exaggerations had only increased admiration for the headman.

But other rumors had also spread, whispered among a smaller group in guarded secrecy. *"They say that this man defied Naldrum. Can you imagine, a thrall, standing up to a chieftain? And Tor defies him still. He's been beaten. Starved. He doesn't care. He's too valuable for Naldrum to kill—and short of that, there seems to be nothing the headman can do to control him."*

. . .

Sám Tor, the 'black mountain,' stood at the traveling-forge he had set up on the common grounds. Thin tendrils of smoke rose from a just-lit fire as Tor set out his blacksmithing tools by the anvil stone. The man's startling appearance had attracted a sizable gathering, who watched his every move in awe.

"You're quite the show here, it seems," Kel noted. "Are you doing sleight-of-hand for them, or is it just your profound ugliness that makes them stare?"

The massive man considered Kel as one would an irritating flea. "Nice of you to come around now that the hard work is done. I could have used help setting up this anvil earlier."

"You know I don't dirty my hands with such work, slave."

"Oh, of course. Those soft paws. Mustn't hurt them."

They glared at one another until Kel saw the twitching of Tor's mouth. He laughed. "You're not as sharp as usual. Travelling must have worn out your wit."

"Spoken by one who looks half-dead with weariness."

"I need something profoundly mindless to distract me. You seemed the best option."

Tor snorted, and the two men gave each other a quick embrace.

Ever since Tor had arrived at Naldrum's compound the prior autumn, this rough banter had become their pattern, albeit infrequently. They never said anything of consequence, only insults. The substance mattered less than the unspoken connection, one that needed to remain hidden, especially where any overheard word might be repeated.

Here, with relative freedom among strangers at Althing, they squatted down to talk. A short wall of split wood offered some privacy. Kel offered a blood sausage, but Tor waved it away.

"Everybody here has brought tidbits of food, as if I was a caged bear. I'm almost too full to work."

"You're far more interesting than a caged bear. They've seen plenty of those. Never a giant dark man."

"Give it a day or so, and I'll be just another sight around here, I'm sure."

"Welcome to your first Althing. How does it compare to gatherings where you came from?"

Sadness filled Tor's eyes. Kel immediately regretted his words. He knew only one thing about Tor's past: for some desperate reason, Tor had sold himself into bondage in some distant land. That much had slipped out one day. Kel had never learned the reasons why. Enslaved people rarely spoke of their former lives, except perhaps to other slaves. Tor did not partake of even that small comfort.

"Never mind. I'm sorry."

Changing the subject, Tor asked, "Has Naldrum the Ghastly appeared this morning to spit upon his adoring people?"

For once, Kel did not laugh at one of Tor's mocking titles. He shook his head. "Still sleeping." He lowered his voice. "Tor?" He started to speak, hesitated.

The tall thrall looked sharply at Kel. Only once had Kel used that tone of voice, on the first day the two men had met.

"What's the matter?"

"There's something I've needed to know. Something Naldrum always claimed was a lie. An opportunity came last night to find out."

"And?"

Kel held his hand over his mouth and jaw, as if to silence himself. Once he said the words, he could not unsay them. Tor gave Kel time. Went to his forge, poked at the charcoal, added wood. When he returned, Kel spoke.

"I heard him force himself on a woman."

Once again, Tor stood, but this time to breathe out his loathing for the headman. He felt the stares of the crowd on him, gave them a quick wave and a nod. A quiver of excitement spread.

"Coals are almost hot enough." This time when he squatted down again, Tor looked Kel straight in the eyes. "Why do you care? Some men buy bed-slaves. Surely those women aren't willing."

"It's a despicable practice, but I don't make the laws." Kel paused. "This woman was free. That makes it a crime." After a bit, he continued. "Made me sick to hear it. Also made me sick that I didn't stop him. A decent man would have." Kel blew out a long breath.

He glanced at Tor. The first time he had laid eyes on the enslaved man, Tor had been ragged, his face haunted and the bones of his tall frame showing from too little food. Cutting the outlaw marks in Tor's hands had sickened Kel.

But Naldrum's idea that he could punish his new property into fearful obedience had failed. Not only had Tor grown stronger, but whispers of his courage had spread. Kel could not help but contrast his own furtive spying of last night with Tor's brazen, brave defiance.

"If I had stopped him, she'd be safe," Kel blurted.

"Report him, then. Weren't you bragging in your little speech about how your laws let '*the weakest stand up to the most powerful*'?

"It's complicated. If I go to the Law Council and accuse him publicly, will the woman speak against him? Not likely, with the way he threatened her. Naldrum walks away. He tells one of his loyalists to get rid of me. And he goes on doing what he does."

Tor shrugged. "Then why all this bother?"

Kel's jaw tightened. He could not say to Tor *If she appears in nine months to say there's a child, Naldrum will order me to kill it so he doesn't have to pay father-fees.* But he couldn't do that. Not again, knowing the truth.

Instead, Kel asked a different question. "That first day you arrived at our compound, when Josson brought you. I was sharpening the knife to cut the outlaw marks in your hands, and you said something to me. Do you remember?"

"Something about you being on the verge of cracking. That the headman was poisoning your spirit. That if you stayed much longer with him, you'd never leave."

"I listened to you, that day. What you said about making my choice. About the Third Way." Kel's eyes, haunted, met Tor's. "The time's come. Not to accuse him; not yet, because I'll need to build a case against him. But I can't stand another day of being in his service. I'm going to tell him today I'm done with working for him. Hopefully

I can get away from him in a way that will still protect—" he did not say her name.

"You *did* set your intention, then."

"Just like you suggested." Lines along Kel's mouth deepened. "It'll be dangerous. Might be the death of me." A laugh with no mirth. "But it'll be a huge relief, if only to just not have to see his ugly face any longer. Which means this may be the last time we talk. I want to thank you for what you've done for me. Because of you, I started having hope again, that first day. You'll always have my gratitude. If you ever need help, find me. I'd ride across the country to help you."

"May the Goodness of the Unknown guide you," Tor replied. "May that Goodness guide us all."

. . .

Kel's misery suddenly lifted. He stood and slapped his thighs.

"Done. Naldrum may be an untrustworthy liar and foul to women, and my only ally is a defiant thrall who has no power beyond the strength of his bare hands...and the woman I love—oh, you didn't know I actually love her? Thought I had a heart of stone? I'm full of surprises today, aren't I? Anyway, I just saw her for the first time in years. She's here at Althing and she hates me and wants nothing to do with me. And I, who was once lauded as a champion here, now feel like a beaten-down failure, and despite that, or because of it, I'm plotting to confront one of the most powerful *gothi* in all of Iceland, a move that will most likely end in spectacular disaster and quite possibly my own murder, and I don't even care. How could things possibly get any worse?"

Tor threw back his head. A great laugh reverberated in his mighty chest. "Sounds like exactly the right place to move forward."

This time, Tor saw a genuine smile on Kel's face. "A fine way to look at things. Now, it's high time I quit holding up your work. The good people in this crowd have waited all morning to gape at you swinging your forge-hammer. When they see you wield it, they'll think they've said 'Thor' wrong all these years."

As he spoke, mischief flickered in Kel. *All those jokes about Thor's hammer yesterday as people set up tents.* Maybe he couldn't undo what had happened to the girl, but he could take a small jab at the headman who had done it. Naldrum loathed Tor and shamed him at every opportunity. No harm evening the score a bit.

"These poor folks know only the nonsense the headman says about himself. Let's show them the real master here." It was all the warning Tor got. Immediately, Kel swung around and raised his voice to the surrounding throng.

"See here! The great Tor," Kel shouted. He blurred 'Tor' to sound like 'Thor', the hammer-god of thunder. "A man from the edge of the world…a man from lands of treasure; of silk, and ebony-wood, and spices, and gold!"

Eyes widened.

"The strength of a bear, and skin as black as the lava-stone that flows from the forge of *Völundur*, the master-blacksmith whose anvil booms below the earth. His soul is as strong as the mountain. See how his hair streams, as dark and glorious as the storm-clouds of the thunder-god!"

The crowd cheered at each exhortation. *Time to plant the seed.*

"He fears no one. Not even his master, the great *gothi* Naldrum. Naldrum outlawed him for defiance, yes—look at his hands, where he holds the hammer, see the marks for yourselves. Outlawed because he showed contempt for the headman, he is still strong and unafraid."

The crowd breathed as one. The rumors were true.

Kel finished. "Behold the might of Tor! Behold the *hammer* of Tor!" The watching people began repeating the words.

"You utter fool," Tor laughed. He stripped off his tunic and tied on a leather apron. His enormous muscles rippled, and the watchers murmured in admiration. Tor put a chipped sword into the fire to heat. He poised his hammer, ready to make the first strike.

"Fearless of Naldrum," Tor muttered to himself. He nearly laughed aloud at hearing the phrase whispered from person to person. He pounded on the glowing red blade, and sparks flew.

Kel could not resist one last exhortation. "Shout for Tor," he shouted. "Show your admiration as he hammers like the God of Thunder. The hammer of Tor! Tor! Tor! Tor!"

"The hammer of Tor!" the surrounding crowd cheered back, fists raised in the air. It was Kel's turn to laugh as he strode away, invigorated.

. . .

The disheveled young woman led Aldís around the corner to her family's festival booth. When they reached it, she stopped and drew a deep breath.

Aldís touched her shoulder. "Courage," she whispered.

The girl nodded and peeked through the tent flap. To her relief, the booth was empty. Everyone had already gone to the festival's opening ceremony.

"Good," she quavered in relief. "I may not have to answer any questions at all."

"Take care of yourself," Aldís said. "And a word of advice?"

"Speak your wisdom, healer," said the young woman.

"If you conceive—I hope you won't, but if you do—under no circumstances let your father or mother go to the headman and ask for child-rights, no matter what. Cast the child off or give it away, keep it, whatever you choose. *But absolutely do not let your family go to Naldrum.* Do you understand?"

"Why not? The law of the land is that a child's father—"

"The law of the land and the law of the headman are two different things," Aldís answered. "*This* is his law." She pulled up her sleeve, and the girl saw angry scars running along Aldís' arm. "I was lucky to survive. He's older and crueler now. Mark my words."

The girl nodded and ducked into the tent, and Aldís left.

. . .

People surged toward the Law Rock, the very stone on which Aldís had sat in such peaceful silence a short while ago. She moved against the flow of the crowd, heading for another destination. As Kel had done, Aldís also sought Naldrum's defiant slave Tor.

. . .

Kel made his way back towards his own tent, letting the crowd push him along this time. The short talk had helped. He couldn't really count Tor as a friend, but then, did he have any friends?

The enslaved man had no fear of pain, of loss, of indignity; none of the tools Naldrum frequently employed. The headman had wanted to flaunt his rare prize at Althing. Instead, the *gothi* found himself with a calmly insolent creature, who Naldrum's pride would not let him destroy.

I could learn a thing or two from Tor, Kel thought. *Fear no power, and one's own power grows.*

He had spent the whole night awake and longed for sleep. But a familiar voice called his name, grating on his nerves. Ankya stood in front of his tent, coquettish, waving. Naldrum's daughter was quite literally the last person he wanted to see this morning.

. . .

She had hovered near Kel's tent since early, intending to trick him into spending the day with her. Clearly, he had not been in bed all night. *Where, then, all this time?* Jealousy burned in her, but she kept her tone light.

"Kel!" she called. "Steward Kel!"

"I'm off duty," he said.

"Where have you been? I've been waiting all morning," Had he made an early visit to the whore-tents? She dared not ask. "Father wants you to escort me through the festival today."

"I'm sorry. Your father will have to find someone else for that duty. I need to sleep." Kel ducked into his tent and tied the flap closed.

Ankya's face reddened. "We'll see about that," she muttered. She spread a bit of linen on the ground and arranged herself on it to wait. When people who might recognize her passed by, heading in excitement to the opening speeches at the Law Rock, Ankya ducked her head down. Her father would disapprove and could not know that she planned to lurk here until Kel emerged from his tent.

"Like it or not, I'm spending the day with you, Kel," she whispered. "I'm a great chieftain's daughter, and I'll not be denied."

. . .

Seeing Aldís had shaken Kel more than he wanted to admit. That unsettled feeling mixed with a sudden desire to be rid of not only Naldrum, but of everything about him: Ankya, the longhouse, everything. Relief at the thought of finally breaking free filled Kel. He made a reckless decision.

"I'm going to skip the opening ceremony this morning and rest instead," he told his servant. "Make sure I'm awake by the midday call. I plan to see if any of the *holmgang* duelers needs a backer."

Kel needed a fight. He wanted blood. He'd find both at dueling grounds.

. . .

By the time Aldís reached Tor, the crowds around him had disappeared. Showers of red sparks flew as the tall man hammered on the anvil. She touched his arm to interrupt his intense focus.

Tor jerked, startled. "What do you want?" he demanded.

He stared briefly before recognizing Aldís. For the second time that morning, a man gasped in pleasure at seeing her face. Tor crushed Aldís in a huge embrace.

This time, she returned the gesture. "I am so glad to see you, Tor. I came to the festival this year specifically to try and find you. Look around. Everyone has gone to the opening ceremony."

Tor glanced about in surprise. "I wasn't paying attention. But what do I care about that? You know what I want."

Aldís frowned. No one was in sight, but still—

"Tor, we should go. It's safer if no one wonders what's important enough to keep us from the gathering. We can talk as we walk."

"The faster, the better, then," Tor replied. He put the hammer down and plunged the glowing piece of metal into a water pail.

Aldís' warm smile flashed. "Besides, slave or not, you're an Icelander now, my friend. Might as well come and see what it means."

. . .

As they walked, Tor asked eager questions. "Tell me as quickly as you can. My children, are they well? Safe?"

"I'll tell you everything," Aldís promised. "Yes, your son and daughter are safe, and healthy. Thriving, in fact. They miss you terribly, but the ache comes less than it used to." She saw him stiffen and spoke a soft reminder. "Many months have passed, Tor. Children find ways to survive."

It would hurt Tor, she knew, to know that his two children had learned to live and laugh without him, but it would also give him a sense of peace. Aldís walked without speaking for a few steps, giving him time to absorb both truths.

As they walked past the horse-grazing meadow, she began again. "Now that you know the most important thing—that they are safe and happy—I can tell you everything else in whatever order you wish. So, what first?"

"The widow Eilíf. How does she fare?"

A good man, to have concern for their caretaker as well. "I actually have very good news about her. When you first met, she was quite...unwell...as you know. She had never recovered from the fire that killed her husband and injured her. But, Tor, it's wonderful now. Caring for your children has given her such joy. She laughs often and smiles constantly. The side of her face that is whole glows with happiness. She has become strong and healthy again, both in body and spirit. She agreed to take your children as a favor to you, but as often happens, the kindness she gave returned even more back to her."

Tor nodded, humble. "I am grateful to her. What do my children call her?" he asked, curious.

Aldís knew the reason he asked, and the correct answer.

"You told them to call her mother, but they use 'Aunt,'" she replied. "At her request. She knows they have only one real mother, and like you, hopes one day that mother will be found."

Tor had felt as if his life had ended the day he said goodbye to his son Nikea and his daughter Nenet. In the past months, the myriad tasks of everyday life had offered tiny respite from brutal loneliness. But seeing Aldís, one of two people in all of Iceland who knew where his children were, hidden for safety, brought it all back in a rush. Without realizing it, Tor moaned in pain.

Aldís took his arm in her hands. "Keep putting one foot in front of another, my friend. Keep walking. You have not lost them. They are safe. Your wife may be, also. We simply do not know." She had known that seeing her again would open the wound for Tor afresh.

He searched for a question, anything to distract himself. "Have they grown?" he croaked.

"Most certainly. Another year and Nikea will stand taller than me. Nenet, too, has grown. She has learned how to—"

A roar of many voices came from ahead of them. Aldís reached up and patted Tor's shoulder. "Listen to that crowd. I promise, I'll tell you more later, as much as you need. For now, come witness what these people traveled so far to see."

Tor suddenly realized he had said nothing to Aldís about Kel. *I'll tell her later how much she means to him,* Tor promised himself. He wondered for a brief instant why they seemed such strangers to one another, but the cheering of the crowd prevented talking, and the thought was soon forgotten.

. . .

Chapter Sixteen

The Opening Ceremony

The Kalendar finished calling *second-eighth* throughout the fairgrounds. He turned towards the *Lögberg* and was soon swept up among the growing crowd. Farmers jostled with artisans hawking samples of wares and bold young men and women eager to prove their skill in games, and families happily reunited with relatives and friends from far-flung valleys. Storytellers and flax-growers, woodchoppers and charcoal-burners, basket weavers and horn-carvers strode side by side with traders from distant lands. Thralls, bond workers, wealthy merchants, brewers, food sellers, acrobats, jugglers, musicians and fire-dancers, their faces eager, pressed together as they streamed towards the stone cliff of the Law Rock.

. . .

On the Rock stood a man known to everyone in Iceland: Mani the *all-sherjar-gothi,* the all-people's-chieftain. He felt proud bearing the honorary title first bestowed upon his grandfather, one of the first families of the Great Settlement. His father had held the title next. His voice had throbbed with pride when he passed the tradition to Mani.

"It is our duty to remind every generation of Icelanders that our leadership lies in commoners, not kings. One day, your son and grandson will bear this honor. Make our family and our land proud."

Mani wore the *allsherjargothi* mantle with respect, but dual duty pressed him. He was also Mani the Lawspeaker, chief leader of the land. He had worked hard to be elected to this post.

Many years as Lawspeaker had taken a toll. Fairness, the bedrock of Icelandic law, ran deep in Mani, but peace had become more fragile of late. This year, Mani feared for the Law as he never had before.

Beside him, a woman watched him, worrying, but when she spoke, she kept her tone light.

"You're thinking of your first Althing, aren't you?"

Mani kept his eyes on the crowd, but she saw the fond memory in his slight smile. "I was just a boy down there in the crowd, watching my grandfather stand up here beside the very first Lawspeaker."

"Did you pay attention?" She wanted to distract Mani, knowing how this particular Althing weighed on his mind.

"Not really. I was far more interested in flirting with you." He did look at her now. Fifty years of love passed between them in a glance. "You did not share the same interest, as I recall."

"I did not." His wife Dalla laughed. "I was just excited to be here. You were a collateral benefit." She took his hand in hers. "Neither of us understood the significance of that day."

They both were silent, recalling the stories of their grandparents: how the ruler of the Nor'way lands had forced his people to convert to a new belief or be killed as Christianity swept from one *jarldom* to another. In its name, rich lands had been seized and people had been killed. Their families had fled the Nor'way lands for Iceland, bringing with them a strong distaste for the absolute powers of rulers.

But this new place required governing, too. On that day when Mani and Dalla had first flirted, the people standing below the Law Rock had listened to a daring new idea: self-governance, by leaders elected by men and women of Iceland's valleys.

"Can you imagine how they felt? Fifty years ago to this day, their feet right here on this Rock, declaring that our people would never bend the knee to a ruler." Dalla wiped her eyes. "As your grandfather and the first Lawspeaker announced it, did they really think such a mad idea would work? No one had ever tried it before."

"Well, it *did* work. It's needed constant improving, but it's been better than a king's whims." Worry again deepened the lines in his face. "We've grown old working to keep it alive. I feel the years."

Dalla squeezed his hand. "Not much longer. One more year and you can retire as Lawspeaker and *allsherjargothi,* and the Council will elect some spirited young woman to carry the Horn of Plenty instead of me. We will finally be able to rest."

Mani grimaced at his lifelong companion. "Will we, sweet Dalla?"

. . .

The festival Kalendar puffed, climbing up the steep rocks to join them. The three waited, watching as the crowd below swelled to an enormous size. The valley rang with happy voices. The sun-goddess glittered on gold and silver finery, carefully stored for this festival.

"You'd never know by how they're turned out today, but mark my words, as soon as the opening ceremony ends, we'll hear the same complaint from every valley: too little land, the soil doesn't produce like it once did, too many mouths to feed. Our land becomes poorer every year," Mani fretted. "For the first time since the Great Settlement, fear has been growing faster than goats do."

. . .

"Time to blow the Horn?" Kalendar asked.

"No. Unbelievably, people are *still* crowding onto the field. I want them all to hear what I have to say. Give it a little while longer."

. . .

Shortly after he had said this, Mani wished he had not. With every breath, his tension mounted. He sighed heavily, needing to talk about something, anything.

"What I'd give to have been in those first-settler days. Clearing fields, cutting trees, moving boulders with oxen. Building hope as they built homes. Such arduous work, but they must have felt such joy."

Dalla agreed. "And excitement! Once they heard of land to be had, Aud's people came from the Hebrides and the Orkneys. Can you imagine, hearing all those different languages? Different customs and faiths, as pagans, white-christ worshippers, followers of the *druid-vitki* came. From wealthy cattle-lords to stone-scrabble farmers, all of them shared one hope: a new life, new opportunity, with freedom."

Her voice caught with emotion. "Look what they accomplished from that chaos. They might have become a horde of rivals, fighting over scraps of valleys. Instead, they created something remarkable, a brave new way of life based on fairness. It has lasted all these years."

Without realizing it, each took a deep breath, full of wonder.

"You should be the one to speak the Opening, Dalla," the Kalendar said.

"It's true," Mani agreed. "It may be my job as Lawspeaker to call Althing into being, but my dear wife has a saga-teller's sensibility." He frowned at the sky. "We're in a different place now. Then, good farmland could be had by any willing to work it. Hills and valleys were lush with trees. Now, some must import wood to build longhouses. Bad crops…how many years can we re-tighten our belts? When people become desperate, they are vulnerable."

"What do you mean?" the Kalendar asked.

"Our Law's great strength is also its greatest weakness. It depends on good human beings, who may passionately disagree yet are committed to integrity and fairness. Once, many *gothi* balanced leadership evenly amongst themselves. Now a handful of dominant headmen control many of the others. I worry that some of them care more about their own wealth than the good of our people. Will they see our people's distress as opportunity? If they gain power, they will trample law and justice into the mud?"

The Kalendar groaned. "My entire purpose in life revolves around keeping order. I call the eighth-segments and count the days. I keep track of the moons and months so that I can be certain when *equal-night-days* come, and the *Sol*-stills of mid-winter and mid-summer. The thought of chaos nauseates me. You must find a way to stop it."

Dalla's practical nature asserted itself. "Even if the sweat of fear runs along our spines, we must appear strong, for people in need crave strong leaders. Mani, you must help them hold faith in the law for just a little longer. We must keep hope alive."

Mani felt weak and old. "Althing barely reached this fiftieth birthday. Clan battles are breaking out. Power is beginning to be more important to some than the law is. Sometimes I wonder if Althing itself might crumble to dust the instant the festival ends." He shuddered, his face pale as that of a man who sees his own death. The ceremonial cloak hung heavy on his shoulders. Mani wished with all his heart that he could be in the horse-field grooming Little Cloud, his favorite mare.

Kalendar touched his arm, and Mani startled.

"The sun is high against the northern sky. We can wait no longer. The time to sound the Horn has come, *Allsherjargothi.*" Kalendar used the formal title to steady Mani. "You must be ready to lead Althing as I call it into being."

Mani squared his shoulders, stepped to the front of the *Lögberg,* and lifted his palms to the sky, silencing the crowd below.

. . .

At Mani's signal, the Kalendar lifted a great horn, gleaming gold worked in runes and ancient symbols. The ceremonial instrument sounded only twice each year, to open and to close the Assembly-for-All. Kalendar drew a deep breath, and the great Horn of Althing sang.

. . .

The beautiful tone lifted the hearts of the people crowded under the Law Rock. Kalendar pushed the Horn's sound towards the horizon, and its bittersweet music raced across the valley and echoed from the hills, its bright blare heralding the love of their rugged, brave land.

Impossibly long the Kalendar breathed life into the Horn, so that those listening marveled. They inhaled of the tune as if they could draw in the essence of the mysterious, empowering melody. Under its spell, differences and worries fell away and they squared their shoulders. For the space of the Kalendar's long, life-giving breath, they knew, *knew,* that all would be well and that everything they yearned for was possible, despite whatever threatened otherwise.

. . .

Cheers built on cheers, every shout celebrating the Horn and the very existence of their Althing. Mani gave them time. These people might forget the discussions and law-readings to come, but this moment they would remember. Finally, he started to raise his hands to speak, but Dalla touched his forearm.

"Give them and yourself all the time you can. No need to rush."

Mani nodded, glad to wait a little longer. Much rode on this Althing. *Grandfather, are you with me?*

Mani wiped his hands on his tunic and lifted them. "We celebrate the fiftieth coming of Althing!" he cried.

Improvising, he signaled to the Kalendar to sound the Horn a second time. *Just this one year.* The playfulness steadied Mani. His eyes twinkled at Dalla, and she breathed easier.

As the Kalendar blew again, the cheering rang even louder. It blended with the Horn to echo from the Law Rock's stone cliffs until it seemed that the valley itself sang with sound.

Finally, Mani raised his hands again to speak. The cheers soon quieted to hear his words. He hoped they would be enough.

. . .

"You have come!" Mani spoke. "You are here—the blood and bone of Iceland!"

Roars erupted from the crowds again. Despite his worries, Mani smiled. "Men and women of our country, you stand here together in muscle and might. Together, in mind and vision. The hopes and dreams of our entire people stand here, represented in you."

They cheered once more.

"For fifty summers, a Lawspeaker has stood here in your service. Half a century we have lived free of the yoke of a king."

Many in the crowd had grown up as he and Dalla had, hearing the stories told by fathers and mothers who had surged towards Iceland in escape of wicked leaders. Mani considered saying something about one. The *Jarl of Lade; how could they stomach a man who used his landowners' daughters badly and then tossed them aside?* Mani had heard the *jarl* had sent an emissary here. No good could come of that.

As he waited for the crowd's cheers to subside, Mani decided against it. *No sense letting rumors about one depraved man diminish our ceremony. I'll stick to the high road.*

His speech began much like the one Kel had given the night before to Naldrum's group. "Since that first Althing, any free person—man or woman, rich or poor—has had the right to stand here on this Law Rock and speak to this assembly. Our own people make our country and our lives better because any of them can challenge the fairness of our law. Who in the Northway can make that claim? Who in the Dane-marked lands? In any other land at all? None of them," he cried.

"None of them!" the crowd echoed. Mani had not expected the response, and it touched him.

"In other lands, a ruler creates the law, and he bends the will of the people to it. The king and his agents take what they want, and the people have no means to stand against him. He tells them how to worship, even, dictating, upon pain of death, what gods the people may call upon in their time of need."

We ourselves divide in the ways we worship, Mani thought. *I would not want a ruler telling me what gods to pray to.*

He continued. This year more than any other, he felt the need to remind people the dangers of yielding their freedom to powerful rulers. "A *jarl* takes as he wishes, and his people have no recourse. He takes taxes from every peasant, not caring if their children starve. He takes their sons as soldiers, to die for his own selfish desires, and his people live in fear of speaking up against him. But here, we are different. *You* are different: we travel forward, not dragged by one man, but as one group, struggling together towards common goals."

Naldrum, standing in the crowd below the Law Rock, pouted. Mani's words would not help his ambitions.

Mani braced himself. *Time for the difficult part.* "And we do struggle, my friends. We disagree. Not on *what* we hope for, but *how* to achieve it. Those struggles are hard. But this summer, as we begin our country's next fifty years, even more difficult challenges face us. So many have come to our shores in search of opportunity that now it feels as if it cannot bear any more. Our fields do not bring forth as much grain as they used to. Despite our prayers and blood-offerings, the gods have again sent us too much rain this spring. Our herds and our crops suffer from it. There is hunger."

He let his voice drop, let the words sink in.

"Free men and women offer themselves as bondsmen, competing with thralls, simply to work for food. But others *still* sail here from other lands hoping to find a home when there are no more homes to find. Each year, mothers bear children they must feed when there is barely enough food as it is."

Dalla balled her hands into fists. Mani had practiced these words again and again. Would he lead the listeners where he needed?

The people listened, hungry to trust. He could see the need in their faces. Could he bring to their eager, hungry, frightened hearts what they needed to help them through the challenges to come?

"As we face this year, and the next, and the next—" Mani let his voice rise in volume each time he uttered the word 'next'— "As we face the next fifty years, we must hold tight to that which has kept us strong all this time. We must rededicate ourselves to our freedoms."

Mani wished he could wipe his eyes. *No one can see them wet from way down there,* he told himself. *Almost finished. Keep your voice strong.*

"Because of our Law, not only are the voices of the rich landowners and merchants heard, but also the voices of those who have little wealth. Not only can the powerful seek fairness, but everyday folk as well—and that, my friends, gives *every single one of us* value. Knowing we have value gives us greater heart and spirit to face whatever troubles beset us—and if every single one of us is stronger, together we have tremendous power. Our strength as individuals forms the foundation of our strength as a people!"

Now his tears flowed freely as he spoke, but Mani did not care. "So, my friends, let me say this: when children hearing these words one day stand before this same Law Rock as old men and women— old, yes, as I am old and as Dalla my wife is old —let us give them a heritage to be proud of. Let us give them the knowledge that *every single one of them* matters, the heritage of true freedom. Long live our freedom! Long live our Law! Long live the blood and bone and the heart of our beloved Iceland!"

The crowd erupted in wild enthusiasm at his words. Sweat poured from Mani's forehead and he drew a deep breath.

It is done, he told himself. *Whether or not it moves our people enough to protect what they have, I have tried my best.*

Mani outstretched his hands once more, but now held his palms upward to the sky, to signify that his opening remarks were an offering to the gods as well as the people. The crowd began to stamp their feet and strike good-luck sticks and shake bells to signify their approval.

Relief flooded Mani. *For a time, we are safe.*

But the relief, he knew, was only temporary. Fine words did not fill bellies, and a genuine danger of starvation loomed. The upcoming harvest this autumn and the next several years, mattered greatly. For many families, every day would be a struggle—and not for freedom, but to life itself. Every morning would matter, and every scrap of food.

. . .

After Mani had bowed slightly and stepped back, Kalendar raised clapped for silence again.

"Listen up, friends, as I recite the schedule for Althing. Most of us have endured grueling journeys, some from the far ends of the eastern quarters. Today, greet other, catch up on news, and relax."

"*Holmgang* duels can take place starting this afternoon, and *only* in the marked ox-hide square. Remember that Althing forbids fighting, weapons, or violence of any kind in any other part of the festival-grounds!" Kalendar gave the crowd a stern look to bolster those words.

"Animal events begin after the supper-time. Tonight, sheep shearing contests, pig- and chicken-catching, and goat races." A scatter of laughter and friendly insults followed.

"Tomorrow, the true purpose of Althing begins. Mani our *Allsherjargothi* will stand here as Mani the Lawspeaker. He will begin the daily morning recitation of a portion of the Law, so that all who wish to know the Law may learn it. Also, the council of *gothar* begins sessions tomorrow afternoon, hearing legal cases to vote on them."

People familiar with the schedule started to chatter, forcing Kalendar to shout. "Trading booths, and the work-lot for free men and women seeking employment, and the slave-trading market are all open the entire Althing. Contests of combat and skill take place each night after the supper-time...and everyone's favorite: bride-fair selections will be announced on the last day"—this to encourage people to stay until the end—"and that evening, the blowing of the Horn will close Althing until next summer."

The long recitation concluded, Kalendar held up a pair of good-luck sticks and struck them together: *fortune to us all!* The multitude gathered below replied by clattering their sticks. They began to chant in rhythm, demanding the final ritual.

Dalla stepped forward with a second huge horn. This one too was carved and shone with gold, but it would not sing. She held the wide end of the horn against an ale-cask and filled it, letting the froth run over the horn cup. The crowd clattered their sticks in delight.

"May we please the gods this Althing and this year," Dalla cried. "May they favor us with good harvests and health. May our people not only survive, but thrive. I give you the Horn of Plenty!"

Dalla took a sip, then offered it to Mani and the Kalendar. Then she raised the horn, gripping it tightly.

"May you have plenty today, and plenty tomorrow, and plenty for all of your life," Dalla exclaimed. She swung the horn in a wide arc over the crowd. A sparkling arc of droplets flew across the gathered people. A final enthusiastic cheer went up as those in the front rows lifted their hands and opened their mouths, hoping to catch a sip.

With that, the ceremony ended, and the crowd began to disperse.

Dalla, Mani and the Kalendar shook hands and clapped one another on the shoulder, then slowly made their way down from the height of the Law Rock. As they reached the base, the Kalendar gratefully removed the ceremonial robe and handed it to a fellow Kalendar from another region.

"I wish I could pull off my cloak and be just another person in the crowd," Mani said. But such could not happen. He took Dalla's hand. They walked without speaking to the first informal meeting of *gothar*, to hear what surely would be depressing, difficult news.

· · ·

Chapter Seventeen

Kel Coesson reached the dueling ground as the final *holmgang* preparations were readied. A thick square of ox-hide, three strides to each side, lay fastened to the ground. Around it, three square borders, each one making the battleground bigger by one pace. As Kel approached, he saw the last detail taking place: hazel-wood stakes pounded in at each corner, to sanctify the dueling ground to the will of the gods.

Holmgang. The poor-man's court, they called it, for those unable to afford court fees and law-arguers, a way to end blood-quarrels, avenge slights to one's honor, and settle disputes—and the one place at Althing where weapons were permitted.

Kel looked over the faces, some of them regulars. Sure enough, old Ora Eettison was there. Always bickering with one neighbor or another, she had induced yet another of her grandsons into battle over some imagined insult.

On one side of the dueling ground stood groups of accusers and challengers, and on the other, the defenders. Kel looked first among the challengers for what he wanted. He soon saw a well-known *holmgang-berserker;* a professional fighter, the type who called a duel against a farmer not for a grudge, but simply to try and win a property with a few strokes of the sword. *There's an example where our laws could improve,* Kel thought. *Such a stupid idea.* Maybe not at first, with the law council overwhelmed by cases and *holmgang* had offered another means of settling arguments. Since the loser forfeited all property to the victor, only the most bitter, protracted disagreements had once ended up on the dueling square. But recently, professional fighters had seized upon *holmgang* as a way to get property for free.

Kel walked among those who were defendants, listening to the conversations.

That group, there. A pitiful excuse of a sword, held in dirt-stained hands of a farmer, and a worried wife twisting at her apron. A too-young son, pleading with his father to serve as shield-bearer. Kel stepped up to them.

"You're accused?" Kel asked. "Of what?"

The beleaguered man had too much on his mind to wonder why a well-groomed stranger had inquired. He groaned, "No accusation. I'm only a land-challenge." He pointed to the professional fighter Kel had noticed. "For rights to our farm and our two daughters."

There were always plenty of girls weeping at holmgang. "Which are yours?"

The farmer pointed to a pair of attractive young women, their faces twisted in worry.

"What's your farm worth?" Kel asked, and the farmer mumbled a small amount of silver.

Kel kept his voice stern. "You don't stand a chance against your accuser. He is going to take your land and your daughters. Why fight a man you can't win against? No shame in walking away."

For the first time, the farmer looked Kel straight in the eyes.

"If I *don't* fight him, he'll take them for sure. I can stand losing the land, but not my daughters. At least they'll know I loved them enough to try. I won't live out my years ashamed of my cowardice." His voice was quiet but determined.

It was all Kel had needed. No sense risking blood for someone not willing to shed his own.

"Friend, tell your wife to stop weeping. Your luck is about to change today." With that, Kel walked away.

. . .

When the dueling master called the farmer's turn, the professional fighter stepped onto the ox-hide, cocky and swaggering. He brandished his sword, laughing and calling to those placing wagers on the fight.

The duel-master called for the farmer, who stepped forward. As required by law, the duel-master repeated the *holmgang* rules before each fight: the first blood spilled upon the leather surface betokened the loser, as well as if either of the fighters put a foot past the edge of the ox-hide. The defendant made the choice of weapons to use; swords in this case, as was generally typical. All property of the loser went to the victor. At the words '*property in entirety, herds, daughters and slaves*', the farmer turned pale and he sank almost onto his knees, whereupon the accuser laughed even more loudly.

The duel-master stood aside and spoke quietly to the farmer. "This man wins land every year. He'll take yours. You could die. Is it worth your life?"

The farmer pulled himself together. "Yes."

"Luck be with you then. But you know I must call the fight fairly. Sympathy cannot influence my judgement."

The farmer nodded. The duel-master read the last rule, nearly always a formality. "If anyone present wishes to fight on behalf of the accused, let him speak now." He hesitated briefly, then raised a gong and hammer. "I now declare—"

"I stand for him." Kel's deep voice rang over the *holmgang* grounds.

People craned their necks to see who had spoken. Kel pushed through the onlookers and walked to the hazel stakes. He carried his sword casually, as one might a walking stick, and planted the tip into the ground at the edge of the dueling ground. His servant followed, laboring under the weight of Kel's three shields.

The farmer collapsed backwards, the sound of his body a soft thud on the bare earth.

"Your name, sir?" asked the duel-master.

"Kel Coesson. Steward to *gothi* Naldrum."

The duel-master breathed a deep sigh. *Thank the gods. About time someone took on this bully.* He turned to the challenge fighter, who now looked much less confident. "Your shield-bearer?"

The shield-bearer, accustomed to fights against farmers carefully selected to lose, backed away. The *ganger* glared at him. "I already paid you. Get back here, you worthless goat."

"And your shield-bearer, Kel Coesson?"

Kel pointed at his servant boy when a voice rang out. "I will carry his shields!"

It was a voice he knew all too well.

"Who speaks?" the duel-master asked.

Goosebumps ran along Kel's arm. He turned and stared straight into the furious eyes of Aldís Robertsdóttir.

"Why are you here?" he asked in astonishment.

"Because you and I have matters to discuss, and you can't answer my questions if you're dead," she replied, glaring.

. . .

Naldrum had declined the many invitations pressed upon him to watch the *holmgang* duels. In truth, fights unnerved him, and the sight of blood often made him nauseous.

Besides, he had more important matters. As the morning's opening ceremony had ended, Naldrum heard the same high-pitched voice whisper in his ear. "Remember your meeting. The tent at the very end of merchant row, the one with red and yellow stripes. Come during the holmgang duels this afternoon," it directed. "And come alone." By the time he turned to look, the messenger had vanished.

Now, the headman combed and combed his hair, gazing at his mirror, rapt in anticipation of the meeting and what it might mean.

"Did the messenger give a name?" Naldrum's favorite daughter held out a tunic and cloak. "This one, I think."

"No, Ankya. I imagine the Jarl has sent someone of note. I only know his merchants, though, not his court officials."

"How very exciting, Father. I wonder what they want?"

Naldrum turned his face from side to side in the mirror. "Your father has a reputation as a shrewd man, Ankya. Whatever offer they bring, I'll get the best of them." He gave her a kiss. "Where is Kel? He should go with me to stand guard outside the tent while we meet."

"I don't know." Her father did not notice her forlorn tone. When Kel left his tent that midday, Ankya had followed him but had lost him in the crowds. She had come back to her father's tent, hoping Kel might be there.

"I'll come with you and keep an eye out for him?" Ankya wished her father would understand how much she admired the strong and straightforward steward, but she bit her tongue. Naldrum might forbid her to associate with Kel. She could not bear the idea of that.

"No, my lovely girl. I forgot; I usually give Kel the first afternoon of Althing off. He goes about greeting others on my behalf. I'll meet my host alone. Why don't you visit the merchant booths? Many lovely things to choose from…remember to be certain to negotiate a good deal in my name. If you happen to see Kel, tell him to find me. I don't want him chasing women instead of doing what I want."

Ankya turned aside, her mood ruined. She would most definitely *not* spend the day visiting the gold-sellers and fabric booths. Kel was out there somewhere. She would walk the festival grounds until she found her father's steward. By the time Ankya waved goodbye to Naldrum, her face was composed again, but inwardly, she seethed.

. . .

Now, Naldrum looked about nervously as he walked to where the messenger had directed. With duels capturing the attention of the crowd, the row of tents stood nearly empty. Even those manning trade booths craned towards the sound of the battles, shouting updates up and down the lanes.

Naldrum ignored them. He strode along the tents with no thought beside clumsy excitement at what a king's messenger might want.

There it was, the last in the row. Red and yellow stripes just as the messenger had described, with the door-flaps tied tightly closed.

He stood at the entrance and coughed. No response. Why did a thrall not open it for him?

"Who wants to speak with *gothi* Naldrum?" he demanded. His voice sounded forced and thin even to himself.

Still no response. Naldrum fiddled with the booth flap, but someone had fastened it from within as well. He grew testy and impatient.

"You said to come here," he bleated. "It's rude to keep me waiting."

Only quiet answered him. Naldrum cursed and turned to go.

The same high-pitched falsetto whispered from the other side of the tent fabric. "I'll be with you shortly. Wait."

. . .

"Shortly" meant an ungodly long time of standing and fidgeting. When Naldrum could bear it no longer, he pressed mouth on the tent.

"I'm leaving if you don't let me in right now. This is ridiculous."

With that, he finally heard someone untying the flaps, but with maddening slowness. His impatience mounted.

. . .

A slave boy lifted the tent door just high enough for Naldrum to enter, then scurried outside and away. With him gone, the tent seemed empty. Naldrum's usual cockiness vanished. He resorted to bluster.

"What's this all about? You said you're from the Haakon. Come out and identify yourself."

Darkness seemed to drift like smoke from one of the corners.

"I speak on behalf of the Jarl. He wants me to assess you." The odd false voice was more normal. The speaker, whom Naldrum had assumed to be male, was not. "My name is—"

Naldrum cut her off. "Assess me? For what?"

She continued as if he had not interrupted her.

"…Rota. I am to determine your potential. Learn your goals. See where your loyalties lie. Discuss goals that you might have in common with the Jarl."

Naldrum, defensive, bristled. "I sell goods to his merchants. What loyalties would he want, besides a cut of the profit from my ships?"

"I've already answered one question for you. Before we continue, I would think a headman might follow proper behavior on meeting an agent of the all-but-king of Norway."

"Haakon Sigurdsson is not the ruler there. Bluetooth is." Naldrum hated his own weakness for quibbling, but he could not stop himself.

The woman leveled a cold look at Naldrum. "Perhaps I will report to Haakon that you are quarrelsome and that I deem you should be of no interest to him."

Naldrum fumed. How had she gotten the upper hand this fast? He tried to regain control. "I have much to offer—if the Jarl has something to offer me."

"I told you my name is Rota." She waited. The spies she had sent last year had told her that Naldrum preferred his business dealings to be with men. On hearing that, Rota had informed Haakon she would go in person to meet the headman.

"Nasty, pushy *fitta,*" Naldrum wanted to say. Instead, he gritted his teeth and made the expected formal response.

"May our words be worthy." Courtesy demanded a bow, slight to a man, deeper to a woman. Naldrum merely nodded his head.

Rota noted the slight. *Doltish imbecile*, she thought. Her spies had also reported on the headman's substantial ego. *Flattery, then.*

"A meeting with great *gothi* Naldrum foretells good," she purred.

Naldrum smiled widely. Rota nearly laughed aloud. *Oh, son of Odin, this fool; one compliment. I'll lead him like a horse by its reins.*

"What interests the Jarl?" he asked. "An exclusive new trade route? A fine ware my ships can distribute for you?"

A wise man would wait to hear and not guess wildly. Rota resisted the temptation to prick Naldrum's self-satisfied pride. She had not come this far just to give this clod lessons in strategy.

"Haakon seeks strategic alliances with certain *gothi* in Iceland," she said. "It would, of course, require some sharing of assets." She would give him a small test, which she intended for Naldrum to fail.

He grasped Rota's suggestion. "Haakon wants me to pay a bribe."

Rota poured ale into a flagon, offered it to Naldrum. After he had drunk, she took the flagon back and pressed her own lips against it but did not drink.

"Bribe is such a ham-fisted word. Let us call it an investment; a sign of your intentions of mutual benefit." She lowered her lashes, pretended to sip the ale again.

"How much does he want?"

"Others pay a tenth."

Naldrum's face reddened and his neck swelled. "*A tenth!* Under no circumstances will I ever pay that much for ware-rights."

"We are not talking about tithes for one of your merchant routes. You are a very wealthy man. A tenth of your annual income might be a trifle to what the Jarl might offer in return. Are you certain, *gothi* Naldrum, that there is nothing of great interest to you?"

"A tenth of my annual income?" Now Naldrum's face purpled and his eyes bulged. "I thought this was a trade negotiation for Harald Bluetooth, Ruler of Denmark and the North-way lands. Instead your trifling Haakon has sent some low-level messenger to extort money from me. You insult me, wench."

"My humblest apologies, headman," Rota replied. She walked to the tent door, her soft, smoky robes flowing, and lifted the flap. "I hope this will not affect our normal business relations."

Naldrum swept past her, full of indignation. If Kel had been doing his job, this ridiculous meeting would never have taken place. "Trade is trade," he sniffed. "As long as I make the profits I expect."

Rota waited until Naldrum, snorting in triumph at besting her, had bent and walked through her doorway before she spoke again.

"I had hoped—a shame. For many years, Haakon has been seeking one capable of holding power in Iceland as he does in Nor'way."

She saw Naldrum stiffen.

"Chieftain of all Iceland?" *Just as he had hoped!* He turned quickly. "I didn't realize—"

"Yes. Chieftain of all Iceland, as you say, with total control. Such a man would need significant resources—and willingness to use his wealth towards attaining such a lofty goal. The Jarl thought perhaps the great *gothi* Naldrum was more than just a common headman, and he sent me to ascertain as much." She gave an exaggerated sigh. "I guess someone else will rule here in partnership with Haakon."

Rota flipped a small coin past Naldrum. It rolled on the ground near his feet.

"A token for wasting your time. Let me know if you think of someone," she said lightly and snapped the tent flap closed in his face.

. . .

Naldrum stood facing the striped red-and-yellow fabric with his mouth gaping open. He scratched his eyebrows and pawed at his nose. What had just happened?

He started to pound on the knock-plate again but stopped. To ask for re-entry would appear weak. His fury at Rota's greedy suggestion turned towards the woman herself. This disaster of a meeting was her fault. She had tricked him. What a dreadful emissary Haakon had chosen in that woman.

She would have to be punished, somehow, that he knew. Needing to vent, he decided to get one of his guardsmen and go to the lakeshore where ship traders congregated. A profitable deal would console him.

Before he left, Naldrum looked up and down the tent row. *No one in sight.* He leaned down and picked up the small coin, put it in his pocket, and turned to go towards the lake.

Rota, listening just inside the tent, heard Naldrum's fingers clawing in the dirt to pick up the coin she had tossed. "You're welcome," she cooed, her lips against the tent wall.

Naldrum's cheeks turned scarlet as he left, mortified and furious.

Rota handed a black pebble to a message-carrier. "Take this to my sister. Tell her that I love her and that I am well," she instructed. "And tell Haakon this: *I have found a willing farmer. I will cultivate his field until it is ready to plant.*"

The messenger repeated her words. She nodded and he left Rota alone in the dim light of her tent, smiling. She emptied the flagon of ale onto the dirt floor and settled herself into a chair to think.

. . .

Chapter Eighteen

At the holmgang dueling ground, shouts of wagering reached the level of screams. Aldís prepared the shields, and the two combatants and their shield-bearers entered the sacred space.

. . .

Kel stepped slowly around in a small circle, his eyes never leaving the *holmgang* challenger. The man stood half a head taller than Kel. His shoulders and arms shone with oil to make his muscles seem larger, and to make him slippery.

Kel would wait until the other man swung his sword first.

"Who is this puny defender?" the holmganger asked the crowd.

Aldís, staying near Kel in the frame that ran around the ox-hide, spoke up. "A puny man who can lift two stone with one hand. Unlike you, whose sword is thin to make it lighter."

Kel's eyes widened. How did she know those things?

"Bah, he has a mouthy woman as a shield-bearer. Surely he cannot think that stupid *fitta* will do any good."

Kel did not take the challenge. Aldís could stand up for herself, Kel knew well. No sense letting the holmganger's taunts distract him.

Aldís, however, responded. She watched Kel steadily, his second shield in her hand to be ready the instant he needed it, as she said, "A woman would not wait such a long time to use her sword. Perhaps you don't feel your weapon is quite firm enough?"

Her insinuation worked and the man, grimacing, swung his sword. Kel was ready for it. He dodged easily and laughed.

This only incensed the holmganger more. Now his sword came fast and hard, as if he felt the need to show his prowess.

Kel parried, thrust, spun, challenged, defended. The clang of metal rang loud in the air, matched by deafening shouts around the dueling ground as the two men fought.

One of Kel's shields broke under the fury of the man's blows. Kel tossed it away without time to worry if it might strike Aldís. She had stayed close, his second shield to the ready. Faster than Kel could have expected, she'd proffered the new one. Immediately, Aldís cleared the broken shield out of the way and fetched his third one, ready again. Kel gave a quick nod of thanks without looking at her.

The sun glared down on the two men. Kel could feel his arms tiring. This challenger practiced sword-work all year long, preparing for these battles. Kel relaxed his legs, keeping a bend in his knees. He was surprised to see the man lift his sword hand slightly to wipe sweat from his brow. *He's tiring too.*

The realization gave Kel a surge of power. He made a reckless move. Lifted his sword high over his head, twisted as if he was going to bring it down, but instead, continued the twist and spun around, his knees bent, his body low.

His opponent had put his shield in front of him to block the blow, but Kel had rotated the opposite direction than the man expected. His sword hit the holmganger's calf, well behind his battle-leathers. The blade, lethally sharp, cut through the man's breeches. Kel twisted the blade, pulled the sword toward him and down in a slicing motion. The man screamed in pain and dropped to the ox-hide, his ankle tendon cut just as Kel had intended.

The duel-master rang the gong to signify that the fight had ended. Kel bent over the holmganger.

"That's the last farm you'll ever steal," he said. "If you're lucky, you'll walk with a limp. Maybe worse. But in either case, you'll never fight again."

. . .

As the dust on the duel-space settled, Kel handed his sword to his servant. Farm families clapped him on the back, exultant that Kel had protected one of their own.

He stripped off his leg-leathers as the duel-master questioned the bleeding berserker about the properties he owned, all obtained through abuse of holmgang. Kel laughed at hearing the astonished response of the farmer as he woke from his faint to learn that not only did he still possess his own small property and his precious daughters, but now owned three other farms in nearby valleys, his to keep or sell, along with nearly a dozen thralls and twice as many bonded servants, plus several herds of sheep, goats, and horses.

Aldís followed Kel. She wiped her face, also listening to the recitation of victor-winnings the farmer would receive. "Well done, Kel Coesson," she said. "You did a good thing there."

He noticed that her eyes sparkled in the old way, her face flushed from the fight. Her lips curved in an easy smile. Not at him, but a smile, at least.

He yearned.

"What made you help me?" Kel asked, keeping his tone careful.

"I didn't do it for you."

"Why, then?"

"I know that family. They're good people," she said. "It was critical that you won. That berserker has good fighting skills. One misstep and you might've lost to him. Your odds were better with me."

"I've never seen a finer shield-bearer," he exclaimed. "No man, and no woman, either." Aldís had moved instinctively in battle as if the exhilarating music of a death-dance flowed through her.

"This changes nothing between us. I want nothing to do with you." Her smile vanished.

"Aldís, please, listen," the hero of the fight choked. "There are things you don't know. Things I should have set right, long ago."

"You poor man, Kel. You think you are the only one who has suffered? There is much more that *you* don't know. And whatever heartbroken tale you are yearning to tell me, keep it to yourself. I really don't care to hear it." Aldís pushed her hair back from the sweat on her forehead, impatient. "I'm filthy. I need to wash this dirt and blood off my clothing."

"I'm fighting again." He pointed to several professional holmgangers.

Aldís flicked a glance over the line of accusers. "You don't need me for any of those."

With that, she was gone. For the second time that day, Kel watched her leave with a mixture of anger and grief. He gritted his teeth and wiped sweat from his own face. For the sake of the gods, could not one thing go right today?

He bent and started re-buckling his fighting leathers. One farmer, one holmgang wrong prevented. Good, but not good enough. Kel checked the lines again. *One? Two, three more? Excellent.* He wanted to be completely worn out when the day was over.

. . .

Naldrum picked his way along the shoreline of the broad lake that filled the center of the Althing valley, thankful that the roar of the dueling-ground had diminished and that that horrid woman Rota was behind him.

Traders from near and far had ferried goods upriver from the ocean. Languages of every sort filled the air. All, to Naldrum's ear, rang with the sweet dialects of profits to make. He made his way from one ferry-skiff to another, greeting some, ignoring others.

To Naldrum's surprise, he saw his daughter Ankya moving among the people thronging the narrow beach.

"Daughter," he called, pleased. "I did not expect to see you here. You have an interest in trade? Walk with me, and listen, and learn."

She ran to him and pushed past his guard. Naldrum offered his arm and Ankya took it, her head high. *So lovely,* he thought, proud.

A cry from a Saxon merchant interrupted Naldrum's thoughts. "You thieving bastard!" The man ran towards the headman. "When will you pay me for the shipload of nails you bought last year?"

"Ignore him, Ankya," Naldrum whispered. "The first rule of business is to avoid payment if at all possible." He grinned widely.

The man sprinted in front of them and planted his feet in defiance. "I'm nearly done in by debt. If you pay me, I'll be able to wipe it clean. I need the payment you owe me."

Naldrum raised his chin and sneered. "If you're nearly done in by debt, the last thing I'm going to do is help. No sense throwing my good silver into a pit. You'll just lose it again."

"I borrowed because of our agreement. You gave me your word. Have you no shame?"

"Do not dare to disparage me!"

The man charged Naldrum. As he reached the headman, Naldrum's guard pulled a short knife from his belt and slid it under the man's ribs. The trader crumped to the ground like scythed grain. He twisted, crying out in agony.

Ankya's mouth opened. Her face swiveled back and forth from her father to the bleeding man.

"Don't be distressed, daughter," Naldrum consoled her. But her face glowed.

"How exciting Althing is," she said. "I wish I had held that knife!"

The guard held the blade, wet and red. "Care to finish him, Miss?"

As Naldrum shrank back, Ankya reached for it, eager. "I'll do it!"

Naldrum jerked her away. "No, Ankya! We don't want his filth on our hands." As always, the sight of blood made him nauseous. He kicked the man's flailing arm. "Come on, Ankya. Time to leave."

"Hey," another sailor called. "You know the rules. No weapons! I'm going to report you."

"The law doesn't apply to the shoreline, does it?" Naldrum asked. "No one knows the answer. Am I the only one here who is on the Law

Council? How dare you assume my guard would break an Althing taboo."

He stretched his lips in a wide, false smile. "But I'm a just man. I'll pay his family a settlement of some kind." He dusted his hands as if free of a troublesome matter and strolled along the shore, a firmer grip upon his daughter's arm.

. . .

As they reached the end of the row of skiffs, a tall Danes-sailor came running and calling. "*Gothi*! *Gothi*!"

The headman turned to see what caused the commotion. The sailor yanked a woven cap from his head. A balding pate shone above a fringe of hair.

"I'm looking for a certain fellow, sir. I saw your garb and I said to myself, a high-placed chieftain such as yourself might know how to find a man." The man's words tumbled out. "I'm carrying a message."

Naldrum puffed at the compliment. "A message? What man?"

The man's eyes shone with earnest desire to discharge his duty. "Very tall. Unusual looking fellow, with skin like charcoal. A thrall called Sám Tor. Means 'Dark Mountain,' I'm told."

"I may know of this man," Naldrum replied.

"Oh, wonderful, sir," said the sailor. "Would it be too much to ask you to pass along a message to him?"

"It would be my honor to help," Naldrum intoned. "What should I say?"

"Only this, your lordship: '*To the slave Tor from the merchant named Indaell: she is found.*'"

"She?"

"I don't know anything more, sir. But Indaell was smiling. Good news, I guess."

Naldrum stretched his lips again. "*She,* whoever the woman is, must be important to Tor. Tell me all you know in case he asks."

"Indaell's ship went up the North-way to Trondheim and put up for repairs there. Coming back to Edinburgh, her ship's sail tore—"

Naldrum, impatient, listened to the tiresome woes of a ship merchant. *Trondheim. Why did that sound familiar?*

"Such bad luck, because it meant she wouldn't get to Althing in time. She begged me, said it was of the utmost importance to get this news to her friend Tor. I promised her I'd find him, but with all these people here, I don't know where to start. I'm grateful to you for helping me." He looked more hopeful than grateful, wondering if Naldrum might produce a coin for such fine effort.

Naldrum ignored the half-proffered palm. "Where shall I tell Tor this woman is located?"

"She didn't say, sir. All I know is where Indaell's traveled this year: along the Nor'way coast up as far as Trondheim, then down to Edinburgh.

The name of the town finally clicked in his memory. "Trondheim? Are you sure?"

"Oh, most definitely, sir. Repairs, there, remember? Only town where she got off the ship, she said, and that she couldn't wait to leave. Liked it there not even a little."

"You've done a good deed, it seems." Naldrum pulled out a silver coin. "I would very much like to surprise my friend Tor by finding this woman for him. To do it requires utmost secrecy. Tell no one that you spoke with me, especially not Tor, should you happen to see him."

The sailor beamed his nearly-toothless grin. "You can count on me, sir." He bowed and walked straight towards where whores and ale waited for those with silver to trade.

Naldrum watched him go. "Follow that man," he instructed his guard. "Let him enjoy his drink. Let him get drunk. That way he won't feel the knife. Then get my silver back."

Ankya listened without saying a word. At the prospect of a second stabbing, she hugged herself in delight. *Althing was wonderful.*

. . .

*Trondheim...*Naldrum's ships put in there every year to trade. And who lived in Trondheim? None other than Haakon Sigurdsson, the Jarl of Lade.

Tor seeks a woman who may be in Trondheim. Naldrum's thoughts spun. Who might she be? Someone from the same distant land as Tor? A friend? A sister? If a fellow slave, she would have cost a fortune which only a person with tremendous wealth could afford.

Naldrum stopped, shocked at what he had just realized. *Perhaps a man who had stopped paying tribute to his ruler?* This woman who mattered to Tor was, in all likelihood, at the house of Haakon Sigurdsson. Naldrum felt certain of it.

Brutal seizing. Well, Haakon knew about that strategy, didn't he? Naldrum, still smarting from his encounter with Rota, cackled and rubbed his hands together.

"Jarl, my ass. I'll treat Haakon in a way he understands. I'll teach him he's dealing with an equal—a superior, not some fool underling he can push around. I just need a ship and the right crew."

Naldrum walked faster, looking along the shoreline for one sailor in particular, a *vikinger* known for taking chances and looking the other way about law. When he saw the man working on a ship, Naldrum forgot his dignity and ran towards him.

"Tiller," he shouted. "By Loki's mischief, I have a job for you."

. . .

Aldís left the dueling-ground and went straight to the bathing tubs. She arrived just as a family stepped away from one of the large wooden half-barrels.

"What are you taking in trade today?" she asked the bath slave.

"Ale-marks, grain-weights, glass beads, wool-skeins. Anything not perishable." He quoted the cost for the tepid water just vacated. "Three times that for a clean hot cask."

"Don't change the water," she said. "I don't have any of those trade items." Aldís had stripped off her jumper and apron before starting the duel. She hung those still-clean garments on a post near the bathing tub and inspected her light linen under-shift. The mud and grass stains were fresh. They would come clean easily.

She soaped and rinsed it quickly in the tepid water, then hung it near a bonfire to dry. That task completed, Aldís stood naked in the water, her back to the festival grounds.

Sweet Freydis, what have I done? All these years of drifting, living like a hermit, avoiding contact with Naldrum, but today she had fought side-by-side with Naldrum's steward right out in the open. The chieftain would know before middle-night. *What was I thinking?*

But Aldís knew she would have done the same thing again. *I am sick of being afraid.* She gazed over the far landscape. Peace flowed through her like wind over a wheatfield. *How good it feels.*

Behind her, the bath-boy watched, curious. Ever since yesterday when his master had set out the wooden casks along the shoreline, people had come and gone, eager to wash off the dust of travel and get back to the festival. But this one seemed different. She looked strong, but there was something almost pitiful about her. She had made no move to wash, but just stood there, staring at the horizon.

His throat tightened. He knew that feeling of looking towards something too far away to see. Lying alone at night, he yearned for the sight of a whitewashed hut halfway up a grassy hill, where his sister would be kneading dough for the oven, where he could smell the sweet smoke of peat burning on their hearth; his father in the fields scything hay and his smallest brother running behind, looking for things in the grass.

The bath-boy glanced left and right. No sign of the mean old man who owned the tubs. He raked two glowing-hot stones from the fire into a bucket and dropped them into a cask of fresh lake water. The liquid bubbled and hissed. He went over to the where the naked woman stood.

"For you, miss," he said. He pointed at the clean hot water.

It took a moment for her to turn to him, to refocus her gaze from wherever she had been. She made no move to cover herself.

A rapid assessment told Aldís that the slave boy had the features of Eire-land people. The looking-inside told more: *grief loss loneliness mother father blood death despair*.

"Born here?" she asked. "Or taken, and brought here?"

"Taken, miss. I was twelve." He gulped and his voice broke. "They cut my father down in the fields where he worked. Mother heard him cry out, and she ran to him. They pulled her mouth open, looked at her teeth, ripped open her blouse. One of them threw her over his shoulder and ran with her to river. My sister too. Tied them both up and loaded them onto the longship they'd beached on my grandma's shore. We never saw them coming. They came out of nowhere. Took everything they could carry and left just as fast."

Aldís said nothing, waiting.

"I tried to fight them." The feeling of being a scared young boy had never left. "But they just laughed at me. One of them grabbed my wrist and dragged me to their ship too. Tied me up with Ma and Sis. After they sold me, I never saw either of them again. I miss them so much." He could not go on for a while. Aldís touched his shoulder.

"My little brother—" the boy's eyes filled with tears. "'*Too small. We'll never sell that one,*' I heard the raiders say. The last I saw of him, he was in the field with my father, standing over my Da's body with his thumb in his mouth, crying. I always hope my grandma found him."

Aldís reached for his cheeks where the fuzz had just begun to show. She pulled his face close to hers. *Her eyes are not like Ma's, but they are just as kind* was all he had time to think before she put her lips on his forehead.

"Darling child," she murmured. "Bless you." The kiss, soft as elf-breath. "Peace to you."

"You were taken too, miss?" he asked.

"My mother was. Same as your sister; young. She gave me what memories she could of her family and her home."

"Did she ever get over it? The longing for what can never be?"

Aldís shook her head, her face gentle in honesty. "You don't get over something like that."

He burst forth, "My master beats me. I'm always hungry. He feeds us only thin oatmeal, morning and night. Never enough. I'm always freezing cold. My hands and feet crack with chilblains in the winter. I'm not even allowed to speak to the others at our farm in our own language. I'll live that hell every single day until I die."

He had not spoken of his devastation so deeply, and now the words poured out. "I carry buckets of water and loads of firewood all day long. Here at Althing, and where he has a lodge for travelers. All day, every day. Fill the buckets from the stream, carry the yoke back to the house, dump the water wherever it's needed, be it the barnyard, or for cooking or laundry. Go back, fill the buckets up again. In between that, I carry loads of firewood. Sunrise until after dark. A hard dirt floor to sleep on, hungry all day, and always cold. But that's not the worst of it. Missing my family is." His young voice cracked. "It's never going to get better. I can't bear it. I don't know what even keeps me alive."

"Some die of a broken heart," Aldís said. "Some, only the gods know why, struggle on." She saw his need for solace and tried.

"That man may treat you as if you don't matter, but you *do* matter. Find something that is of yourself only. Tell no one about it. Let it be your secret, something you care about, that only you know. You're a bathing-tub thrall, and you carry heavy buckets of water and firewood all the livelong day, but even a tub-thrall can sing to himself as he works, or think of poetry. Even a slave can make a ritual of offering a kind word to every single person he meets each day, or asking elders to share their stories. Just something that you like; something that you do, that you create."

"What is the purpose, if you don't mind me asking?"

Aldís gave a gentle smile. "It will nourish your *yggdrasil*—you, know, the tree of life that grows within every human being. Where this hard and grim life will take you, I can't say. But find something to hold onto *yourself* as you go through each day. Something the man who bought you doesn't know about. Something he can't take away."

"Will it ease the pain? Fill the hole where my family used to be?" His question, so sadly hopeful, yet so afraid to hope.

"No, sweet boy. It never will. But the *trying* helps. Start with something small. Something constant. Something to get you from one heartbeat to the next, from one sunset to the next. Having that focus will help you survive."

Aldís had never felt the pain that this young enslaved boy did, but her mother had lived it. She felt ashamed. *Look at me, bewailing my woes, while so many tread this heartbreaking path. Their entire lives are an abyss of unhappiness.* Her own trouble seemed somehow smaller, more bearable, beside such loss.

As the bath-thrall started to walk away, Aldís grasped his hand. "You have the gift of understanding. Across this festival, and across our country, boys and girls like you and your sister, and women like your mother, and men, too, are all drowning in the same fear and despair that you feel. They are like you. They need something,

something, to cling to, in order to simply survive. Reach out through your own pain to offer them kindness. Befriend them."

He stood staring back at her, not trying to pull his hand away.

"Your family is gone, and your family's clan are far away," Aldís said. "Welcome the enslaved here as your new clan. Welcome those you cannot even see and will never meet. Even on a distant farm with only the night stars as companions, you can reach out in your heart to the pitiful, heartbroken, wretches who also had their freedom snatched away. Send them greeting and encouragement. My child, you will never be really alone ever again, if you do that."

She patted his hand. "You are stronger than you know. You have survived every day that threatened to cut you down. Let your strength grow by helping others. Reach out, to those near to you and those far away. Your little brother, especially. Reach out to him, as if he can hear you. He can."

The thin young lips did not smile, but he squeezed her hand, nodded, and went back to work.

. . .

Aldís had already used too much of her energy in the holmgang battle. Now, this giving to the bath-boy had cost more than she could afford. She knew the feel of the void that came from being exhausted: the sharp edges of the cliff inside, the crumbling walls that dropped to depths threatening to suck her in. They called to her, tempting her with the emptiness of nothing.

She had been to that dangerous place before, more than once. Sometimes the way out took long weeks.

Let go of the past. Aldís told herself. *Let go of the future. Be only now.*

She reached for the block of tallow soap, a small lifeline to hold her to the present. In slow deliberate movements, Aldís soaped each finger, each hand, each part of each arm and leg; her shoulders, belly, buttocks, back. Soon she had covered her bare limbs in a froth of suds. Soaping and slow rinsing in the hot water soothed her, working a quiet healing. By the time Aldís left the bathing tub and pulled on her dry clothing, the sucking void had gone. She had gained a small precious sense of calm—and was starving for something to eat.

. . .

"Make your bets!" The dueling-judge wished he could make a wager himself, but the rules forbade it. He had never seen such frenzied betting as took place for each of Kel's fights.

The second holmganger had assumed that Kel would be fatigued from his first battle. An imprudent mistake, as Kel's fury at Naldrum and frustration with Aldís fed each thrust and swing of his sword. He seemed to gain strength rather than lose it. That duel lasted nearly as long as the first one, but was lost poorly. The holmganger had not anticipated such fierce opposition and did not want to really risk his *own* life and limb for a bit of land. He tried to make it look as if he stumbled when his foot landed outside the ox-hide square and ended the match. Another poor farmer found himself suddenly a much wealthier man instead of a dead one.

Kel, resting for the next challenge, called to the people around him. "I'm going to run out of shields. Who will lend me some?"

"*Lend*, you say? Since you've been breaking shields left and right, we'll not actually be getting them back from you, will we now?" A clear voice, stating the facts.

"Not likely."

"Well, then, if you're askin' for folks to *give* you perfectly good shields with expectation of naught in return, that's a whole different thing than lending, isn't it? Because in that case, you can have mine. That last farmer was my cousin." A strapping young man handed a shield to Kel. "Who else?"

Many of the surrounding crowd were simple folk, merchants and farmers themselves. Kel had taken on the glow of a bit of a hero to such ordinary people. Shields were readily donated, and soon Kel had as many as he would likely need for the remaining fights.

The betting on his third fight favored the holmganger, a sinewy man flexing his sword overhead to show his prowess. But the farmers who place bets for their new protagonist once again found themselves the winners. The challenger stood taller, but Kel moved faster. Soon a slash along the man's shoulder ended that battle.

As his fourth fight came up in the roster, even with some rest in between battles, Kel had wearied, and it showed. But when the challenger appeared, bets flew again. Little more than a poor, strong boy who hoped to have a chance of a farm through dueling, he was no match for Kel's seasoned skills, but clearly too ashamed to withdraw. Kel gave the frightened lad a few easy rounds, then tripped him. The boy fell off the ox-hide where he yielded with some sense of dignity.

The evening feasts had begun, and the smell of roasted meat made Kel's mouth water. "We're all finished here," he told his servant. "Go to the eating tent and get a platter filled and ready for me."

As Kel sheathed his sword, bone-weary and glad to be finished, the dueling judge announced one last fight for the day. *Even if it's a farm-challenge, I've done enough,* he told himself. *It's not my job to fix every sad situation in this country.*

The defender, fetched from the sheep pens, affirmed his name and farm. Right away, Kel could see that the man moved badly from some prior injury. With him came an elderly couple, likely his mother and father.

Oh, fukking Odin, Kel groaned, longing for rest. *I suppose I have one last fight left in me.* The duel-judge was already looking hopefully at him. Kel held up his hand in wearied acceptance, and the holmganger he would fight stepped forward.

Kel knew the fighter by sight. The burly man had often shown up at Naldrum's holdings, spoken privately with the headman, and quickly left. He had a reputation for cheating in every kind of matter, including holmgang duels.

The duel-judge repeated the rules as he had for each fight of the day. "No biting, kicking, or scratching. Punching, walloping, and hair-pulling are permitted." He lowered his voice, saying in an almost-inaudible aside to Kel, "and recommended." He continued, announcing, "Three shields each, and when the shields are broken, the shield-bearer must leave the duel-ground as well."

Despite the earlier offers, Kel was down to only two shields. *No help for it.* He tightened the leathers protecting his thighs and stood. A quick prayer might help, but to whom? Kel respected the gods but had a distant relationship with them. Still, against that brute…

Forseti, the god of justice, came to mind. Kel prayed rapidly.

He looked around for his servant who had carried his shields after Aldís had left, but the young man had followed orders and left for the food tent.

"I need a shield-bearer," he called. People eyed the holmganger in dismay. None of them replied.

"Who will help these good people keep their farm?" he asked. "Have none of you any honor?"

"It's not about honor, just plain good sense," someone answered. "That man's unbeatable. He'll kill a shield-bearer just as quick as he will a dueler, just for spite."

"The rules say I can give you to the count of one hundred," said the duel-judge to Kel. "If no one volunteers by then, I have to start the fight, whether you have a shield-bearer or not."

. . .

Aldís leaned against a tent pillar in the shade, scooping succulent roasted carrots into her mouth. She ignored the first roar from the holmgang grounds, but the second came louder.

"Are they still at it over there?" Aldís asked a man lugging a small barrel filled with beer.

"Aye, they are. I heard they called one last claiming-fight. A big fellow. Goes for land-rights every year. He's gotten rich from it."

"Always has seemed unfair to me," observed Aldís.

"Me too. But I don't make the rules." He grunted off, shouldering his load.

She meandered back towards the dueling ground, chewing another juicy carrot, delicious from meat broth cooked rich and brown.

The crowd had grown enormous. Aldís decided it was not worth the effort to push into it. She turned to go, but a flash of blue caught her eye, and she spun back around.

Was that Kel's cloak still on the fence where he had put it at midday? He couldn't possibly still be here, she told herself, but a sudden impulse overtook her. Aldís dropped the bowl of carrots and began to run.

. . .

"Atti-atte...atti-ni...nitti...nitti-en..." the duel-judge counted. "Ninety-two...ninety-three..."

He was counting for a shield-bearer. In that instant, Aldís knew.

. . .

"Wait!" Aldís shouted. "Wait!" She clawed at people who blocked her way. "Shield-bearer!" she screamed towards the duel-judge. "I am here!"

He paused in his counting. "Did I hear someone volunteer?"

"Yes! Let me through!" Now the crowed parted easily, excited to see this spectacle grow even more dramatic. Aldís bent over, her hands on her knees, panting and out of breath. She raised one hand enough to give the signal. "I'll be shield-bearer."

"Give her a chance to catch her breath," the duel-judge proclaimed. He waited. As the wagering clamors began afresh, Aldís stood and went over to the marked-off dueling area. To her horror, she saw the holmganger that Kel had recognized, but the man standing in the defendant's corner and holding Kel's sword was not Kel.

"I thought—" she stammered to the thin farmer. "My gods, that man will kill me."

"You have volunteered," said the duel-judge. "Once you are inside the lines, if you leave, the fight is forfeited."

"Come closer, pretty lady," the holmganger leered. He thrust his hips towards Aldís. "Maybe you'd like a taste of what you'll be getting later, when I beat your hero to a pulp?"

"A little early to be calling the fight, isn't it?" she replied. "Don't talk to me. I don't want to hear your voice."

He cupped his crotch. "Oh, stomps her little feet! Amusing."

"You're a stupid troll." Aldís turned to the judge. "I thought Kel Coesson—"

"Who asks for Kel Coesson?"

Aldís whirled, and relief flooded her. "You *are* here."

"I am. What are you doing back?"

"I saw your cloak. I heard the judge counting. I didn't think it through. Something in me sensed danger, and I ran."

Something in her sensed the danger. That ability Aldís had, of knowing-without-knowing-how in strange but often-accurate ways. Kel wished he had given more credit to it years ago.

He leaned close. "Are you sure you want to? Against that thing?" Kel nodded towards his rival.

"You don't think you can win?"

"I don't know, Aldís. This fight may not go well. On a good day, and fresh, I could barely go against him. I'm drained to the bone, and that man doesn't wound his opponents. He's a killer. But I gave my word. I'm not going to back out. Doesn't mean you have to help."

They stared at one another, desperate, caught in the instant, unable to think clearly.

Aldís—" *Damn it, he* would *say it, finally, whether she wanted to hear it or not.* "If this fight gets the better of me, I have to tell you, Aldís. I love—"

She wasn't listening. "Kel...I just remembered. I once saw this man fight at a local *thing* near us. He has a trick—it makes him vulnerable if you see it in time." She put her mouth close to Kel's ear.

"Watch for when he bends his knees and begins to sway back and forth like a bear," Aldís whispered. "Once—twice—three times, he will do it. Then he swings his shield about wildly to distract his opponent. He'll fling away his shield and his sword, and while everyone looks towards where he threw them, he pulls out his short knife to leap on his opponent and stab at close range."

Kel nodded, and Aldís continued. "Don't look at his shield or his sword when he starts to sway. Watch his feet. When he throws his shield and leaps, he is vulnerable. Be ready."

. . .

Screams erupted from the crowd at each powerful swing from the combatants. The challenger had not fought already as Kel had. His arms were fresh to the fight and as strong as iron, and he swung his sword relentlessly, determined to break Kel's shields as quickly as possible, to leave Kel open and remove Aldís from the fight as well.

The first of Kel's two shields shattered. Kel whirled, threw off the broken one, reached with his open hand and Aldís slipped the fresh shield onto it and darted back out of the way. Kel squatted, rose quickly, caught the other fighter mid-turn, and with a quick blow, broke the challenger's first shield as well.

They hacked, thrust, parried, surged against each other, each man sweating and grunting. The opponent swung his second shield like a weapon, but Kel blocked it, and both men's shields split in two.

The challenger called for his third, and his shield-bearer slipped it on his hand in a flash. Kel now had only his sword. He pulled his short-knife from its sheath as the duel-judge shouted to Aldís to leave the dueling space.

A woman pressed up against the marked lines, grabbing at Aldís, shoving a shield at her.

"Here," she screamed. "It was a gift for my betrothed. Take it!"

Aldís snatched the brightly painted shield and whirled towards Kel. The two men already were circling one another at close range again as they caught their breath. As they moved, Aldís saw it: a deep bend in the holmganger's knees, a swaying from side to side.

"Kel! The bear!" she cried, as the attacker threw his shield.

. . .

Later, Aldís could not understand how she had moved, or how her body had spun through the air towards Kel, her back flat to the ground like a cloud floating over a mountain, or how the betrothed woman's shield had slid from her hand onto Kel's as he dropped his dagger.

She had flung herself towards him, the shield-grip barely in her grasp, and Kel had leaped towards her, reaching for it. He and Aldís had twisted, impossibly twirling past one another in mid-air as time stopped for Aldís. She saw Kel's well-honed knife slowly tumbling end-over-end to the ground, saw the sun gleam along the sharp edge as it fell, admired the many strokes on the whetstone that had created such a fine *scramasax*.

As the challenger sprang though the air, Kel met him, roaring. With the new shield, he slammed a tremendous blow to the side of the holmganger's head. The man dropped like a sack of barley. He flopped against the ox-hide, unconscious. Wild cheers burst from the crowd.

"The fight is not over," the judge said. "They are inside the ox-hide and blood has not spilled.

Aldís, breathless, reached over to where Kel's dagger lay. She gripped it in her palm. "This man needs to be lightened a little," she announced to no one in particular. "We need no more of his kind."

Kel bent over, too exhausted to understand. "What do you mean?"

Aldís bent and pressed the scramasax against the man's earlobe. She cut with the knife, *quick quick,* and a second time *quick quick* on the other ear*,* then stood admiring her work. Satisfied, she wiped the blade against the ox-hide that covered the duel-ground and handed the knife back to Kel.

"Blood has touched the hide!" the duel-judge declared. "The fight is over." He began to list the farms and property that the challenger had forfeited. For a final time that day, an almost-certain victim ended up with more gain than he could possibly have imagined.

As the judge spoke, the defeated holmganger began to thrash about on the ox-hide. He sat up holding his head, his eyes unfocused.

"Did I win?" he asked. "Is he dead?"

The circle of people, absorbed in listening to the judge, glanced over at the fallen holmganger. A snicker sounded. One by one they began laugh and point as loud guffaws rang out.

"What?" the man demanded. "What makes you laugh like drunken boys?"

They pointed to his ear. "Barrow-pig," they laughed. "Balls-gone!"

He felt it, flinching at the cuts. A pig-herder, holding his sides with laughter and his eyes streaming, mimicked for the crowd how to remove the testicles of a male piglet, and the notching of the pig's ears to indicate the absence of sex organs.

"You know, ye great warrior," he said, doubling over with laughter and wiping away the tears, "we notch the ears of pigs *just as yours are now,* to show which of our boars have balls, and which do not." He staggered off howling with humor, and the challenger shouted with impotent fury.

Kel sheathed his sword and wiped his face. "You wanted to talk?"

"I'm too tired," she replied. She could not begin to talk now, not after all that had happened that day. Aldís gripped Kel's tunic, feeling the rough linen in her hand. She stared into his face as if searching for something and then abruptly turned and drifted away.

Kel could almost swear he heard the words 'when I'm ready' floating on the evening air behind Aldís.

Wishful thinking, fool, he told himself. Still, he had done good today, and she had helped. It was something.

. . .

Chapter Nineteen

Once again, Naldrum hovered outside the red-and-yellow striped tent. *Ridiculous that I must stand here asking to come in like a common man,* he fumed. Still, better to negotiate.

He had sent his guard away with Ankya. Being alone made him defenseless, an unwelcome sensation, but it was better not to have anyone witness if Rota mocked him again.

He cleared his throat. "Let me in. "It's Naldrum, of Bull Valley."

Rota, inside, ignored him. She trailed her finger over a tray of beads, admiring them. "The amber ones are lovely," she murmured to herself. "People say they carry druid-magic. But these foil-glass ones gleam beautifully." The shining layers of gold, silver and copper sandwiched between layers of glass required expert work.

Rota murmured each type of bead as she touched them with her fingertip. "Carnelian. Jet. Glass-eye. Thousand-color."

Naldrum called again, and wiped sweat from his brow, wondering if anyone heard him.

"Be patient," she called and returned to her pleasant perusal of the expensive wares. After she finished, she sat for a short while with her eyes closed, exhaling, deciding.

"Return these to your mistress," she directed the bead-seller's assistant. "Tell her I want a necklace made with three of the foil-glass and ten of the amber beads, to be delivered tomorrow."

Haakon Sigurdsson would pay handsomely for her work here, but he would not mind—or know about these beads.

. . .

Naldrum perched on the edge of the tiny bench Rota offered. For the life of him, he could not turn the conversation as he wished. He had gone in intending to bluster and threaten, but Rota slithered away each time he pressed her. Not a patient man, and anxious to leave, Naldrum burst out. "Just say what it is that Haakon wants me to do."

Rota made her voice soothing. "Only this, fine sir. To ask yourself which matters more: loyalty to your country, or to something greater?"

Naldrum tried to think of an answer that another chieftain might give but failed. Rota saw, and the honey in her voice dripped sweeter. "Perhaps I might help. Perhaps you feel loyalty to yourself. To …supremacy."

He smiled widely. "I do value that. More than anything." Naldrum rushed ahead. "In exchange for what? I tell you know, I cannot—" he stopped himself to correct his words, "will not pay the tenth you demand."

"The gaining of supremacy comes dear. But the *having* of it pays us back a thousand-fold."

He felt confused. What did she mean? "Yes, of course, everyone knows that."

"One can use authority to do good, so that poets flock to compose songs in our honor."

Naldrum found that thought attractive. "Of course, but I already have that."

Rumors say you pay your skalds poorly and their work is mediocre. "Or perhaps one uses authority to gain more authority."

He fidgeted, unwilling to say that again he did not understand. Rota ignored his fingers drumming on the table and continued.

"Think what you could accomplish if those who disagreed with you could be silenced."

Naldrum tipped his head and considered Rota from the corner of his eye. Who had told her that many of the *gothi* disagreed vehemently with him? The idea of silencing his critics appealed to Naldrum.

"How does one make that happen?" he asked.

Rota saw eagerness fill Naldrum. She pictured her new necklace. *Perhaps a longer one. The same number of amber beads but each of them alternated with pure gold ones.* She would have this imbecile pay for it himself before she left the festival.

"I can teach you the path to control others," she said. "You have some control, but not nearly as much as you want—or need. Now, some might think you need more gold, more weapons, more followers. But these are crude tools; nothing beside true weapons of control."

Naldrum almost salivated in his longing to hear what she said. Rota paused, making him wait.

"You long to know, don't you? Well then, I will tell you, but the telling comes at a cost."

"Anything," he said. "Tell me."

"You do not wish to know the cost first?"

"Tell me. I can afford whatever you want."

Rota's eyes narrowed slightly. *Can you, my arrogant friend?* "Then we have an agreement, and I will collect what you have agreed to when I choose. Now, for your lesson."

Naldrum leaned forward with his mouth open.

"The path to ultimate authority is simple. First, one must spread three darknesses, like grains of seeds cast onto a field. From them, your control of others will grow."

Naldrum rubbed his shoulders, chilled despite the fire crackling in the floor pit. Was Rota a *scinlaece,* one of those hated Saxon wizards who claimed to work with dead phantoms and evil spirits?

Rota saw his unease and smiled to herself. She spoke low, forcing Naldrum to bend forward to hear her. "The three darknesses are these: *Fear of change. Assignment of blame, whether deserved or not. Punishment of those who oppose you.*"

"Such nonsense? Just words! Nothings," he blurted. Maybe this woman had magicked the Jarl of Lade. He smelled an odd odor, felt dizzy. *She's just trying to frighten me. This wench is no match for me.* "You've given naught but a bit of mumbling. Let's talk about what I want: there's a woman—"

Rota ignored him. "Spare me your stupidity, *gothi,*" she snapped. "We can discuss what you want another day. P*ay attention, you fool.* After you have spread darkness, you must divert those who are afraid with something to hope for…something you control."

Naldrum lunged from his seat towards her, his face contorted in a snarl. Rota remained motionless, her own features disdainful. Her calm composure halted Naldrum. He meekly took his chair again.

"For now, gothi, do your work. Across this autumn and winter, bend your attention to things that annoy you or worry you. Don't tell me nothing does; no man is that brave. Things that fret you at night. Focus on those things, how they threaten your life with unwelcome changes. Teach others to feel the same. Instill *fear of change.*"

He did not protest again, just sat listening, vexed by her distain.

"As you point out your dislike of such things, you must also accuse your enemies of promoting these troublesome ideas…and then assure your valley people that *you will punish those responsible.* Sow these three darknesses across the seasons to come. At the same time, find something that will inspire people to hope. Come the spring, I will seek you out to learn what harvest you have reaped for the Jarl, and we will discuss the next steps to happen at next summer's Althing."

"Your plan seems ridiculously childish. And what do you mean, 'harvest?' I have weapons and men who will do my bidding—" but Rota cut off his words.

"Would they die for you at this point? Lay down their lives in anger at those who oppose you? If not, then you have no real control. Do not disappoint me by thinking you understand these things." Her voice had the sharp brilliance of cut tin. "I give you this advice in order that you may begin to understand just how powerful I am. In the spring, we will speak again of what your tribute to Haakon will be. For now, just do as I tell you. And since you said you can afford whatever cost is needed, you may thank me for my gift of knowledge today buy going to the bead-seller and telling her you will pay for the necklace she is making for me."

Rota stood and indicated the tent door. Naldrum staggered out, confused, like a bull that had charged a haystack and no longer knew where to aim its horns.

. . .

Tor finished the last mending work of the day and scattered the coals of his forge fire. He had enriched Naldrum by many cattle-marks, repairing everything from cooking cauldrons to plows. True to the prediction he had made to Kel that morning, the initial fascination with him had diminished. Now only a few children hung about, hammering at scrap bits of metal with stones, along with several girls who would be in the bride-fair. They made flirtatious glances, hoping the handsome blacksmith might happen past them later.

Tor intended to go to the shoreline, where he would do as he had many times across the years: describe his wife and ask those from distant ports if they had seen a woman like her. The quest had carried him to this distant island, far from his homeland.

But he felt famished. *Just some pottage first, and then I'll go.*

Tor pushed his way through the crowd at one of the common-tents, looking for a table with a bit of space. People already sitting along the bench edged a little closer, making room for him.

He sank down. The hard wood of the trestle seat felt good against the backs of his tired legs. Tor realized this was the first time he had sat down since before dawn. He dug hungrily into the food.

A woman across from him whispered to her companion. "That's the one, you reckon?"

The man didn't even lift his head from his meal. "That's the one."

She tapped Tor's arm. "Fellow's been looking for someone who matches your description."

Tor felt too tired to care about those who had not yet had a chance to gawk at him. He handed his already-empty bowl to one of the passing serving-girls in exchange for a full one. She cringed a little, seeing on his hands the marks of an outlaw, but the woman across from Tor spoke up.

"Yah, he's all right. His headman cut 'm there, and his headman's brought 'im here to the Althing, so don't you get in a fret about it." She had heard Kel's exhortation of the crowd but had been as impressed by the calm concentration in his eyes as by Tor's strength.

"Thank you," Tor mumbled, his mouth full.

"Did you hear me? Fellow looking for you. Fellow from a ship."

Tor stopped mid-chew. "Who?"

She pointed to a man sagged in a corner, clearly intoxicated, his toothless mouth wide open. "That one. Kept saying how proud he was to have gotten a message from someone named Indaell to you. Looks as if he drank up every bit of whatever reward you gave him."

"He says he gave me a message? I've not spoken with that man."

"Well, he seems to think he talked to you."

Tor rose and put down his bowl. He climbed around and over the other people eating until he reached the toothless man.

"You there," he said, shaking the man's shoulder. "Hey."

The man did not respond. Tor shook him harder. "Wake up. You have a message for me?"

The man's eyes flickered open. He saw Tor's face, the dark skin, and he smiled.

"…found her…" he slurred.

"Indaell told you? She found someone? A woman?"

The man nodded, happy to help. "Found her…"

"Found her where?" But the man did not answer. He shook his head from side to side.

"You told someone. Who was it?" Tor pressed. The man's breath came rapidly, too light.

"*Gothi*," he said. "Secret."

Tor's blood ran cold. *No one must know about her.*

"Which *gothi*?" he cried. "What color cloak?"

"Don't know," said the man. "Friend said tell *gothi*...find you."

"His name...tell me," Tor shouted. People paused, food halfway to their mouths, wondering what the commotion was about.

The man's face fell forward towards his chest. Tor shook him again, rattling his head back and forth on his neck. "Please. His name." He held the man's head up, tried to focus his eyes. "Please!"

To his horror, he saw blood drool from the man's gaping mouth. Still, the sailor tried.

"Nal-something," he said thick and slow. Then his eyes sharpened, and he looked straight at Tor. "Naldrum. He's going to get her for you.

. . .

The trickle of blood became a flood gushing from the sailor's toothless mouth, and he sagged lifeless in Tor's hands.

. . .

Naldrum had learned about his wife? Did he know about the children too? Tor's thoughts, normally so controlled, spiraled towards terror. His strong faith buckled under a wave of fear.

Indaell knew I was searching for a place to hide the children. She would never say a word about them, he reassured himself. *Don't panic. Think. Be calm.*

But calm would not come. Tor slid his hands up along the sides of his head, grabbed handfuls of hair, and strode from the tent, wracked with anguish.

. . .

He went straight to the lake where merchants congregated and rushed from skiff to skiff. "A man with no teeth and no hair," he said to the first merchant he encountered. "Any idea who he is?"

To the next skiff and the next. Most were empty. Some had a sailor watching the wares. One man thought he remembered a fellow with no teeth but could not be sure. Tor sank down, his back to a *byrder*, and prepared to wait. A deep fog began to rise from the lake, and exhausted, Tor fell asleep.

. . .

A kick woke him. "What the—?" A man was picking himself up, having tripped over Tor.

"I'm sorry," Tor said. "I fell asleep waiting for someone."

"Why do you sleep on a damp bank instead of up at the tents?"

"A toothless sailor said he had a message for me from a woman called Indaell. She often works the route from Hedeby to Dublin. Was hoping someone might know how I can reach her."

"Why don't you ask your toothless fellow? I've seen him around."

"He's—" Tor stopped. No sense mentioning that the man lay dead, murdered in the food tent. It would put Tor at the center of unwelcome attention. "It's Indaell I need."

"Well, you're in luck, sort of. I heard she's in quay in the Faroe Islands. I'm heading up the North-way when I leave Althing. We'll probably come back via the Faroes. I can try to find her there."

Only a sliver, but at least it was something. "I'm indebted to you. Can you get word to her?"

"Sure enough. Costs nothing to carry messages back and forth."

"Just say this: her message reached the wrong man. The woman is in danger, and I cannot help."

Tiller, not knowing anything of what the toothless sailor had told Naldrum, misunderstood. "I don't think any of us needs to worry on Indaell's score. She may be tiny, but she's as tough as they come. I highly doubt she's in any danger."

Tor dared not correct him. "Just give her that exact message. She'll understand."

Tiller shrugged. "If you say so. Now you ought to get off this shoreline. Folks say that lake-spirits drift in the fog can make you sick, lying down like that in the damp." He laughed, unwilling to believe the stories. "Besides, now you owe me a favor. You can start by spotting me to a brimming ale-horn. I've just gotten some profitable work, and I want to celebrate."

. . .

Tor paid for Tiller's ale out of what he had earned for Naldrum that day. They walked out of the crowded tent and found seats on flat boulders nearby. This *vikinger* was such a slim connection to his wife, but because of it, Tor found himself unwilling to leave.

Do I say something? He wondered. *Ask him to keep watch in his travels for a woman whose skin looks like mine?* He struggled with the pros and cons of it. Better to say nothing of his wife or even Naldrum. The headman likely had spies everywhere, and this man might be one.

Likewise, Tiller said nothing of the voyage he was about to undertake for Naldrum. He drank his ale, looking at Tor's skin. It was dark, like the woman Naldrum wanted him to fetch. The market for Gaelic and Scoti slaves had dwindled. Maybe exotics were the only profitable trades now.

They talked about port towns they had each visited. Tor had the gift of storytelling, and repeatedly made Tiller laugh at sardonic portrayals of wealthy seaside burghers and shrewd hagglers from the Scoti-lands. As they talked, Tor stayed alert for any mention of a dark-skinned woman, but Tiller said nothing of the sort.

When the ale-server brought another flagon, Tor reached a point of desperation. Just as he opened his mouth to ask Tiller directly about any dark women he'd seen in his travels, a third man joined them.

"Dragon's teeth," said Tiller. "Thorgest, how'd they pry you away from your valley?"

The graying farmer snorted. "My new wife informed me I was taking her to the fiftieth Althing or she would divorce me. I told her to come on her own, but—" His voice trailed off. "You know."

"I'm glad she got her way. Good to see you." Tiller clapped Thorgest on the back. "Since I know you're only happy at home with your flocks, let me get you an ale-horn to ease the pain of being around this many people." He disappeared into the crowd, leaving Tor and Thorgest alone.

"You sail with Tiller?" Thorgest asked.

"No. I used to work for a ship-merchant, but now I work here on a farm."

"What *gothi*?"

"Naldrum, a chieftain of Bull Valley."

Thorgest snorted and spat on the ground. "That's what I think of him. But there's plenty that seem to think highly of him."

Tor said nothing. Soon Tiller reappeared with two brimming horns. "One for you, Thorgest, and one for you, my new friend."

Tor shook his head.

"What? No ale for you?"

"My people do not drink spirits that cloud men's minds." At their dismay, Tor laughed. "Trust me, many days I wish I could join you."

"Who would know?" asked Thorgest, but Tor did not reply.

Tiller leaned forward. "I need to come to your farm soon, Thorgest, to finally get my high-seat pillars. You've done me a huge favor to hold them for me this long. When I get back from my next trading run, I'll be ready to start on a longhouse of my own. They'll make a fine display in it."

Such long travels those pillars have seen. Tiller wondered if they would erase the pain of his past.

"When might you be getting them?" Thorgest asked, his expression even more glum than before.

"I intended to come to you straight after Althing, but I have work I need to do first." Tiller silently calculated the days needed: a straight shot up the North-way current to Trondheim, search for the woman he'd been told to find, then back across the Nor'way sea. The return always proved harder than the trip north due to fighting the sea currents. He'd have to go down to the Orkney Islands, then across to the Faroes, then back up to Iceland. He added in the time for a horseback ride up the Bull River valley to Naldrum's to deliver the woman, ride back down the valley to his ship, then around the southern and half the western coast of Iceland to reach Thorgest's valley.

"With great weather, I'll be back in a few weeks. Even if storms delay us, I'll get there no later than autumn. Equal-night-and day, at the latest," Tiller predicted. "You told me not to worry about how long it took me to take them back, but gods, Thorgest, I'm just now realizing they've been cluttering up your place nearly a year already. I promise I'll come straight to you after I get back."

"That's too long. You know the rule," said Thorgest. His friendly demeanor became abrupt. "You know the law. After a year and a month, they become mine. You need to pick them up before you go on that voyage, or you'll miss the deadline."

Tiller ignored the change in Thorgest's tone. He shook his head. "I have to go. You have my word, friend, you'll see me as soon as I get back." He laughed, not noticing that Thorgest was now frowning into his ale-horn. "You're just threatening me because you think I'll postpone again and your wives will be complaining at you about tripping over them for another winter."

Thorgest lifted his ale-horn and drained the contents.

"Always good to see you, Tiller," he said. "Do what you must but mind my words. Law's on my side. Don't be late. *Please*." He nodded at Tor and walked off.

Tiller watched him leave, mildly perplexed. "Thorgest's not usually moody like that. We've been friends for as long as I can remember. He was like a second father to me. I taught all of his sons to sail." He slapped his leg. "That old fox was just joking with me.

He's probably annoyed because he hates to leave his farm. He knows how much those pillars mean to me. He would never keep them."

In not much longer, Kalendar walked among the tents and lane calling the *seventh-eighth* in the bright sunlight.

"Agh, nearly middle-night. I need to sleep," Tiller yawned. "Always too little rest this time of year."

The enslaved man Tor sat fraught with worry as servants cleared ale-horns from trestle tables in the empty beer tent. *What should he do?* Indaell might be anywhere. His wife might be anywhere. He could not just run after Tiller, ask to go on the first ship to leave Iceland and madly cast about the ports looking for her. *I did that for years,* Tor reminded himself. *Not one trace, ever, as to where she was.*

He looked across the sky, full of color and light. In the winter months, he often pictured the moon or starts shining on both his wife and him, binding them somehow in light. But no comforting night-time stars twinkled during the endless light of mid-summer.

Things appeared and disappeared in the sky. Perhaps life and humans were the same. One day she was there. One day she had disappeared. Perhaps one day she would appear again, and all would be well.

"The Almighty One brought me to this land," he told himself. "He led me to a safe haven for my children. Today I learned that my wife is still alive, and Indaell knows where she is. For now, there is no clear course I can follow. I must stay in this land where my children live, and trust that the same Allah who has kept her alive and protected our children will help us."

Breathe in. Breathe out. But the practice that normally helped Tor find peace within eluded him tonight. To profess trust in The One was one thing, but actually feeling it under such circumstances seemed quite another matter. Tor left the ale-tent and headed back to the common grounds, distraught and exhausted, yearning for his family.

. . .

Chapter Twenty

Naldrum paced back and forth across his large tent, shouting in temper, his face florid with fury. Servants pretended to work as they tried to stay out of his way. One of his wives directed them, but she, too, was trying to avoid Naldrum's notice, even as she murmured responses to his tirade.

Only his daughter Ankya seemed oblivious to Naldrum's anger. She watched Kel, fuming where he stood in front of Naldrum, and considered several things.

Why had her father become so angry when she said she'd seen Kel fighting in the holmgang duels? Who were those two new guards? She had never seen them before, but they now wore the colors of her father's household. Why ever had they bound Kel with a rope? Who was the woman who had been Kel's shield-bearer? Was she the one Kel was 'chasing'? Hiding intense jealousy, Ankya lounged on rich bedding of silks and furs, arching her back and turning her elegant body this way and that in hopes of attracting Kel's attention. He could not help but see her and wondered how Naldrum could ignore his daughter's ridiculous posturing.

Naldrum glared at his steward, his mouth turned down in ugly lines. "Get out of this tent, all of you," he shouted at his wife and servants. They left in relief, but Ankya ignored him and stayed, preening herself.

Naldrum erupted at Kel. "My steward fought like a common brawler in the holmgang duels today? Tell me I heard wrong."

Kel glared in return. "You heard correctly. What of it? And why have these guards bound me as if I was a common thief?" *Toad*, he thought.

The headman seethed in rage. He could not admit to Kel that the duels today had cost Naldrum dearly: nine farms, all told, plus thralls and livestock.

"The holmgang is for people too poor or too ignorant to make use of the council trials," Naldrum bawled. "My own steward, fighting among such rabble? You make me look small." He kicked his dog.

Kel stood unmoving. "No law forbids any free person—steward, farmer, trader or even gothi—from participating in the duels."

"You defy me? I will not have my household besmirched by such lowly affiliation."

"Then perhaps you need a new steward." Kel's voice was flat and hard. In the corner of the tent, he could see Ankya react in dismay. She ran to Kel and flung her arms around him.

"Father, no," she cried to Naldrum. "You must keep Kel. I only feel safe when he guards us. If you release him, I'll…I'll run away!"

Naldrum blanched. "You wouldn't."

"I would, Papa." Her lashes were wet with tears. "I'll throw myself into the waterfalls."

Naldrum turned to Kel. "Do not threaten my precious daughter's happiness. Servants worthy of the house of Naldrum come few and far between. I—only I, not you—will decide when I intend to replace you."

"Then we have a problem, sir." Kel slid the words between his teeth. "Not being a thrall, I can do what I want. And what I want is to leave your service, now." He pushed Ankya away.

"You cannot. We have a contract that binds you."

"Refresh your memory. Our contract started during Althing, all those years ago. That means it expires at Althing. I no longer owe you any loyalty."

"We'll see about that. Bring her in," Naldrum screeched. Another man Kel did not recognize appeared, pulling a woman.

Kel froze. Aldís, her arms tied and a rough gag in her mouth, fought the man who dragged her.

The woman from the fight. Ankya covered her mouth in delight at this splendid development.

"How dare you hurt her?" Kel lunged at Naldrum, but the guards behind the steward jerked the rope tight.

Naldrum smirked. "I understand that this woman assisted you in the holmgang duels. Perhaps she will assist me also." He looked over a dish of imported dried fruits on his table, choosing a plum. He bit into it, found it sour, and threw it to a piglet that lay grunting in the corner.

"Your knife," Naldrum directed the guard. The man pulled out the knife he had used on the Danish sailor.

"Oh," said Ankya. "Another cutting!" She clapped her hands in excitement.

"Ankya, stop it," Naldrum reprimanded his daughter. "Your behavior is unseemly."

"You wouldn't," Kel shouted. "Don't hurt Aldís, I beg you."

"Oh, I have no intention of simply *hurting* her. You have a choice: stay as my steward and obey me, or my guard will put the knife in her throat. It matters little to me."

Kel could see the blade pressing against a vein that pulsed in Aldís' neck. One move and her blood would spurt.

The new guard's eyes were small and cold and cruel. They drilled into Kel's. *I'll have that steward's job one day,* he thought. *If Kel even blinks, I'll slice this woman.*

Kel could tell the man's intentions. His jaw hardened. "Let her go," he retorted. "I give you my word, if you hurt her, I'll destroy you. I'm only warning you once, you monster."

"A monster I may be, perhaps," Naldrum agreed, selecting another fruit, "but one wielding all the power right now. I have no intention of letting her go without your guarantee."

"Threatening to murder a woman just to keep me in your employ is madness. You can get any steward you want."

"But none skilled as you, especially in certain matters I require."

Kel saw fury in Aldís' eyes. She shook her head, *don't do what he says.* But Kel knew he could not bear to let Naldrum hurt her. Revolted at his choice Kel went down on one knee to the headman.

"I yield, *gothi.* You win. I'll do whatever you want. Please let her go without harm."

Yield. The ancient term of giving respect to one's better, of pledging fealty to a deserved leader. Aldís looked away, repulsed.

Naldrum heard the compliment in the word, and he puffed. "A wise choice. For the life of me, I can't understand what this rough woman means to you." He nodded to the guard, who pulled the gag from her mouth and untied the rope.

Naldrum waited for a torrent of abuse from Aldís, almost gleeful to hear the anger she carried. But Aldís said nothing. She walked slowly around the headman and never took her eyes from him, even though Kel could see her visibly trembling. As she completed the circle, Aldís muttered something, too quick for Naldrum to catch, and then she spat on the front of his rich tunic.

When he struck at her, Aldís leaped back, as if his touch would be poison. Naldrum staggered, unused to fighting, and fell against Aldís. He clutched at her tunic, his expression almost pleading with her to remove whatever curse she had invoked.

"Quit pawing at me, vermin," she cursed. "You're so vile that your spirit feels rotten to me. I pity you. Odin's wolves would refuse your carcass." She backed away, revolted.

Naldrum staggered to his feet. "Get out of my tent, both of you. And Steward, I expect to see you in full regalia tomorrow morning for the start of the Law Circle. I intend to make a suitable entrance. This was your last warning. Cross me and I *will* have her killed. I told you when you first agreed to work for me that you were to stay away from her. Did you think I had forgotten?"

Kel did not answer. Naldrum snatched at his sleeve. "You doubt me? Did you see the marks on her wrist, Kel? I had that done to her, years ago, because you ignored me."

Kel blanched. "Why? I did as you said. I never saw her."

"Yes, you did," Naldrum retorted. "Admit it."

Kel did not answer. There had been that one time. How did Naldrum know?

"Do you want her death on your conscience?" the headman taunted. "Be clever and forget about her, once and for all."

Kel shook off Naldrum's clawing fingers. "I'm a man of my word. I'll stay on as your steward, for now. You just won another year for yourself. But don't think you can tell me how to feel. And if you hurt her, our contract terminates—and I'll revenge her pain, with interest."

He turned to Aldís and pulled her from the tent.

. . .

Naldrum stood staring at the door flap after they left. "That cursed steward has worked for me too long. I need someone I can trust to do my bidding—and someone who doesn't steal a fortune from me in the holmgang duels." He nodded to the man who had held Aldís. "You're ugly, with your little pig-eyes, but if he crosses me again, you'll do."

This Althing had barely begun, and so much mess already. Naldrum sighed, annoyed. He had barely had a chance to talk to the other valley leaders to see if they, too, had heavy rains, and if it had affected their farms. Famines might come. They would mean fewer sales and smaller profits, maybe even a loss for the year. Frustrated by Kel's disloyalty, disgusted that Aldís had spat on him, and now feeling anger at the idea that starving people could spare no silver for trade goods, Naldrum flung off his cape and sat heavily on a stool.

"I'd have cut that strange woman for you, Father. Would that make you happy?" Ankya stroked Naldrum's hair, eager to placate her father, her cheeks pink with excitement at the thought of blood again.

Naldrum shuddered. *On top of everything else, Ankya's oddness.* But the words 'strange woman' reminded Naldrum of his triumph today, worth far more than any miserable farms: the creature of whom the toothless sailor spoke, the woman so important to Tor.

I am going to acquire her. I'll flaunt her in front of my beastly slave. Maybe use her as a bed-warmer. That, certainly, would finally humiliate that damnable mountain of a man. Cheered, Naldrum rooted in the dish for another dried fruit, but only plums remained in the bowl. He threw the expensive treats to the piglet and cursed.

. . .

Ankya followed Kel and Aldís out of the tent. She mimicked Aldís, spitting on the ground behind them. "The curse you put on my father returns to you," she said, wishing she knew some magic.

"Go inside, child. You know nothing of how to bind a curse. And you know nothing of what your father does to women," said Aldís.

Returning inside, Ankya sulked at Naldrum. "She's mean. You *should* let me cut her."

Naldrum blanched and backed away. "Go shopping," he said. "Leave matters of fighting to men; we're better suited to them."

Men such as that holmganger Aldís humiliated? But Ankya kept her face docile. "Of course, father," she murmured, her voice sweet. "You always know best."

. . .

Aldís, stubborn and unrelenting, stood rubbing where the rope had chafed her arms.

"You know why he did this?" she asked Kel.

"Cut those marks on your wrist, you mean?"

"No, Kel," Aldís interrupted. "Why he is angry about the *holmgangs.*"

"I have no idea. I was just fighting because I needed a distraction. Maybe I wanted to do something decent for somebody. Why does Naldrum care about the cursed holmgang duels?"

"You honestly don't know?"

He shook his head, and Aldís snorted in exasperation.

"How is it possible that you work for him and still do not know about such things? Your Naldrum has his allies and spies ride about the entire country to select farms he might want to acquire. Instead of buying them—because they usually are not for sale, for where would the farmer and his family go? —Naldrum hides behind professional holmgangers like that one. They're not claim-fighting for themselves, Kel. They might issue the challenge, but the winnings go to Naldrum."

Kel's stomach turned over. "That's why I've seen some of those men at his compound. They trade the farms for some reward."

"Exactly. The farm stays in the holmganger's name, but Naldrum reaps the harvests and the profits."

How the rich get richer, Kel thought.

"But it's worse than that," Aldís continued. "He doesn't just target vulnerable or elderly freeholders with the best land; Naldrum does it as an act of revenge against those who speak against him. You don't want to give half your piglets up for the quarter-tax? Don't want to pay the butter-tithe he demands?"

Kel interrupted her. "Quarter-taxes and tithes are collected to help those who are in need. All *should* pay their share."

"You deluded imbecile. Those taxes and tithes are *supposed* to go to anyone whose pigs sicken or whose herds don't give milk. But who gets them? Naldrum's wealthy favorites! Anyone who protests his cheating usually find their farm challenged the next year by one of Naldrum's holmgangers. That's why he was angry today. You inadvertently took back quite a bit of land and wealth he had collected."

Kel groaned again. "Everything you say makes it harder for me to work for him, and I must. Stop, Aldís, please."

She ignored his request and continued, pacing across the tent.

"You don't want your sons forced into labor for him? Don't want your daughters forced to open their legs for him when he's in your house and you've fallen asleep? Don't want him running his hands over your wife when you turn your back, and then claiming she made it all up? Everyone who stands against Naldrum does so at their own peril. But he's not even brave enough to be honest about it. He has others do his dirty work for him."

Kel knew that last fact only too well. *Ones like me.*

"I hate that man," he said, full of vehemence.

Aldís frowned in surprise. "Your anger sounds real. I thought you knew all this."

"What made you think that?"

"Because you have worked for him for years." She spat the words as if they burned her mouth.

Kel took her wrist and turned it over in his hand. Traced the long scar hacked along her forearm. "Poor Aldís," he said. "Why do I feel that this was somehow my fault?" How had Naldrum found out that Kel had betrayed him that one time to see Aldís again?

"I wonder." His voice had been gentle, questioning, but hers was hard and furious. But even in her anger, Aldís felt the ground under her swaying as the thought came, *have I been wrong all these years, thinking it was Kel who had told Naldrum about my daughter?*

Kel cleared his throat, made an attempt, his voice gruff. "So many things I wish I could go back and do over. I was young and stupid back then. That summer I saw you, here at Althing. Never had a feeling like that before. Hit me in the gut. I had come to look for work, wanted no attachments, nothing to distract me from my future. But there you were, and suddenly everything changed."

She made no reply. How stupid it would sound to admit the same feeling had happened to her? Aldís could not humble herself to ask, even after this long, why he had left without even saying goodbye.

Kel talked hurriedly, as if he had to get the words out. "I had never even looked at the women and girls in the bride-fair before. Really didn't want a wife. I was a free young man. Plenty of—" he skipped the vulgar term, and instead said, "plenty of opportunity to be with any number of women." He drew a deep breath remembering Aldís laughing and talking. *The way her eyes had cut over to me. The way she had sized me up.*

"I knew in that instant I had met my match. You glanced at me and with that one look, invited me and challenged me and dismissed me, all at once. You never stopped talking to your friend. Just the barest hint of a smile on your mouth. You didn't look at me again, but I knew that smile was for me. Every gesture after that, every twirl of your fingers in your hair, you did knowing I could not take my eyes off you. You played me like a fish, waiting to see how long it would take for me to yield. Every line of your body, flaunting, ruthless, teasing me. You were heartless. You were brazen. I wanted you the moment I saw you."

"And you *had* me. Naïve girl that I was." Old bitter resentment in her voice.

"I know," he admitted. "But then—"

"But then *you disappeared.* I thought you were going to woo me, but you didn't. You got what you wanted, and you left. I don't need you to remind me how stupid I was. I had dreams back then, too, Kel. But your loyalty to Naldrum came first back then, and it still does. Between you and your despicable headman, you've ruined my life." She pulled her sleeves down over the marks on her wrist.

"I'm staying with him to protect you." Kel heard his voice grow louder, accusing.

"You can't. I'm a very convenient threat he uses to control you. One day he'll destroy both of us when we no longer serve his purposes. I didn't want you to yield to him, but you bent your knee anyway. Kel, he basically owns you, as if you were one of his thralls, and you let him get away with it. I might have hated you all these years for choosing him over me, but I could at least respect a man who finally had the courage to stand up to Naldrum. You didn't."

"You're right. He *does* use you to control me. And you're right that I don't have the strength to willingly allow him to hurt you. As long as you're alive, I'll never escape Naldrum."

"So ironic, Kel," Every word from Aldís' lips came bitter as poison. "I'm a healer, but I'm powerless to help myself. I'm trapped in what happened between us. You're a strong man, a renowned fighter, but you're weak in the one place I need you to be strong. We never had a chance, did we? We were just two fools tricked by lust."

"No, Aldís. It wasn't just lust and you know it. I loved you the moment I saw you, and I still do. Don't you dare turn your face away when I say it. Call me weak if you want, but it takes every bit of strength I have to keep serving Naldrum when I loathe his very breath. Leaving him means your death. Do you really expect me to abandon the thing most precious to me in all the world?"

"How sad for you," she mocked. "Because of you, the thing most precious to me is gone forever. My little daughter who once breathed and laughed and does no longer, was taken away from me by Naldrum. Could *you* survive *that?* It has taken every bit of strength I have—and I am beginning to lose the battle, Kel. I can feel it in myself. You should have given me over to him. My work keeps me alive at this point, but it won't much longer. What will be your excuse when I'm gone? You should've gotten away when you had the chance just now."

Her anger had built a wall to protect her. Beyond that wall was the place Aldís dared not look. Impossible to descend, too wide to cross, it was a glacier, treacherous, cold, and dangerous, that ground day after day against her wall of iron, rusting it with unyielding pain.

Aldís felt suffocated. "I need to leave."

. . .

Kel watched the purple-blue of her dress until Aldís disappeared from his sight. Despite the brightness of the midnight sun, a killing darkness filled him. But there would be no more holmgang duels left today in which to seek mindless solace. The ox-hide had been taken up and put away until tomorrow. But inside, Kel knew that even a fight to the death couldn't fill the inner chasm left behind by hope held long and now gone forever.

Kel swore and turned towards the horse fields. He would saddle Thunder and they would gallop far from the festival grounds. Being with his beloved stallion would not bring Aldís back and would not restore his once-innocent faith in Althing, but at least he could be with a creature he trusted that did not leave every time he tried to explain.

. . .

Thunder pranced at the far edge of the horse-fields. Kel whistled and the stallion's ears pricked. It half-reared, proud head lifted towards the sun-goddess as if to acknowledge an equal being.

Another piercing whistle. Thunder wheeled and raced across the field, his hooves pounding on the grass.

"There, my fine fellow," Kel said. The bit of carrot disappeared from his outstretched palm, and the horse nuzzled his face. Kel gripped the gleaming mane in his fists and buried his forehead against the muscles of its neck. How to explain to this fierce, magnificent creature that he, Kel, would choose to bow and scrape to Naldrum, to live a life of deceit? How to convey to the stallion how deeply he detested the idea of walking behind Naldrum into the Law Circle tomorrow, pretending to be loyal to his loathed chieftain?

No words. "Ah, Thunder. Let's leave this place for a bit. I need to be away from people."

He sprang onto the horse, tightened his thighs against Thunder's back, and leaned forward, gripping his mount's mane. No need for a saddle or bridle. The wilder this ride, the better. The farther from traps and manipulation, the better. The more animal, the less human corruption, the better. He urged the stallion to go, and they galloped forward, seeking oblivion.

. . .

While Kel rode, Aldís searched for Tor.

"I have to leave, right away," she told him. "I just wanted you to know. I'm going back to the widow to tell her and the children that I saw you—" she stopped at the haggard expression on his face. "What happened, Tor? You look awful."

"She's been found, Aldís. Kandace, my wife. The merchant woman who brought me to Iceland—the one I sold my freedom to, to let me keep looking for Kandace—she sent a message through another *vikinger.*"

Aldís' eyes lit up with joy. "That's wonderful news, Tor. Why do you look unhappy?"

"Because I didn't get the message. Naldrum did."

The sickening news filled Aldís from head to toe. "Oh, no."

"I don't know what to do, Aldís. I don't know what to do." His big hands shook.

Aldís thought quickly. "He hasn't said anything to you or asked you any questions?" When Tor shook his head *no,* she tapped her fingers against her lips. "That means something. He doesn't want you to know he knows. Why?" Her eyes widened. "I'll wager he's going to try and get her."

Tor lifted his head. The idea offered both horror and slim hope. "Do you think?"

"You have no way of finding her, right?"

They both knew the answer. Aldís continued, "If he's looking for her, it's dead certain that Naldrum will bring her to his homestead."

"Then what? He will have her as his slave. I cannot bear thinking what he intends with her."

"Then we will find a way to get her away from him. Somehow. I don't know how." They stared at one another in grim acknowledgement of the massive challenge they faced.

"Listen, Tor," said Aldís. "I'm leaving Althing today. I'm on my way to the lake to look for a boat. I'll tell widow Eilíf that you're alive and well. I'll tell your children you love them. And I'll let her know she may have more mouths to feed one day. Let's leave it at that for now. You need something to hold onto to stay sane."

Three short conversations, yet he trusted this woman completely. Tor watched Aldís hurry towards the shore, then knelt right in the path, touched his forehead to the ground, and thanked Allah.

. . .

When Kel returned to the festival grounds, sweat soaked his tunic and Thunder's flanks shone wet. Kel led the stallion back to the pasture, rubbed it with the dry bits of his tunic, brushed it. Then he went towards the beer tents, where late-night revelers lingered.

"Here's our hero of the holmgang!" One of the landowners Kel had saved leapt up from his table to clasp Kel, pounding him on the back. Someone pressed a frothing ale-horn into Kel's hand, and a cheer broke out.

"To Kel Coesson!"

"To Kel!" Toasts rang in the air. Drink after drink arrived, until Kel had to laugh and decline. "I have to work tomorrow, my friends. My body is weary from the fights, and I cannot afford a splitting headache as well."

Other gifts came. Meat, bread, cheese. Wrist cuffs. Beads for his hair.

And more, these from women. Men peered into their ale flasks, pretending not to notice but silently supportive at what they knew was a thank-offering. *The steward of one of the richest men in the land, standing up for us, the poor.* Kel had put his life in danger for them. Anything they could give back, he deserved. *Anything at all.*

A woman, handing Kel a dish of sausages, let her hand linger on his shoulder. Another sat next to him, combing his hair, re-braiding his hair. One across the table took a bit of roasted chicken from her own plate, held it to Kel's lips. After he had eaten it, she put her fingers in her mouth, tasting. Licked them clean.

The touches spoke without words. *Anything we can do to thank you. Anything at all.* After a while, Kel let them lead him to a tent.

He smiled, but it did not erase the sadness in his eyes. He took what was freely given and savored it, and thanked them for their attentions. The release gave another kind of oblivion, for a while, at least.

· · ·

Chapter Twenty-One

Aldís's boots crunched on the wet edge of the lake shore. Across the past few days, small *byrder*-boats had furiously shuttled goods up from the merchant ships at the coast, but with booths all filled with fresh wares, the little vessels now sat idle. She knew it unlikely that any would head downstream to replenish supplies again, so she was grateful and surprised to find three men and a woman at one byrder making preparations to leave.

"Are you taking passengers?" Aldís asked. "What's your fee?"

"If you work, you can come for free." Tiller hummed as he worked. He threw a length of rope into the vessel. "We're short a deckhand because nobody wants to leave Althing this early."

"I can work."

"Good. We need to get across the lake and to the Ölfusá river in time to catch the outgoing tide and ride it down to the sea. That means we won't be portaging at any of the rock-falls. It'd take too long. Running rapids in a *byrder* is fast and dangerous. Ever done it before?"

"Yes." *When did I become such a liar?*

"Good. Then you know what to do. Just stay on your knees when we hit the white water, keep braced, and have the oar ready to push against rocks. Don't fall overboard."

Aldís tossed her small bundle into the boat and climbed over the thwart. Tiller raised the byrder's sail and a fresh breeze pushed them across the waters. In almost no time, the portage-boat had reached the other shore of Althing Lake.

Desperate to distract herself, Aldís pictured the flow of water starting from where she had sat on the Law Rock this morning, listening to the gurgling *Öxará*, the Ax-river, fall into Thing-valley over the cliff of god-rocks. The Ax broke into little streams that crisscrossed the Althing valley, some so small that Aldís remembered a childhood game of jumping across them, and then rippled into Althing Lake.

On the opposite side, another small flow exited, the very beginning of the *Sog* river, in whose water the byrder soon floated. The Sog widened ahead of them, pouring first into the *Úlfljót*, Wolf-Lake, and then the Swan-lake, *Álfta*.

From there the ever-larger flow tumbled south to the frothing white-river, *Hvítá*. The enjoined waters became the *Ölfusá*, where the byrder would race on the outgoing tide to the sea, where Tiller's ship lay waiting on the sand.

I'm allowed to be happy. I'm allowed to feel safe. Aldís said the words that had pleased her only this morning, but now they gave her no comfort. What did give comfort was her next thought: *I'll take that ship on the sea, and I will never have to see Kel Coesson again.*

. . .

Aldís heard the roar of the rapids ahead and braced, waiting for them. Soon the small craft plunged through the foaming water and rocks in a dizzying drop. When the byrder reached a calm stretch,

Aldís leaned over the side of the boat and reached her fingertips towards the *water-nixies,* the spirits of the flowing stream.

"Daughters of Freydis," she prayed, "please watch over Tor. Please bring his wife safely to him. And as for Kel Coesson…" she hesitated, then plunged her whole hand into the water, her palm wide, beseeching the nixie. "Let me forget him, once and for all. Hide his memory from my thoughts. That man…" she choked in fear. "Hide my path from him, please. Keep me safe from him. Please, I beg you." Aldís pulled her hand from the water, kissed the wet on her fingertips to seal her entreaty to the *nixies.*

She suddenly remembered she had not spoken to Kel about the matter she had intended. *Too late now,* Aldís told herself. *Not that it matters anyway.* She flicked the words she should have spoken to Kel into the waters and let the river-nixies carry it away. *Too, too late.*

The sound of more rapids approached. Aldís braced her knees against the side of the ship again and held out the oar towards the foaming rocks.

. . .

Tiller watched the sail fill with fresh ocean air of the North-way winds. They lifted the merchant *knarr* over the waves as it rode the sea currents.

Odin's eye, it felt good to be away from land. On the open waters with none of the confining rules and filth of the barnyard. *On the waves, everything clean. No pigs burrowing, no smells of the outhouse, no stable manure to rake and trundle to the fields.* Just the fresh wind and the simple rhythms of water and wave. Raise the sail, adjust it, lower it. Ride the sea as a bird rode the wind, effortless and free. No paths, no narrow tracks where a horse had to pick its way through lava fields, just wide-open water and sky. *Perfection.*

But then, the other matter: one could not sail forever. *Sail first, till after,* the saying went. Most *vikingers,* men and women, eventually found a place on land to call home, married, had children to care for them in old age. Farms were more and more scarce, but this voyage would make it possible to build a decent longhouse, buy sheep and horses—and to get his family's ancient high-seat pillars from Thorgest. Maybe one day establish a chieftainship of his own. How fortunate that he had been on the lake shore when Naldrum came by.

Tiller stood at the helm, the steering board in his hand. *You, a headman?* The sarcastic voice in his head, always cutting. *I came from a line of kings,* Tiller reminded it.

Your father was a killer and an outlaw, it reminded him.

I am not my father. The same conversation, year in and year out. Now, with a chance at last to realize his dream, Tiller could hardly believe his luck. Of course, it all depended on getting safely out of Trondheim with Naldrum's stolen thrall. If that went awry, all those big plans would go back to being just dreams—if he and his crew even survived getting this woman back for Naldrum.

Tiller turned his thoughts on exactly how to acquire her. Could he really sail into Haakon's harbor, find the Jarl's house, find the woman, get her back to the ship, and get out to sea before anyone knew what had happened? Haakon Sigurdsson reportedly lived in a large dwelling surrounded by a tall wall and guards. Even if Tiller could find a way in, she might be anywhere. A single startled onlooker might sound an alarm. It might be returning Naldrum's stolen property, but Haakon would declare it thievery. If caught, he'd be run through with a sword.

On the other hand, he could bargain. From what Tiller knew of Haakon, that, too, would be a doomed effort. He had nowhere near the silver the jarl had no doubt spent to acquire her and Naldrum had made it clear that he would not pay until Tiller delivered the woman to him.

The last option, which Tiller liked least, involved some reconnaissance and trickery. *Never thought I'd be sneaking around like a common cattle-reaver* he thought, his jaw set.

Tiller adjusted the steering-board and eyed the sail. It billowed full. The members of the small crew worked at small tasks, and the sun shone.

It would take a bit of time to make the voyage up the Nor'way coast. He'd use those days to plan how to find and steal Naldrum's slave. Tiller needed *that* before they reached Trondheim, or none of his other plans stood a ghost of a chance.

. . .

Chapter Twenty-Two
Seacoast of Iceland

"Land!" The unmistakable forms of the fire-mountains Helgafell and Eldfell jutted from the sea.

Konradsson's stomach tightened. As the ship approached the shoreline and the call came to bring down the sail, Konradsson wished with all his heart that he could stay on the ship, or better yet, take it safely back to Germania. The sailors had been decent to him, but they were not the people of that land that lay ahead, menacing and gray.

Iceland grew larger and larger on the horizon. Konradsson sweated in the cool air. He could not tell Fredrich that he felt reluctant to put on his alb and become a priest again.

. . .

The inflowing tide bore their ship up the Ölfusá river. Twist by turn, Konradsson and Bishop Friedrich moved towards the greatest gathering of Icelandic peoples that had ever occurred. At last they beached at high tide on the river shore. *No escape now,* Konradsson thought over and over.

. . .

The bishop directed the unloading of their baggage, which included several large kegs of beer, onto the portage-skiffs that would carry them up the shallow rivers to Althing.

"The porters say that we've missed nearly all of the festival. Unfortunate, but at least we will have a brief chance to meet folk from distant parts of this land," he said to Konradsson.

"What is your goal, Your Grace?" Friedrich had instructed Konradsson during their voyage to call him *Brother*, as any ordinary monk, but in nervousness, the young monk reverted to formal language.

"My goal, son, is to simply say hello. To greet all in the name of Our Lord, and to show that we come offering the love of Jesus to all." *Perhaps that was not entirely honest.* Friedrich tried again. "To forgive them for their pagan ways, and to instruct them in true devotions." That still did not indicate the extent of his intentions. The bishop patted the front of his surplice, serene and calm. "Then we can proceed around, traveling from place to place, preaching."

Konradsson was not as relaxed. "The people of this land…"

"Are some of them rough, and wild, and unruly, given to fighting, and blood feuds. Yes, yes."

"Yes. Feuds, and vengeance, and more. They kill—" but the bishop interrupted Konradsson.

"But not all kill, else how would they have survived? Put that trunk with the others over there," he directed the men hefting cargo. "The Twelve who followed Our Lord faced all sort of dangers, scattered to many lands after His crucifixion. Some were martyred. We work in the service of God. Trust that to whatever trials he brings us, he will also give us armor of faith, to keep us safe."

Konradsson shook his head in confusion at the combination of *'some were martyred'* and *'God will keep us safe.'* If God hadn't seen fit to keep Saint Peter safe, why would He trouble Himself with one formerly-pagan Icelander? Konradsson crossed himself in fervent self-chastisement for impudence.

"Of course, Your Grace," he bowed. "Here, let me carry your box of sacraments."

. . .

Naldrum hurried to the red- and yellow-striped tent for a third time. Althing would end in a couple of days. He had fretted, wanting for reassurance from Rota that Haakon Sigurdsson would keep his promises, but she had eluded Naldrum. Thank the gods she had sent him another summons: *my tent, today. Alone.*

Why does she make me run to her as if I am a common messenger? But the temptation of being ruler of Iceland proved too great to resist. What was a little hardship if one gained much in return?

To Naldrum's surprise, Rota's tent flap stood wide open. He stuck his head in, peered around. Every bit of the riches of the Jarl of Lade, every piece of furniture that Rota had brought to Althing, was gone. In the empty space stood only two thin sleeping pallets. A candle flickered on an odd little table in the corner. Someone knelt there.

"Rota?" he asked.

A man turned, startled. "Rota?" he echoed.

"Rota had this booth. Where has she gone?"

"I know no one by that name. I am renting the tent." The man stood, made a sort of motion across his forehead and chest, and strode towards Naldrum.

"I know that gesture. You're one of the white-christs," Naldrum said, annoyed. *Where was Rota? She had summoned him.*

"White-christs?"

"You have the white robes. You worship a god called the christ, so we call your kind white-christs," Naldrum explained, testy. "When did you take this tent?"

"We arrived this morning and were told that it was available. Since Althing is over after tomorrow, I was glad to get it. I hope to meet many of the leaders here. What's your name?"

"I really don't care about your business. I'm the headman Naldrum, and you're wasting my time. I need to go and find Rota." Naldrum spun around to leave.

The man ignored Naldrum' rudeness. "You're *gothi* Naldrum? How fortunate."

Naldrum stiffened. "Who are you?"

The man did not answer. He simply stood gazing at Naldrum, hands folded across his robes, a calm smile upon his face, as if he was lost in thought.

The awkward silence grated on Naldrum. He sized up the monk, looked for something with which to make a quarrel. Before he could speak again, the bishop closed his eyes.

"Father, bless this successful man, who holds the fortunes of many in his hand. May our words together find favor in your sight. Amen."

Bishop Friedrich opened his eyes again and clapped his hands together. "Now, let us talk. May I invite you to share a beer with me?"

Naldrum squinted, uncertain.

"I assure you it is an excellent brew. We produce it in our community. I brought a few barrels for the good people of your land to sample. Come," he clapped a hand on Naldrum's shoulder, "let us drink a toast to Althing."

. . .

As the two men walked across the Thing-valley grounds, Friedrich asked many questions of Naldrum. The headman, still irritated at Rota's disappearance, made only cursory answers, annoyed that this troublesome white-christ was wasting his time.

A woman wearing a thrall-collar nearly tripped Naldrum as she fell to her knees in front of Friedrich. "A bishop," she breathed, looking reverently up at him.

"Yes, my child," he said.

"Father, it has been such a long time since my last confession…"

"It is not your fault, daughter. I will hear confessions in my tent this evening," the bishop replied. "Come when you are able." He held out his hand. She took it, trembling, and kissed it.

Friedrich trembled as well. He had seen many slaves since he had arrived at Althing, but this was the first to whom he had spoken. The visible pain these people endured wrenched Friedrich's heart.

Naldrum did not notice. "Why did she kneel? What does that word 'bishop' mean?"

Friedrich indicated the simple wooden staff he carried. "This is the sign of my office."

"The crook of a common shepherd? I've heard that your kind gives up all possessions. You own nothing. Why did she bow to you?"

"We *do* give up all possessions. But love and respect do not derive from wealth." As the bishop spoke, another thrall dropped a basket of charcoal, crossed himself, and knelt.

Friedrich blessed the man. They continued walking. "The woman. What did you see about her?"

"She's a thrall," Naldrum replied, testy. "Old. Gray hair. She carried a load of something."

"Did you see the depth of sadness in her eyes? Did you notice how she moved, with pain in her body?"

"Her master probably beats her." Naldrum's tone indicated that he did not very much care.

"She's the age of a grandmother. How unkind, to beat an elder—to beat anyone in that way. Do you see her only as a tool, to use until she breaks—and that man with the charcoal, the same, just a possession? Think of it: in whatever land they came from, they had a life. Maybe she was once a young mother. Maybe he was known for his ability to play the wood flute. A girl, practicing with her first bow and arrow. A boy, fishing along the shore with his brother. Just a happy child, like the children you must have…just living their lives when one day slavers arrived to snatch them. Now, nothing remains of what they once were. They barely live through endless work and beatings, unseen by people like you. What a cruel change to bear."

Naldrum had never thought of thralls in that way before, as people who once had entire lives and families before someone captured and sold them. He thought of his daughter Ankya, pictured her in bondage, and pushed the thought away. *That could never happen to her.*

The bishop continued. "You asked why they bow to me. In their homelands, many people worship the God I serve. When they see me, it is not I who matter, but their memories. A man wearing robes like mine may have married them, or baptized their children, or buried their loved ones. My clothing and cross are a reminder of beloved places, of people they will never see again. That is why they are overcome with emotion."

I must work on this matter as well as bringing the light of Christ to the pagans here. Those who trade in human lives and put God's beings in such godforsaken conditions must learn to see that their actions are wrong. The slaves themselves must strive for better conditions. It all must change. I must not fail in this work.

Friedrich had only envisioned the task of converting pagans to Jesus. This second large issue complicated matters. He felt overwhelmed at the idea. *Lord, I do not have the strength to do what you ask of me.*

Naldrum did not notice the bishop's distress. "How fortunate they see you," he said. "Makes everything all better for them, I guess."

. . .

The bishop had had his kegs delivered to one of the brew-tents. Friedrich had struck an arrangement: half the payments to the beer-seller, and half to the bishop to support their journey. The brewer, his barrels nearly depleted by the unexpectedly large crowd at Althing, had been happy to shake hands on the deal.

Konradsson wiped sweat from his forehead as he leaned against the barrel he had just rolled out of the brewer's tent. At the brewer's insistence, Konradsson had tied an apron over his robes and gone to work. At first it had felt strange, filling horns with ale and taking cattle-marks and trade beads, but the brewer shouted commands too rapidly for Konradsson to think. He had worked without a break for most of the day.

"Konradsson, two more ales for this group."

"Konradsson! Clear those empty horns and get that table ready."

"Konradsson, take a pitcher of ale around and try to sell refills."

"Konradsson? Is that *you?*"

. . .

The last question had not been a command of the brewer. It had been half-disbelief, half-scorn. The young monk, his fists full of dripping ale-horns, knew the voice right away.

It all came back in a flash. Randaal, nearly a full-grown man, sneaking along the field edges of the farm where Konradsson lived, intent on taunting the younger boy. Lurking, hiding behind the stone wall of the sheep pen or the chicken-house, waiting for Konradsson to finish his chores in the dark. Randaal would always throw a pebble against something, tormenting. Konradsson had come to despise the sound.

After that, always, the low call. *"Ásuauth*! Ewe-boy!"

He would flinch, trying to figure out where Randaal was hiding. Wondering if he could make it to the longhouse door in time.

"Ready for me, ewe-boy?"

He had never been brave enough to accuse Randaal openly, and too ashamed to admit to anyone what Randaal made him do or had done to him with those big dirty fingers. No one knew of the pain and the self-loathing. Finally, Konradsson had run, blindly heading from river to sea, searching for a ship, *any* ship leaving Iceland willing to take him on as a deckhand.

With nowhere he could run now, Konradsson turned, his heart thundering. *Our Father, who art in heaven.* Randaal must not see his terror. Randaal relished provoking fear. It made him even more cruel.

The young monk forced himself to stand tall. He dropped the empty ale-horns on a table in an untidy pile. Forced himself to drag his gaze to where Randaal stood, to meet his tormentor's eyes, as if the unspeakable things between them had never happened.

Forgive our trespasses as we forgive those trespassing against us.

"Randaal." It was all he could choke out. At least it sounded calm.

"Why are you dressed in that long thing. It looks like a woman's dress." An exaggerated mocking of a woman's walk, a jeering laugh, pointing. "Ewe-boy, dressed like a woman, how hilarious. I always knew you were that kind." He guffawed, squinted his small eyes.

In his youth, Konradsson would have backed away from the older man, stuttering, his shoulders down. Would have tried to deflect. Would have failed. Would have felt Randaal's fists, his kicks and then what Randaal referred to as 'your punishment for being so weak.' Konradsson feared nothing in the world as much as he feared Randaal.

. . .

But he dared not show that fear. Konradsson prayed for the Holy Spirit to be with him and unexpectedly, the right words came. *You preparest a table for me in the presence of my enemies.*

Konradsson felt the table of the beer tent under his fingers. He gripped it, hearing the inner words again. *A table. For me. In the presence of my enemy.* The young monk lifted his chin and spoke in a clear voice. "It is the robe of my work. I live in a community of ..." He stopped. This stupid boor probably did not know the word '*monks.*' "I live in a community of white-christs."

Randaal still pointed, but his jeering stopped. "Wha—where?"

"In Germania."

"*Germania?*" Randaal's forehead creased as he tried to work out where that was.

Time stopped for Konradsson. He held onto the table as if only it would keep him alive. He could feel the warm sun on the skin of his shaved head. Men and women around him played knucklebones, shouting and slamming the pieces against the wooden planks that made the tables. He could smell ale spilled on the ground, the stale beer odor mixing with the smoke of cooking fires.

His tormentor stood right in front of him, the embodiment of the fear that had whispered *randaalllll* across the long sea voyage. But Randaal was not pommeling him now. Not grabbing at Konradsson's tunic or pawing at his breeches. Not dragging him towards the pig-yard to throw him into the muck.

He was just there, staring at Konradsson in stupid confusion.

The strangeness of the whole thing threatened to start the terror-tremors again. Konradsson burst out with the first words that came to him. "We make good ale. We brought it to sell. Let me get a horn."

He dashed off before Randaal could reply. When he reached the back of the tent where the big barrels stood, Konradsson leaned against them, shaking.

After a bit, the urge to vomit had passed. He took an ale horn, steadied himself, pulled the bung from the barrel, filled the horn. Walked from the back of the tent to the tables again as if he was in a dream, concentrating on putting one foot in front of the next. Walked straight towards that hated, dreaded, feared face. Proffered the flagon.

More words came from his mouth, he wasn't sure how.

"Germania lies far across the North-way seas. Past the Faroe Islands, past the Northumbrian lands, past the Dane-mark lands. About twice as far as the Nor'way coast. I've lived there for a while."

"Well, aren't you the far traveler," Randaal said. He tried for mocking disdain but failed.

"I am." Konradsson said nothing else. He walked to the next table to clear it. Kept his head high, his back erect. Fought the nausea.

Later, he noticed that Randaal no longer stood in the beer area.

I survived. Konradsson knew he was not a brave man. But he had just faced his worst tormentor, and it had been Randaal who walked away, not himself. *You faced him with dignity,* the inner voice said.

He had trembled. He had feared. But still, he stood.

Konradsson rushed to the back of the tent and emptied his stomach onto the ground. He wiped his mouth and rinsed it out with a swallow of ale. "I survived," he told the horizon.

Something that resembled a brief smile of wonder crossed his lips. Konradsson straightened shoulders long used to stooping and went back to work.

. . .

"Konradsson, please fill a horn for our friend headman Naldrum, and one for me, will you?"

Konradsson bowed to the bishop, suddenly overjoyed to see the man who had insisted he come here. "Your Grace," he enthused. "How may I serve you?"

"No need to bow, my son. This man and I will be talking for a bit. Please keep our flagons filled—and find us food to eat, will you?"

. . .

Naldrum sipped the ale and marveled again at how this Friedrich, who wore only simple clothing, had no rings or arm bands or any servant following him, was constantly treated as if he were noble. *Profit might result from him in some way. I'll tell him of my trading prowess.*

Naldrum droned on. Friedrich half-listened, undeceived. He could see Naldrum for all the headman was: petty, insincere, ham-fisted, brutish. For years, the monk had schooled himself not to judge. Such things were God's concern, not his. Friedrich had one charge, and one only: to love all, unconditionally, as his Savior had loved others. *Do unto others as you would have others do unto you. Love your neighbor as yourself.*

But this one might prove hard to love. For the entire conversation, the same gentle smile stayed on Friedrich's face, the same kind tone in his voice as he struggled to understand what inner failings had made the chieftain feel it necessary to brag so incessantly of his worth and esteem?

He does not yet know the love of God. Friedrich sipped his beer and his heart swelled at the thought of the tremendous good he—no, the Lord—would bring to the people of this land.

. . .

Despite his intention to love his neighbor Naldrum as himself, Friedrich soon felt uncomfortable at how Naldrum's eyes narrowed whenever someone knelt and asked Friedrich for a blessing. Each time, Naldrum followed with even wilder claims about his prowess and achievements. Friedrich wished the headman would stop talking about himself. *Anything else,* he silently beseeched Naldrum. *Please.*

Another servant. Another *'bless you, my son'* to a man in his prime, who replied in Latin.

"Excuse me," Friedrich interrupted Naldrum monologue. To the man, "You speak the Church's language?"

The man kept his head bowed. "I was a priest, Father. Taken with others from Eire."

Friedrich shook his head in dismay. "And what fills your days now, brother?"

"I've become a stonemason," he answered. He glanced furtively at Naldrum. "I share when I am able." Friedrich realized it meant secret meetings for prayers.

"Look at his enormous strength," Naldrum exclaimed, misunderstanding the man's distress. "I'm planning to add a room to my longhouse for food storage. Come to Bull Valley after Althing. I'll hire you." He felt pleased that he had distracted the man from an almost-worshipful adoration of Friedrich.

"More of this excellent ale," he called to Konradsson. "And bring us some of the honey-loaves from that baker's tent. I cannot resist the fragrance any longer." He leaned in close to Friedrich, as if to impart a great secret. "It's made with wheat from one of my farms, you know. The best wheat makes the best bread."

. . .

As Naldrum continued talking of his successes, an idea occurred to Friedrich. "What do you know of my faith?" he asked.

Naldrum stopped, his mouth open. "Ah...um...I don't...um..."

"Perhaps I could teach you some of it." If Friedrich could lead *this* pompous braggart to Christ, many others might willingly follow.

"Always wise to learn of new gods. One never knows from what corner good favor may come," Naldrum answered, thinking *he can take his white-christ ways and shove them up his...*

Friedrich spoke of faith, his face glowing.

Naldrum did not listen to as the bishop droned on and on. Friedrich did not respond to Naldrum's attempts to interrupt and turn the conversation back to himself. As each considered the advantages the other might offer, their intentions entwined, gliding over one another, seeking advantage...just as Konradsson's smoke-snakes and dragons had done.

Konradsson, carrying beer and bread, stopped in his tracks, struck by how similar their expressions had become. Without knowing why, he crossed himself.

. . .

Chapter Twenty-Three

The track to the widow Eilíf's house had all but disappeared under lush summer grass. Berry vines sprawled over the boulders that marked the turning. A passerby might never notice them.

As she approached, Aldís hallooed, a special call that Eilíf would recognize. She caught a whiff of a hearth fire, but no smoke drifted on the air. *Good. She's careful. Tor chose well.*

The longhouse lay tucked so snugly against a small hill that it, too, could easily have escaped notice. More berry vines draped over the door, and the roof was one long thatch of green grass. Aldís hallooed again, knowing full well that she was being watched.

"Come on. I know you see me, and you can see I came alone."

Still, nothing moved in the landscape. She frowned. Vague worries flitted through her mind, but nothing felt awry in her inner sight.

Her dog, joyous to see her again, came running across the path. As Aldís knelt for it, a great cry sounded behind her. She whirled, not in time to avoid being tumbled to the ground by two racing children.

"Oh, an ambush, eh?" she laughed. Squeals of delight sounded as Aldís hugged first one and then the other of Tor's children. "Wait until you hear the stories I have for you!"

"Hush! Hush that yelling!" Now Aldís saw the widow Eilíf, her skirts tied up for farm work, running towards them. "Someone might hear you. Stop it!"

The two children immediately obeyed, looking behind them towards the main path to see if anyone approached. "No one's around, my friend," Aldís reassured her. "I was careful."

"Aldís," cried the widow, rushing forward with her arms open.

"Eilíf," smiled Aldís, delighted afresh at the young widow's renewed health. Eilíf's face—the part not scarred, at least—bloomed with the happiness Aldís had described to Tor. The women linked arms and walked to a sunny patch beside the longhouse. They sat on the grass, talking excitedly. Eilíf had shooed the children away. No sense disappointing them until she learned what updates Aldís brought.

"You look full of yourself. I take it you managed to find Tor at Althing?"

"Managed? I should say so. He was surrounded by crowds every day. And I'm so glad to tell you that even though his lot is terribly hard, he has found his way to strength and calm. He is no longer seems wracked with misery. And how overjoyed he was to hear news of the children and you."

At this, Eilíf clapped her hands and called the children to come back. "Nikea, Nenet, come quickly. Aldís brings word of your father."

They ran up, eager. Aldís swept Tor's children into her arms once more. "Wait until you hear!"

The little girl, her face Tor's in miniature, bounced on Aldís's lap. Her eyes filled with tears. "Please tell us," she begged. "Will Papa come soon?"

"I cannot say that, Nenet," Aldís answered her. "But I can tell you he loves you every bit as much as he always has." She launched into a lengthy description of everything about Tor, from his work to the way so many people at Althing had admired him. She omitted the part about the loathsome man who had taken ownership of their father; no need distressing them with Naldrum's cruelty.

"He asked of you, too," Aldís told Eilíf. "He is grateful to you."

"It's I who owes thanks to Tor," Eilíf replied. "Look what joy he has given me." She blushed. "And there's a bit more news. I wish you had known in time to share it with him. too."

"What?" Aldís asked. As she did, a flash of understanding shot through her. "Oh…where is he?"

"Come, and I'll introduce you," Eilíf blushed. "The goddess Freya has sent me the perfect man."

She set the children to throwing sticks for Aldís's dog and led her friend around the back of the property.

. . .

"Shhh." Eilíf put her finger to her lips. A man bent over her sheep pen, lifting heavy stones into place along the wall. He gave no indication that he heard anyone watching as he carefully fitted a rock into place. Aldís admired the work, a neat pattern that showed his skill and care in craftsmanship.

"Just the one guest for supper tonight?" he called to Eilíf. A slight smile crossed his lips. "I'm guessing this is the famous Aldís of whom you speak?"

Eilíf laughed. "How did you know?"

"Not often I hear the children shrieking in delight like that." He stood, brushed off his hands, and turned to greet Aldís. She backed up, startled.

"Please forgive me. I'm sorry, I forgot," he said, tying a length of linen around where his eyes had once been. He reached towards Aldís again, his hand somehow in exactly the right place to grasp hers. She wondered how he managed that. "I'm Petr. Good to meet you, Aldís."

Eilíf moved to his side and slipped her arm around the man's waist. He brushed a kiss against her hair, and she tucked her face against his neck, sweet and shy.

. . .

They worked on the wall through the long pleasant afternoon. Rather, Petr placing stones by feel and by instinct as the two women looked for the shapes requested, all talking the whole time.

"An awful holmgang duel over sheep that became a stupid, ongoing blood-feud between two families," Eilíf explained. "First his grandfather, then the other's father, then an uncle and a brother...all of them caught up in one of those everlasting cycles of hate and revenge. That's not what holmgang is for. It's supposed to settle disagreements, not prolong them. Petr was the last casualty of the feud. They followed him home one night after the spring cattle brandings, carrying their fire-marks."

Aldís flinched. "They blinded him instead of giving him the honor of a fighter's death."

"Yes. But I'm glad of it, now. Petr drifted after he lost his sight, living on scraps of work and food. Somehow his path brought him here. The children saw him sitting in the yard, playing his harp, just waiting. He said he smelled the pottage I was cooking all the way up from the river, which of course is impossible. Cabbages and smoked pig's feet, it was. Anyway, after he supped, the afternoon turned wet and miserable. I offered him shelter for the night, as I would any traveler. He never left."

They both smiled, as if at a familiar old joke. "You never *let* me leave," he corrected.

"You never *tried.*" A gentle chuckle.

"We make a strange pair, but we are right for each other. After the fire, so many people stared at me in horror that I knew I must look a fright from the scars—yet this man cannot see my hideousness. He thinks I am beautiful because he likes the sound of my voice."

"Don't forget that cooking," he teased. "That's really why I stay."

Another sweet smile. "And I, made ugly through by my own greedy fault, understood that a person whose face had been destroyed could still have a good heart, and need love. Petr treats me kindly. He takes diligent care of our farm. There is nothing he cannot do. These two little ones do not mind if their guardians look more like hideous trolls than human in appearance. Even those, if they had kind hearts, might have a sort of ugly beauty, I hope." A lingering wistfulness, which Eilíf brushed off. "Petr, my love, that wall seems finished. Time to give Aldís some of that wonderful *sup,* yes?"

. . .

The air stayed warm enough that they took their bowls outside, and when finished, lay on their backs, looking at the sky, talking through the long bright evening.

Petr, it turned out, a poet's gift as well. His pleasant voice gave them familiar stories and songs, along with new ones he had worked out. Fairies, *norns*, and elves danced in their imaginations, and he entranced them with tales of warriors, men and women pitted against evil foes, and of love.

"And you, dear Aldís?" asked Eilíf. "Tell us about yourself and Althing. I know you would never go to the bride-fair, but with many men at the festival... might anyone have caught your fancy there?"

Aldís shook her head. "No. I think I will be like the *norns*...liked by many, but beloved by none."

"A man loved you once. Perhaps he still does."

"Perhaps I don't love him."

"Did you talk to him?"

Aldís knew perfectly well what Eilíf meant. She reached for Nenet, pulled the sleepy little girl onto her lap. "I talked to Kel. But no, I did not tell him."

The widow shook her head, sad. "You can try to deny it all you want, but you will never heal until you do."

"Then I will never heal. Because I am a coward. Besides, he hates me as much as I hate him."

Eilíf reached for Aldís's hand. "Nonsense. I don't believe that, about either of you. You must not give up hope. Look how things worked out for me."

"I don't believe a man could make me happy," Aldís protested. "Besides, I love the work I do." She nuzzled Nenet and stared at the setting sun.

"And your work loves you. All of us cherish the healing gift that flows from you. I would selfishly hate to see you give it up. But Aldís," she touched her friend's arm. "I may be blind in one eye, but even I can see a thing or two. Some people really are happy alone. But others are alone because the right partnership has eluded them. And you, my friend, are not of the former kind."

She patted Aldís again and got up. Dew had begun to wet the grass. They carried the drowsy children and their food bowls back to the longhouse in the still-light air. "You needn't go chasing after Kel, but don't be so afraid of love that you drive it away if a second chance ever comes. Promise me?"

"I promise nothing." Aldís shrugged off her friend's serious words. "We'll just have to wait and see. Now let's get some sleep. I can only stay one night, and I intend to be up early, disrupting your marital bliss." She kissed her friend on the cheek, and assured the children, yes, of course they could sleep with her.

. . .

As the longhouse settled into nighttime quiet, Aldís lay awake, fingering the scars on her wrist and letting herself remember. Kel had come to see her, just once, a few years after that first Althing when they met. He had seen the child toddling around her. Aldís had tried to hide the little girl, afraid, but Kel had spied the child before Aldís had time.

He had mumbled through a description of his work. She had half-listened as Kel described traveling the countryside to get to know the farmers who rented land from Naldrum. *He was gaining responsibility...there was talk of him being Naldrum's steward one day...he didn't spend much time at the headman's main compound, but that might change when the current steward retired, whoever he was...Kel had never met the man but Naldrum had said 'Kel had what it took'*... Naldrum, Naldrum, Naldrum...as if she wanted to ever hear that name again.

At first, Aldís had been glad to see Kel's face, hopeful that the magic which had first connected them would bring them together again. But as she heard him praise the chieftain again and again, and compare himself to Naldrum, and speak of Naldrum's pleasure at his work, Aldís's anger burned afresh at how Kel had left the festival without even saying goodbye to her and had not spoken to her since.

Once the bitter words had left her lips they could not be unsaid, nor the sharp cruel tone of her voice or Kel's answering anger.

She had told him to get out, and he had left. Not long after, the two men had arrived at her door.

"It is equal-day-and-night," Aldís had greeted them. "Are you seeking shelter for the *álfablót* tonight? The farm up the road has enough space for guests. I was about to go there for the harvest supper. I could show—" but the older one had cut her off.

"Word has reached the headman Naldrum that you made a father-claim. He has sent us regarding it," he said. "We are to inspect the child for flaws."

Even after all these years, the devastation of those words gutted Aldís. *My little girl,* she grieved. But worse than the sadness was the fury she felt towards Kel. *Why in the name of all the gods had he tattled to Naldrum about her daughter? Just to gain favor?*

That long-ago day, Naldrum's men had informed her that her perfect daughter was somehow unfit. The one who called himself Sauthi had pried the child from her arms.

Aldís dropped to her knees when she realized what was coming. She could see the man's distress and had clawed at his legs, sobbing. "I know you don't want to do this." But her pleas went unheard.

"I'm sorry," the man said, unable to meet her eyes. "I'll ride off a way, so you won't have to see."

He had mounted his horse, holding the child carefully in one arm. The sounds of the little girl's screams diminished as he rode away. The quieting had cut a fjord-sized hole in Aldís's heart.

When she had no longer been able to hear her daughter's cries, the younger man—the one with the small cruel mouth and the evil eyes— had wrenched Aldís to her feet and shoved her against one of the pillars in the longhouse, tying her to it. He had taken out his knife and heated it in her longfire.

I'm *not* sorry," he sneered. "I'll enjoy this."

He had taken his time. Her arms had healed across the long months of autumn and winter that followed, but her spirit had been irrevocably broken. She had never learned his name—but that face had burned into her memory as deep as the scars on her skin.

. . .

That face. She had not seen it for years, until this summer.

The man who held the knife to her throat in Naldrum's tent this Althing had the same small cruel mouth and evil eyes. Seeing him again brought not just the grief of losing her daughter but memories of the agony he had inflicted on her. Yes, she had wanted to get away from Naldrum. Yes, she needed to give up on Kel, once and for all. There was no longer even a shred of hope there. But most of all, she had fled in panic because of that man.

Aldís listened to the murmur of the waterfall behind Eilíf's longhouse. She pictured the long river road that had borne her away from Althing, away from the danger of that small cruel mouth and those evil eyes. She hoped that her escape had been fast enough and far enough away, and that the *water-nixies* would honor her appeal.

. . .

The long night wore on, and still Aldís could not sleep. She kept thinking of the man who had taken her daughter, and of Kel.

Cast off. Those who could afford to feed many offspring never used the practice unless the newborn showed serious flaws. Poorer folk with lesser means, however, braced themselves to do what they must. Whether from a hand held over its mouth or from lying naked and shivering in the cold or from scavenger foxes, a cast-off infant soon wailed no more.

Cast off or exposed, it meant the same thing. Neither of the bland terms indicated the small creature's desperate, kicking struggle, or the mother's anguish—or the sadness that never went away.

Aldís touched the marks on her wrists again. Did Kel cut women that way too, when Naldrum told him to? Did he take away perfect children, declaring they were unfit? She had so wanted to ask Kel about that, to throw the words at him and see if he denied it.

Now she could not, so she had to assume the worst.

What kind of man could do that? She could hardly bear to think of such a thing. Worse, what kind of woman could love such a man?

"Kel was not what I thought he was," Aldís murmured to herself as she had so many times. "I thought he loved law, and me. But he only cared about one thing: his chance to ride the tail of a powerful, horrible man."

But still. *Kel, I did love you,* she whispered into the night, full of anger and chagrin. *Why do you stay with Naldrum? You once seemed to care about fairness and goodness, about law, about doing right. You seemed strong. What happened? Was I* that *wrong about you?*

She had searched her heart and mind and memories too many times to know anything for sure. But she had been certain once. In kindness, Aldís offered the only thing she could manage.

Find your way back to who you once were, Kel Coesson. Not for me. For yourself.

. . .

Nenet's sweet breath came soft against her cheek. Aldís forced herself to stop thinking and try to sleep. The music of the small waterfall comforted her now, gurgling down the rocks to the stream. Aldís pictured the sparkling little flow, rushing ocean-ward in search of its welcoming sea mother. Little by little, she was able to fall asleep.

. . .

Chapter Twenty-Four

Kel felt no ease at all. Each day had he searched for a glimpse of Aldís among the festival crowds, asking others if they had seen her. She had simply vanished. Why? And why did he even still care? Kel teetered between hating Aldís and worrying. Able to bear it no longer, he went to a seeing-woman.

. . .

Banners around the sooth-sayer's tent snapped in the wind, tattered and torn. Charred bits of offering-bones littered the yard. Kel stepped carefully, trying not to tread on any, and winced when he heard something crack beneath his feet.

. . .

A ribbon hung from the door, to show that someone was already with the seeing-woman. Kel waited at a distance, embarrassed that someone might see him. But someone else like him, whose life was in disarray, clutching at hope, might not judge. Kel pulled his cloak over his head and turned his face. *Agh, a saith-woman. I have sunk low.*

A young man came out, and a woman followed him. The saith came out after them and stretched in the sun, holding her hands up to the warm light. "Feed me, mother Sól," she said.

Kel picked his way over to her, and she sized him up. "What brings a strapping healthy man such as yourself here?" she asked.

"Uncertainty," he growled.

The woman stood close, sniffed as if the air around Kel would confirm his words. "Not like others this week. Not uncertainty about crops. Not weather…"

"A woman," he growled.

The woman paused, sniffed again. Shook her head. "No, not that."

"I'm telling you I came to ask you about a woman."

"No," she insisted. "I sense that concern. But there is something else, something deeper."

She put her hand on his stomach, moved towards his hips. Stopped at his lower abdomen. "You ache here. You have lost your bearings. Your uncertainty is about…" she frowned and looked at him. "Are you struggling with truth about yourself?"

Of course. It was clear when she asked it that way.

"I am, sooth-sayer." Suddenly, coming here did not seem quite as ridiculous. "Tell me what to do."

. . .

In the dim light of her tent, the seeing-woman sat facing Kel. "Tell me about the woman first," she said. "Get that off your mind first, and you will be able to let it go."

The woman. "There have been many across the years. But when I am with one of them, if I close my eyes, they all have her face and her body. But I cannot even pretend that any have the mind she does." The attraction to Aldís had been instantaneous, wild, irresistible.

"Why?"

Kel had never spoken of his feelings for her. Choosing the right words came hard. "I had never thought of a woman to love before, or to marry. When I saw her, in my bones, I could feel that something was different. I wanted to *be* with her. Not just for pleasure, although the gods know, I wanted that. But even more, I wanted to share things of the mind that I had never been able to before with any other woman. How I felt about Althing itself. What it represents to our people. I'd never found anyone who understood what it means to me, but she felt the same way. I wanted to be with someone like that, in a way I never had before. I wanted her to be with me always. I wanted Ald—" Kel stopped abruptly, worried.

She guessed the reason. "Don't worry what will overhear. Summer-spirits don't find amusement in taking love away. If anything, they encourage it. You're safe speaking aloud. The beings that harvest from humans only take during the waning months, and in winter."

How had she known he did not want a culling-spirit to overhear? "That's a relief."

"You felt a connection. Did she?"

"I thought so. Who knows, though? But from the instant I saw her, every breath I drew I looked to see her again, thinking of when we could next talk of our ideas, of dreams. Then came the first touch. The first kiss. With the talking came desire."

"That desire for her has never left you, yet she is not with you now. Why?"

The old hatred for Naldrum. "She chose another."

The seeing-woman showed surprise. "That seems strange. In my experience, such strong attraction usually finds itself reflected in the other."

"Strange or not, that's what happened. I could not get enough of her that Althing. Then I saw her with another man."

"You are certain?"

"Certain."

The saith's tone sharpened. "We draw close, now, to what really troubles you. This other man. You loathed him, but he held you in some way. He holds you still."

Once again, Kel regretted how little regard he had held for sooth-sayers. Perhaps some of them really did have the true sight.

"Yes. I had come to Althing to find work. One chieftain offered me a position I could not refuse, more silver than I had ever dreamed of earning, especially with my youth and inexperience. I had to promise to one day perform certain duties for him. '*Perhaps distasteful, but nothing illegal*,' he assured me. He would not say clearly what they were."

The woman said nothing.

"I gave him my hand, and we shook on it. Shortly after I pledged to my new chieftain, I started seeing him with this woman. Standing next to her at the livestock fields or talking to her in the food tents. Always touching her, somehow. I had seen how she loved men. She loved to laugh and talk with them. I asked her about it. She said it was nothing. But one day, I saw them …together. She was stumbling, as if she had drunk too much. He had his arm around her. They went inside his tent. Did not come out for a long while."

"And did you ask her about that afterwards?"

"I didn't have to, because *he* told me what happened, almost as if he couldn't wait to brag about it. Said that she had mocked me to him. Said that she preferred a man with plenty of land, and prospects, a man like him. And he told me to stay away from her…that she was his."

"Ahhh," The seeing woman's voice, soft and eager. "Good. Here is the hatred. Now I can see how it turns in you. Hate and love, twisted inside. But there is more."

"Yes. I wanted her so much. I told myself that if he was what women wanted, I would be like him, and one day would have all those things: silver, land, wealth. If he had been a worthy competitor, it would have hurt less. But he had disparaged her. I disliked him for that, but I had already given my pledge to work for him. Break a contract, and no one will ever hire you again. Besides, who was I to tell her who she should choose? I was young, and poor."

"You felt your only choice was to honor your contract, and believed that your best way of winning this woman back was to make yourself as much like him as possible, even though there were things about him that troubled you."

Now Kel wanted to hide from the woman's eyes, large and luminous in her face. "Yes. That very day, he told me to leave the festival grounds immediately, to ride to his holdings to start work. I wanted to ask Aldís if what he said was true—that she had mocked me, and that she preferred him to me—but I couldn't find her anywhere. She seems to have a habit of leaving abruptly. The entire ride home, the only thing I thought about was that if I ever saw her again, I might have another chance."

"But you never did see her again?"

"No, *saith*. I *did* see her." Now came the hardest part. "One time only."

"Tell me."

"As I said, my headman had told me that Aldís was his, and he had told me in no uncertain terms to leave her be—or he would cut *her* to punish *me*. I tried not to go, but I could not stand wondering why she had deceived me. It ate at me. I ignored him and rode in secret to see her. I had to know. I told myself that he would never find out."

"And?"

"I learned where she was living. Went there. I was surprised to see a little girl with her. Tiny, clutching Aldís's skirt. Two, maybe three years old. Looked exactly like her."

Kel had stared at the child in dismay, unwilling to see physical evidence that she had lain with Naldrum.

"And?"

"She met me coldly. Harsh words passed between us. She told me that I was a liar and a cheat. I said unkind things as well. I told her that she might have waited, that I was trying to make myself as much like him as possible, that I might never be as rich as he was, but one day I would be a man of means, someone she could be proud to call her husband. She just laughed at me, mocking me. I realized it was just as he had said. I called her despicable for choosing the *gothi* over me."

Her hateful words still rang in his ears. "*'Me, despicable? How little you know me.'* She told me to go home. And as I left, she delivered a last cruel blow."

"And that was?"

"She proved my master's words about how she had lain with him."

Kel had never forgotten how strong and beautiful Aldís had looked, her shoulders back for battle and her eyes blazing.

"She said *'Tell your headman he owes me child-rights. If he'd been a decent man, my daughter might have had a chance to know her father. Instead, I've raised her alone. It's time he paid for what he's done.'*"

A long pause. The betrayal still cut deep.

Kel continued. "It's no wonder she hated him. He got her with child, and then abandoned her. But I've never understood why she hated me too."

The seeing-woman frowned. "Something is not fitting together properly, but I don't know what it is." She bent her head, concentrating, then shook it. "I can't get it. Later, perhaps. Did you tell your headman that you had seen her?"

"No. I didn't dare. Remember, he had threatened to hurt her if I contacted her. What kind of man makes such a lowly threat? There was no way I'd have told him."

"Did you ever see her again?"

"No. I suppose I could have kept track of her whereabouts. But she made it very clear that she wanted nothing to do with me. I asked others about her, from time to time. Just never could let it go, I guess. I heard sometime later that the child had died. I'm ashamed to admit that I felt a little glad."

He rubbed his hand over the stubble on his chin. "Bad though that might make me seem, I'm glad that I at least protected both of them from a crueler alternative."

"What do you mean?"

"Because not long after that, the headman promoted me to be his steward. I moved to his main compound, and I learned then what he did to women who demanded child-rights. The 'certain duties' I had promised to perform, the ones he would not clearly explain in our contract? Naldrum has much gold. Men of wealth such as him—well, women accuse them of things to get a bit of that gold. He taught me that if he allowed it to happen even once, more and more people would levy false charges. At least that is what he always claimed, and what I always believed. But what he expected… It was… unpleasant work."

The soothsayer could see the regret in Kel, deep as his marrow. *This man speaks the truth.*

"Once he told me what I he expected me to do, I tried to get out of my contract, but he threatened Aldís again. I stayed with him to protect her…but in doing that, I lost her forever."

. . .

The sooth-sayer stood and smoothed her apron. She went to the tent door and looked out. No one waited to see her. She put a handful of charcoal on her brazier and sat again.

"You've spoken only of your past with this man and this woman, but not what brought you to me today. Let's talk about that."

. . .

They emerged from her tent some time later. Both stretched in the warm sun. Kel felt a deep sense of relief. He did not have to judge

302   Katie Aiken Ritter

whether Naldrum was innocent or guilty. That was the job of the council of *gothar*. Nor was it his job to confront Naldrum and demand an explanation.

But it *was* his responsibility to tell the head lawspeaker. Kel sucked in the fresh summer air. He looked around, as if seeing the wonderful festival with new eyes. Of course, there were problems in the land. There were always problems in the land. But the land had its laws. One worked with problems within the context of the law, and one resolved them. One kept going.

It was what he had always loved about Althing, the untidy, back-and-forth balance of a country based on honor and law instead of one person's selfish whims.

The sooth-sayer protested Kel's offer of silver, but he pressed it into her hand anyway. "Use it to do some good. You have helped me."

He struck out for the horse meadows again, knowing Mani the Lawspeaker always went there after the day's courts, to clear his mind for the next day. He would talk with Mani, and he would groom his stallion Thunder. He would find a path forward, one way or another.

. . .

Mani had indeed gone to the horse-meadows. Nothing soothed him as did a quiet, careful brushing of his mare Little Cloud. The slow strokes of the pig-bristle brush and the fragrance of the horse's coat helped him relax and forget, for a short while, the endless struggles that ensued from humans living with one another.

Kel had grown up in awe of the Lawspeaker. Across many Althings, the two had bonded over love of their horses and the fine points of imported mead. When Mani saw Kel, he hailed the steward, happy to spend the evening with someone he liked and respected.

The two men admired the fine afternoon, talking of their favorite topics: horses, horse breeding, and horse training.

Kel watched his stallion with a mixture of love and pride. The envy of the stable-yard, Thunder pranced along the far stone wall, his head raised in haughty challenge against the other males. Mani's beloved old mount ignored the beast and nudged at the Lawspeaker, nuzzling him so that he would brush her where she wanted.

"Little Cloud and Dalla own you, Mani," Kel laughed. "They both pretend to be docile creatures, but they know what they want, and they're both as headstrong as the day is long."

Mani laughed as well. "It's true. I should tell my sons to look for wives that resemble their favorite horses. It certainly worked for me. But maybe you should get yourself a nice mare instead of that beast Thunder, showing off and snorting over there."

Kel's eyes shone as he watched Thunder. "He may be feisty, Mani, but he's the only creature I really trust." Kel pulled strands of long grass, began to twist them idly in his fingers. "I can't imagine life without him. Sometimes he's all that stands between me and the abyss. He's been with me through much."

"The abyss…" Mani said softly. He brushed Little Cloud in silence, thinking of the challenges that faced Iceland.

Kel twisted, twisted, twisted the grass. "Strange how we cannot speak the same language as our horses, but they understand us so well."

"Speaking of speaking, you came here for a reason, young fellow. What is it?"

"Mani, I'm sorry to trouble you with this. But I had to tell you." Kel repeated to Mani all he had seen and heard the night before about the girl in Naldrum's tent, the sound of forcing. The old lawspeaker stared aghast at Kel as he spoke.

When Kel finished, Mani tipped his head back and closed his eyes. *What a mess. Kel was right to come to him, but aie, the difficulty of such an accusation against a headman like Naldrum.* After thinking for a while, Mani spoke.

"The court schedule is already full for this Althing. The spring or autumn *thing* held in Naldrum's valley could normally hear a charge of rape, but if it's against him, that's impossible. Local folk might ignore testimony against their own *gothi* if they hoped to curry favor with him, or vote against him because of personal grudges, in which case his law-arguer would claim Naldrum didn't get a fair hearing."

Mani made a sound of frustration. "Yet to ignore such a vile act is also not possible. But this is not one of those cases that could be settled in the time needed to drink an ale-horn. We would need much time witnesses to speak and for law-arguments to be made by each party."

"Is it because he is powerful that you find this issue inconvenient? What if the woman was a *gothi,* and Naldrum a common bondsman?" Kel asked, concerned. "You said yesterday that the law belongs to all Icelanders. Were those just words with no meaning?"

Fire flashed in Mani's eyes. "Do not dare preach legal matters to me, Kel."

"I'm sorry, Lawspeaker."

Mani could hear the sincerity of the apology. He resumed grooming his mare. "Kel, this has nothing to do with Naldrum's wealth, except that a wealthy man can afford a much more skilled law-arguer. It's that I won't consider bringing a charge against *any* man or woman unless the case has a reasonable chance of winning. I'll not waste the court's time, nor will I hold up Althing based on your say-so. There has to be likely proof."

"What if I have evidence?"

"Tell me what it is, then. You say you heard her resisting, but you didn't see everything. It would be his word against yours. What if the woman refuses to testify, as well she might, out of fear of Naldrum? Then there would be a sensation and much gossip, but little else; much harm done, and no good. I know you will not like hearing this, but I am going to offer this counsel: come to me next year before Althing begins. Bring credible evidence and witnesses, and I'll put your accusation on the court schedule. A year may seem an eternity to wait, but in the end, building a careful case is better than an impulsive gesture made in frustration."

Mani fixed his gaze on Kel. "And make no mistake, sir," he said. "Going up against Naldrum may be within the law, but he has resources you don't. Expect every possible bad outcome. You'll need to be as strong and determined as you've ever been in your life."

"I understand, Lawspeaker. Were he just any man, I'd be offended at his action. I'd confront him directly, but this troubles me even more, because each spring…" Kel stopped. Just as with Tor and the saith, he did not elaborate on the distasteful work he had done for Naldrum.

But Mani's ears sharpened at what he heard in Kel's voice. "Because why? What happens each spring?"

Up until now, Mani had continued to groom his horse's flanks, soothed by the repetitive swish of the pig-bristles against the mare's glossy hair, but now the brush had stopped moving.

Staring at it, Kel saw something he had not noticed earlier: the smallest tremor in Mani's hand and the whiteness of his knuckles gripping the brush. With a shock, Kel realized a staggering truth. Mani, too, had a secret. The Lawspeaker knew something he was not saying.

Before he could stop himself, Kel burst out. "You already have evidence! You know of such a girl."

Mani's expression, clear, honest, and sad, admitted as much.

"You *do*," Kel practically shouted. "Why are you protecting Naldrum?"

The grooming brush clattered against a stone underfoot. Mani's hand, now openly shaking, covered his eyes. "It is not the headman I protect," he said. "It is my wife Dalla. But I cannot speak of it to you. Not now. And as Lawspeaker, no matter my personal feelings, I must be impartial. I cannot help you to win your case." Mani wiped his eyes. "But do your best, my honorable friend. Swallow your pride and stay with Naldrum where you can watch him. Build your case, and hope for luck—because we will need all the good luck we can get."

. . .

Chapter Twenty-Five

Swallowing his pride grew harder each day-eighth for Kel. As the end of Althing approached, he found himself longing for it to be over, yet dreading that. *I used to love Althing,* he told himself. Now, everything about the festival unrelentingly reminded him of Naldrum, Aldís, farce, and lies. It seemed an eternity stretching ahead.

Just get through it. Just take it one day-eighth at a time. But each one found Kel imagining putting a knife in Naldrum. Could a man survive a year with such intense anger filling him?

. . .

At last, the final day of the festival arrived, and the drums for the Law Council beat a final time for the year. *Boom… boom… boom… boom…,* the same solemn rhythm that had sounded for each morning's law session. Thirty-nine beats, one for each leader.

Mani watched as the *gothar* for the East, West, and South quarters of the land walked ahead of him, nine apiece for each quarter, and the twelve that represented the North quarter. Flanking every *gothi* walked two law advisors. The group marched in silence across the flat ground below the Speaking Stones. The only sounds came from the muffled tread of their shoes on the trampled-flat grass.

Mani came last, as symbolic servant of all present. With him walked his two sons, the oldest, Bright, and the much younger Mothur. Mani carried the ancient and sacred ash-wood staff, reputed to be an actual branch of *Yggdrasil*, the First Tree of the World.

"I must start the process of ending my service today, my sons," he said to them. "Soon, Mothur, you will bear the title of *Allsherjargothi,* the honorary descendent of the first Lawspeaker. You must practice so that you are ready to open Althing each year."

Mothur smiled to himself. His father had said the same thing to him several times each year since he was a child. He replied dutifully, "Of course, Father. I will do my best to fulfill the honor of the title."

Mani sniffed. "I trust you will." The remark bore equal amounts of rebuke and praise. *So typical,* Mothur thought. *Always cautious. Never trusting us to do our work properly.*

Mothur would never inherit Mani's other role of Lawspeaker, to preside over the Law Circle council. That responsibility must go to Bright, his far more serious brother. Bright had studied the law his entire life. He loved working with the complexities of it as Mani did.

Mani had wanted to retire the term before, but Bright had disagreed. "Yes, of course I am ready, Father," he had said. "But after all your service, you deserve the honor of ushering in the fiftieth anniversary of the Althing. Besides, with the poor harvests and the unrest in the valleys, our entire way of life may be at stake. At such a critical time, our people need to look to a seasoned leader, not a brand-new Lawspeaker. Who can better steer us through this rough water than you and your experience?"

This is exactly why Bright will make a fine leader, Mani had thought. Just that sort of careful, unselfish logic. Bright was universally well-regarded. The vote for his nomination as the next Lawspeaker would likely be only a formality.

. . .

Now, that conversation weighed on Mani's mind. *Perhaps Bright was wrong. Maybe we needed fresh leadership right now, at the start of our next fifty years…should we be lucky enough to have that many.*

Mani, Bright, Mothur, the thirty-nine *gothar* and their seventy-eight advisors reached the Council ground. They filed forward into the three rings of benches, the *gothar* to the middle ring, and their advisors to the inner and outer circles of benches.

As they stood in place, the drums ceased their slow pounding briefly. Mani pounded the ash staff on the ground, once, and the drums erupted again in furious thunder.

. . .

As he had done on the *Lögberg*, Mani raised his hands. "I call this Council of Gothar into order for our final session this year," he said. "One last time, my friends: in order that all may know their fellow council members, call out your name and from where you come."

The voices rang out around the ring, proud and strong, as they had each morning.

"Járni of Vik!"

"Helga of Egilsstadir!"

"Gunnar of Ránger-valley!"

"Viglund of Stong!"

Most of the faces and names were familiar, but each year, some were new. The roll call served not only to keep track of who had come to vote on each matter or avoid it, but to learn the character of the thirty-nine who led the people of the far-flung valleys.

"All are present," Mani decreed. "The Law Council is in order for our final session. Our last business is to ensure that the position of Lawspeaker will continue, filled by one of us who knows and honors the law. Today, we ask for nominations for the person who will serve as our next Lawspeaker. Use this time to get to know those who are nominated, because at the end of *next* Althing, you will vote for my successor, who will serve our people in years to come."

"I nominate Bright!" Mani had barely finished speaking when multiple calls came from voices around the circle.

Mani tried to keep from swelling with pride. "I present Bright, who many of you know as my son. He has studied the Law with me and others for many years. Any of you who do not know him well, I welcome you to visit our home, or to invite Bright to travel to your valley to assess his abilities and character." Mani nodded to his son and the council applauded.

The vote for Bright would really be only a formality, but Mani did as the Law required. "Are there others who might want to serve?"

He waited the required time, but no one else spoke. Mani was not surprised. Few would stand a chance in a vote against Bright.

Naldrum could feel his face grow hot as blood pounded in his head. Those fools with all their tedious wrangling about the fine points of their law understood little of human nature and actual power. The things he could show them.

Now or never, Naldrum told himself. He leaned to a companion and whispered furiously.

As Mani raised the ash staff, ready to signify the close of nominations, the man stood. "I nominate Naldrum of Bull Valley to become our next Lawspeaker," he shouted.

As if by a signal, the mouths of almost every headman, their advisors, Mani, and his two sons sagged open. Even Naldrum's law-arguers could not conceal their astonishment. Only Naldrum and the man who had spoken sat unsurprised, with smug smiles.

The man who had nominated Bright stood, furious. "*Gothi Naldrum?* I hate to be rude, but he has never once indicated any interest in legal matters. How could he possibly serve as Lawspeaker? He does not even know our Laws enough to observe them, let alone to recite them aloud and teach as the Lawspeaker is required to do."

A great churning started in the pit of Mani's stomach. What had he said in his opening speech this year on the Lögberg? He had rehearsed the words over and over. They came to him, a terrifying foretelling of this unseen possibility. *The Law's great strength is also its greatest weakness: it depends on good human beings who may passionately disagree, yet are committed to integrity and fairness...*

Naldrum was widely known as the opposite of integrity and fairness. Mani re-heard his words: *"Headmen who care about their own wealth...seize our people's distress as opportunity..."* And then his worst fear. *If they gain power, they will trample law and justice into the mud.*

Oh, by the gods, no, anyone, *anyone* but Naldrum.

The nomination must have been a stupid joke, Mani told himself. Yet here came Naldrum, walking to the grass center of the council, explaining his reasons. Worst of all, some of the other chieftains seemed to be nodding their heads in agreement, listening with interest.

"Father," Bright whispered behind him. "Father...stand up."

In his dread, Mani had begun to sag, holding onto the law-staff for support. At his son's whisper, he straightened.

Well, I'm still Lawspeaker for this year and next. Naldrum can strut about in his pompous finery; we'll see what happens when the council votes next summer. That's a long time away, and we have a near-famine facing our country. He almost laughed in bitterness. *As if Naldrum would care about leading people through that.*

Mani carefully kept his face impassive. Appalled, he found himself wondering if his sixty-five-year-old arm was strong enough to put a *sax* into Naldrum's soft throat, unaware that Kel, watching in cold fury, was thinking the exact same thing.

. . .

In the common fields, Tor loaded his blacksmith anvil into one of the carts that would form part of their entourage back to Bull Valley. He put his tools and leather apron on top of it.

The trip back to Naldrum's holdings could require any number of requests for his services, from filing hooves to repairing harnesses. He had checked everything he possibly could, but things always broke.

Tor hoped things *would* break. Any distraction, any work, would help. Otherwise, he would have few duties along the trail. Since his brief encounter with the toothless sailor, he fought daily to keep his thoughts under control. *How long until his wife might arrive at the headman's home? What if bad weather forced the ship to wait until spring? What if she never arrived in Iceland, drowned by a storm at sea with no one to know or grieve?* One worry after another beset Tor.

When slavers had first stolen his wife Kandace, every breath had been torture. Tor put his hand flat against his chest where the old familiar pain now burned again. *How had he gotten through those early days?* He had forgotten how intense the pain had been. Strange to realize that he had actually grown numb to living without her. Now even that comfort eluded Tor.

The children. Aldís said they were safe. I'll think of the children. But immediately, his thoughts returned to Kandace. *I hope she comes to the compound soon after we get back.*

The irony of anticipating his return to the place he loathed was not lost on Tor. He wished he could talk to Kel about it, to ask him if Naldrum had said anything about the merchant Indaell, or about a new slave woman who had dark skin like himself. But the two men could not easily talk on the trail without Naldrum's other servants and thralls taking note.

Probably just as well, Tor sighed. He and Kel had not spoken with one another since the first day at Althing. Despite Kel's declaration of his intent to leave Naldrum, Kel had clearly stayed on as the chieftain's steward. Whatever his reasons, Kel had kept them to himself.

Tor shook his head. Everything was a mess, and no one to help with any of it. For the first time, he did not turn to prayers for relief.

. . .

The fiftieth anniversary of Althing ended in heavy rain. Despite that, a sizeable crowd stood in drenching wet for the closing rituals.

The night before, Naldrum had summoned Kel. "Steward, bad weather threatens. I've decided that our people will not attend the final ceremony. We'll get an early start before the roads are a mess of churning mud. Put bells on all the horses and have our entourage ready to depart first thing in the morning."

But they did not leave at the Kalendar's early-morning call. Instead, Naldrum kept them waiting for no apparent reason, the horses stamping and chuffing, roosters calling, and herders frantically trying to keep their animals together, with everyone anxious to be moving instead of just standing about wet and cold.

Kel clenched and unclenched his reins, irritated and wanting to be on the way. At the advice of the sooth-sayer and Mani, he had gone through the motions: pretending to be a responsible man who held an important position, pretending to have respect for Naldrum, but he had seen his face at a mirror-merchant's tent yesterday. Dark circles under his eyes had deepened to blue-black hollows.

Rain dripped on his face, increasing his annoyance. Next to Kel, Naldrum sat on his own horse, a faint smile on his face. He ignored Kel, looked at nothing, spoke to no one.

Kel heard the Horn of Althing sound over the valley. "Since we're not leaving, our people might appreciate attending the closing ceremony," he said to Naldrum. *Anything to not just sit here with him an arms-length from me.*

"Do you think I want your advice, steward? No, we will not attend the ceremony. I have decided that we will leave right now," Naldrum snapped. He spurred his horse. Instead of taking the shorter route out of the valley, Naldrum rode directly towards the Law Rock, gesturing his entire entourage to follow.

Kel grimaced in disgust as he realized what Naldrum was doing. To what depths would this man sink? Naldrum's bells were causing everyone to turn and gawk at him instead of observing the closing of this fiftieth year. *Yet he claims he wants to stand as Lawspeaker? How little respect he has for anything of honor.*

Kel pulled his cloak over his face and kept his head low, wanting invisibility against such a disrespectful action.

Mani's son Bright, standing with his father, shared the same thoughts. He had never spoken to Mani about his dislike for the headman Naldrum, and he did not comment now.

But Bright knew that Naldrum had forced Mani to pause in his speech and to wait for the long train of riders, walkers, animals and ware-carts to pass. It made a great noise of bells jingling, hooves thudding on the ground, herders calling and shouting, as Naldrum's group churned mud right against the heels of the crowd who stood below the Law Rock.

Bright put his hand on his father's arm. Even across the duration of Althing, Mani seemed to have grown more stooped, grayer. As they waited an interminably long time for Naldrum's noisy caravan to pass, the rain soaked the Lawmaker's hair and cloak. Mani forced himself to stand tall, but Bright could see his father shivering from the cold.

Bright's heart hardened to iron. Silence did not mean acquiescence—and self-control did not mean weakness.

. . .

Chapter Twenty-Six

Kel called for the middle-day break in riding. All along the line the command repeated, stretching back from where Naldrum's wives rode to the walking servants and thralls to where the herdsmen at the rear of the caravan drove livestock Naldrum had bought at Althing.

Traveling on horseback would take only a few days of hard riding, but Naldrum had spent heavily on new breeding stock. The traveling herds of sheep, goats and cattle moved far more slowly and needed regular time to graze. Slowest of all were the pig-drovers.

Kel had given orders when they left: they would travel pig-speed each morning until middle-day when the sun was directly overhead, then a stop to graze the livestock and rest the pigs. Move again until the sun dropped half-way to the horizon, still in the north during these long summer days. Rest and graze again. He had estimated the journey would take at least a week, perhaps a little longer. *Days of semi-freedom out in the open air.* With dread, he thought of winter and the stone walls of Naldrum's compound closing in.

As he did every day, Kel pushed away thoughts of Aldís, but they returned, mice nibbling at his sanity.

She fought beside me at the duels.

Then she left you, his inner voice contracted. *Just like before.*

This back-and-forth had done nothing but increase Kel's bitterness at still being forced to serve Naldrum. *Because of her,* that inner voice chimed. *Because of her, you're stuck.*

. . .

Kel heard shouts of an argument and looked around to see what had caused the commotion. Naldrum's son Drikke was screaming at his new young groom. Kel muttered an invective and walked back.

"I told you to take my mare over *there,*" Drikke shouted. "Are you deaf? Do I have to do everything for you?" he jerked the reins from the groom's hand and dragged his horse to the greener spot.

"No, sir, this is better," the boy argued, following him. "The grass grows greener there because it is swampy. We should keep your horse on the dry ground. It already has a limp."

"Don't you dare argue with me."

The boy, had, in fact, heard a noise from the tall grass. Fearing a troll or some kind of local spirit, he did not want to venture closer.

"It's not too wet. Get over here and hold the reins," Drikke demanded. As the boy took the reins, however, he saw three things very quickly.

A nest of some kind. Wild dogs, he realized almost immediately, and young in the nest. The mother dog, her shoulders hunched and hackles up. The horse, stepping on one of her pups, and it squealing.

As the horse reared in alarm, the mother dog leaped. The groom felt her teeth tear his calf. At the same time, the horse lost its balance and tumbled on top on him. A loud crack, and everything went black.

. . .

Aldís had been slicing cabbages into barrels of vinegar for sauerkraut when something had clicked in her head, hard enough that she felt it in her chest. Aldís hesitated, wondering as she always did if she had imagined the need.

Again, the sensation. *Broken,* it insisted.

Aldís put down her knife. "I have to leave," she said to her farm friend. "Can you finish without me?"

The woman took the knife and resumed slicing the same cabbage Aldís had dropped. "If you're needed, go. And stop doubting yourself. I can see it in your face." The two women had been friends for years. Aldís had spoken with her openly of the uncertainty of the random, indeterminate impressions that sometimes flooded her.

Still, the call felt strong. Aldís struck out from the farm, unsure of which direction to follow. Where the farm track joined the valley roadway, she hesitated, reached out in her thoughts. A slight inclination to go to the left. Aldís followed the sensation *broken* along the stone and sand bed of a dry stream, feeling foolish, and wondering if she really had sensed anything at all or if her own imagination had caused this. Should she run? *Agh, to trust myself would be such a comfort."*

A horse came galloping towards her, the rider barely in control as the horse's hooves sprayed gravel into the air. Aldís stood aside to let them past, but the woman jerked on the reins. The horse reared, its hooves pawing the air.

"Yellow scarf?" she asked. "A healer! Thank Freya!"

She leapt from the horse and handed the reins to Aldís. "River-fork Farm," she panted. "A horse spooked, and a boy—his leg—"

Aldís leapt onto the horse in one swift movement and kicked her heels into its flanks. She wheeled on the river course and rode hard.

. . .

Aldís followed the riverbed until she came close to the farm. She veered off, cut through a meadow, and headed towards the road, still pressing the horse to go as fast as it could.

A long train of people. So many wagons and carts. Her heart sank. Only one possible group cutting across the flatland towards Bull Valley could be that large. *Naldrum's entourage.* Right after that, the next dismay: *Kel will be with them.*

But *broken broken broken* demanded that she come. Someone ahead, hurt, needed help. Even if it was Naldrum himself, she could not refuse.

. . .

A crowd had formed around the boy. Drikke fussed over his horse, worried that it might have injured its lame leg, ignoring the too-pale boy stretched out on the grass. Aldís pressed her way through.

"How long?" she asked. She felt for the boy's heartbeat. Put her ear to his mouth, listened for breath.

As someone answered, Aldís half-listened, examining the long bone of his thigh as much with her inner-vision as her fingertips, trying to hold his spasming thigh steady, hoping not to feel the grittiness of shattered bone signifying a break which would never heal.

*There. T*he leg had already begun to swell, and she had located the break under where the muscles jerking as they tried to hold the brokenness together.

She looked up at the group of people crowded around. "Who is responsible for this boy?"

"I am," Drikke replied, not bothering to look at Aldís. "I bought him at Althing."

"His leg is broken," she started, but Drikke cut her off.

"I don't need to know the details. Just tell me if he'll get better or if I've wasted my silver."

Such a loathsome family. "He'll get better. I'll bind it up. He'll need to rest for two moons."

"That's impossible," Drikke snarled. "As soon as we get back to my father's compound, he's needed for the harvest."

"He won't be able to help. He can't even be moved there." Aldís stood her ground.

"What do you know?" Drikke clapped his hands, called for one of the carters. "Load him onto that. He's just being lazy. We'll bind him up when we get home, if he lives that long."

Aldís felt sick. But the law gave Drikke the right. She could not resist a parting shot. "He might not have broken his leg if was better fed." The boy's ribs showed clearly, and his limbs were too thin.

Drikke reddened and his lips pressed together. *I remember this woman,* he realized. He had been young, had stopped at a tiny longhouse where she and a child lived, needing water for his horse. She had stared at him, odd and intense, and had asked his name.

Drikke, son of the headman Naldrum, he had told her, lifting his chin and looking down his nose. She had narrowed her eyes.

"Get off this land."

"You must do as I say. Law of hospitality!" he demanded.

"Tell your troll of a father I'll obey the laws when he does. Tell him to pay women the child-rights of which he deprives them," she had spat at him.

He had been forced to ride nearly until midday for his horse to slake its thirst. All the way home he had stewed in fury, practicing the angry words he would use to report the insolent creature to his father. Naldrum had promised to revenge Drikke's inconvenience.

Now, Drikke strutted over to Aldís, his chest out and arms back, looking for all the world like a bantam rooster. Without warning, he struck her full-fisted on the face, and Aldís dropped like a stone.

. . .

Kel, keeping the crowd from stepping on the boy, had not seen Aldís ride up. She had not seen him either, all her attention on the injured groom. Now, he grabbed Drikke's tunic from behind and hauled him away from Aldís.

"How dare you!" he bellowed. Kel whirled Drikke around. Naldrum's son put up his hands in front of his face, whining and cringing. "How *dare* you!"

Kel shook Drikke hard enough that his cap fell off and his neck-chains rattled. "Father," Drikke screamed, and Kel let him go.

"Get out of here, you coward," Kel muttered. He bent to Aldís. Her eyes opened, but she looked around, confused and unfocused.

322   Katie Aiken Ritter

"You're safe," Kel said.

. . .

Aldís stared up at a fuzzy image. *I know him.* She blinked, tried to focus, tried to think, tried to sit up, but nothing seemed to be working.

Kel, her mind said.

"Kel," Aldís repeated.

"Yes," he replied.

She lay in soft grass. *Kel. We must be at Althing.* Aldís smiled. "Did we just…?" she laughed and blushed.

Kel's heart nearly stopped. Years ago at Althing, she had woken next to him to ask the exact same question. He wished fervently that he could say 'yes' again. Go back to that day. Start it all over again.

"No, Aldís," he said instead. "It happened long ago. Not today."

She stared at him for a little while, trying to figure out what he meant. The boy on the ground groaned. Aldís turned her head, looked over at him.

Suddenly it all rushed back. She sat up, fell back. Pressed her hand to her head.

"Oh gods," she said. "We have to help him."

"Tell me what to do," Kel said.

. . .

Naldrum's daughter Ankya, seeing that Kel had gone back to the thralls and herds, had at first not followed. She waited for him to come back to where she rode with her father at the head of the column.

"What is taking him so long?" she asked her maid. The girl shrugged her shoulders.

"Go back and see."

The maid ran back, and soon returned to Ankya. "Someone is hurt. There's a woman there. She's hurt too. Kel is helping them both."

A little flicker of jealousy. "Stay here. If my father asks where I am, tell him I'm lying in one of the litters taking a nap."

She kicked at her horse. The crowd was a little way back at a straight stretch in the roadway. As Ankya rode up, the little bells on her horse jingling, people made way for her.

"Drikke, you look a mess," she said to her brother. He turned his face away and did not answer, sulking.

Ankya saw Kel's tunic and pushed to get close. To her horror, she recognized the woman he was helping was the same one from the holmgang duels, the one her father had threatened to kill.

"Kel, what is *she* doing here? You know Father said you were not to ever see her again or he would—"

Kel blanched. "I'll be right back," he said to Aldís. He walked Ankya a little distance from the throng.

"I didn't ask her to come. There's a boy there with a badly broken leg and a dog bite. That farm there," Kel gestured to the not-too-distant longhouse. "We asked them for help. They sent someone to ride to the next farms along the valley and look for someone who knows how to fix bones. It's only a mad trick of Loki that she's here. I swear I did not send for her."

Ankya gazed into Kel's earnest eyes. "You don't want me to tell Father, do you?" she asked.

"I don't. She didn't come here for me. She's helping one of your father's slaves. He's valuable property, so there's no reason to hurt her for it. As I said, Loki is playing tricks on us." Kel forced a smile.

"Do you love her, Kel?" Ankya could not hold the burning question inside, try though she might. "It seemed at Althing that she was helping you in the holmgang battles, and Father said something about he'd warned you before about her. It seems—" Ankya stopped, jealous and distressed.

Kel gripped Ankya by both hands. The thrill went straight to her loins.

"You have to believe me, Ankya. I didn't seek her out at Althing. She sought me out." *Almost true. It fit the facts as Ankya knew them.* "And not now, either. I have no—" he choked. He'd told the truth his whole life. It's why he'd trusted Naldrum, he suddenly realized. *We see others as we are, not as they are.*

Kel found he did not want to say the lie, and instead chose words to make it mostly true.

"I've had no intention of seeing her for years. And I have no intention of seeing her in the future, either."

"Oh, Kel. I'm glad I asked Father to keep you. You are such a faithful steward to him." Ankya rose on tiptoe, offered her cheek for a kiss. Kel could smell the perfume that rose from her breasts. It sickened him.

To his relief, someone called him back to the circle around the boy. "Steward Kel. they want us to carry him into the farmhouse."

Kel forced another smile at Ankya. "Go on back up to your father. This messy business isn't fit for a pretty girl like you to see."

Ankya's mouth opened in delight at what sounded like a compliment from Kel. She made a show of walking off as he turned back to the injured boy, but then swung around and watched. *After all, there might be blood,* Ankya thought, smiling.

But such delight did not come. Instead, eager hands loaded the boy onto an improvised litter and carried him to the farmhouse. Ankya saw Kel and Aldís following. Aldís walked unsteadily, and Kel put his arm around her waist to steady her. *The way a man might if he loved a woman,* Ankya realized.

Her own blood turned to ice. For a moment, she hated Kel with all her girlish heart. Then she saw the woman lean away from Kel. Push his arm from her waist. The woman bent over, her hands on her knees. Shook her head at Kel when he tried to help her walk again.

That horrid woman. She doesn't know what a wonderful man Kel is. The hate Ankya had just felt for Kel doubled, tripled, quadrupled—and shot straight as an arrow towards the woman wearing the yellow scarf.

. . .

"I hear that Drikke had a bit of trouble with his groom when we stopped for the mid-day," Naldrum said. He had dropped his reins. No need to hold them on such a straight roadway. Instead, the headman peeled a fruit that Kel did not recognize and ate it. He sounded bored at the idea of whatever the trouble had been.

Kel wondered if Ankya had said anything. Best to be careful. "Not sure how it all happened. The break appeared to be a bad one. Not much could be done."

Drikke, Kel knew, would have said the exact same thing to his father. When they had carried the boy to the longhouse, Kel had dragged Drikke in to negotiate a care fee.

"Just give him to them," the arrogant young man had said. "He's a slave. They help his leg mend, and they keep him. They kill him, they don't. It's a good enough deal."

"If they care for him and he dies, they have spent much effort for your foolishness, and for no gain. Your father is the first to seek profit for himself in anything. You will pay them what they ask."

For now, the entitled son of Naldrum still held Kel in some regard. Another year or two, and he'd not be able to talk to Drikke this way.

The farm family had settled on an amount that Kel thought more than fair. When Drikke threw the bit of hack-silver on their table and stormed out of the longhouse, Kel dug in his pouch.

"Here." He held out his other hand for the thrall collar, knowing the amount Drikke had paid for the scrawny lad. "Promise me you'll set him free."

"Good man," said the freehold woman. She undid the collar and handed it to Kel. "We're not of those who treat men and women and children like work animals."

Kel had bowed. As he left the longhouse, he started to throw the slave collar deep into the brush along the road, but instead tucked it into the waistband of his pants and pulled his tunic over it and went back to the head of the caravan. Foot in stirrup, he mounted his horse and shouted for the break to end.

. . .

The grim stone walls of Naldrum's compound loomed in Kel's mind. The big longhouse that boasted Naldrum's renowned glass window was a sinister pit in which family, servants and slaves fed the chieftain's all-consuming pride, knowing that to survive meant pretending to admire Naldrum's arrogant pronouncements and murmuring compliments loudly enough so the headman could hear.

After what had happened at Althing, the thought of going back to such dishonesty sickened Kel to his core. Brittle anger filled his throat, making it hard even to eat. Not only had he had to bend the knee to save Aldís, but before they left Althing, Naldrum had insisted on the formal handshake that signified agreement to duty. "I want you to remember who's the headman here, Kel. Swear fealty to me."

He had put out his hand and nauseated, had forced himself to say the words. Afterwards, Naldrum had grasped Kel's arm, smiling broadly, relieved to be back in control. "Let's have this unfortunate matter of that woman behind us. She's left anyway, I hear."

"What is it about her that makes you hate her so?" Kel had asked.

He had seen Naldrum clench his jaw. Had seen the way the headman's neck thickened and reddened in anger. But Naldrum had not answered. "We'll all get back to normal, shall we?"

Kel let himself think of Aldís. She was gone, and then today, she was suddenly here. He felt youthful joy remembering her question *'did we just…?'* Then the frustration when, once again, the cold mask had slid over her features, shutting him out.

He thought through his conversation with the sooth-sayer at Althing, letting himself remember, slow bit by slow bit, each interaction with Aldís, seeking a part that he clearly was missing.

Aldís's angry resentment, that long-ago visit when she had her child. How she'd sent him away, choosing Naldrum over him. How he'd made himself a model servant to Naldrum, doing even Naldrum's appalling 'spring duties' for the headman without complaint, because young and foolish, he had wanted Aldís to see him as a man of ruthless power, the kind of man she seemed to want...the kind of man she now claimed she loathed.

Images of being with Aldís came and went, as did images of her and Naldrum and the child she'd claimed was Naldrum's. *How could she be so sure,* he suddenly wondered. *We lay together—*

No. She'd have told me. Her daughter—Naldrum's child, much as it sickened Kel to think those words, must have come from a later coupling with the headman.

Some strange rope bound the four of them together, but for the life of him, Kel simply could not see how to cut through the angry tangle that tied them to something in the past.

Just keep going forward, he told himself. *Do what Mani said. What other option do I have?*

. . .

But the thought *I could just kill Naldrum* occurred to Kel more and more often. *Just have it done with. Get myself outlawed. Leave the country for a few years. Come back and live a life of peace.*

Who was he fooling? Naldrum's cronies would never let him live in peace.

Go to Eire then, or to the Scot's lands. Somewhere else. Somewhere far away. Maybe take Tor with me. Set him free.

He flicked a glance back to where Tor walked near the cart that carried the portable forge. Tor's words came again. *Set your intentions, and the way will open to you.*

Kel straightened in his saddle, bored with the slow pace and wanting a gallop. He had tried to get away from Naldrum, and Loki had dragged him back. *So be it. Whatever path the gods have laid for my destiny, I am going to walk it, come what may,* Kel told himself. Mani had told him to watch and learn. *So be it.* He would stay close to Naldrum and watch and learn, no matter how distasteful that might prove. One day it might all make sense. If not, at least one day, he might stop the headman from future wrongs. It would have to be enough.

. . .

Naldrum glanced in turn to where Kel rode, wondering what his steward was thinking. *He's so weak. I made one threat to that hag-witch at Althing, and Kel buckled like a newborn foal. What was her name? Oh, yes, Aldis.*

Naldrum knew perfectly well what her name was. The curse she had put on him long years ago still plagued him, and now she had spoken it again. He shivered.

If Kel proves disloyal, useful or not, I'll have no choice but to get rid of him. Naldrum realized, surprised, that the idea of Kel leaving his service was mildly unsettling. Annoyed, he pushed the idea away. *I should have replaced him while we were at Althing. Made that new fellow my headman. Kel's a liability. I can't trust him any longer.*

Naldrum, backing rapidly away from admitting that he had acted unwisely, thought of Rota. Her words drifted across his thoughts. *Be aware of things that disgust you.*

The order still made little sense, but Naldrum made an attempt. *I'm disgusted with Kel. He isn't completely loyal to me.*

What had she said to do next? *Point out your loathing and your dislike. Make sure that people see those things the way that you see them. And finally, show your people that you, their leader, will find whoever is to blame for their fears, and whoever is responsible for the things that upset them. Show that you will punish those responsible.*

Why hadn't that irritating woman told him exactly what to do? Such nonsensical wanderings. It all felt like a waste of time. He decided to let Kel do the work for him.

"Steward, approach."

Kel pulled on his reins, drew his horse back alongside Naldrum's.

"Steward, there are people in my service whose loyalty I can't trust. Not a good thing for a leader, to have people whispering against him, is it? How do you propose I address such issues?"

Kel flinched. Was this a trap? Did Naldrum know Kel had spoken openly with Tor, and Mani, and the sooth-sayer, or had Ankya told Naldrum she'd seen Aldís just now? Kel chose his words with care.

"Every leader has these concerns, *gothi*. Old sagas tell of rulers who killed even their own sons, fearing betrayal. It is a hard thing to tell if people are just grumbling—as people will, who work hard—or they would do actual harm. Food is scarce these days and work equally hard to find. Winter is coming, and people need food. Those who sound disloyal may simply be expressing worry."

A good answer. Naldrum congratulated himself for keeping Kel. "But if some do more than grumble, what then?" *Punish,* Rota said.

"One might try and focus their thoughts on hope. Let them know that even if the harvest is bad, they will not go hungry in the winter."

What a weakling. Good harvests came from those who worked hard to make them happen and to those the gods favored.

"Enough, Steward. Let me ride alone with my thoughts now."

Kel kicked his horse and moved to his position at the front of the column again. Naldrum watched his steward as they rode along the flat gravel riverbed, pleased. Kel had inadvertently given Naldrum the answer he needed. People were worried they might go hungry that winter? *Bah. Only cowards wanted coddling.* He would do exactly the opposite: let people know that the harvest and fall slaughter would *not* feed them all. Only those who were loyal would eat.

Naldrum beamed. The excellence of his plan astonished even him. Those who did not support him would not eat, and those who did not eat might not survive the winter. Such a plan would handily eliminate many he disliked and help his allies. Thanks to his graciousness, those would be even more loyal than before. *What a brilliant strategy.*

Naldrum straightened up in his saddle and spent the last hour of riding considering which of the landowners he might keep and which of them had fine farms Naldrum might have for his own.

King of Bull Valley…and one day, king of all Iceland. His dreams soared. Naldrum smiled. *People will know how important I am.*

. . .

Chapter Twenty-Seven

The caravan wound up the river road to the headman's longhouse. At each settlement or farm, people who lived there had left the caravan. Now only Naldrum's own household plodded along the last weary stretch.

For the headman and his family, the sight of their lands coming into view in the far distance brought relief. They would sleep in their own home tonight, safe and dry with the long-fire crackling, and the quiet interior of their longhouse a pleasant change after the relentless daylight of the trail.

For those who served as Naldrum's bondsmen and thralls, the sight had a different effect. Gone were the days of light duty at Althing, and the pleasures of companionship with other travelers on the road, not least of which had been the joy of speaking in their native languages with slaves from other homesteads, a mixed bag of languages from distant shores that mingled in a pleasant patois.

Today, the sun and warmth helped to soften the transition between the pleasures of Althing and what lay ahead: backbreaking weeks of work haying the fields and digging root crops in the upcoming harvest season. After that, the grim night of the *álfablót* again, gateway to the cold isolation of winter. To a person, they shuddered as the caravan made the last turn to Naldrum's holdings.

. . .

Ankya did not regret the thought of long nights cloistered in the longhouse. To the contrary, she relished the idea, thinking of Kel. Whenever weather limited travel, he would work at her father's compound for days at a time. Last year Kel had resisted her efforts to seduce him. Ankya vowed that this winter, she would not fail.

Ankya's mother continued her steady low mumble of complaints. She loved the bright excitement of Althing and dreaded leaving it.

"Stop fretting, mama," Ankya said. "We will all be busy and working hard through the upcoming weeks. The days will go quickly. Before you know it, the time will come for the autumn's *equal nights and days* feast, and then the *álfablót,* and then the sheep-gathering. There will be lots to enjoy."

Her mother clutched at the idea in relief. Her tone grew more cheerful as she considered which of the silks she had bought at Althing would be her new dress for the harvest feast. Soon she stopped chatting with Ankya and mumbled about mead, meats, and meals.

Ankya kicked her horse and moved up to where her father rode.

"What is making you smile in that happy way, daughter?" Naldrum asked.

"Nothing, father. Just glad to be getting home. Everyone celebrated you at Althing, and now you can tell the stories to all who did not attend. And I was wondering if perhaps you will let me ride out with you and your steward when you visit the farms to collect the harvest tithe. I would love to help tell them about your exciting tales and new plans."

"Such a brave girl you are," he said. "You understand my job as *gothi* far more than your brother. Of course, you may come with us on some of them."

Her heart beat faster. Perhaps now was a suitable time to launch her next objective. "I'm glad you kept Kel. I like him so."

"Silly child," Naldrum reached over and caressed his daughter's hair. "He's not worth your infatuation, but if he makes you happy, I'll keep him around."

"I'm not a child. Why won't you ever put me in the bride-fair? I've been old enough for years now. I had hoped you would make Kel choose me."

"My dear Ankya," Naldrum smiled indulgently. "Even my love for you will not permit such a pointless match. You are too fine for my steward. I have far greater plans for you. Princes in other countries will beg to make a match with you. Trust your wise father to choose what is best."

Ankya's breast swelled with anger. "I don't want a stupid prince. I want Kel." She kicked her horse and wheeled around to ride back where her father could not see her pout.

. . .

Even though Naldrum's compound now lay in sight, it was still at some distance and the herds still needed to rest and graze. Kel called for the midday pause, a last one before they reached the property.

Naldrum sighed in relief and jumped from his horse.

"Here, Ankya, look what arrived just before we left," Naldrum pulled a parcel of exotic fruits. "I had them brought to Althing specially for you. I've been saving them as a gift."

She hid her frustration and obediently took a fruit from the mix. "What is this one called? I forget."

"Pomegranate, my darling." Naldrum tore the flesh open and showed his daughter the jewel-like red droplets twinkling inside.

She laughed, an unnatural, eerie sound.

"Stop that, Ankya. It makes my head hurt."

"It should be called 'drops-of-blood' fruit!" she laughed again, ignoring him. "I would have seen *real* drops of blood if you had cut that woman in your tent."

Ankya blanched. She had almost blurted to her father about seeing Aldís caring for the wounded groom. To cover her error, she popped bits of pomegranate into her pursed lips, one by one, licking her fingers each time. "Does blood taste this sweet?"

She's just teasing. Just playful, Naldrum told himself.

"Speaking of women," he said, "I'll have another surprise soon."

"What is it? Tell me." Ankya held up a morsel of pomegranate against the sun, admired how the light gleamed red through it.

"I have sent for a new thrall. Like this fruit, she is exotic, and from far away. Like Tor."

"Will she look like him? Dark, like the lava?"

"I think so. We'll find out together, shall we?"

"And her blood? Will it be red like Tor's?" Ankya wrestled another scarlet morsel from the fruit, held it between her white front teeth. She bit down and the red juice stained her lips. Again, she gave the eerie laugh, had the strange look in her eyes.

"Give me that! I'm trying to give you a gift and you mock me." Naldrum snatched the pomegranate from Ankya. For the thousandth time he told himself that there was nothing the matter with his daughter. The torn fruit lay wet against his hand, juices staining his palm. Naldrum threw it as hard as he could into the rough grasses along the roadway.

Kel might not want to be in his service, but by the gods, Kel was *going* to be in his service. Ankya's infatuation with his steward was the one normal thing about her. Whatever ploy Naldrum could use to protect his daughter from her own strange impulses, he fully intended to use.

. . .

Kel had barely unsaddled his horse before Tor approached him, looking about. No one was nearby. Tor hazarded a whisper.

"Have you heard of anyone new joining the household soon?"

Kel felt annoyed at everything these days. He started to snap an answer but restrained himself. His situation was not Tor's fault.

"Not likely. Hard work until the harvest will keep most people on their own farms. A rush of people will come to the harvest festival. It'll slow to a trickle across the winter."

"No...I meant...perhaps any new slaves?"

"Only the ones Naldrum bought at Althing. They're roped together near the goat herds." At Tor's downcast look, Kel endeavored to give him a little more answer. "But the headman doesn't tell me his plans."

Tor wandered off, chewing on his thumbnail. His normal stoic calm had disappeared ever since seeing the toothless man at the food booth. Again and again, he had knelt in prayer, asking for advice, but the Almighty had given no indication of what he should do.

What to do when there is no choice, and no help? *You sold yourself into bondage to be able to keep searching for her,* Tor reminded himself. *You knew what being a slave meant. Just because your first master was your friend didn't mean it was always going to be easy.*

Confused, Tor paced back and forth during the rest break. It occurred to him that had the trader Josson never bought him, had Naldrum never taken him, had he never gone to Althing with Naldrum, he might never have met the toothless sailor.

Was all this the Almighty's plan? he wondered. There was no way of knowing, but the thought gave him some consolation. Tor found a place to lie in the sun and half-slept, his thoughts ever so slightly less troubled as he waited for the call to ride again. *Third Way,* Tor told himself. *Find your intentions. Make your choice.*

. . .

Chapter Twenty-Eight

Two months later, the last full moon of summer began its rise, round, massive, and glowing scarlet just above the horizon on a cloudless night. From valley to valley across all of Iceland, people turned out of doors, calling to one another to come and see the god-of-the-night in his shining glory.

Not only its beauty brought them. A full moon was the best time to ask for blessings from the moon-god.

Two weeks ago, he had been no more than a thin sliver in the night sky. People across the land had whispered encouragement to the growing young moon, each night leaving small gifts to nourish it: a bit of turnip laid on a stone where the moon's light would touch it, or a morsel of bread. A few grains of barley, a crust of cheese, a fish head…a bit of carved wood or a fragment of fresh-made soap, or a broken comb.

They fed the moon-god, helping him to grow plump and round. Now, this night of fullness, those who stood outside held up their hands to bathe in the moon's beams, hoping that it would answer their requests—because, tonight, too full to hold any more blessings, the moon would spring a small leak, and like a waterfall, the boons it had absorbed would flow back down.

They would drift, those moonbeams of promise. The moon-god knew not where, nor cared. Some would land on rocks and keep them strong. Some would bless the flow of streams and rivers. Some would glimmer on the broad waves of the sea, and some would strengthen sails. Some would feed land-spirits and river-nixies and nourish the living essences of grottoes and fields. Some would gleam on geese, or goats, or horses or piglets, and give them vigor.

And some would bring brightness to a fortunate human. The moon-god's bounty was impartial in this regard as well. Chieftain or thrall, well-intentioned or cruel, thoughtful or careless, all might benefit equally. The moon smiled down on all creation, exquisitely unseeing, blind to fault as well as to virtue, dispensing goodness without bias, for who knew where goodness might take root and grow?

So across the whole land, from valley to valley and farm to farm, people lifted their hands in supplication to this creature of generosity. Climbing from the horizon to the high night sky, its great round face changed from rose to orange to yellow to white. It lit valleys and mountains of the land beneath it, happily dispersing of all the offerings it had taken in. From tonight and for the next two weeks, the moon would give until it had given all of itself back to the land.

Then, thin and hungry again, it would need sustenance. The little gifts would begin again, and the moon would absorb them into its great Presence. It would grow and glow fatter each night, become full once more, send fortune once more, and then grow thin once more, again and again in an endless, gentle cycle of taking and giving.

In his settlement near the shores of *reykja-vik,* the bay-of-clouds, Mani the Lawspeaker asked for what he always did on the night of the full moon: nothing. Instead, he stood watching the eastern horizon, waiting to offer grateful greetings to his foster-father, the god with whom he shared a name.

Mani. Such a tremendous honor to have been given the same name as the moon-god. Mani's father had bestowed it knowing his infant son would one day be the *Allsherjargothi,* and possibly Lawspeaker, hoping to inspire in the boy the ways of his godly namesake: impartial to all, generous and kind. The name had shaped his life, had caused Mani to study hard, fervent in his determination to be faithful in serving an unbiased Law.

In the two months since Althing, the old Lawspeaker had found himself yearning to ask Mani the moon-god for help, just this once, dreading what havoc Naldrum might wreak on Iceland should he become Lawspeaker instead of Mani's son Bright.

Not for myself, Father Mani, and not for your god-son Bright, but for this land I love. For the Law.

Instead, he prayed to Forseti, god of justice. *May I find the right course.* To Odin, for wisdom. To Thor, for bravery: *I am Lawspeaker until the vote next summer. Give me courage to serve our people well.*

When the fullness of the moon-god showed on the horizon, Mani the Lawspeaker found in himself the strength to *not* ask for blessings.

I will wait to see what Kel says, come next summer. If he needed anything, it was patience.

. . .

In the seas off the northern fjords, the young priest Konradsson sat with his back against the side of a small merchant ship. He watched the moon rise over the rising and falling waves as they lapped against the *knarr* taking him and the Bishop Friedrich to yet another remote fjord to greet others in the Lord's name.

Seeing it, the sailors on the ship paused briefly in their work. They turned towards the moon, lifted their hands. Friedrich did not notice, and Konradsson did not draw his attention to the small invocations. He was not sure why, exactly. But the monastery in Germania felt incredibly remote, and carved dragons on doors somehow no longer felt as threatening or as wrong.

Konradsson found himself, too, wanting to make the age-old gesture of lifting his palms to the rising brightness and saying a word of prayer. It would be to God, of course, not Mani-the-Moon-God, but the action, so out of place in the monastery, somehow felt fitting and right on this ship riding the swells of Rán the sea-mother.

I am waiting to learn my destiny, he thought. And then, unable to resist, he opened his palms in his lap. *Please show me how I can serve. I am waiting to be Your messenger.*

. . .

On the other side of the land, in Bull Valley, Tor closed his forge for the night. He walked outside the small stone shed. Its walls shone white, bathed in moonlight. Tor thought of Nikea and Nenet. If only he could hear their laughter; were they, perhaps just now, chattering as they helped Eilíf harvest her fields of barley and rye, the moon lighting their beautiful ebony faces with the color of oranges? The same moon smiled on them as him, Tor reminded himself. *I must feel grateful for even that small connection.*

And Kandace? Perhaps she was on a ship tossing somewhere in the rough Nor'way seas. Tor sent a prayer for the moon to light her way. *Almighty Goodness, keep Kandace safe. Bring her to me.*

He thought of his own Third Way, the decisions he had made. Somehow, they would all be together as a family again.

Breath in. Breath out. Live for a moment, and then an eighth, then a day, a week, a month. moon after moon until she comes. Do not trouble yourself with how it will happen. Trust it will somehow, somehow come to pass.

. . .

Kel, overseeing thralls laboring at Naldrum's harvest, watched the moon rise over fields heavy with grain. It was a clear night, so Kel sent word back to the longhouse that the harvesters would eat their supper in the fields, since the brightness of the moon-god would allow for extra work that night. He then promptly announced that toils had ended for the day, and to lay down their scythes and rakes.

To the supper-runners, Kel directed, "Bring an extra measure of *sup* and a full cask of beer for these good folks. The *gothi's* storehouse will not miss it."

Kel did not know the workers had a secret name for him now, one that had spread in whispers since the holmgang duels. The harvesters—a mixture of Scoti, Saxon, Northumbrian, Frankish and Gaelic women and men—shared it carefully, trusting the name only with those they knew would not betray them to Naldrum.

As the *sup* and beer arrived, Kel saw their forefingers going to temples, indicating silent thanks. He nodded back, an equally silent, equally meaningful acknowledgement.

Kel could not do much besides give them a bit of rest here and there and a full belly to make life a little easier. Still, he felt a simple pleasure in it, a small repayment for staying in Naldrum's service.

Kel realized with a start that more than sixty days had passed since Althing. The young woman he had seen with Naldrum would know soon enough. In seven months, perhaps, he would have a witness.

I will be here waiting, Kel told the moon. *Please bring the luck and courage I need to challenge Naldrum next Althing*

He was surprised at how calm he felt. "Apparently, Tor is right about the Third Way," he told the moon. "I haven't worried about Aldís and Naldrum at all. Somehow, it will all work." A flicker of doubt came, a shadow of the old fears Naldrum had always used to control him. Kel pushed it away.

Aldís had come to Althing. Maybe she would again. Maybe the break between them would somehow heal. *What did Tor say? Not only is anything possible, everything is.*

Kel turned his palms to the moon again. The first request had come from his decision to do what was right even if difficult. This one came from somewhere deeper, a place of spirit where the slow drumbeat of destiny, muffled through it had been for so long, had never ceased its sonorous, intoxicating call to be with her. *Please keep Aldís safe— from herself as well as from Naldrum—and let us be together, somehow.*

. . .

Naldrum, a golden wine-flagon in hand and his youngest wife at his side, strolled and watched the moon-god rising. He thought of pouring a bit of the wine out as homage, but it was an excellent beverage from a Frankish trader and he did not want to waste a drop. He spat on the ground. The moon would not know the difference.

*Still...*becoming a ruler might be worth a splash of wine. Naldrum tipped his flagon, intending to pour, but a messenger panted up from the field, bearing Kel's message. Naldrum squinted, trying to see the multitude of workers in the far fields but they were too distant.

"Kel says he'll keep them working long into the night," he told his wife. "Good. Just as it should be. Our fields, high up in this valley, have escaped the worst of the wet weather. Others will want for flour this winter. Kel will ensure our slaves pick up every single grain from the earth. I shall make a fine profit after all, my love."

Naldrum considered his wife. Still attractive, certainly, but she had grown past the bloom of youth. Lines had begun to show along the sides of her mouth. When he was king, he could have any woman he wanted. No one would dare refuse him.

Come spring, I'll take another wife, he promised himself. *Younger, and even more beautiful.* He had his eye on one or two maidens he'd seen in the bride-fair at Althing. One, especially, had attracted him enough that he had bribed the bride-fair matron to keep all offers from reaching the girl's parents. *I'll have that girl.*

A younger more beautiful woman would be an asset. *She'll help me win the vote to be Lawspeaker. It's the first step in my plan.* In the meantime, he would imagine those fine round young breasts as he lay with his current wife. *They're as round as that fat little moon-god,* Naldrum snickered to himself.

Beside her father, Ankya skipped a little. "You know, it's a shame that we don't have a *blót* offering for the moon-god each month. Just a little blood of some kind would be nice, don't you think?"

Naldrum left off thinking of the pleasures of young women and gripped his daughter's arm.

"Ankya, stop!" He turned his face to Mani in the sky. "Make her stop," he ordered the moon-god. Inwardly, fearful that even his wife might hear, he added a small plea. *Make my daughter be ...normal.*

Ankya shook off her father's grasp. She turned her palms up to the moon, keeping them hidden so that Naldrum would not demand to know what her wish was. *Kel,* she breathed. *Give me Kel. I am waiting.*

She glanced sideways at Naldrum's wife, barely older than herself. *I will throw her out without a backwards glance when my father gets old and dies. I will be the* gothi *of this valley...and we* will *have blood-ceremonies, every single moon.*

Ankya smiled, and a thrill of power swept through her.

. . .

Aldís saw the moonrise only as a bright glow across the open door of the longhouse where Drikke's former groom lay. The break had been bad, but clean. She had been able to set the bone and had braced his leg with birch branches and linen strips to hold everything in place.

"It's healed well. Let's remove the brace tonight."

"Will it hurt?"

"Not a bit. But look, your helper is coming to comfort you in case." Her faithful dog and the boy had become fast friends. He patted its soft ears while Aldís removed the linens, then took a tentative step.

"Well done! That break might've crippled an older person, but you young folk recover better. You'll be as good as new soon," she said. He tottered off, the dog at his heels, nuzzling him.

Young folk can withstand so much.

It would be *álfablót* next month again. *Young folk...*

Something in her still held the slenderest sliver of hope, as tiny as a crescent moon. *I will always be here,* she said to the night.

Surprising Aldís, another thought came, but this one was of Kel: not the anger that she had felt for so long, but a quiet sort of kindness.

He had been good to this boy. Was it possible she had been wrong?

Aldís was surprised to realize she felt something akin to warmth towards Kel. *He fought bravely in the holmgang duels, and none of it for himself.* Her round cheeks turned as softly pink as the rising moon as she remembered moments of stolen passion when they had met.

Perhaps next Althing—

She could not bring herself to finish the thought, but left it as it was, neither denying the idea or accepting it. *Perhaps.*

. . .

In distant meadows, far past Naldrum's compound, Kel's friend the shepherd Sauthi leaned on his stick. The moon-god's rising cast a reddish glow over the grazing sheep. Almost time for the roundup and sheep-count, which Sauthi dreaded for it meant being close to Naldrum's compound for a few days until the count was over and he could escape to the remote valleys again.

Sauthi thought of years past and wished he could not remember.

Forgive me, he prayed to the moon. For years he had made the same plea, month after month, but had found no release. *Forgive me. I don't deserve forgiveness, but I long for the peace it brings.*

Since Kel's visit earlier that year, Sauthi had added another prayer each month. *I ran in fear. Let Kel be stronger than me. Let him find a way to do what's needed.*

. . .

Even farther away, Rota watched the moon lift across a wide beach of black sand. She had hired people who knew the area well and after Althing had explored valley after valley.

She had delighted in the place called *reykja-vik,* the bay of clouds, and then *reykja-dalur,* the mist-valley where she had lain naked in the soothing waters of a steaming hot river. She had seen waterfalls so immense they boggled the mind, and steam that shot from the underworld straight up into the sky. She had stood inside a cave of ice of clearest, richest blue, so beautiful it had taken her breath, and had eaten the succulent flesh of a pig roasted in scalding sands.

I may never go home, Rota sighed in contentment. Haakon and his intrigues seemed far away. *This wild land is magical.* Haakon had no idea that Iceland's treasures lay not in its trade goods, not in linen and iron and carved ivories. No, its treasures were the land itself.

As if to prove her point, the moon suddenly came free of the sea, its light transforming the black sands into dazzling glory. Rota wrapped herself in a fur. The sand was dry and the night mild. She would stay right here and watch the sparkling sands until dawn.

Come next Althing, she would learn if her plans for Naldrum would work. Swords and power schemes had nothing to do with Rota's true goals; they were just a deal she had struck with Haakon for another purpose. Only Mani the Moon-god would hear her true desire.

. . .

Farthest of all, on wings that gleamed silver in the night sky high over the great North-way current, a falcon flew. It peered, searching the seas far below. In the distance, it spied the striped sails of a ship, miniscule in the immense ocean. The ship labored, fighting the current that flowed to other lands.

None of the crew working on the ship saw the bird as it swung lower. In the unknowable way of wild things, the gyrfalcon understood a truth: two beings that belonged together drew nearer with each gust of the wind. Satisfied, it flicked feathers of one wing, curved in a great arc, and headed back to land. Ahead on a high precipice its mate waited. They would watch together. The bird gave a cry of harsh joy as its powerful wings beat under the rising moon. *I did as asked.*

. . .

Above all of them, above the entire land and sea, the round gleaming orb of the moon-god drifted across the sky.

Hope, it gleamed. *All is possible,* it shimmered.

Far from human distress, the moon-god could see across the long past and the endless future, both marked out in patterns of his growing full and ebbing to a sliver. Mani kept faithfully to his duties: raise the tides and mark the days and weeks and months. Urge seeds planted at his waxings and wanings to grow; yes, the seeds must break free to grow. Most of all, Mani took and gave, first of all those tiny offerings, and later returning them, purified and cleansed.

He did not experience the passion and heat of his fiery sister *Sól* the sun, but knew only a serene stillness, balance and calm.

Be steady, Mani glimmered to those who looked up. *Stay the course. Trust in the Great Pattern that has been since the world began.*

The humans below, some of them quite desperate, still felt the moon's tranquility. Without knowing why or even that they did, they absorbed his quiet calm. Mani's great face smiled down as he sailed across the night, placid and serene.

What was to come, would come. Fearful people did not need promises, or even certainty. What they needed was faith that the great pattern of life would not fail them, and hope for better days to come, utterly simple things that could not be held or measured or even described, but only felt.

Tonight, as he shone down on them and they bathed in the beams of his light, Mani the moon-god offered what they needed: faith that life would go on, and hope that troubles would end…and love, for only that great force might have the power to bring together those things which were meant to be.

The End

A preview of Book II

VIKING: Thunder Horse

Iceland, circa 979 A.D.
The north-way seas, just after the midsummer festival of Althing

Tiller Thorvaldsson had not sailed to Trondheim since his youth. How had he forgotten the wickedly tight entry into this fjord?

His ship had cleared the marker island that morning, the one topped by a hulking stone that resembled a gigantic sea turtle. Once past it, they had dropped sail until the tide turned. When the waves lapped hard forward against their hull, Tiller called for the sail to be hefted again, made a hard-to-starboard pull, and their merchant *knarr* slid into the narrow mouth of Trondheim-fjord.

Imposing bare hills stood guard over both sides of the fjord entry. Atop them, armed men scrutinized every passing vessel. Crews on ships also cast suspicious looks towards Tiller's unrecognized knarr.

The lookout called back from the fore. "Nearly every one of these ships shows the same flag. Do they *all* belong to Haakon Sigurdsson?"

"Don't worry about them," Tiller replied. His casual tone belied his thoughts. *Don't worry about them? Gods, how were they ever going to get out again past that nosy fleet?*

Another hard turn, this time to the ladder-board side. The wind freshened and filled their sail, pushing them fast fore-ward. By afternoon, the rooftops of Trondheim came into view.

Tiller's throat tightened as they came approached shore. He had remembered a tumbled cluster of huts, barns, trading tents, but nothing of any great note. Now, buildings of every description stretched as far as he could see, a great clutter of structures large and small. Around them, people swarmed like ants. The wind came alongside them now, and it carried the smell of habitation: smoke from innumerable cooking fires, fetid outhouses, and the good green-smell of crop fields.

How was he ever going to find one woman in all that mess? *I should never have listened to that cursed headman Naldrum or his promise of money for me to fetch her back. I'm a fool for taking this job, and I've brought this crew on a fool's errand.* But no going back now. The only way forward lay in figuring out how to find the woman, get her out of this place bristling with Sigurdsson's men, and make it back to the open seas alive. *Just that; nothing much.*

It occurred to Tiller that of all the gods, only one might appreciate what he was about to do. A prayer to Loki, then: *if you ever loved this errant human, now would be a fine time to show it.*

Tiller swallowed hard, grasped the steering-board, and pointed the prow toward the teeming shoreline.

. . .

Chapter Two

Lade Garde, the home of Haakon Sigurdsson, Jarl of Lade

The *knarr* slid perfectly onto the smooth beach of Trondheim harbor. Tiller turned the steering board just before the hull made contact to allow the ship to keel over onto the sand on its port side. As the crew lowered the sail and coiled ropes, Tiller dropped the ramp overboard and hopped onto the shore.

"I'm going out for a bit to see what opportunities might be here. I need you all to stay close to the ship for now." Tiller ignored the groans that ensued. Most of the crew would spend the day making salt, searching the shoreline for driftwood, hauling out small cauldrons for boiling. They could groan all they liked, but by evening, they would each be richer by a mark or two. Salt was always an easy sale and a highly profitable return for a day's work simmering seawater.

Tiller shouldered a pack of trade goods and headed towards the cluster of buildings. Lade Garde, Haakon's seat of power, stood somewhere ahead in that hive—and in Lade Garde, perhaps, was Haakon's thrall woman, the one Tiller had sailed all this way to steal.

This entire town belonged to Haakon, Tiller reminded himself. None of the people he was passing were free in the way he always took for granted. The awareness that all these lives hung on one man's whims gave Tiller an uncomfortable sensation of being followed. *Nobody rules Icelanders like that,* he thought.

His father had had the same stubborn streak, but with a contentious nature. Always brawling. Always on the wrong side of a fight. Defiant to the end.

I won't share his fate. Won't fail as he did. Old bitterness clouded Tiller's thoughts.

Always the struggle. Always one man trying to steal what he envied from another. Only the names changed, generation to generation. Men like himself always at the bottom, scrapping to survive, while ones like Fairhair and Bloodaxe and Haakon prospered and ruled. Why?

Tiller trudged along the path, past ship-building sheds and barns where barrels of trade goods were stored, straight towards the heart of Trondheim where the woman might be—and if so, where the greatest danger lay.

. . .

Mother of Odin, why does Haakon's place have to be so far from the shore? The further Tiller walked, the more somber his mood became. Trondheim had grown into an even larger settlement than it looked from the shore. Assuming he could wrest this woman from Haakon's home, how would he ever get her back to the ship? The quick sprint from house to ship that Tiller had envisioned would never work. *We'd need a hundred swords to fight our way out. I'll have to come up with another idea.*

And even then, once they reached the ship, he would still have to sail back through that confounded fjord with its long thin passage. It bent twice at hard angles, much like an arm at elbow and wrist. Not an easy waterway on which to gain speed and outrun pursuers.

We just have to stay ahead of Haakon's men long enough to reach the open sea, Tiller reassured himself. Once he got back to Iceland, he'd unload the woman as fast as possible on Naldrum. Then she'd be the headman's problem, not his.

. . .

A bent beggar held out his palm and whined. Tiller dug in his pouch. "Which way to the home of the Jarl of Lade?" he asked

The beggar seemed to think the token Tiller offered deserved more than simple directions. He started limping along after Tiller, poking with his stick.

"Anything else you'd like to know about Lade Garde, seeing as how you're headed there?" the man asked. "I know the place well. I used to work there."

"Best way to get in without being accosted by a trove of guards?"

"You'll want the kitchen entrance," the man said. "Behind the main building. Merchants are always coming and going, so the guards there tend to be a little lax. I'll show you." He straightened and surprisingly spry, matched Tiller's gait.

"What's your business with Haakon?" the beggar asked.

"Nothing I care to discuss," Tiller said.

"Oh, then," the man replied. "Not good business, I take it."

Tiller remained silent, which did not detract from his companion's wheedling. "Not as though many *have* good business with the Jarl, if I may say so."

"And why is that?"

"Haakon takes care of those who make him wealthy, but he steps all over those who don't. Cheats them, steals from them, appreciates nothing, does not know the meaning of the word 'truth'."

"You've no loyalty to him, it seems."

"I'm a beggar. What does my loyalty matter to anyone? But you're right. I'd cut his throat if I could get close enough," the man sneered. "I won't trouble you with the reasons why. Suffice to say that if you mean him any harm, I'm happy to help. For free." He fished the token back out of his own pouch and with a half-hearted gesture, offered it back to Tiller.

"Keep it. What do you know about the Jarl's household? About people who live in it? His wives...his thralls?"

"He has a wife, Tora. A sprawl of children, mostly not hers." The man looked about, although no one walked near them. "He takes the daughters of nearby farmers as a tax. Prefers the younger ones best. He uses them for a bit and then throws them off. Any kids end up with him, by law. House is full of them, running like wild young dogs."

"And his slaves? Anything unusual there?" *Too dangerous to come right out and ask if Haakon had a dark-skinned captive.*

"Plenty of slaves. Most hate him, of course, but they fear him, too, so they'll rat out any threat to the house. He has a new slave now that's the talk of the town. A woman from far away. They say she has skin the color of a seal's fur, dark brown. Eyes, the same color. Said to be beautiful. His wife Tora hates her."

"Interesting," Tiller said. "What does she do there? Where does the Jarl keep her? I'd like to see such an unusual creature." *Excellent. The woman Naldrum wanted was here.*

The beggar shot a sharp look towards Tiller. "As would many. Word has it that Haakon keeps her under guard, deep in his household."

"'Deep in his house? Just how big is it?" Tiller asked. Turning a corner, his beggar companion pointed ahead.

"Lade Garde," he announced with some pride. "Home to Haakon Sigurdsson, the Jarl of Lade." A different voice at this, and he spat on the ground.

A building the size of ten longhouses loomed ahead, two stories tall, and the whole of it surrounded by a thick fence that stood just over Tiller's head. Without meaning to, he groaned.

. . .

The beggar grabbed Tiller's elbow, every movement eager. He pointed to a path that led through a small copse of trees. "We'll avoid the attention of the front-gate guard this way," he said. "Kitchen's this way. Look, here's a bit of luck." A cart filled with linen-wrapped meats passed where they stood. "We'll just walk along behind. Keep your head down. The gate guards will assume you're with the meat smoker's crew."

Tiller did as the beggar suggested. Soon they stood in the crowded alcove of a cooking room. The tantalizing aroma of big being roasted over a spit came from an enormous fireplace.

After the cook finished haggling with the meat-smokers, the beggar sidled up to her. "Hey, Svienne. You remember me, don't you? I've brought a fellow from a trade ship who might sweeten your palm," the beggar announced. "New to these parts and has some goods to sell."

The cook ignored him. She directed the cinder-girl to turn the spit more slowly, then, wiping her hands on her apron, she lifted a cloth on a wooden tray of rising dough. The fragrance of yeast mingled with the roasting meat. Tiller's mouth watered. *Wheat bread, aie.*

"What sort of goods?" the cook asked, never once glancing at Tiller.

"Amber beads, perfume, carved combs," he began.

"Women's stuff, then. Luxury."

"You could say that, yes."

"Ever traded with the Jarl before?" she asked.

"No."

She held out her hand. Tiller placed a bit of hack-silver in it. She waited, her palm still extended, and he added more. Her eyes finally met his, but they held no welcome.

"I have some advice for you," she said. "If you want to *sell* your wares—or at least take your unsold things back with you—show them to his new favorite, the one he calls the Nubian. If you want to "donate" your items," she laughed without humor, "show them to his wife Tora. She'll thank you for your loyalty to Haakon, and that'll be all the payment you'll see."

"Wise advice. I think I'll show my things to the Nubian. How does one arrange that?"

"You can't. I can't. Absolutely no one can visit the Jarl's new prize. But there's always a way to screw a man who screws others, isn't there? Cindergirl," the cook barked. "Go tell Mistress Tora that a trader has arrived with fresh goods." The cook laughed again, this time with real mirth. "That'll get you inside, at least. It's up to you to figure out how to make your way from one woman to the other."

. . .

It did not take long for a summons from 'Mistress Tora' to arrive. Tiller left the beggar in the kitchen whispering with the cook and followed the cinder-girl through one hallway after another until they reached an upper room. He could feel sweat rolling down his back between his shoulder blades. Getting inside Lade Garde had been unexpectedly easy. Getting back out would likely be the opposite.

"That door," the ash-girl whispered. She darted back towards the kitchen. Tiller knocked.

"Come in."

Tiller bowed as he entered the room. A woman, attractive and middle-aged, lolled upon a chair covered in fur.

"I'm told you have fine goods of interest to women," she said.

"Yes, mistress. The Jarl told me to show them to a lady in his household. His favorite lady, he said. Thank you for receiving me."

Tora's smile warmed to flirtatiousness, increasing her beauty. "You flatter me. My husband has excellent taste. Spread your wares." She gestured to a table.

"Your husband?" Tiller feigned confusion. "You are the head lady here?"

"Haakon's wife. Yes, of course."

"I think there has been some mistake." Tiller coughed. "These are…lesser goods."

"Then who *did* you come intending to sell to? The ash-girl said you asked for me."

Tiller had opened his bundle of wares and had started putting items out on a small table. He hurriedly scooped everything back into his pack.

"I am thinking I misquoted him. Perhaps he meant one of his favorite lieutenants' wives? Or one of your personal favored slaves, who might have a bit of coin to spend? One who would see a bit of glitter and think it gold?"

The slight line between Tora's brows deepened. "But I thought—didn't I hear you say he specifically told you to show them to me?"

"My apologies, mistress. Your husband is a powerful man. I don't wish to offend in any way." Tiller backed towards the door.

My husband is a man besieged by his lusts. A hot flush began to spread up Tora's neck. "Tell me who exactly you thought you were meeting with."

Tiller edged out the door, the latchstring in his fingers. "No one, madam. He did not give a name."

"Now I remember." Her face grew angry. "You said 'his favorite lady,' didn't you?" Tiller ducked as a wooden plate flew past and broke against the wall. "*Didn't* you?"

"Perhaps he meant one of your daughters?" Another plate. "His mother?" A spoon clattered.

"I know exactly who he meant." Tora's voice rose to a shriek. "You brought your trash to dangle in front of his horrid new amusement."

She jumped from her chair and leaped for Tiller, her fists battering his head.

"Come with me," Tora cried. "I'll take you to her, much good that it will do you or my husband." She dragged Tiller along narrow corridors until they reached a door at the opposite end of the house.

A guard stood at the entrance. Tora shoved him aside and opened the door without knocking. She jerked her chin. "There she is! Show your cheap wares to his 'favorite lady'—and then get out of my house."

Tora wiped angry tears from her cheeks and whirled out of the room. She slammed the door shut, then ran down the hall. Tiller could hear her bare feet thudding on the pine boards.

. . .

The woman Tiller sought stood alone in the center of an empty room. He had never seen such sadness in a face before, but that was not what captivated his attention. What made him stop in his tracks was her attire.

He had encountered women wearing clothing such as this when he had traded in other countries—always at a distance, always in a group. Never alone, and never close at hand.

An unadorned brown robe fell from her shoulders to the floor. Another cloth served as a simple headdress, white, and neatly folded over across her forehead. She wore no ornamentation, not in clothing or jewelry, save for a carved bit of wood hanging on a thin leather string around her neck.

"By Odin," Tiller breathed. "Naldrum never mentioned that his stolen property was a nun."

Enjoy this preview?
Find your copy of VIKING: THUNDER HORSE
via Amazon or at your local bookstore or library.

If you like exploring more deeply, some book club discussion topics and a few author's notes follow.

Thank you for taking the time to leave a good review at Amazon.com

Contact Katie via:
Facebook
Instagram
Goodreads
BookBub
Amazon Author Page

Find a typo? I loathe those rascals. Please email me via KatieARitter@gmail.com and I'll fix it right up. Thank you!

BOOK CLUB DISCUSSION TOPICS

Have you or someone you know experienced things such as Aldís's visions? Where do you think this 'second-sight' or intuition comes from? What do you think of Aldís's struggle to accept and trust the confusing gift she possesses?

Who or what do you think is 'calling' Aldís the night of álfablót?

What is your opinion of Kel staying with Naldrum? Should he have made a break earlier, or was staying his only real option?

How loyal do you think Rota is to Haakon? Why?

Konradsson clearly suffered emotional trauma from Randaal's abuse. Should he confront Randaal about it?

Does Tor's belief in the Third Way apply today? Why or why not?

What do you think of Tor's decision to leave his children with Eilíf?

What do you think might cause Ankya's odd behaviors?

AUTHOR'S NOTES

First: how NOT to write a book series

Every historical-fiction writer wrestles with a delicate balance between known history, suspected history, educated guesses based on solid research, and places where no research will take you—aka, pure fiction. Each writer approaches it her or his own way.

I wrote the 'first' novel in this series—*VIKING: The Green Land*—after an unexpected, life-changing epiphany. When I went to write the sequel, I realized to my distress that the sequel needed additional fully developed characters I hadn't created yet, so I set out to write a prequel.

But I got stuck. Author friend Louisa Locke suggested a short story of a minor character in *The Green Land.* I knew immediately that I would write about Tor.

Why him? I had no idea, but from the moment Tor showed up in *The Green Land*, I knew he was 1) a man of color, 2) a person of good character, and 3) someone of very few words. Beyond that, I knew nothing about him as a character, or what might be true of a real person in his circumstance.

I wrote a novella about Tor entitled *A Man Called Black Mountain,* then went back to work on the prequel. In a year, I had a completed manuscript, or so I thought. But beta-reader-first-class Bibi Bendixon announced something I had begun to secretly dread: "You need to include Tor's story in the prequel as part of the book," Bibi said. "Then you need to break the prequel into two books."

OhHolyMotherOfGodNoNoNoNoNo may have gone through my mind at that point…but she was right.

I took the carefully constructed plot arc of my prequel, rewrote the beginning, incorporated AMCBM, and found a point at which the now-200K-word manuscript could be cut. Despairing, I broke the book in half and reworked it into two separate novels. For anyone writing a book, this excruciating process is definitely *not* recommended.

Lots of good characters had come along to join in this effort. I particularly liked Kel Coesson, a man who changes from a dutiful servant to one determined to stop his brutal, corrupt chieftain. Kel, like Tor, is a decent man trapped in a difficult situation. Aldís, the woman Kel loves, has secrets and struggles of her own. The widow Eilíf appeared, strong but tormented—and although terrified to try a new course of life, finds the courage to do it.

Tor, Aldís and Kel each brought tough questions to the story. For instance, the world's first true democracy in Iceland was also a culture in which slavery was commonplace. What was life like for enslaved people in the medieval ages? What brutal realities did they endure? Was slavery completely accepted by all people in Iceland, or did many of them, just as we do now, find slavery repulsive?

There were deeper social questions to consider. What forms the basis of power…character, or wealth? And what happens when corruption and character collide?

You've met the characters caught in these very questions. They, and others, return in *Thunder Horse*.

After that, some of them will go on the epic voyage of *The Green*

Land. When we get to the end of *The Green Land*, you'll meet most of this gang again via two sequels—and each of them will be even more determined to do good, or evil, as the case may be.

So here we are: two full prequels, then *The Green Land*, then two sequels. If anyone wants to say "um, George Lucas / Star Wars much?" I won't stop you; it's deserved.

I hope you enjoy these books. I've shared my thoroughly disorganized process as a writer with you. I hope you share your experience as a reader with me.

Human Enslavement: breaking the color connection

As I researched the myriad details needed to authenticate this story, I slammed point-blank into a shocking fact: slavery was not only present, but *widespread* throughout Europe in the medieval age. A decade ago, we barely knew this—but as more and more Viking-era research came to light, it's now an undeniable fact that Vikings and other traders dealt regularly in the capture and sale of humans.

The vast majority of enslaved people in medieval Europe were likely Caucasian: across present-day Denmark, Norway, Russia, England, Ireland, Scotland, France, Germany, the Baltic countries, Spain, Portugal, Istanbul and other lands, we know that pagan tribes, Christians and Islamic people repeatedly fought for power, riches and land. Whether taken in battle or profit-driven raids, people were snatched from every country and fiefdom. Many came from family farms along riverways. Raiders sailed in, grabbed whatever people and goods they could, and trundled them away to sell them, sometimes in another part of the very same country and sometimes far away.

Everyone was complicit, whether capturing slaves or buying them. Literally anyone could be caught and held in thralldom. The British Isles and Scandinavian communities appear to have been among the very last to give up slavery. While many factors influenced social change, the spread of Christianity (which made it illegal to own another person) doubtless played the biggest role.

(An aside: in one appalling moment—already aware that Baptist-funded George Washington University and Jesuit Catholic priests of Georgetown University owned slaves and/or supported human enslavement in the US colonial era, I wondered if abbeys and monasteries of Germanic and Nordic lands of 1000 A.D. may have done so as well. While the spread of Christianity eventually ended slavery in Europe, when did churches outlaw it and how, across the sprawling and fragmented kingdoms of the time?)

I also realized that slavery in medieval Europe has been largely ignored in western literature. This body of work usually deals with slavery in two ways. First, we have novels of ancient Greece, Rome, and Egypt, in which enslaved people are often supporting characters whose tragic lives (with some exceptions) remain unexplored.

We also have novels set in the Americas from the 1600s era up to the Civil War. This era co-mingled enslavement and racism. When complicit tribesman and Europeans snatched African people and sold them to British sugar plantations and then to colonial era Americans, the word 'slave' became profoundly intertwined with race and color.

I found myself mulling over the fact that before that, enslavement was not based on skin color or race as it was in the modern era. Might this matter, somehow? An idea came to me very gradually as I wrote these books, difficult to accomplish but one I hope was worthy.

Let me explain.

I live in a country that has not examined enough the short-term and long-term effect human enslavement has had on individuals, families, communities, and the country as a whole. It is an ugly topic. Some want to look away from the past, and some try to hide the horror by whitewashing it as the Lost Cause. Just *talking about talking* about race and slavery is fraught with tension: say "BLM" to see the divide.

Human enslavement is appalling. It is horrendous to think that people, even today, romanticize it, or worse, actually *like* the idea. It is also appalling that one race of humans has been made to feel of less value than others. I hoped to influence those attitudes in two ways.

By having most of the enslaved people in this book be European, I hope that white people who have not yet grasped the long, ugly ramifications of slavery might suddenly see it differently. If I removed race from the issue, might they think of their own Irish or Scottish ancestors snatched away and forced into a life of lonely servitude, never to see their loved ones again—and finally realizing the horror of slavery, instead of romanticizing or excusing it, might they begin to see differently the plight of those who suffered as slaves in America? I hope so.

Likewise, Tor gave me a chance to challenge some beliefs in the minds of people who do not grasp the challenges faced by many people of color. Tor is the master of his own destiny, even though he is a slave (by his own choice, albeit for agonizing reasons.) He has no fear of Naldrum. Too often people of color have been represented as somehow being weak because of the powerless position into which they were forced. But they were strong enough to endure tragedy and horrors we can only imagine. Their very *survival* demands respect. I want to show how strong they were in no uncertain terms, and Tor allowed me to do that.

So, as I worked through writing these books, I decided to subtly and deliberately (and I hope, sensitively) show their circumstances to readers, to write some of what their day-to-day lives might have been like in the context of the story.

My work regarding this may turn out to be an epic fail—but I would rather fail attempting to do good than be too afraid to try.

My humble hope is that their human experience enriches the depth of the story—but more importantly, I hope that in unexpected and helpful ways, it helps to encourage more dialogue—open, unflinching, and decent—about matters of humanity and equality.

...But was it realistic to include a man of color in Nordic lands?

If one considers the rich resources in Africa (including gold and salt, desired all over Europe) and add the far-flung trading practices of the Viking-era Norse, it becomes a certainty that Africans, Arabs and other Mediterranean peoples engaged regularly with Viking traders. Unfortunately, part of that trade almost certainly included slaves from Africa who were captured and sold by their own countrymen, as well as European slaves sold to African countries of the time.

History and archeological research in fact confirm that individuals of color made their way—as merchants, by marriage, and as slaves—to the very northernmost edges of European civilization. A famous (or infamous) description comes from a first-hand account of Viking slavers, written by a 10th century Arab traveler in what is now Russia.

In addition, burial clothing in 800s-900s A.D. Sweden has silken bands embroidered with 'Kufic characters referring to Allah and Ali, an important figure in Islam.'[1] Icelandic sagas include people called "the Black;" Erik the Red reputedly had a dark-skinned member among his companions. So this book has slaves, and Tor is one of them. The bath-boy and Aldís's mother come from what is now Ireland and Scotland, while Tor comes from Morocco. My goal is to touch on their lives and struggles so that we may better understand their powerlessness and engage with their humanity. We have people who need that understanding.

Details, Details

I've tried to verify every detail in these books. Did monks wear robes back then? Did Icelanders have access to honey, and therefore mead, as the sagas suggest, or not? Unlike now, were there trees in Iceland during the Great Settlement—and if so, what kind? When during the year do gyrfalcons mate, and when do they live solitary? How did longhouse doors open and close? What type of hinges were used? What were their locks like? How was food preserved and cooked? How did people pay for things? Vikings were famous for portaging entire ships long stretches along partially navigable waterways; how exactly did this happen, and where?

Research even one small topic can take a couple of hours. It's fascinating—and endless: after all my digging, when I start on a new manuscript, often the very first paragraph will require yet another dive

---

[1] https://www.atlasobscura.com/articles/viking-clothes-with-allahs-name-embroidered-in-silk

into Google. There are so many questions still to answer, but I hope you enjoyed learning just as I did.

Transparency

Being transparent about my work is important to me. If you found these notes interesting, we are kindred spirits. Thank you for that.

ACKNOWLEDGEMENTS

My husband Mark has endured the sighing, the dawdling, the pre-occupied working, and the endless worrying for years. Our sons Zach, Gabe and Ben believe I'm doing good work. Their love helps, a lot. They save me from the Fire Swamp of Worry.

Thanks to author Louisa Locke, author of Victorian cozy mysteries, for her unflagging support of indie writers like me, and also to Bibi Bendixen, wonderful beta reader, as well as the stalwart Gordon Giffen. Both endured a series of messy drafts to help me reach the final product.

I'm indebted to Emily Sweet @SweetBookObsession on Instagram, who has kindly recommended me to her followers and introduced me to rainbow-arranged book shelves.

Gratitude to Soffia Arnadottir and Gérard Chinotti (and Skuggi lol) for welcoming us to Iceland and being such lovely hosts for dinner.

Another group of special friends follows on the last page, where they can be easily spotted.

There's only so much one can do via internet research. I needed a boots-on-the-ground trip to Iceland to see sites about which I was writing. To breath the air there. To *feel* the land.

Wonderful friends stepped up to help fund the needed trip via Indiegogo. They travelled with me in spirit, from a freezing-cold September pre-dawn landing across the approximately 1600 miles my husband Mark and I covered in four days. This book could not have happened without them. I'm honored to share their names with you:

Cynthia Ballard	Bibi Bendixen
Susan Stiles Dowell	Winnie Drier
Ricardo Druillet	Rick and Robin Duszynski
Leslie Fortune	Ari Gabinet
Savitri Gauthier	Mairi Giffen
Bill Guerin	Lisa Jan
James Johnson	Lynne Jones
Donna Katunick	Michael Katunick
Gary Levine	Mary Lou Locke
Don Lyman	Sarah Mackie
Joe Newcomb, posthumously	Nancy Palmer
Dave Richter	Meg Pohe Rose
Janet Schiller	Peggy Taliaferro
Steve Van Holde	Tobyanne Ventura
Mary Frances Wagley	Cathy West
Rebecca St. Croix	333Mellan

Finally, thank *you* for choosing to read this book. With gratitude, Katie

Made in United States
North Haven, CT
30 December 2021